Edwin Paxton Hood

Lamps, Pitchers and Trumpets

lectures on the vocation of the preacher. Second Series

Edwin Paxton Hood

Lamps, Pitchers and Trumpets
lectures on the vocation of the preacher. Second Series

ISBN/EAN: 9783337313791

Printed in Europe, USA, Canada, Australia, Japan

Cover: Foto ©Andreas Hilbeck / pixelio.de

More available books at **www.hansebooks.com**

Lamps, Pitchers and Trumpets.

Second Series.

Lamps, Pitchers and Trumpets

LECTURES

ON THE

VOCATION OF THE PREACHER.

ILLUSTRATED BY ANECDOTES, BIOGRAPHICAL,
HISTORICAL, AND ELUCIDATORY, OF EVERY ORDER OF PULPIT
ELOQUENCE, FROM THE GREAT PREACHERS OF ALL AGES.

BY

EDWIN PAXTON HOOD,

MINISTER OF QUEEN-SQUARE CHAPEL, BRIGHTON, AUTHOR OF WORDSWORTH:
AN ÆSTHETIC BIOGRAPHY," "DARK SAYINGS ON A HARP," ETC.

SECOND SERIES.

NEW YORK:
M. W. DODD, No. 506 BROADWAY,
1869.

CHARLES HADDON SPURGEON,

MY DEAR FRIEND,

It is very natural that I should inscribe this volume to you, as it is composed of Lectures mostly delivered to the Students of your Pastor's College ; and you, who heard most of them, expressed yourself most kindly about them. I will not deny myself this pleasure, although I have devoted a paper, not delivered as a Lecture, to yourself in the volume. I will only say these Lectures do not aim to be a Course of Lectures on Homiletics, I may possibly attempt this more ambitious task some day. Please to take this volume as an affectionate and reverent acknowledgment of that extraordinary work you have been called upon to perform. With earnest desires for your long-continued life and usefulness,

I am, my Dear Friend,

Heartily yours,

EDWIN PAXTON HOOD.

CONTENTS.

LECTURE I.

I.

The Pulpit of our Age and Times.

THE subject of this lecture presents the pith of the whole matter. *Our Times; the Preachers and the Times, and their relation to each other.*

I wish to review those weaknesses which we may avoid or strengthen; but I wish also in doing so to avoid that tone of insolent assumption in which some have spoken lately of the pulpit, and its men. What are preachers? Well, let us say at once that what the prophet said of old is true of them, "They are men and not gods, and their bodies are flesh and not spirit." It is probably true that the pulpit is not what we could wish it to be—perhaps not what it ought to be; but still I believe it is with infinite disadvantages, all circumstances considered, the holiest, noblest, and finest thing in the country; it is the most hardworked; it is the most unselfish; it is incomparably the worst paid thing within it. It has the largest demands for the most manifold labors, and, on the whole, as compared with all things it is successful. Successful it is with all its shortcomings—never so successful as now. It has been, of course, the usual policy of the wits and the evangelists of the Church of England to depreciate our ministry; let us not do so. Sidney Smith, that able minis-

(11)

ter of the New Testament, and high priest of the profession of small jokes and large dinners, used to say :—

Any man may depart from the Church of England, and preach against it by paying sixpence. Almost every tradesman in a market town is a preacher. It must absolutely be even this with them—the butcher must hear the baker in the morning, and the baker hear the butcher in the afternoon, or there would be no congregation. We have often speculated upon the peculiar trade of the preacher from his style of action ; some strike strongly against the anvil of the pulpit; some have a tying up, or a parcel packing action; some bore; some act as if they were managing the needle. The occupation of the preacher's week can seldom be mistaken.

This is poor stuff, but is is a very good specimen of the wit of Sidney Smith. The evangelist of the Church of England, Charles Simeon, the author and framer of a greater quantity of dreary, bony, school-of-anatomy style of preaching, than any man that ever lived, was not more complimentary to us. He says, "How diffusive, and heavy and overwhelming, is the style of Dissenters' preachings !" (witness the four vols. of the Skeletons, just published) they endeavor to collect as much as possible together into a sermon. Robert Hall is reported to have addressed a young St. John's man thus: ' Do not imitate our style ; you have plenty of good divines in your own church. Never attempt to aim at our style of wordiness, diffuseness and declamation.' " The advice is good from wherever it came. I do not believe that Robert Hall ever passed such a criticism, or gave such advice, the language is surely not his ; and if he did give such advice, it does but prove he knew not of what he was talking. At a time when Collyer, and Robert McAll, and Alexander Waugh, and Bogue of Gosport, and John Griffin, and Cooke of Maidenhead, and Angell James, and William Jay, and James Parsons, and Stratton, and Andrews of Walworth,

and Guyer, and Hamilton, and Ely of Leeds, were in the
zenith of their power; to characterise our pulpit thus was
impossible to the genius of Robert Hall, though quite in
harmony with the narrowness of mind and heart of so good
a man as Mr. Simeon. The depreciation of the pulpit now
is still more remarkable. Such depreciation, in almost all
instances, emanates from ungodly editors and laymen
belonging to the Church of England, whose estimate, of
course, of pulpit success and power, is the measure of flash,
or of finish in a sermon; and with them, Dr. Dodd in one
age, and Mr. Bellew in another, are typical of the highest
order of excellence. Or such depreciation comes from the
minister who, without much faith, perhaps unsuccessful
himself, has grown envious, and sneers at every kind of
success, in the department in which he has failed.

Prominent among these quarrellers with the pulpit is the
Saturday Review. It has expressed itself thus, "There is a
gulf between the clerical mind and the ordinary male
mind, which is deep and daily deepening; on the one side
it is a pity akin to contempt, too apathetic to form itself
into words; on the other, there are pious hands uplifted
in meek spitefulness." The same pious and respectable
organ says, "The mass of the male sex look upon religion
as a womanish kind of thing." Another of these insolent
and unworthy attacks is from the pen of one who calls himself "A Dear Hearer;" it has received the most encomiastic
eulogies from *The Homilist,* which, in its usual inflated style,
speaks of it as having the ring of Luther and Junius. This
expletive style of praise is very cheap and very easy, yet the
thing contains hints which may be used, although it is to be
deplored that the editor of a periodical, himself a preacher,
can only set his hand to endorse the bill filed against all his
brethren, and his whole profession.

When I read these things, I enquire whether the difficulties
we have in the pulpit of to-day are a whit less, or even a

whit different from those which met the apostles in the first age. The progress of the ages does not advance man one step towards a more favorable view of divine things and truths. Recollecting that Paganism is in the human heart, and Positivism in the human mind. These are the two enemies that Paul had to attack ; and he will be the most successful preacher who sets himself most deliberately—not to beat round the bush, complimenting human nature, on its progress in art, in civilization ; but who attacks these two strongholds of error. Infidelity in man, which tells him to lean on law—Positivism, the hardness of our times ; and Paganism, which tells him to clothe himself in superstitions and formalities, the effeminacy, the softness of the times. And certainly to storm these castles, "Innocent Young Sermons,"* will be of little avail.

And still, as I have already said, I shall in no case yield to the impression, that the pulpit is behind other professions in the average number, and eminency, and use of its professors ; for while in every other profession everything makes way, against this everything helps to erect a barrier ; other professions educate the animal and the devil in man, this does all to repress both. The eminence of the preacher, when he makes his way to eminence, is often in the very teeth of all that helps to eminence elsewhere. The bar is thronged with men, and the House of Commons has its continued succession of members ; there are very few Burkes and Cannings, and Chathams, in either one or the other ; no, the mantle of Erskine and Curran does not seem to fall more frequently on men at the bar than the mantle of Paul, or Chrysostom, on men in the pulpit. Whatever we may say of the eloquence of the present day, I suppose it is higher and better than the eloquence of the bar or the senate ; and I suppose, in the history of eloquence, in the literature of our country, the eloquence of the pulpit far

---

* See *Chronicles of Carlingford—Salem Chapel.*

transcends that we meet in any other arena. We deplore our want of success as a class, but we can still afford to say to those who sneer at us, "Physician, heal thyself;" and this Nonconformists may especially say. What can invoke and beckon a man to the Nonconformist ministry? Let a man attain to the largest and highest position amongst us, and his emolument will be poor compared with that he might obtain by push and tact in trade; but, ordinarily, he will have to pare down all his wants to an income barely sufficient to keep body, and soul, and family together. He is to be the leader of public opinion, and he will receive the income of a fourth or fifth-rate clerk; on this he is to keep his information and books abreast of the philosophy and the reading of the age; he will have tastes far above his circumstances, his education and the spirituality of his nature will give these, and he must mingle with men of taste, but he will have no means of gratifying them. Pictures, busts, books and instruments, furnishing the avenues and inlets to the great world of knowledge, can rarely come into his house. He must be the chief in chapel rearings, and the extinction of chapel debts, or the erection of school-rooms, and he must be content to see his income and salary dwarf down to the merest minimum, while the debt remains. With all this there must not be a whisper that his tradesmen's bills are overdue, for there is more consistency expected from him, and therefore less mercy will be shown to him. Moreover, his worst work, his sermon, is most in sight—always before men for their remarks; his most valuable, his pastoral labor, all out of sight and unknown, his attendance to prayer-meetings, and cottage meetings. His self-consciousness will be trained by incessant criticism, and he will be expected to be humble and meek before captious remarks in private and public criticisms and sneers.

It is not possible to do more than glance slightly at some of the influences which have operated on the formation of the pulpit method of our day. One of the most prominent is one of the most unfortunate; it is that of CHARLES SIMEON and the mighty regiment of Simeonites. His sketches and skeletons have been well compared to a great bone house, and however vigorous they were when Simeon himself lived in them, and made them effective and affecting, they are simply now very many and very dry. It has also been well said that he sent his young disciples forth to a sermon-fishery, not to a field of battle, and he gave to each a present, not a sword, but an oyster-knife; that is just the Simeon method—it was to *open* texts—it was not possible that this method should ever make great preachers, and from Simeon's disciples never came forth a great preacher. Let us speak of them with honor; they have been good, earnest men, and as narrow as good; while I do very much fear and think, that the end of that oyster-knife style of preaching has been to create Colensos; it is a style that stakes all usefulness upon the mere letter of the Scripture. Never was there a more little, pretty, chimney-ornament sort of shell, or fossilised and osseous fragment, than produced by this being great at opening texts, and feeble at saving souls.

This is an influence in our day confined chiefly within the walls of the Establishment, and there, principally, to what is called the Low Church school; our circle has been touched by another influence. I fear we must give to the late Dr. HARRIS the honor of introducing very largely into our pulpit that other—which perhaps I may be pardoned for calling the most objectionable and fatal thing in the pulpit of modern times, *The Religious Essay.* It was a beautiful and affecting thing to hear Dr. Harris; but the style in other hands really became as impressive as sweet oil on marble. I believe for consciousness and for conscience the thing was and is useless. In most men it has become a mere monotony of pointless words; there is nothing to stick, and, as Watts has well said, "Can an arrow wound when it will not stick?" I am far from denying that this style, or that Dr. Harris's style, is remarkable for its elegance; but give this praise, this is but poor praise for the preacher—what is elegance? It is the doctrine of the curve, the never too much of any creed; but curves are not points, and we often need the impressiveness of angles. Now, a great deal of the criticism of men of the world, scholars and statesmen, just brings to this result, the testing of the eloquence of the pulpit by its repose, its rest, its elegance, and unity. You must feel that there is something far more, and far higher than elegance in preaching. Choice of pretty words, pretty combinations of unity of speech and sentiment. Robert Hall was a great man: I suppose he was a wonderful preacher; but what a far more wonderful preacher he would have been if he had broken his style from the frequently tame magnificence into the grand, rugged, and abrupt coruscations which shine in such jagged, but lightning-like majesty in his *Table Talk*. Now, if there is anything a real and working mind disdains, it is the spectacle of prettiness in the pulpit, it is usually the assurance of *moral* infirmity. Did it ever occur to you to think of the Unitarian pulpit, and of the really eminent and able men who have filled it; but how powerless, how utterly powerless? The Unitarian pulpit has busied itself with the composition and the preparation of these same pretty little essays; indeed, I will say, that Unitarianism is only cold and icy, when talking of Christ and His Cross. On the great truths of civil and religious freedom, the Unitarian kindles with rapture and eloquence; and I shall not hesitate to say, that there is something in the Divine breath, when it blows the soul, which gives a magnificent and sublime contortion to the style, the contortion of the Gothic frieze, and the groin-work of the Saxon arch. Chief of this cold style, I think

I must mention William John Fox and James Martineau. A man can only preach well when he is moved by "the powers of the world to come," when he preaches as "seeing Him who is invisible"—visible truths—but an invisible, although real world, this makes a great preacher.

But I have spoken of the difficulties of the pulpit in our day. Chief among the difficulties, I place the peculiarities of the age itself; it is not merely that so much is expected from the minister, such a tax of brain, to bring out perpetually something new, so much necessity to keep the mind fresh and awake, and so little sympathy with all this; in addition to all this, there is such a *subtle* power abroad, *thought* is finding men *out;* we live in such a conscious, such a self-conscious age; it is not merely thoughtful, I say it is subtle, it is introspective, and very much of this must be, I believe, sadly diseased. Amidst all this, poor preachers are expected to be always healthy. I am inclined to think, that the preacher who has embodied all this in the most remarkable manner is Thomas Binney; to my mind he has stood revealed as in many, and most particulars, the greatest preacher in England in our age; he has not attracted the greatest number, but he has searched most deeply and thoroughly those whom he has attracted; his words have had the effect of magnetism in finding their way to the brain. I think of modern ministers he has ministered most to the thoughtful. What sights some of us have seen at the Weigh House—sights, the like of which we shall never see again, a whole congregation bowed to tears; sometimes, it must also be admitted, moved to laughter, the man fighting his way through all the phases of the text, following his thought in conception into every imaginative corner, now refining, it may be, too much, now throwing out some daring thought, throwing your mind, almost your moral nature, on itself in a recoil, and now a strain as of some lofty hymn, some bardic rapture, in a word, a lofty preaching to *thought.*

If you go into large towns, if you—as I trust you will—enter into the company of men, you will find that you too must minister to the thoughtful. How will you do it? You will only do it by yourselves becoming men of thought and prayer—"there is a kind that goeth not forth but by prayer and fasting." You can only answer the problems of the soul by experience. Experience is the truest and best exposition, this will give the readings of many a text, and often many a difficulty, and only so will your auditors feel that you are their teacher, while feeling that you have been into the furnace and the difficulty before them.

Once more I remind you of your difficulties. Science has displaced wonder, there is no strange place, there is no strange thing, everything and every spot is now made familiar to the mind, hence our difficulty has greatly increased. Yet, you still have to meet both natures in man, his understanding and his faith. You will notice how many preachers permit the subtle to predominate over the practical, they fancy that in this they satisfy by entering into the essential reason of things ; on the contrary, in others the merely practical becomes turgid. We should rise to ideal views of all truth. Is it not true, that that which satisfies the understanding, leaves, in fact, the whole nature unsatisfied ; leaves the infinite heights and breadths in which the soul may sublimely exercise herself ? Rise to the ideal, the wing in the cloud, but drop in harmony and happiness refreshed to earth again. You would secure belief—now, all preaching to be successful must always be based in common sense, but especially now ; begin first to secure belief by laying down her principles, and defining and showing the reasonableness of her grounds, and then that which we call rhetoric, eloquence, sets the logical framework in a blaze. This is just the image : look at all the arrangements for an immense magnificence of fireworks ; all those sticks are arranged, and, most necessarily ; they contain all the combustibles for the display, but unignited ; but the fire kindles, and there and then rush forth all the splendors of the many-colored flames. A rocket stick is a poor substitute for fireworks; true, but we cannot do without the stick ; it is a pity that in the matter of preaching many persons mistake the stick for the rocket. And this leads to another remark : you must in this day relate together the theology of the intellect and the theology of the feelings.* You must do homage to both, all things demand that you do homage to both ; it has been well said that the sensitive part of our nature quickens the perceptive, the theology of the intellect enlarges and improves that of the feelings, and is also enlarged and improved by it. I am happy to think that you will have no difficulty in using as yours language which the Holy Book and the holiest hymnologists have used : intensely sensuous ; but if you see the law it represents, if you recognize and understand such expressions in the spirit that prompted them, even in the spirit of the schools, you will make your meaning felt. John Foster has well said that "when a man prays aright, he forgets the philosophy of prayer," and so when men are deeply affected in preaching, they very likely disturb the logical proportions of their subject ; but it is in such moments they give the truest impressions of it. I have little hesitation in saying that the finest illustration of this inflamed logic is VINET.

That the ministry is often unsuccessful is to be deplored,

---

* See, upon this topic, an invaluable essay or discourse by Dr. Edwards Park " On the Theology of the Intellect and the Feelings," reprinted in the *Eclectic Review* for 1865 (January—February).

and it should be remembered that many neighborhoods need the Evangelist, and this is a character of ministry which may need some special remark. While letters and papers have been teeming from our denominational organs on the evangelization of our rural or neglected population, I have myself become aware of a little circumstance which has put the method of doing the desirable work in altogether a new and affecting light. In a watering-place—the best known, most frequented, and most densely populated, near London—in an outlying district, a chapel, a mission chapel, has, within the last two years, been opened by the united services of Thomas Binney and Samuel Morley; the ministrations conducted since by the ministers of the town, and especially by the earnest, indefatigable work of a local lay laborer; but, unhappily, some Sabbaths since, the place needed a supply, and there was a necessity for falling back upon one, and that one of the very best known of our Colleges. Our friend, the local lay laborer, himself a man of very clear and well-informed intelligence among books, as well as men, penetrated into the vestry, and behold! the young neophyte, to his undisguised commingled horror and amazement, draped, and swathed, and wrapped, and flowered in all the adornment of gown, cassock, bands, &c., &c. It was all in vain that our friend remonstrated that a gown had never been seen in the building—that the ministers of the town, who wore the cloak in their own temples, left "their cloak at Troas" when they came there —the young brother was obstinate—it was in vain to remind him that the people might laugh at it; that they were a poor plain race of artizan folk. The gown was an essential part of his individuality. On that very spot, in the streets round about, something more than Puseyism was seeking to pervade and leaven all things; it was argued that it was necessary to keep perfect the simplicity of our system—it was all vain—the service was in the gown. Our young friend even became affecting as he declared that he could not preach without the gown, the whole virtue of the business would be lost without the gown, and in that pulpit, before the astonished audience, he really disported himself in that fashion.

The incident is, we are half afraid, characteristic. This little notice of it has been pressed upon us by the numerous efforts now made to reach the ear and the heart of the people. I am afraid that this little circumstance indicates the principal barrier in the way of success, in the evangelization and conversion of the people. The instinct of gowns is greater than the instinct of souls ; perfunctoriness is death to vitality ; and what can touch so living a thing as a soul, save life—a living soul ? And how is England to be evangelized ? Has anybody much hope of it ? It seems all our work goes to holding fast the ground we say we have. We seem really to break into very little new ground. The saints have to be fed ; and that feeding-time absorbs all the labor and thought of many of our churches and ministers. The feeding-time is really like that in the Zoological gardens ; it is the chief thought and object of attraction ; and the catching of animals from the desert, and training "lions and beasts of savage name," enters as little really into the thought of nearly all the Christians we know, ourselves included, as the catching of an African lion or Bengal tiger enters into the thought of the visitors standing before the cage in the menagerie. This being "fed" and being " built," is the death to all true progress and life amongst us ; and we greatly fear that whatever plans may be devised and adopted, they are likely to fail, because they do not spring from, and find their satisfaction in, that instinct for souls. For instance, of what avail is it to lay down rules and programmes to guide a man or men in the achievements of great ministerial works ? Churches have a favorite theory that ministers possess an order of piety beyond the lay members of the Church, and they test their theory by trying the faith, patience, piety, and self-denial of their ministers ; while their own little slips of those "plants of renown ," are left, for the most part, uncultivated. I believe, if most ministers spoke honestly, they would say, "That which we preach is a faith with us. We believe it really, but we don't believe it more than you. You call for extraordinary work from us ; we really have it not to give. We mete out our labors as best we may ; we are not pressed upon by burning desires and affections ; nor are you. A decent, orderly, well-conditioned, decorous faith is all that either of us have. It is all to which we can minister ; all that you can appreciate." Hence, when to a temper like this, mighty propositions are presented about the worth of souls, and the salvation of souls, etc., the language rises altogether above the knowledge or the conception. It certainly would not do to say "This is all nonsense, souls are of no value ; we see them plunging out into the great night that lies round this world —by millions, every day—we don't believe in their value— God does not seem to care about them." It would not do to say that bold audacious thing, and hence men, unable to perceive and not in earnest themselves, create perfunctory instrumentalities, and they say to ministers, "We will collect a certain quantity of money, you go and do the feeling, the believing, the loving, the praying." In fact, it will not be wrought that way. Religious action must bear up like the waters of the great Geyser, mountains high, boiling from the deep central spring, and woe betide the pots, pans, kettles, or beefsteaks (*vide Travels in Iceland*) that stand in the way of it. Yet, sometimes the Geyser has seemed to be a well-conducted, well-behaved little thing, and travellers have boiled and washed over its bubblings. This is even that which many of us, in this way, have done by our Committeedoms, &c. We have used that great Geyser, the

religious instinct in man, as a means for keeping our pot
boiling, and almost all our modern designs about religion
look in that direction. "Oh! Clarkson," said William Wilberforce to his great *collaborateur*, when he called upon him
one Sabbath morning, and found him sitting before his
table, which was covered with papers about emancipation
and slave-trade—"Oh! Clarkson, do you ever think about
your soul?" and Clarkson replied, "Wilberforce, I have
time to think about nothing now but these poor negroes."
The irrepressible instinct of the man, the divinely self-ab-
sorbed unselfishness of the man; something like this is the
only power which will tell in Evangelistic movements. We
do not know how to do that which we desire to do.
Protestantism in England has lost the art of converting
souls. My readers and friends will not suspect me of
Papal bearings and tendencies; but it is in that Church,
which numbers, assuredly, holy, blessed, and devoted men
among its members, we must look for illustrations of the
instinct for souls. Catholic home Missions are very successful. It behoves us to enquire—Why and how? What
are their ways and means? So many requirements go to
success in such labor; it would represent a power for hard
work, and that is a rare faculty; an aptitude and felicity of
speech; a command over sharp, pointed words of wisdom;
fertility of illustration, to take the stand on the village
green or in the market-place; to talk like a gentleman, so
that the man should feel the presence of one well instructed
and able to guide; and to talk like a brother, so that the
hearer should not imagine the speaker as living in one room,
or belonging to one family, while he belonged to another;
and what would be the use of all this without the button-
hole power? It is the coming to close quarters that tries
the stuff in a man—the ability to be insulted meekly, and
to get the best of it, that is a rare faculty—the ability to
let disputations and grumbling stupidity, ignorance, and in-

fidelity growl or talk themselves out, and then slip in a word boggling them, putting things in a new light, so that they feel that the man knows more and has thought more than they; and then, what is the use of all this, unless it is picked up, followed up, drawn and coalesced into communities? All success must depend upon fitness and adaptation, and the chief thing of all needed would be not an instinct for thoughts, nor an instinct for books, nor an instinct for æsthetics—all these would hurt and hinder the work; there must be chief, and before all else, an instinct for souls.

And what would that represent? The preacher would feel, or the converser, he had a piece of knowledge real to himself to give to the people before him—the people would become individualized to him in one soul, and he would feel that as the adding of one chemical to another entirely alters the quality of that to which it is added, so that piece of knowledge created within the person to whom he spoke a new consciousness, an entirely different perception of himself—life, and all his and its relations. Could a man, feeling this, be finicking about his instinct for gowns or modes of speech? Would not the thought give to him a divine abandonment? Would he not be, as Paul said, beside himself? But without something of this kind it is vain to think that people, rural, artisan, laboring, plain, poor cottage people, who have not been baked into Ecclesiastical shape and order, are to be met. We have a morbid horror of eccentricity, and I will be bound to say, that any one of our brethren going down to evangelize a rural district, would either in the village chapel or on the village green, give out a well-approved hymn, sonorous, long measure, and make a prayer, a kind of creed or confession of faith of a quarter of an hour's length, and then deliver a sermon, from which should studiously be eliminated anything that could create a smile, not to say so horrid and ungodly a

thing as a laugh, every touch of humanity or of humor—
almost everything that could convey the idea that the man
was at freedom and ease in his work. Alas, what would
the brothers of the Oratory say to an attempt to win over
England to Popery and Rome, conducted after this fashion?
Truly I wish they would try this fashion; instead of that,
they try the method of the Pauline madness—"beside
themselves." Snatches of profane song made sacred;
walking to and fro in courts and alleys, and out-of-the-way
nooks; winning by a strong word, accompanied with a
kind smile; by a piercing lightning-like truth conveyed at
the end of a most entertaining anecdote, and so, in the
course of a year or two, behold a church, a cathedral, and
Rome flourishing in that neighborhood! This goes on
while we twaddle upon committees and read minutes of the
last meeting, and get out our reports, and wonder who will
subscribe. And where are the reports of all the Roman
Catholic affiliations? What printer prints them? Where
are the magazines that glorify them? The thing rises as
silently as a fog, creeps up like an autumn mist over the
whole landscape, never says "I'm coming," only says, "I'm
here." Gentlemen who are interested in these matters, as
who with a Christian heart is not interested, would do very
well to read the late Father Faber's *Essay on Catholic Home
Missions.* It would seem that Romanism, too, has its members, to whom these things would be simply disgusting;
to whom graceful cowls, and matin bells, and vesper chimes,
and swelling chants, and swinging lamps, and stern old
crusader's tombs, and all the poetry of religion, are most
attractive. There are members of that Church, as of our
own, who would look with contempt if they met the Church
upon the road, out of breath, pursuing souls with bleeding
feet, hands rough and chapped, and perspiration streaming
from her brow. In all bodies there are those who prefer
the elegant to the prophetic in religious matters. Father

Faber tells a story, not inapt, howbeit it may provoke the smile of some:

> Once upon a time, as story-tellers say, there was a great missioner in France, of the name of Morcain. Now it came to pass that this great missioner was going to give a mission in a certain French town, whose inhabitants were very much opposed to missions. The Devil did not at all relish the prospect of the aforesaid M. Morcain; and, after due deliberation, entered into the ouvriers of this French town, and inspired them with a design quite worthy of himself. They met together, and they were not few in number, and they set out with their arms bare, and their teddytiler caps upon their heads, as nice a specimen of sansculottism as may well be conceived. The reader may divine the interior life of this procession, which marched out to salute in somewhat peculiar fashion, the approaching missionary. They advanced along the road chanting a parody of the popular song :—
>
> > C'est l'amour, l'amour l'amour,
> > Qui mène le monde à la ronde,
>
> to this effect—
>
> > C'est le Morcain, le Morcain, le Morcain,
> > Qui dam ne le monde à la ronde ;—
>
> The unsuspecting missioner came quietly along in his vehicle, very likely getting up his evening discourse, when lo and behold! he is in the middle of this delectable crowd. However, a Frenchman is not often at fault. Forthwith he descends from the carriage, jumps into the middle of the crowd, takes hold of their hands, and commences dancing in the most brilliant style, at the same time joining in the chorus with right good will, "C'est le Morcain, le Morcain." Away he goes dancing and singing, and his sansculottes with him, till they reach the door of the church; into which he also dances, irreverent fellow! and the crowd after him. But there he is on his own ground, and straightway he mounts the pulpit, and preaches a most tremendous fire-and-brimstone sermon, at the end of which he proclaims that if, during the whole course of the mission, any one who has sung that song wants to go to confession, he has only to cry out, Monsieur! j'ai chanté le Morcain, and he

shall be heard immediately before any one else. No waiting for
turns! No weary delay! No besieging the missioners' confes-
sional for hours! No! he has gained an immediate hearing!
And so it was. Ever and anon, during the mission, from the
outermost edges of huge crowds of women and others, no matter what was going on, came in a loud voice the appointed signal, Monsieur! j'ai chanté le Morcain. No sooner said than done.
It is as though he were some royal personage: a passage is formed through the Red Sea of people for him; every one else gives
way; no one claims his turn; it is a bargain; it is fun and consolation and earnestness all in one, and there is Monsieur! j'ai
chanté le Morcain, foreshadowing his own arrival and acceptance
one day at his Saviour's feet in heaven, in tears at the feet of
him, who thus knew how to be all things to all men that by any
means he might gain some.

We quite think this story carries our principle to an extreme, it illustrates Rome. Wisdom should be justified of
her children and wisdom may be. We are not fastidious
ourselves, and we are persuaded, that those in whom is unfolding the instinct of souls will not be fastidious. We
must recollect that we approach sinners, all of whom are
about an equal mixture of savage and child. How ridicul-
ous the method which should deal with them as scholars,
or in the highest sense, as men. It was St. Charles Bor-
romeo—a great example for us all—every way a Cardinal,
but a great Sunday-school teacher, perhaps the first of Sunday-school teachers; a beautiful and blessed laborer among
the poor; it was he who said :—"A parish priest should be
like a French milliner, always bringing out new modes, in
order to keep up the interest, and stimulate a languishing
taste." Why not? This is the use of excitement. The
Roman Catholic Church acts upon the principle of periodical missions and excitements; feels that every Church needs
an occasional visit from a mission to re-awaken its energies.
We want new modes for ourselves now, and without them,
and a fresh and free soul, able to use them, it will be quite

vain to think of being useful in visits of evangelization.
One thing must pre-eminently be borne in mind, as that
which alone will make us successful, that we follow the instinct for souls. Ecclesiastical politics and the like, will
come after if they come at all. It is neither an instinct for
a creed, nor an instinct for an ecclesiasticism, we must follow to be successful in this work. It really seems to us
that we have done our best to kill the religious instinct ; a
fervent conviction dares scarcely show itself ; it is instantly
called to order; our feelings are made to order too ; our
eloquence cut out after a pattern. We are afraid of indi-
vidualism. We must label ourselves sect fashion. We
have innumerable little crochets, and if the working of
these be interfered with, we walk off, talk nonsense about
our religious liberty, which, for the most part, means determination at all hazards to have our own way. We shelve
our responsibilities in the cupboards and desks of commit-
tee-rooms—an awkward, plain-spoken infidel tells us we
don't love souls, etc., and we point him to our name down
for a guinea in the report of the Circumlocution Society.
We estimate all divine things after a money standard—not
that we contribute so much as sects, after all—even here
we do not test our own resources ; and meantime, in the
depths and on the fringes of the forest land of our country
on the wastes of moors, in out-of-the-way hamlets, in villages, there are men and women it is well known, growing
up who know no more about Christ and His salvation than
their cows and pigs. To meet this, it will be of no use
thinking of any usefulness without such a baptism in the
worker as shall really be equivalent to the creation and
calling into existence of a new instinct. I read a little volume which I am glad to see is its fifth edition, called,
Strange Tales, by John Ashworth.* It is a marvellous little

---

* *Strange Tales from Humble Life.* By John Ashworth. 5th Edition.

book. It is a wonderful home missionary report, and we know how usefulness may be perilled by pointing at it the finger of prominency. It is the recitation of the work which I believe has to be done, and the way in which it ought to be done. Mr. Ashworth realizes what I have meant all along by this instinct of souls—that love for immortal mankind, and belief that we have the power to reach it, and to do it good, which overwhelms all obstacles and bears down all before it. It is really the story of the life, walk, and triumph of faith. Thus a simple man sets to work—a plain, working-day sort of man, meets with laughter and contempt from the people who do salvation by committees, and so, after waiting awhile, sets to work himself, opens his chapel for the destitute, following meantime his own trade, expecting to make no worldly gain out of his labor of love ; continues to hold and to fulfil all his offices and duties as a layman in the church to which he belongs.

We depreciate no means for effecting an entrance into souls. The man bathed in power, all his faculties alive, and on the stretch with the intensest ardors of poetry and argument,—the massive man, using his words like projectiles or weapons derived from some great arsenal, for assaulting the inmost recesses and sophistries of the intelligence—even the neat and fastidiously careful man, who wraps up his feelings in small sentences, and polishes away all the angles of expression—the hesitating, clumsy, but scholarly man, who feels that he only fulfils himself as he enters the neighborhood of scholars—for all these men, in the degree in which the instinct for souls is stirred within them, we have veneration and affection. But JOHN ASHWORTH will be the best type of man for the evangelist ; especially there is a great deal of work best done as the " saints" and " serious" people keep out of the way. Their criticisms, and remarks, and physiognomies are very often not a help to a man, but a great hindrance. We would have all these things pondered, in efforts made at teaching either artizans in towns or laborers in villages. The principal interest of Congregationalism in this matter is, that Congregationalism alone, for the most part, can effect it. We want a band of men, gifted with a free spirit, able to preach with a gown or without a gown—able to use a liturgy, or let it alone without detriment to their devotion—able to pitch a tune themselves, and carry a congregation aloft upon the wings of it, or to yield themselves with as much pleasure to the subduing powers of an organ or a choir. The Church of England mode of conversion, as we very well know, proceeds upon the assumption of the younger brother who happily furnished us with our text—it must be done in chasuble or gown and bands ;—the principal feature of Congregationalism, to our mind, is, that it is *versus* sacerdotalism. There are two chief foes to the religious life in England everywhere, —indifference is one, sacerdotalism, which is an easy lapse from indifferentism, is the other. Congregationalism is the corrective for both ; it is the corrective for indifference, for it strikes at the individual conscience ; it is a corrective for sacredotalism, for it places man above all dependence upon sacraments and forms ; but then it is necessary that the spirit of the instructor should be itself charged with the life it aims to convey. Where the ministry of the word is not an instinct, it will be, as it was promised Jerusalem should be, "a burdensome stone." Even at the best, how difficult it is to bear up the spirit in the midst of bodily depression and weariness, the captiousness of a diseased thirst and morbid curiosity, the fainting of the spirit before the unfaithfulness and sometimes the treachery of friends ; all these difficulties have to be thought of, for they have to be encountered ; but these trials will be greater still when there is a demand for large resources of bodily strength ; the call upon nervous energy for repeated visitation, and

constant conversation where conversation is to be a reality.
Most persons hope to get through life with ease some day,
this the true-hearted minister can never hope to do ; to
him his work must be always toilsome and anxious, for
ever haunted by the instinct of souls ; his very ground of
anxiety not comprehended ; perhaps, by even his friends
around him regarded as a mystical vagary, a half-diseased
dream, fearful of himself, fearful for others, impelled and
moved by a restlessness caused by that brooding spirit,
which of old hovered over the face of the deep. When I
think of all these things, I confess I do not hope great
things from any mere new effort, rather must we use, as
best we can, the very poor, inadequate, and incompetent
machinery we can command. Perhaps God may have
some resources of great men, strong instinctive souls—yet
—who knows? But, certainly, in the light of our modern
poverty in all the great things of soul, we may express our
hopelessness "till the Spirit be poured out from on high,
and the wilderness be a fruitful field, and the fruitful field
be counted for a forest. Then judgment shall dwell in
the wilderness, and righteousness remain in the fruitful
field."

But, if Christ is the great power of God, it is clear that
the preaching will be the power as *he is in it.* Hence I
shall have to beg you to notice how different, how infinitely different, the influence and the effect of controversy
in the pulpit, to conscience. Polemics have, I believe,
never, or but seldom, been power.

I have heard how once upon a time, the Christian faith
heard of the threatening and formidable incursions of her
foes, so she determined to muster her preachers and teachers to review their weapons, and she found beyond all her
expectations every thing prepared. There was, namely,
a vast host of armed men ; strong threatening forms,
weapons which they exercised admirably, brightly flashing

from afar. But as she came nearer she sank almost into a swoon; what she thought iron and steel were toys; the swords were made of the mere lead of words; the breastplate of the soft linen of pleasure; the helmet, of the wax of plumed vanity; the shields of papyrus scrolled over with opinions; the spears thin reeds of weak conjecture; the colors, spiders' webs of philosophical systems; the cannon, Indian reed; the powder, poppy-seeds; the balls, of glass. Through the indolent neglect of their leaders, they had sold her true weapons, and had introduced these; nay, they even made her former warriors, whose armor, faithfulness, and strength, were proved, contemptible; bitterly did Religion weep, but the whole assembly bid her be of good cheer; they would show their faith to the last breath. "What avails me," she cried, "your faith, since your actions are worthless; of old, when I led naked unarmed combatants to the field, one martyr, one warrior faithful to death, was worth more to me than a hundred of you in your gilded and silvered panoplies."*

* Quoted from *Historical Enquiry into the Theology of Germany.* By E. B. Pusey, M.A., 1830.

2*

Pulpit Monographs.

I.—Frederick Robertson.

I DO not go too far, I believe, in saying that no preacher has so touched the heart of the thoughtful, earnest classes of our day? and I am greatly mistaken if the published life be not the noblest sermon of all; at any rate, confidence in all the previous printed words will be deepened and strengthened after reading this record of a most real and brave battle. To the world at large, Robertson did not speak until after his death; only one sermon, and a lecture or two were published while he lived. The period of his absolute influence was very short; it was comprehended within the little better than five years he ministered in Brighton: he was not a pulpit star; was unknown for the most part away from home; would not have been at all likely to have created much stir by his name in any town to whose churches he might have been invited to preach for society purposes. In Brighton, while he struck down to the very roots of the reverence of those who knew and listened to him, he was in a far more eminent degree the target for calumny, scorn, and persecution; his church was one of the poorest and most obscure in Brighton—only about equal to, and not quite so handsome, as the second-rate dissenting chapels in the same town; yet from that town, and that little Trinity Church, went forth words which, for penetrating and searching sweetness and strength, for subtle power of at once awakening to a sense of, and reconciling the spirit to, the mysteries of the kingdom of heaven, have had a most singular influence.

FREDERICK WILLIAM ROBERTSON was the eldest of seven children; he was born February 3rd, 1816. He came from a military stock; he was born in the house of his grandfather, Colonel Robertson, in London. His father was a captain in the Royal Artillery; he had three brothers all military men, and by one of those hairbreadth chances, as some would speak, but which we should rather trace to "the Divinity which shapes our ends," Robertson himself escaped the Seventeenth Dragoons. Many elements in his nature compelled him through all his after life to look back, not unregretfully, to this. There was much of the soldier in him, and far on, when nearly at the end of his career, he writes, how, "as I walked home in my dragoon cloak, I thought that I ought to be at this moment lying in it at rest at Moodkee, where the Third fought so gallantly, and where spots of brighter green than usual are the only record to mark where the flesh of heroes is melting into its kindred dust again." I have heard expressions of regret even from Christian folk, that his desire to enter the army was disappointed. I cannot understand the feeling; surely however great a soldier may be, and however mean and inferior personally many ministers are, the knighthood of a life of holy earnest endeavor to lift lives, to inspire them, convert them, console them, to make them brave and true, must be greater than that of the mere profession of arms.

In his boyhood he was a wanderer. The first five years of his life were passed in Leith Fort; then his father left Leith, and settled, on half-pay, at Beverley, in Yorkshire.

Subsequently, the family resided at Tours—was again compelled to travel home, by the revolution which broke out
in 1830. At sixteen years of age, he was placed in the
New Academy, Edinburgh. Notwithstanding this scattered
existence, he seems to have been very carefully and watch-
fully trained, and the almost romantic variety of impressions of the days of his childhood and boyhood always
stood out with great distinctness in his mind. I can well
believe how fond he was of wanderings over downs and
moors, how he cherished almost a passion for animals, but
especially for birds. The frame, consumed at last in the
intense furnace of soul, was, as a boy's, almost iron in its
stoutness and strength ; he was as Carlyle would say, "A
radiant being pulsing auroras ;" animated, too, even then,
by a dreamy brightness of chivalry and young imagination
in which the lad liked to conceive himself a knight seeking
adventures, and redressing wrongs ; also, there is proof of
the possession not merely of a fine sensitiveness of nerve,
but of a clear sense of duty ; a fine sense also of devout-
ness and reverence there must have been in him : *prayer*
seems to have been quite an actual fact with the little lad
from his child's days. The following extract from a letter
written when in Brighton puts the intense reality of the
boy's early religious feeling in a strong light :

I remember when a very, very young boy, going out shooting
with my father, and praying, as often as the dogs came to a
point, that he might kill the bird. As he did not always do
this, and as sometimes there would occur false points, my heart
got bewildered. I believe I began to doubt sometimes the
efficacy of prayer, sometimes the lawfulness of field sports,
Once, too, I recollect when I was taken up with nine other boys
at school to be unjustly punished, I prayed to escape the shame.
The master, previously to flogging all the others, said to me, to
the great bewilderment of the whole school—"Little boy, I
excuse you ; I have particular reasons for it," and, in fact, I was
never flogged during the three years I was at that school. That

incident settled my mind for a long time; only I doubt whether it did me any good, for prayer became a charm. I fancied myself the favorite of the Invisible. I knew that I carried about a talisman unknown to others which would save me from all harm. It did not make me better; it simply gave me security, as the Jew felt safe in being the descendant of Abraham, or went into battle under the protection of the Ark, sinning no less all the time.

Many years afterwards, when only taking part at a debate in Oxford, at the Union, when a young student, he was about to denounce the moral tendency of the theatre; before he spoke he was quite nervous; his friend, afterwards the Rev. Mr. Davis, Vicar of Tewkesbury, was sitting next to him, Robertson pressed his knee, and whispered in his ear, "*Davis, pray for me!*" But before reaching Oxford he passed through several phases of possible destiny in life; for a little time he was in a lawyer's office; this he utterly detested and abominated; his heart yearned towards the army. "I was rocked and cradled," he writes, "in the roar of artillery, and the very name of such things sounds to me like home;" but his father very naturally thought that his character and deep religious feeling well fitted him for the Church, and he proposed this to him as a profession; his answer was decisive, "Anything but that, I'm not fit for it." And there seemed a difficulty in his entering the army, but his mother's family having some influence with the king, his name was put down on the list for a cavalry regiment serving in India. He was enraptured, and immediately set to work to prepare for that profession. Before his departure for India, he made the acquaintance, apparently in a most casual manner, of Mr. Davis, whose name we have just mentioned; the casual acquaintance changed the whole current and course of his life. It could not be expected that such a change could happen to a man like Robertson without its producing a singular impression upon his mind—*in fact, it came about from the barking of a dog.* Lady Trench resided next door to Captain Robertson ; she had a daughter seriously ill ; the young lady was prevented from sleeping by the barking of Captain Robertson's dog. The families were strangers to each other, but Lady Trench wrote to beg that the dog might be removed ; the dog was not only removed, but in so kind and acquiescent a manner that Lady Trench called to express her thanks. She was so much struck with the bearing of the eldest son, that an intimacy sprang up between the families, which resulted in the introduction of young Robertson to some of Lady Trench's clerical friends; one of them, Mr. Daly, now Bishop of Cashel, was no sooner introduced than he struck at the question whether it were definitely fixed that he should go into the army ; the im-pression of his unaffected piety convincing Mr. Daly that he ought to be in the church. It seems to have been an amazing self-sacrifice to Robertson, but so it came about, that to the barking of a dog we probably owe those wealthy volumes of fine instinctive teaching and exhorta-tion. There is an extract from one of his posthumous papers showing how deeply this circumstance impressed him ; he is speaking of his favorite theory, that all great truths consist of two opposites which are not contra-dictory :—

"All is free," he says,—"that is false; all is fated—that is false. All things are free and fated—that is true. I cannot overthrow the argument of the man who says that everything is fated, or, in other words, that God orders all things, and can-not change that order. If I had not met a certain person, I should not have changed my profession : if I had not known a certain lady, I should not probably have met this person : if that lady had not had a delicate daughter who was disturbed by the barking of my dog ; if my dog had not barked that night, I should now have been in the Dragoons, or fertilising the soil of India. Who can say that these things were not ordered, and that, apparently, the merest trifles did not produce failure and a marred existence?"

So he went to Oxford; and he was studying in Oxford during a great period of its history, when Dr. Newman was in the full heat and excitement of his influence there. The strong reaction of Robertson's mind against Romanizing, Puseyistic, and High Church influence rendered him, we believe, unconscious to the almost involuntary power Newman's mind had over him. But we think it is impossible to run over the pages of those admirable and most extraordinary sermons, heard those days within the walls of St. Mary's, and Littlemore, without feeling that, probably, more to Newman than to any other teacher, Frederick Robertson was indebted for the first seeds of his peculiar thought. Two scenes also in Oxford impressed him much: while he was there, he heard Arnold of Rugby give his well known Lectures on History, when all that was brilliant, wise, or distinguished, thronged the University Theatre in order to listen; a still more sublime sight he saw when the patriarch, Wordsworth, was introduced by John Keble to receive his honorary degree. There were wonderful tempests of acclamations, and the lesson in either instance, to one able to receive it, would be the same, of gladness in the hour of triumph, and sympathy with those who had loved these men when the world despised them. Like Newman himself, he seems to have entered the University either as an evangelical, or with strong tendencies to evangelicalism; he narrowly escaped Newmanism, and for ourselves we marvel—it is to us even almost a psychological puzzle—how one constituted as he was, could have escaped that strong influence.

We hurry along through those days, oppressed even then by an early and premature sadness of heart, not wanting in brightness, college friendships, and in that which we should suppose always most essential to Robertson, the possibility of companionship with pure and noble women; so he says at that time, "the woof of life is dark, but it is shot with a warp of gold." His first work as a pastor was at Winchester, and he seems to have worked well. He says he was conscious of having developed his mind and character more truly, and with more fidelity, at Winchester than anywhere; there he led a life apparently of much austerity; he was but a curate—rather, we believe, a deacon—and his income probably was but very small. He submitted to austerities not merely for the purpose of keeping himself under, but that he might have more money to spare for the poor. He established a system of restraint in food and sleep; for nearly twelve months he denied himself the use of meat; he compelled himself to rise early; he inspired himself by the lives of Henry Martyn and David Brainerd. When he was at Brighton he turned back with envious feelings to the peace of his mind in the obscure Winchester days. Also, as the little lad had prayed in earnest before the terrible school-master, with much more intensity of earnestness prayed the young minister now. He disliked forms of prayer, yet he felt the necessity of them to sustain the spiritual life within him; and here is a prayer he wrote when at Oxford, and used when at Winchester—how very real and earnest it is! There is something very touching in reading these lines—disentombed from among his papers —record of the wild beating heart that knew its danger and wanted its Saviour:

"The enemy has come in like a flood. We look for thy promises. Do Thou lift up a standard against him. O Lord, here in Oxford, we believe that he is poisoning the streams which are to water Thy church at their source. Pardon us if we err. Oh, lead us into all truth. But, O our God, if we are not mistaken, if the light which is in us is darkness—how great is that darkness! Lighten our darkness in this University with the pure and glorious light of the Gospel of Christ. Help, Lord, for the faithful are minished from among the children of men. My Father, I am like a child, blown about by every wind of doctrine. How long shall I walk in a vain shadow, and disquiet myself in vain? Let not my inconsistent, selfish conduct be a pretext for blasphemy against Thy saints and persisting in heresy. Hear me, my Lord and Master."

Also, in his own mind, he set apart in those days particular days to pray for particular things. It is, perhaps, clear, that he was in the period of his apprenticeship, becoming an individual, scarcely an individual yet. He seems to have worked hard in his parish, but all his work dissatisfied him; he even quotes and applies to himself Byron's well known lines—but perhaps we may read in the complaint a prophecy rather of what he became:—

> As it is, I live and die unheard,
> With a most voiceless thought, sheathing it as a sword.

And when his sister died, he speaks of "longing to share her quiet shroud and her departure to be with Christ." But it was about the year 1840—when by the death of his rector there came an end to his curacy at Winchester—he was quickened into a new life by a continental tour. Geneva fascinated him; his letters from the Hotel de la Couronne show, too, that objective theology had laid hold upon him, and from the exercises of a holy life he was now reviewing more clearly the successive strata of religious opinion. He threw himself into his new field of work at Cheltenham with his whole energy—his private journals reveal the holy life of the man—reading indeed admirable books—Dante, German metaphysics, Niebuhr, and Guizot; but also marshalling himself especially to self-denial in eating. He says in his journal, "It is a paltry trial for a child of glory to fall in, it is a base return for the washing of the blood of Christ." Also in disciplining himself in early rising, because "it gives calmness to the day; late rising is the prelude to a day in which everything seems to go wrong." I am very well aware of the pie-crusty character of good resolution and rules ; but perhaps Robertson found it easier to obey them than some of us have found. Surely the following resolves in so young a minister exhibit a painfully earnest and exemplary conscience :—

Resolves.—To try to learn to be thoroughly poor in spirit, meek, and to be ready to be silent when others speak.

To learn from every one.

To try to feel my own insignificance.

To believe in myself, and the powers with which I am intrusted.

To try to make conversation more useful, and therefore to store my mind with facts, yet to be on my guard against a wish to shine.

To try to despise the principle of the day, " every man his own trumpeter ; and to feel it a degradation to speak of my own doings as a poor braggart."

To endeavor to get over the adulterous-generation-habit of seeking a sign. I want a loud voice from Heaven to tell me a thing is wrong, whereas a little experience of its results is enough to prove that God is against it. It does not cohere with the everlasting laws of the universe.

To speak less of self, and think less.

To aim at more concentration of thought.

To try to overcome castle-building.

To be systematic in visiting; and to make myself master of some system of questions for ascertaining the state of the poor.

To listen to conscience, instead of, as Pilate did, to intellect.

To try to fix attention on Christ, rather than on the doctrines of Christ.

To preserve inviolable secresy on all secrets committed to me, especially on any confidential communication of spiritual perplexities.

To take deep interest in the difficulties of others so communicated.

To perform rigorously the examen of conscience.
To try to fix my thoughts in prayer without distraction.
To contend, one by one, against evil thoughts.
To watch over a growing habit of uncharitable judgment.

His mind, on many matters, was undergoing change ; from some cause in those years which we might have thought would have looked bright to him, he was still racked by moral suffering. He writes to a lady, " What worthy crown can any son of man wear upon this earth except a crown of thorns." And there is abundant evidence that some gnawing disappointment was plaiting for him a crown of thorns ; partly, perhaps, this arose from an intense religious disgust which began to possess him ; he found the religious life in Cheltenham so widely different from the simple spiritual life he had seen among his poor parishioners in Winchester. He was separating himself from evangelicism ; even then he began to say severe things about the evangelicals ; " They tell lies in the name of God, and others tell lies in the name of the devil, that is all the difference," he says. He soon relinquished his charge at Cheltenham ; his health began to fail, and for some time we find him on the Continent, doing duty at Heidelburg ; returning, the Bishop of Calcutta offered him a chaplaincy in his diocese, with the promise of a canonry ; he did not, however, now desire to leave home. He placed himself at the disposal of the Bishop of Oxford, and he offered him the charge of St. Ebbe's in the city of Oxford. It has been supposed from his connection with the Bishop of Oxford, that at this time he sympathised with the views of the High Church party : but,

" Before my son," writes Capt. Robertson, " went to St. Ebbe's, he saw the Bishop in London, and frankly told him that he did not hold, and therefore could not preach, the doctrine of Baptismal Regeneration. The Bishop replied, "I give my clergy a large circle to work in, and if they do not step beyond that I do not interfere. I shall be glad, however, to hear your views on the subject." An hour's conversation followed, and at the close his lordship said, "Well, Mr. Robertson, you have well maintained your position, and I renew my offer.' It was at once accepted."

In fact, Robertson had no sympathy with the views of the High Church party, but great sympathy with the men holding these views. Clearly and naturally he had more fellowship of heart with them than with the men of the evangelical party. He utterly distrusted and repudiated *their* views on baptism, and perhaps did them but scant justice ; nor can I see that he thought unfairly or un-righteously if he regarded the *Record* as embodying and exhibiting not only their sentiments but their character. The *Record* was always Robertson's aversion ; it soon became his bitter and malicious foe. While thus his mind was veering between these two extremes of his church, and cutting its own way through tempest and fogs into seas unquestionably lightful and peaceful to him, if not alto-gether the region of the happy isles, Trinity Chapel, Brighton, vacant by the retirement of Mr. Kennaway, was offered to him. He considered himself pledged by having accepted St. Ebbe's from the Bishop of Oxford, and refused at once ; the Bishop, however, gave his consent to the trustees, Lord Teignmouth, Rev. James Anderson, and Mr. Thornton, to open their negotiations with him again ; the result was, that in the August of 1847, he became the minister of Trinity Chapel Brighton, the scene of his last brief pastorate, of his most collected energies. In each of the other spots of his ministry, we have seen him more especially engaged in educating himself, and feeling his own way ; henceforth there is no hesitancy ; whether people liked the sound of the " trumpet" or not ; one thing is certain, it gave no "uncertain sound." He rightly appreciated upon his entrance into the town the career of difficulty before him. It was a sphere, to a nature like his, so conscious and sensitive, at the same time so humble, earnest and real, full of besetting pains. A watering-place can never furnish to any well-constituted mind a happy pastorate. Usually, the ministers of watering places are those whom Robertson himself satirized as "never being able to forget the drill and pipe-clay of their profession, and speak with a living heart to the suffering classes." Usually, the ideal minister in such places is "not one of the same flesh and blood, vindicating a common humanity, but a policeman established to lecture the suffering into propriety." His Cheltenham education had a little enlightened him as to the difficulties he would meet with here, but he threw himself ardently into his work ; he lived in Brighton, lived for Brighton ; Trinity Chapel and its work instantly became the one absorbing object of his thought and endeavor. Scarcely, indeed, had he entered upon his labor than he lost his little daughter. One of his first letters speaks of his "perfectly beautiful little thing," and of his "returning from putting my little beautiful one myself into her grave, after a last look at her calm, placid countenance lying in her coffin. It was by starlight, with only the sexton present ; but it was more congenial to my heart to bury her so than in the midst of a crowd, in the glaring daylight, with the service gabbled over her." The following passages, apparently from a journal, indicate the spirit and resolve with which he entered upon his work in his new field :—

1. I want two things—habit of order and *de suite*. I begin many things and re-begin, each time with greater disrelish and self-distrust. At last, life will be a broken series of unfinished enterprises.

Hence, I must resolve to finish : and to do this, I must not undertake, till I have well weighed, *e. g.* I will not now give up German. I will study Scripture-books thoroughly through, histories separately and thoroughly.

I am conscious of having developed my mind and character more truly, and with more fidelity at Winchester than anywhere. Looking back I think I perceive reasons for this. First, I went out little : hence, perfected what I undertook before fresh impulses started up to destroy the novelty and interest of the impulse already set in motion. It came to its limit unexhausted, *e. g.* in studying Edwards.

Hence, I think, it will be wise at Brighton to go out little ; and even to exercise self-denial in this. But I will not commit myself to any plan by *expressed* resolve. I have now only a few years to live.

My danger is excitability—even in Scripture conversations was it not so ? This makes me effeminate, irresolute, weak in character—led by circumstances, not bending them by strong will to my own plan and purpose. Therefore, I must seek calm in regular duty, avoiding desultory reading—desultory visits.

2. *Artificial excellences.*—Goodness demands a certain degree of nerve, impulse, sudden inspiration. Characters too much trained miss these. Some turn their eyes perpetually on self in painful self-examination. Suspicion destroys the *élan* of virtue, its freshness, grace, beauty and spontaneousness. Artificial merits are like artificial flowers—scentless. Cultivate natural and not unnatural excellences.

3. *Explanations* are bad things. You preserve your own dignity by not entering into them. The character which cannot defend itself is not worth defending.

4. *My mind is difficult to get into activity.* Therefore, in order to prepare for speaking, preaching, &c., it is good to take a stirring book, even if not directly touching upon the subject in hand. Love is all with me. Mental power comes from interest in a subject. What I have to set in motion is some grand notion—such as duty, beauty, time in its rapid flight, &c.

Also he felt, with a true presentiment, that his work would kill him in a few years, and he determined to crowd as much as possible into those few. Scarcely had he commenced his work, when, as our readers will remember, in the February of 1848, the waves of the great European revolution broke forth in Paris, and rolled over the nations of Europe. Robertson was one of those, naturally, who sprung up as if inspired by what he, perhaps, too precipitately regarded as a "bridal dawn of thunder peals." His utterances and sentiments created more attention, possibly, than sympathy; but they gathered round him a number of persons of liberal sentiment, and his strong sympathies with liberty, and especially freedom of thought, and his fellowship with the working classes, and grief for their condition in England, and in other nations, made him well known, and proportionately slandered and misunderstood. Robertson, unlike Kingsley and Maurice, had no sympathy whatever with any kind of socialistic or communistic theory; he, with great respect, declined the fellowship of opinion. Yet the *Record* newspaper not only raised the cry of socialism against him, but continued to reiterate it after his disavowal, and loudly reasserted the charge after his death. There seem to have been favorable circumstances, partly created by the events of the time, and undoubtedly responded to by his own spirit, which made Robertson especially a centre of attraction to a large number of the working classes in Brighton. He became the animating brain and heart of an Institute numbering some twelve or fifteen hundred members. And even in his life seeds of dissension began to bring forth fruit, as is manifest in the strong discussion upon the proposition to admit infidel books into the library of the Working Men's Association. His biographer gives a striking and graphic picture of his appearance in the Town Hall to oppose the introduction of such works. A large number of sceptical socialists had come prepared to hoot him down :—

He began very quietly, with a slow, distinct, and self-restrained utterance. He explained the reason of the meeting. When he spoke of himself as the person who had summoned them— as one who was there to oppose the introduction of the infidel books, knots of men started up to interrupt him ; a few hisses and groans were heard ; but the undaunted bearing of the man, the calm voice and musical flow of pauseless speech, powerful to check unregulated violence by its own regulated quietude of utterance, went on, and they could but sit down again. Again and again, from different parts of the room, a man would suddenly spring to his feet and half begin to speak, and then, as if ashamed or awed, subside. There were murmurs, passionate shuffling of feet, a sort of electricity of excitement, which communicated itself from the excited men to every one in the room. At last, when he said, " You have heard of a place called Coward's Castle—Coward's Castle is that pulpit or platform, from which a man surrounded by his friends, in the absence of his opponents, secure of applause, and safe from a reply, denounces those who differ from him," there was a dead stillness. He had struck the thought of the turbulent—the very point on which, in reference to the address, they had enlarged ; and from that moment there was not a word, scarcely a cheer, till the last sentence was given. It seemed, said one of them, and what he said was confirmed by others, as if every man in the room were thrilling with the same feelings, as if a magnetic power flowing from the speaker had united them all to himself, and in him to one another. The address was the most remarkable of all his speeches for eloquence, if eloquence be defined as the power of subjugating men by bold and persuasive words. It was remarkable for two other reasons which may not occur to the ordinary reader. First, in it he revealed much of his inner life and character. He was forced by the circumstances under which he made the address to speak of himself. The personal explanations into which he entered were an overt self-revelation. But there was one passage in the address in which, without the knowledge of his hearers, he disclosed the history of the most momentous period of his life.

To speak in a provincial town-hall to an ordinary meeting of a thousand persons is an event common enough ; but

the tact of Robertson's speech on that evening; his powerful subjugation of his blatant antagonists, especially by his
clever allusion to "Coward's Castle;" the touching revelation of the history of his own mind, and what dark
thoughts had been to him; the reverence with which he
treated himself, and the perfectly overwhelming reverence
with which he spoke of his Saviour—"I refuse to permit
discussion this evening respecting the love a Christian man
bears to his Redeemer—a love more delicate far than the
love which was ever borne to sister; or the adoration with
which he regards his God—a reverence more sacred than
man ever bore to mother;" then the free, unclerical appearance of the man in his black cravat, hurling back the
charge of infidelity, "I have learned to hold the mere
charge of infidelity very cheap;" his fine expressions of
pity over Shelley, his defence of the works of Dickens and
their moral significance;—altogether we heartily envy those
who had the opportunity of being in that packed hall that
evening; and we suppose his appearance is worthy of being mentioned as one of the most astonishing and effective
pieces of popular eloquence in our day. The Society in
connection with which it was called together, continued in
existence a short time after his death; but it has long since
fallen to pieces for want of support. He soon found that
by a course of conduct like this, however, he was before the
bar of what he called the "Brighton Inquisition for heretics;" in truth, he was in a region eminently unfavorable
to freedom of thought and expression.

Our preacher came into an unpleasant world of things.
It was late in his ministry that he wrote, "I do dislike
Brighton; but it is my present sphere, and I must make
the best of it. The ministry is nowhere a bed of roses, and
if there was so delectable a spot, it is not open to me to
change to, instead of this." Soon after his settling I find
him regretting that his life was not passed in the risk and

3

excitement even of Kaffir land—"more real than the being badgered by old maids of both sexes in a place like Brighton," He aimed to be true; "What is truth?" he says, "the path to the pillory of ridicule." I think had his heart not been so sore from some unprobed wounds, he perhaps, would not have spoken thus. I honor the manliness of Robertson ; and, therefore, it is not so much with reference to him that I say I have little sympathy with sentimental mewing and pecking over either want of excitement, or deteriorated character, or unromantic scenery. Robertson, however, like some sweetly-shining and pendulous dew-drop, transparent and refreshing, has a world of awful and daring lightnings in him, and the disagreeable people with whom he met, we expect caught a scathing sometimes. Thus, one Monday morning, an elderly gentleman of evangelical and asinine proclivities waited upon him, introducing himself by saying he had been of great service to young clergymen :—

He arraigned the sermon he had heard in Trinity Chapel the day before; spoke of dangerous views and the impetuosity of young men; offered himself as a weekly monitor, and enumerated in conclusion, the perils and inconveniences to which popular preachers were subject. Mr. Robertson, who had remained silent, at last arose, "Really, Sir," he said, sternly, "the only inconvenience I have experienced in being what you are pleased to call me, a popular preacher, is intrusion like the present;" and he bowed his censor out of the room.

Another day, a lady, with whom he was slightly acquainted, assailed him for " heterodox opinions," and menaced him with the consequences which in this world and the next would follow on the course of action he was pursuing. His only answer was, "I don't care." "Do you know what 'Don't Care' came to sir?" "Yes, madam," was the grave reply, " He was crucified on Calvary."

Anecdotes like these reveal at once his weakness as well

as his strength. He had a flashing, vehement, and I suppose, even a cruel scorn for all that looked like cant, simulation, or unreality. Moreover, he was too real, which, with our natures and in this world, is quite possible. I find many instances in which he put an unnatural restraint upon himself, exhibited an unwise scornfulness of the surrounding sentiments of things, and was, perhaps, too severe and exacting in his treatment of those who were really not unreal themselves, while falling verbally or apparently into some relationship to unreality. Perhaps he thus sometimes needlessly provoked hostility. How strange it seems, one of the gentlest of creatures, always alive with the divine afflatus of affection, the vidicator of the wronged, the gentle soother of sorrow and suffering, he, more than any minister in the town—far more than any of whom we have knowledge of the same order—provoked hatred and bitterness. Unnatural as this seems, it is most natural. The divine qualities of truthfulness, reality, and gentleness in a man have been, in all ages, from the time of the Master and the Lord, exactly those which have called out and given active potency to their opposites in human character, just as it is the very beam of light that shows the surrounding gloom. Hence I notice an intense bitterness and scorn in him of sectarianism. He could apply to the *Record*, and its miserable but mischievous imbecilities, the words of the prophet, "Will a man lie for God?" or "Do not I hate them, O Lord, that hate Thee?"

"I have just had sent me the *Record*, in which your letter appears, and thank you heartily for the generous defence of me, which it contains. The *Record* has done me the honor to abuse me for some time past, for which I thank them gratefully. God forbid they should ever praise me. One number alone contained four unscrupulous lies about me, on no better evidence than that some one had told them, who had been told by somebody else. They shall have no disclaimer from me. If the *Record* can put a man down, the sooner he is put down the better. The only time I have ever said anything about Socialism in the pulpit has been to preach against it The evangelicalism (so called) of the *Record* is an emasculated cur, snarling at all that is better than itself, cowardly, lying, and slanderous. It is not worth while to s'op your horse and castigate it; for it will be off yelping and come back to snarl. An evangelical clergyman admitted some proofs I had given him of the *Record's* cowardice and dishonesty, but said, " Well, in spite of that I like it, because it upholds the truth, and is a great witness for religion." " So," said I, "is that the creed of evangelicalism?" A man may be a liar, a coward, and slanderous, and still uphold the truth."

As I read his life, it seems to me we are reading a story of Christian knighthood. There was a chivalry in his character like that we associate, either in truth or error, with the pure brave knights of the middle ages. All meanness was detestable to him ; all suffering was interesting to him, either for the purposes of love or pity ; the waters of discipline in which he had bathed, had so purified his nature and his vision, that it was greatly from this that he was able to give those subtle glances into the pathways of intricate truth. His love and honor for women was of the true knightly description, chivalrous and pure, and must have been very purifying to his own nature. Something like this from his very earliest days haunted him. He sympathised deeply with woman's frequently too abject condition in modern society, and as he talked to his sisterhood, he shed upon them in private the light of ideas which must have lifted them. " Woman's subjection!" he would say, " What say you to *His?* Obedient —a servant ; *wherefore* 'God hath also highly exalted Him.' Methinks a thoughtful, high-minded woman would scarcely feel degraded by a lot which assimilates her to the divinest man. ' *He* came not to be ministered unto, but to minister.' " He watched all those slight circumstances which revealed the nobility of woman's character ; he thought he saw plenty of the real poetry of life and inarticulate sorrows, far more pitiable than those of an Alfieri, in many a broken-hearted washerwoman, pining under the brutal treatment of her husband, and lost among her soapsuds. The grief, perhaps, could not be spoken ; but, in all its depths it was there, Here is one of those fine tender glances, in which he shows himself so able to appreciate a woman's character, and so sympathetic with her sorrows, true minister that he was :—

"There is one in whom I have been deeply interested; a married man with a family, his wife was a very superior woman. He has been reading very hard, hoping to take his degree ; but, to my sorrow, failed in his examination—to him a severe trial on many accounts. I called, he was out; but I found her very much overpowered, and suffering intense anxiety for her husband's bitter disappointment. I sat some time, hoping to soothe ; his tread was heard at the front door, and the whole woman was changed. I did not hear another sigh, and she calmly and quietly spoke on the subject, and held up a brighter view of it than she herself saw. The hour of weakness was past, and the deep strong current of a woman's affection bore her up. It was the reed rising from the storm when the oak was shattered."

This respect for womanhood as womanhood — what Charles Lamb calls, in one of the delightful *Essays of Elia,* "the reverence for the sex"—manifested itself not merely in his sympathy with ladies, but in his regard for the feelings and profound respect to servants, winning for him, his biographer testifies, extraordinary devotion while in Brighton ; servants, also, especially appreciated his ministry. Not long after he went to Trinity Chapel, on a Christmas day, on going into his reading-desk, he found a set of handsome books—Prayer Book, etc.,—which had been presented to him by servants attending the chapel. In the course of his sermon, he delicately alluded to the subject of presents, and drew a picture of the delight which would fill the heart of a brother, who, on the morning of his birthday should awake, and find in his chamber a rose, placed there by sisterly affection. Those who had contributed the gift would well understand the beautiful and delicate allusion. He acknowledged it in a letter, in which he says, "I shall never read out of those books without the inspiring feeling that there are hearts around me." This brotherly feeling for womanhood knit his character to a proportionate intensity of indignation over her wrongs, or upon the manifestation of any attempt to injure her. "I have seen him," writes one of his friends, "grind his teeth, and clench his fist when passing a man who, he knew, was bent on destroying an innocent girl." "My blood," he writes himself, after a conversation on the wrongs of women, "was running liquid fire." The following little extract illustrates also that chivalry of expression which, there is evidence enough to show, would readily have turned to chivalry in action :—

"I read a melancholy story to-day. A young English lady, who had been sent from Australia to finish her education in England, was returning to her parents, when the vessel was wrecked, and all the party with whom she was, except herself, was slain. She was taken prisoner by the natives, and has been forced to live with them ever since. She has been seen more than once, vigilantly attended by a black. She is hurried away instantly when the whites are seen. All efforts hitherto to penetrate the forest, and discover her, have been unavailing. The Australian savage is almost lower than the Bosjesman in the scale of humanity. Conceive such a lot for a refined and educated girl. Poor poor thing! I should like to be in Australia. In my present mood, I would lead the forlorn hope in search of her; I would not recommend any black to come within reach of my rifle. How much better a virgin grave in the Atlantic would have been for her!"

With this, or because of this, there was no misconception of the proper and social position of woman ; ho had too much reverence for her to chatter about her rights, after the fashion of some who affect to reform her social influence. While he reminded some of his friends that their theory about woman reduced her very much to the position of " a merely unemancipated negro," he humorously described the difference thus, " as *you* say, Woman is to man what the gristle of a child is to the hard skull of an adult : as *I* say, what the brain is to the skull, or the flesh to the ribs."

The biographer of Robertson (Mr. Brooke) reveals the character of Robertson, not by reciting a story, but by grouping together into harmony and consistency extracts from his papers, and journals, and multifarious letters. Externally, his life does not show much ; internally, they are a wondrous revelation of mental and moral conflict, and work attempted and done. To me, I confess, Robertson seems a mystery : I could almost feel, as I lay down his life, as though its story were yet untold. Such revelations break forth of constant internal wretchedness ; the life was so faithful, the trust in God and in Christ so unbroken ; yet the heart was so hungry and unsatisfied. It will be said, this arose from the exquisite structure of his nature, a kind of Cowper of the pulpit, composed of harp-strings so fine, that the finger or the wind touching them soon turned the strain to discord. Then, if any nature ever had a profound sense of the wretchedness of life and the world he had. Does this satisfy us as to the cause of his sorrow? We are told :

His sensitiveness followed him into society, and constituted his pleasure and his pain. He was easily jarred ; but when in tune with those around him, when in the company of those he loved and trusted, the harmony of his nature imparted itself to all around him. In his happier moods he was as radiant as a

child : he joined with a fascinating cheerfulness in the games
and merriment of young people; it seemed a relief to him
to throw off with them the whole burden of life, and to forget
the sorrow and disappointment with which his career was be-
set. His whole being blossomed under the sunshine of love
and comprehension : in such society he diffused peace, and
drew out from each all that was best and purest; but where he
felt that he was suspected and misunderstood, he would often
sit silent for the whole evening.

It seems undoubted that in his views he sometimes became morbid. He refreshed himself by visiting the poor;
but the terrible contradiction which sorrow, pain, and sin
seemed to give to the truth that the Ruler of the world is
love, pressed upon him with a fierce force; "Shall not the
Judge of all the earth do right?" he perpetually asked.
He thought life not worth living unless that question could
be answered. He was reckless of life : one day, while riding
with his wife and some friends, he put his horse at a lofty
hedge; it was a very dangerous leap, his friends earnestly
dissuaded him, but he could not be conquered, and did not
believe in danger; he urged his horse, took the leap, and
came down with a crash on the other side. The lookers-on
thought that both rider and horse must have sustained
injury; he got up smiling, but he owned he had been too
rash. Robertson was not a fool, but in the presence of
loving hearts, a man who could, without a cause, for no sake
of humanity, encounter a frightful risk before an anxious
wife, should be a fool or something far more sad. Circumstances like these occurring in his life seem to reveal that
he had no zest in living. I have no doubt that in a very
high sense he was a martyr; he used to say, "It is perfectly
true that whenever there is a great soul pouring out its
utterances to the world there will be a Calvary." Yet he did
not advise purposeless martyrdom. "Be sure," he would say,
"that the truth is one worth suffering for, or that the people

to whom you speak are worth its illumination. Thus you may save yourself the irritation of attacking the prejudices of Pharisees, which exhausts and does no good ; like a great horse kicking at flies, every kick covering him with sweat, and enough to break twenty men's lives. You always get the worst of it when you kick at flies ; squash them, if you can, without more effort than the switching of the tail ; if not, let them alone." Yet he suffered enough of more than irritation in the buzzing and the stinging of the flies. Great as was his success from the pulpit, I have no doubt, that, while grace and Providence placed him there, nature had rather fitted him for a poet ; he had every faculty, it would seem, which would have made him a great poet—the exquisite flow of rhythmic and penetrative speech ; an eye of exceeding sensibility for the finest shades, and groupings, and powers of natural scenery ; a deep acquaintance and fellowship with souls ; an absorbing sense of the Infinite Presence always walking by his side ; a synthetic faculty by which he held in his hand the great generalization of things ; and a fine power of analysis in detecting the differences of things, and separating them into proportions. We have called him the Cowper of the pulpit, in allusion to his sadness, his power of satire and of scorn, his sensative, shrinking delicacy of touch ; but there the analogy ends. His indebtedness to Wordsworth his homage to Tennyson, united to his own mighty power of assimilation, and especially to his sense of the mystery of things, and the perpetual shadows reflected by them from unseen worlds, gave to his sermons more of the character of those two great teachers—especially the elder and the higher of the two—than any preacher with whom we are acquainted. But there was a wild and passionate dealing with nature, that de-conventionalizing an audience, tearing aside its veils, and masks, and that pouring forth, through the deeper recesses discovered in human souls, rays

of light or waters of consolation. Robertson always seems
to us the poet in the pulpit. I have referred to his power
of depicting scenery, and that which is the true poet gift,
the synthesis of the human heart with a scene, making
soul and sense the tubes or chords of the great instrument
sending forth the tones of melody. Here, for instance, is
a walk to Hove churchyard :

"I went out this afternoon to get some fresh air, and cool a
little feverishness. After a walk I bent my steps to the spot
most congenial to my feelings at that time, the churchyard at
Hove. It was quite dark, but the moon soon rose and shed a
quiet light upon the long church and the white tombstones. I
went in and was pleased to hear not a single human sound far or
near. The moon was rising, like glowing copper, through the
smoke at Brighton. Above there were a few dense clouds,
edged with light, sailing across a marvellous blue, which
softened towards the zenith into a paler and more pearly cobalt,
with clear innocent stars here and there looking down so chaste
and pure. I heard nothing but the sea ; that, however, very
distinctly chanting no "sea psalm," but falling with a most
dissonant, heavy, endless clang upon the shore. It found for
me the expression I could not put in words.

"I went to the tomb, and stood beside it quietly for some
time. I felt no bitterness—infinite pity and tenderness—that
was predominant. I did not kneel to pray; I do not know
why. I passed E. M——'s tomb, and paused one moment. The
bridegroom lies beneath the hillock where so many fell at
Chillianwallah ; the bride is desolate. Two who were there are
dead, both young. That marriage and that death are singularly
joined in my mind, for poor E—— was planning her own wed-
ding then, and settling that I should marry her. Young R——,
too, has gone, but I do not envy any of them, except the soldier,
perhaps. I wish I had been with my own gallant, wondrous
regiment in that campaign.

He had certainly a morbid nature. His sins were all
sins of pride—an over-sensitive nature—it is not uncommon. It was hence that he scorned his task as a preacher :

"I wish I did not hate preaching so much; the degradation of being a Brighton preacher is almost intolerable. 'I cannot dig, to beg I am ashamed;' but I think there is not a hard-working artizan whose work does not seem to me a worthier and a higher being than myself. I do not depreciate spiritual work. I hold it higher than secular; all I say and feel is, that by the change of times, how humiliated and how degraded to the dust I have felt in perceiving myself quietly taken by God and men for the popular preacher of a fashionable watering-place; how slight the power seems to me to be given by it of winning souls; and how sternly I have kept my tongue from saying a syllable or a sentence in pulpit or on platform *because* it would be popular!"

This is sad, and it is wrong. Yet Elijah fled to Horeb, and said, "Oh, Lord, it is enough, let me die," and Moses, and Jonah, alike shrank from the prophet's office. But all beauty saddened him, made his heart ache; he says, and truly says, "No man can attain the highest excellence who is insensible to highest beauty." He moralized nature, his biographer says, not wilfully but unconsciously. Impressions of scenes were reproduced from the haunted chamber of his soul where they had continued in waiting, or were thronging, as in that magnificent passage in one of his lectures on Poetry:

"I wish I could describe one scene which is passing before my memory at this moment, when I found myself alone in a solitary valley in the Alps, without a guide, and a thunder-storm coming on; I wish I could explain how every circumstance combined to produce the same feeling, and ministered to unity of impression: the slow, wild wreathing of the vapor round the peaks, concealing their summits, and imparting in semblance their own motion, till each dark mountain-form seemed to be mysterious and alive; the eagle-like plunge of the lammergeier, the bearded vulture of the Alps; the rising of the flock of choughs, which I had surprised at their feast on carrion, with their red beaks and legs, and their wild shrill cries startling the solitude and silence, till the blue lightning streamed at last, and the shattering thunders crashed as if the mountains must give way. And then came the feelings which in their fulness man can feel but once in life : mingled sensations of awe and triumph, and defiance of danger—pride, rapture, contempt of pain, humbleness, and intense repose, as if all the strife and struggle of the elements were only uttering the unrest of man's bosom : so that in all such scenes there is a feeling of relief, and he is tempted to cry out exultingly, There ! there ! All this was in my heart, and it was never said out until now."

It is manifest that we might go on quoting illustrations of such walks and reflections, but we must forbear. Rich, gloomy, or beautiful natural scenery had to him the moral significance it has always to the true poet. It became an embodying and unbosoming, like Byron on the lake of Geneva, amidst the wild thunders and the phosphorescent dances on the waves, and the uproar of cloud and mountain, when everyone found a tongue. It was as if the poet had said, " There, there," I have had all that within me that is the picture of it, that is what I have felt and feel. And my readers, perhaps, will remember there is a passage in one of Robertson's sermons, in which he appropriates some such expressions as these :—" When we gaze on the perfect righteousness of Christ, and are able to say, There, that is my religion, that is what I want to be, that is what I am not, that is my offering, that is my life as I would wish to give it : My Saviour! fill up the blurred and blotted sketch which my clumsy hand has drawn of a divine life, with the fulness of Thy perfect picture,—I feel the beauty which I cannot realize ; robe me in Thine unutterable purity—

> Rock of Ages, cleft for me
> Let me hide myself in Thee ! "

But he has been charged with being *unevangelical*, and no wonder, for he says :

"In proportion as I adore Christ, exactly in that proportion as I abhor that which calls itself Evangelicalism. I feel more·at brotherhood with a wronged, mistaken, maddened, sinful Chartist, than I do with that religious world which has broken Popery into a hundred thousand fragments, and made every fragment an entire, new, infallible Pope—dealing out quietly and coldbloodedly the flames of the next world upon all heretics who dispute their dictum, in compensation for the loss of the power which their ancestors, by spiritual descent, pleasingly exercised for dispensing the flames of this world. Luckily the hope remains that they are not plenipotentiaries of the place with which they seem so familiar. More and more, day by day, one's soul feels itself alone with God, and resolved to listen for His voice alone in the deeps of the Spirit."

What a pity we do not take care of our words. Yet assuredly, Robertson was what we mean by *evangelical*, that is, he was a *Christian*, and not a believer in *sacerdotalism*, or the limitation of divine gifts to priestly channels. He sought to speak to, and to awaken, and to convert *consciences;* he believed in the message of Christ to the world.

Thus we have reached to the defective side of Robertson's theology. He was a poet, he was not a theologian; he interpreted faith entirely by feelings; he protested against dogmatic theology. There must be a religion of feelings; of the two, better a religion of feelings than a religion of dogmas, if one have to exist alone and apart from the other. But there is not therefore the less to be found a religion of dogma. It is remarkable, upon this point, to contrast together the two men who most naturally suggest comparison and contrast, John Henry Newman and Frederick Robertson. I have already suggested some points of resemblance. I am acquainted with no other sermons which will bear comparison with Robertson's, besides those all-strengthening and light-bearing discourses, which were his counsellors to his close. Yet, while Newman declares that "Dogma has been the fundamental principle of my religion. I know no other religion. I cannot enter into the idea of any other sort of religion"— Robertson, as we have said, resisted the idea of dogmatic teaching. It must have been, and it is still, very charming to find how he opens human spirits; that was his characteristic. The proper opposition in the pulpit to the dogmatic is the suggestive; he was eminently suggestive; as a theologian, I can have no hesitation in saying, he was eminently ignorant. I am sorry to see, and I wonder to know, that the Fathers held so slight a space in his esteem: "I know their system pretty well," he says. I have no proof that he knew Augustine at all, and I must think that his mind brought resolutely into harness by a course of Augustine, would have made another man of him. How much in Augustine would have ministered to his peculiar idiosyncracy of character! Strange to say, of so strong a nature, he really wanted robustness; he fed upon his feelings; they were right noble and glorious feelings; but such food or drink turns out to be a real Amrheeta cup at last, and so Robertson found it. It seems remarkable that a nature constituted like Robertson's, with a spirit of instinctive and implicit homage to the principles of obedience, did not so distinctly recognise the necessity of lines and laws, settled and established at once for the measurement of truth and the furnishing a standard in the preception and reception of it. Of course, I am quite aware that he would have said, and his biographer would perhaps say on behalf of him, such laws were recognized. It is clear, however, that the very catholicity of his own nature, its intense freedom, its independence, led him to renounce all external dictation, not only arising from that, it seems to us, which tradition had established, but that which had been wrought out from the careful, and patient, and elaborate processes of thought. Hence it was that, to him, highest truth rested ultimately on the

authority neither of the Bible nor of the church, but on
the witness of God's spirit in the heart of man ; and this
was to be realized not by the cultivation of the understanding, but by the cultivation of loving obedience. It is
a dangerous standard, although substantially it is the
doctrine of Fox, and of all the holiest of the Society of
Friends, also of the great mystics of the Romish Church,
like Henry of Suso, and St. Theresa, and St. John of the
Cross. It is an utterly dangerous standard, for it must
surely follow that truth is not anywhere fixed and absolute
to the mind without itself ; it is as if because we may be
unable to deal with the great laws of weight and mensura-
tion, they have no absolute and actual existence. Hence
he says of his own views on inspiration :—

"I hold that a spiritual revelation from God *must* involve
scientific incorrectness ; it could not be from God unless it did.
Suppose that the cosmogony had been given in terms which
would satisfy our present scientific knowledge, or, say, rather
the terms of absolute scientific truth. It is plain that, in this
case, the men of that day would have rejected its authority;
they would have said, 'Here is a man who tells us the earth
goes round the sun; and the sky, which we see to be a stercoma
fixed and not far up, is infinite space, with no *firmament* at all,
and so on. Can we trust one in matters unseen who is manifestly in error in things seen and level to the senses ? Can we
accept his revelation about God's nature and man's duty, when
he is wrong in things like these!' Thus, the faith of this and
subsequent ages must have been purchased at the expense of
the unbelief of all previous ages. I hold it, therefore, as a
proof of inspiration of the Bible, and divinely wise, to have
given a spiritual revelation, *i. e.*, a revelation concerning the
truths of the soul and its relation to God, in popular and incor-
rect language."

I give this, for it is a fine illustration of what we get to
when we relinquish dogmatic teaching. But let me not be
unjust to Robertson himself; he walked in the light; in

well known words, in one of his sermons, he testifies as to
the course to be adopted for the obtaining purest light and
highest rest.   It seems to me that he separated too much
that favorite text of his, "If a man will do his will, he
shall know of the doctrine whether it be of God;" he
greatly isolated it, but let us be just to him to remember
that he acted upon it nervously, and painfully sought to
do, and thus to *know:*—

But there are hours, and they come to us all at some period of
life or other, when the hand of Mystery seems to lie heavy on
the soul—when some life-shock scatters existence, leaves it a
blank and dreary waste henceforth for ever, and there appears
nothing of hope in all the expanse which stretches out, except
that merciful gate of death which opens at the end—hours when
the sense of misplaced or ill requited affection, the feeling of
personal worthlessness, the uncertainty and meanness of all human aims, and a doubt of all human goodness, unfix the soul
from all its old moorings,—and leave it drifting—drifting over
the vast Infinitude, with an awful sense of solitariness, Then,
the man whose faith rested on outward Authority and not on inward life, will find it give way : the authority of the priest, the authority of the Church : or merely the authority of a document
proved by miracles and backed by prophecy : the soul—conscious
life hereafter—God—will be an awful desolate Perhaps. Well ! in
such moments you doubt all—whether Christianity be true :
whether Christ was man, or God, or a beautiful fable. You ask
bitterly, like Pontius Pilate, What is truth ? In such an hour
what remains ? I reply, Obedience. Leave those thoughts for
the present. Act—be merciful and gentle—honest : force yourself to abound in little services : try to do good to others : be
true to the duty that you know. That must be right whatever
else is uncertain. And by all the laws of the human heart, by
the work of God, you shall not be left to doubt. Do that much
of the will of God which is plain to you, " You shall know of
the doctrine, whether it be of God."

And here it must be said, that it is at this point the dangers of Robertson's whole system of thought and theology

emerge. He unquestionably believed in the sacrifice of
Christ ; but it would need far greater space than I can
here bestow to notice the points of his departure from the
more generally received systems of theology. From the
reasons we have assigned, it followed that Christ, appre-
hended by the human spirit, was rather Infinite Wisdom,
and, if we may say so, Infinite Example, than Power.
Christ, in Mr, Robertson's system, becomes an illustrious,
to use the word again, infinite, revelation of the mind and
Providence of God. But, with all the touching lovingness
and purity of our Brighton teacher, we apprehend his
message would fail to meet and convey comfort to millions
of poor, weak, sinful souls in whom the seeds of grace were
very small and few, and the proclivities to damnation very
fierce and certain. His system seems to remove the method
of salvation from the Divine strength and place it in human hands. Of course, such a man would see the necessity
and strength of the great conservative elements in theology
we call Calvinism ; but his appeal was to human will, and
our comfort in religion, and almost our salvation, depended
on the equanimity of our own affections, the enlightenment
of our own perceptions. I say it with a profound sense of
indebtedness to Robertson for many gleams which, across
his pages, have been like sudden sunlight across the mists
of mountain lakes, and vales, still I am compelled to feel
that the element wanting in his sermons is Christ, the
power of God. But, while we say this, and attribute this
defection to him, we confess to infinite surprise that he has
been made to suffer so severely in popular estimation.
Something like the same defects would be noticed in all
Arminian teaching, and to the same extent. His theology
assimilated to much that is most popular in the Romish
Church, which, in spite of the great Western Father, Augustine, has never been very Augustinian in its teaching ;
was not John Wesley charged with defect? It is the pow-

er to perceive Christ as *imputed righteousness* which is, and has been wanting ; and this will always prevent Robertson's sermons from being the consolation of the large number of sick rooms, and places where the utterly weak, crushed, helpless, but penitential are.   They brace for action ; their words sound through the halls of the soul like a morning trumpet to sleeping hosts ; they are as grand and refreshing as winds on lonely seas, or solitary heights ; but for the consumptive and the weak, they are like sea breezes, too strong for the system.   Read from this point of view, perhaps it is not wonderful that Robertson's ecstacy of vision, his own purity of heart, and his perpetually brooding and profound sorrow over human lives and lots, consumed him : he took no refuge either in the heartless sentimentalism of universalism, or Heaven-made-easy-for-all-and-sundry, and eternal amnesty to, Newgate calendars : or in the still more, to my thought, inconceivable dream of annihilation, or the infinite ash-pan for the greatest multitude. He says, and it was much for such a nature to say, when we remember the principle rather of internal light from which he would in such a case speak, "My only difficulty is how *not* to believe in everlasting punishment."   The processes by which such a mind arrived both at its convictions and truths are most interesting ; and it would be especially interesting to notice how he and Dr. Newman, starting from centres so opposite, arrive very substantially at the same result.   It was a canon with him, and a well-known passage in the *Apologia* declares the same sentiment, that God cannot be found by the understanding.   Strange that it should seem surprising to us when the scope of Scripture seems to maintain the same impossibility.   "I do not think that where such men as La Place, D'Alembert, Hume, Voltaire,—have never seen any demonstration, that understanding can be the real court of appeal."   And thus it follows, as he says :—

There are men always talking of rights, and never of duties; I do not expect that they should believe in God, nor could I prove God to such. But, let a man once feel the law of duty in his soul—let him feel within him as with the articulate distinctness of a living Voice, the Absolute Imperative, "Thou shalt," and "Thou shalt not,"—let him feel that the only hell is the hell of doing wrong, and if that man does not believe in a God, all history is false. Brother men, the man who tries to discover a God outside of him instead of within, is doing just like him who endeavors to find out the place of the rainbow by hunting for it. The place of the rainbow depends upon your standing point; and I say, that the conviction of the being and character of a God depends upon your moral standing point. To believe in God is simply the most difficult thing in the world. You must be pure before you can believe in purity; generous, before you can believe in unselfishness. In all moral truth, what you are, that is the condition of your belief. Only to him in whom infinite aspirations stir, can an Infinite One be proved.

And in the following words he finely expresses how clearly he has grasped the truth that God is infinitely greater than human faith in Him :—

I think we shall become content to wait—a great lesson ; and let God teach us by degrees, instead of fancying we can find it all out by effort. Do you remember Wordsworth—

> Think you, 'mid all this mighty sum
> Of things for ever speaking,
> That nothing of itself will come,
> But we must still be seeking?

We do not trust God, we trust ourselves. We do not believe that He seeks us ; we fancy we have to seek Him. We are anxious to know *all about* God, and meanwhile we never think of knowing God. God, instead of religion, and much more, God, instead of theology, is what we need to believe in. . . . . . . I myself follow this plan as much as possible. I mix little with the religious world, and so avoid discussion. I read little of divinity, much more of literature, though that, from mental prostration, is now next to nothing. And I try to trust in God—

God and our souls ; there is nothing else to trust to. And I am
sure I should be giving you dreary advice were I to say, read on
all sides of the question. No, I rather say ; trust in God—live
in Him—do His will—and rest.

But this also would save him from the hard scepticism of
the college-school, as he says again to the workingmen :—

There have been great mistakes made in this society, and there
are many difficulties ; but you will weather the difficulties yet.
The mistakes will become your experience. Nay, I believe that
the discipline of character which many of you will have gained
by this struggle with an evil principle, and the practical insight
which it has given you into the true bearing of many social
questions, in which I personally know that wild and captivating
theories have been modified in your minds by this recent experience, will be invaluable. If only this had been gained, I believe the institution would not have been established in vain.
But if men say that all these difficulties tell against inquiry
and education, I can only say that it proves we want more education. If I wanted a proof of that, I should find it in this—
that the *workingmen of Brighton have not yet got beyond Tom
Paine.*

No doubt it is painfully true *conscience and faith are
twins* ; one is born with the other, with the one the other
expires too.

Robertson did not find land in Rome ; of Romanism he
spoke as " an infinitely small and sensualistic embodiment
of truths—a living human form shrunk into a mummy,
with every feature hideously like life." He was not, indeed
uncharitable to ancient Rome ; purgatory, absolution, ma-
riolatry, were, he says, to him "fossils, not lives ;" but
for " chanted services, and innocent gentlemen with lilies
of the valley in their dresses "—for the whole procession
of Christianity done up in haberdashery—he had, if not
contempt, then the fulness of a scornful pity ; from all
these, from the illusions of the senses, and the iron vices
of the understanding, he turned to feeling ; as we have

seen, to obedience. Let those who quarrel with Robertson's faith, first rival him in the heroism and beauty of his obedient life. Prayer was his solace, and perpetual strong consolation : he recommended this to all who expected to derive light and strength from his teaching. We read of his continuing in prayer until he realized the presence of God. "The love of God," he would say, "is the end of all, and I suppose all must drop off, leaf by leaf till that fruit is matured." In this spirit he prayed and commended prayer ; hence came to him the light within. It would be to malign God, and the dispensation of the Spirit, to believe that he was led astray by the light in which he walked ; his faculties thus became almost passive in their perceptions.

> The eye, it could not choose but see.
> He could not bid the ear be still.

With this also, in all his sense of misery arising from relation to the outer world, came the thought—the more than thought—the overwhelming feeling and assurance that God's idea of humanity always was what humanity is in Christ. Thus he would speak :—

Dare to be alone with God, my dear ———, trust Him, and do not fear that He will leave you in darkness long, though His light may dazzle. Was not HE alone in this world ?—unfelt, uncomprehended, suspected, spoken against ? And before Him was the cross. Before us, a little tea-table gossip, and hands uplifted in holy horror. Alas ! and we call that a cross to bear. Shame ! yet still I do admit that, for a loving heart to lack sympathy, is worse than pain.

He maintained that God could only be seen in Christ ; but certainly seen in Him. "That God's idea of humanity ever was and is—humanity as it is in Jesus Christ—that so far as it fails of that, His idea may be said to have not been realized."

The life of Christ and His death, after all, are the only true

solution of the mystery of human life; to that, after all, all
the discords of this world's wild music must be attuned at
last. There is sharp pain—past pain— in that letter which you
sent me, but yet, how instinctively one feels at once that the tone
of Christianity is wanting. I do not mean the cant expressions
but the genuine tone which numbers of real men and women
have learned by heart.

It may be hereafter mellowed into this as I hope my tone
will; but neither are as yet, though I have got what your cor-
respondent has not, the words of the Song; only I have not the
music. And what are the words without? Yet it is something
to feel the deep, deep conviction, which has never failed me in
the darkest moods, that Christ has the key to the mysteries of
Life and that they are not insoluble; also, that the Spirit of the
Cross is the condition which will put any one in possession of
the same key: "Take my yoke upon you, and ye shall find rest
for your souls." It is something, much, to know this, for, knowing it, I feel it to be unphilosophical and foolish to quarrel with
my lot, for my wisdom is to transmute my lot by meekness into
gold. With God I cannot quarrel, for I recognize the beauty
and justice of His conditions. It is a grand comfort to feel
that God is right, whatever and whoever else may be wrong.
I *feel* St. Paul's words, "Let God be true, and every man a liar."

The most admirable thing I noticed in his life is the holy and lofty spirit in which he fronted life. I read his own
character in the words he used in addressing the workingmen of Brighton:—

The cry of "*My* rights, *your* duties," I think we might change
to something nobler. If we could learn to say, "*My* duties,
your rights," we should come to the same thing in the end; but
the spirit would be different. That not very dignified feud between Nabal and David is only a picture of that which, hidden
under fine names, men are calling now patriotism; public spirit,
political martyrdom, protection, free trade—miserable enough
in my mind.

All we are gaining by this cry of Rights, is the life of the
wild beast and of the wild man of the desert, whose hand is

against every man, and every man's hand against him. Nay, the very brutes, unless they had an instinct which respec's Rights even more strongly than it claims them, could never form anything like a community. Did you never observe in a herony or rookery that the new-made nest is left in perfect confidence by the birds that built it? If the others had not learned to respect those private and sacred Rights, but began to assert each his right to the sticks which are woven together there, I fancy it would be some time before you could get a herony or a rookery!

Two thousand years ago, there was One here on this earth who lived the grandest life that ever has been lived yet, a life that every thinking man, with deeper or shallower meaning, has agreed to call Divine. I read little respec'ing His Rights or His claims of Rights; but I have read a great deal respecting His Duties. Every act He did He called a Duty. I read very little in that life respecting His Rights; but I hear a vast deal respecting His Wrongs—wrongs infinite—wrongs borne with a majestic, Godlike silence. His reward? His reward was the reward that God gives to all His true and noble ones—to be cast out in His day and generation, and a life-conferring death at last. Those were HIS Rights!

I have dwelt thus at length because I am really desirous that Robertson should not be misunderstood. I can have little hesitation in saying, that, as in life, so since his death he has been wickedly treated, and his views wickedly perverted. And now we must hasten to the close. He bore his own personal cross, and wrought out his work bravely in Brighton, until August, 1853. There, some have told me what a cheerful thing it was to see him walking even through the town; his bright face, his elastic step, and a fine yet affectionate bearing and presence, seeming to do a spectator good, while the noble, unclerical looking clergyman was hurrying along on his way. The volumes of his life will reveal what was going on in him and with him then. I have implied that his nature was really consumed by its

own intensity and zeal ; at last, the frame fell down, worn
out by the extraordinary flame of soul. Those causes
which more immediately brought this about I have not
time to attempt to detect or put in order and place before
my hearers. He felt all unkindness ; had he been an Independent clergyman, as in many instances with us, his
pulpit would have been filled for a year or two ; and he
would have been sent to the continent, if possible, to recruit his exhausted nature ; but he was unpopular with the
high and dry Church factions in the town ; especially it
was determined to make Brighton a perfect vestibule to
Popery, covering it with a network of nunneries and women in black, religious haberdasheries, and churches which
when the spectator enters, seem, by candles on the altars,
flowers and wreaths, fald-cloths, and all the infinite raggery
and rubbish of modern Tractarianism, to transfer him instantly from Anglicanism to Romanism—those who loved
this were not likely to sympathise with the fine appeals to
man as a living conscience and consciousness, emanating
from the lips of the preacher of Trinity. How can men
whose long course of vicarage never resulted in a single
ministration to a human heart, whose history is only one
record of hard, incarnate selfishness, without a single echo
of one loving heart, breaking the monotonous and desert
solitude of their own dreary, unmeaning, do-nothing career
either know or sympathise with such men as Robertson ?
Mr. Robertson appointed his curate to relieve him of his
burdens while his life was wasting and his heart breaking :
the vicar possessed the legal power of putting an interdict
on Mr. Robertson's choice. We can understand the natural dislike a man like the vicar of Brighton would feel towards a man like the minister of Trinity ; in addition to
this, it seems the vicar had some personal dislike to the
clergyman Mr. Robertson had appointed ; the vicar, no
doubt, knew his opportunity. The very presence of Rob-

ertson in the town to a man capable of the career of the
vicar of Brighton, must have been as unpleasant as the
voice of John the Baptist to Herod. Now was the moment; Robertson could not preach—of course he could
not yield—he was compelled to relinquish Trinity. That
scene, no doubt, in-wrought with a host of affectionate
memories, where so many of the most illustrious and gifted had hung upon his eloquent lips, of every order of rank,
and of every grade of spiritual and moral excellence, had
to be relinquished; the desk, hallowed by the gift and
prayers of the servant girls, the classes of the young men,
the members of his congregation, some of them gifted women, related to him by the great bond and tie of useful life
and labor—all this had to go ; in fact, Robertson was sa-
crificed to the much-lauded parochial system of the Church
of England. It was the parochial system of the Church
of England which prevented that fine life from expiring in
the harness of its uses and affections. Some misconcep-
tions seem to have spread about his death which may, perhaps, be cleared up by the closing pages of his memoir.
With patience, thoughtfulness, and faith, he trod along
that dark valley he had so often sought to illuminate for
others. I am glad to believe that his humble trust never
deserted him ; God, Christ, and immortality were sustaining thoughts to him. He felt still the beauty of the outer
world he had loved so much, the beauty which had made
his heart ache so much. When scarcely able to move, a
day or two before he died, he got up at four o'clock in the
morning, and crept to the window, to see, as he said, "the
beautiful morning." A night or two before his death, he
dreamed that his two sisters, long since dead, came to
crown him : "I saw them," he said earnestly. All reverent kindnesses were heaped around his dying bed ; "how
different," he said, "the lot of Him who would fain have
slaked His morning hunger with green figs:" His dear and

attached friend, Lady Byron, left a sick bed to see him ; but was permitted only to be with him a few moments. At last came the day ; it was on a Sunday, the 15th of August, 1853. Shocks of intense pain, unbearable in agony, came upon him ; feebly crying at intervals, "My God, my Father! my God, my Father!" he fought out the battle, which sooner or later, all have to fight. This lasted for two hours, during which period, however, he never lost his clear consciousness. I am glad to know that his mother, the "my dear little mother," the "dear little motherette" of his letters, and his wife, and one friend, with his physician, watched over him. When they sought to relieve him by changing his position, he could not endure the touch : "I can not bear it," he said, "let me rest, I must die ; let God do His work." They were his last words ; immediately afterwards, a few minutes past midnight, all was over. Fatal thirty-seven! The age of Byron, the age of Burns, the age of Raphael, and of what a long procession descending into the tomb in the prime of their majesty, the fulness of their insight and vision! I am glad now to see, beneath the steady light of that midnight lamp, the quiet which sheds itself over the features of the dying saint.

Brighton knew how to appreciate its loss. It had been resolved that the funeral should be private ; but it soon became manifest that this would be almost impossible. The circumstances of his death too, the harsh, legal cruelty of the vicar, roused the spirit of the town. The congregation of the departed clergyman, of course, desired to follow his remains ; a number of local societies, and Jews, Unitarians, Roman Catholics, Quakers, and Churchmen, followed to his tomb this noble gentleman, this ardent Christian minister, this saintly and gifted man. All the shops were closed in the line of the procession ; the principal tradesmen assumed mourning, and all sects and classes merged their differences in a common grief around the grave so honored—to our thought, so premature. It surely should be a lesson very helpful and suggestive, not only that "he being dead yet speaketh,"—but really he did not begin to speak from his present influential platform at all until after Brighton, suddenly smitten with an astonishing sorrow, followed him, in long procession, to his grave in the hollow of the Downs he loved so much ; and it surely adds something to the pathos of that procession to know, as I have gathered from residents in the town, how among the followers was one remarkable lady, wending her way on foot —Lady Byron—who would not go in her carriage ; "unworthy," as she said, "to ride after such remains."

It is the story of one whom many call the Arnold of the pulpit, where he signalized himself as that great man did in the schoolroom. Truth, I hope real to my own convictions, presents itself in many aspects differently to those in which it was beheld by Robertson : but *the man*—his earnestness—his reality—his consecrated genius—his self-denial—his sympathy—his wonderful glances into the places from whence, before his vision, not only the obscure flies, but gives place to unexpected and reconciling light— his nobility and his tenderness—all unite together to seize on the imagination, and to quicken and impart life to all who come beneath the spell of his influence. Does he not seem to thee perfect? Oh, art thou perfect? Have we not often said our gothic architecture is a thing of sublime incongruities, contradictions and deformities, but how sublime ; and, to generations long beyond the present, will be not only fascinating, but helping in some of the deepest needs and wants of the soul, the life-giving words and character of Frederick Robertson.

As specimens of preparation for the pulpit, the sermons of Mr. Robertson are very instructive to preachers.* I

* *Sermons, Preached at Trinity Chapel, Brighton.* By the Rev. Frederick W. Robertson, M.A.

understand none of them to have been prepared for the press, perhaps few prepared with any idea to another eye than that of the preacher. Some are recollections, notes taken down by friends, fragmentary and incomplete, yet with directness and earnest practicalness of aim, and, for the most part, unmistakable transparency of meaning. Now, I suspect, had Mr. Robertson prepared more elaborately, with a nice eye to finish ; had he brought his cultured and fastidious taste to bear upon these compositions, so far from increasing in power, their efficacy would have been almost lost. He seems to have resolved his topics, and to have used his notes, chiefly, for the purpose of giving freedom to his own mind. As we have intimated, a fragmentary character attaches to most of the sermons—paragraphs unfinished, words penned evidently to awaken and re-collect within the preacher's mind the chain of thought, association, and discourse—from this broken and incontinuous character of composition, it is, we feel, that we cannot, even in any very adequate sense, know the mind of Robertson. His bright glance rapidly pierced the recesses of subjects hither and thither. Then he returned into himself and mused ; then the fire burned, and he shot forth those flakes of living speech which do not always seem part of a symmetrical whole. That, too, which is put upon paper might be so incomplete compared with that which the preacher intended it should be, when the written word of the pen became the uttered word of the tongue. Here, for instance, is a short paragraph—it is the close of the sermon on the appointment of the first king in Israel, and the preacher finds a lesson which looks out upon the evanescence of human life.

A very pregnant lesson. Life passes, work is permanent. It is all going—fleeting and withering. Youth goes. Mind decays. That which is done remains. Through ages, through eternity, what you have done for God, that, only that, you are.

Ye that are workers, and count it the soul's worst disgrace to feel life passing in idleness and uselessness, take courage. Deeds never die.

Now this is surely a truth stated very boldly. Sufficient for a preacher's note-book—certainly not sufficient for a reader. Mr. Robertson says, "Mind decays, 'it is fleeting and withering as life,' we are only what we have done for God; deeds only never die." If Mr. Robertson were with us, we suppose, he would say, while we ventured to point his attention to such a paragraph:—"You know you are attributing to it a meaning I never intended; I never meant to get rid of the fact of man's substantive being." I do not suppose that when he asserts the perpetuity of deeds and their consequences, that Mr. Robertson intends to deny to man the possession of an inherent and an immortal consciousness. The sentence, in fact, was never intended to be printed; it was simply a succession of catch-words to the preacher for his pulpit. I suppose that from many such sentences he suffers in a similar way; readers forming impressions of what the man really was, from broken hints and fragmentary words. Moreover, with the greatest respect we should say it, especially in the recollection of the rare delight these posthumous works have given to us and to thousands, we have sometimes wondered whether so vigilant, and reverent a conscientiousness has presided over the executorship of these remains as there ought to have been. Would Robertson himself have ever sanctioned the publication of the notes *In Memoriam?*

I must make up my mind that the whole of Frederick Robertson cannot be known; his mind, too, was essentially of an order that does not shape itself into system, or the system may be there, but the mind does not know itself. It is like some wonderful organism out of sight. There are minds, like men observing the heavens, they see constellations dip and constellations rise, because they look intently and earnestly; the heavens present different aspects on different nights; or they visit different latitudes, and so become possessed of different scenic effects in the celestial spaces. It is so with men who watch the "heavenly places" and states of the human soul, while, to some, all experiences are one and the same; to such men no experiences are possessed of sameness; they all have essential differences, while they are all illustrative of the great life of God in the human soul. It, perhaps, would have been a very difficult thing for Coleridge to shape his spiritual observations and ruminations into one consistent Cosmos; it is certainly a difficult thing for any one from his *Friends*, *Aids to Reflection*, and *Table-Talk*, to do it for him. The glory of the man was his marvellous super-fecundity of thought, life, and vision, and very much of this is the power of Robertson's sermons, they are living and they give life to souls, they shoot their own volitions and thoughts into the minds of men; possessing in an eminent degree that power of expressing pregnant truths—truths, not only true in themselves, but which illustrate and conform together other truths—truths, which, like daylight, not only give light to our own room, but enable us to look upon the world without, which is just the difference between truth from a sectarian point of view, which is a most useful, and by no means to be despised parlor-lamp or candle;—and truth from the Church point of view, which is like the sun, a light for all the households of the universe. His views of the atonement are not mine; he seems to me, and I say it with great respect, partly, because in the memory that he is no longer with us, and partly, because I am disposed, from the reasons I have mentioned, to doubt how far we have a perfect view of his mind—he seems to us, I say, however, to plant the fact of the atonement less on what God has done for the world than on what man is doing in the way of sacrifice and atonement for himself. Is not the following, now, a defective statement of the thing?

My Christian brethren, hell is not merely a thing hereafter, hell is a thing here; hell is not a thing banished to the far distance, it is ubiquitous as conscience. Wherever there is a worm of undying remorse, the sense of having done wrong, and a feeling of degradation, there is hell begun. And now respecting this. These words, "banishment from God," "alienation," though merely popular phrases, are expressions of a deep truth, —it is true they are *but* popular expressions, for God is not wrath. You are not absolutely banished from God's Presence. The Immutable changes not. He does not become angry or passionate whenever one of the eight hundred million inhabitants of this world commits a sin. And yet you will observe there is no other way in which we can express the truth but in these popular words. Take the illustration furnished to us last Sunday: it may be that it is the cloud and the mist that obscure the sun from us; the sun is not changed in consequence; it is a change in our atmosphere. But if the philosopher says to you, the sun in its splendor remains the same in the infinite space above, it is only an optical delusion which makes it appear lurid: to what purpose is that difference to you? to you it is lurid, to you it is dark. If you feel a darkness in your eye, coldness in your flesh, to what purpose, so far as feeling is concerned, is it that philosophy tells you the sun remains unchanged? And if it be that God in the heaven above remains Love still, and that Love warms not your heart, and that God is Light, in whom is no darkness at all—yet He shines not in your heart: my Christian brethren, let metaphysics and philosophy say what they will, these popular expressions are the true ones after all; to you God *is* angry, from God you *are* banished, God's countenance *is* alienated from you.

All true without any doubt, but not completely true— leaving out of sight what God does on His own part to reconcile His own character with man's salvation—in fact, with the most beautiful and elevating views of Christ, and the most subduing and lovable views of God, there is in Mr. Robertson's system the want of that element which meets us alike in the Old and New Testaments; which, to quote his own language in the extract we have just made, whatever it may be in itself, is wrath to us, and ruin, and condemnation, but for the supernatural means which God appoints, passing through the fire to stay the wrath of the fire and by "the law of the spirit of life in Christ Jesus," to overcome "the law of sin and death."

It is in his sermons on Scripture characters in which the preacher so eminently displays his power of using the old biographic story for the purpose of unwinding the history of the human heart in any age. The sermon on the *Character of Eli*, and the *Calling of Samuel*, is a beautiful illustration of this. From several illustrations we take two or three. The following passage on the docility of Eli before the teaching of the inspired lad is very beautiful, and all in Mr. Robertson's style.

Eli might with ease have assumed the priestly tone. When Samuel came with his strange story, that he had heard a voice calling to him in the dark, Eli might have fixed upon him a clear, cold, unsympathizing eye and said, "This is excitement— mere enthusiasm. I am the appointed channel of God's communications, I am the priest. Hear the Church. Unordained, unanointed with priestly oil, a boy, a child, it is presumption for you to pretend to communications from Jehovah! A layman has no right to hear Voices; it is fanaticism." Eli might have done this; he would have only done what ordained men have done a thousand times when they have frowned irregular enthusiasm into dissent. And then Samuel would have become a mystic, or a self-relying enthusiast. For he could not have been made to think that the Voice was a delusion. *That* Voice no priest's frown could prevent his hearing. On the other hand, Eli might have given his own authoritative interpretation to Samuel, of that word of God which he had heard. But suppose that interpretation had been wrong!

Eli did neither of these things. He sent Samuel to God. He taught him to inquire for himself. He did not tell him to reject as fanaticism the belief that an inner Voice was speaking to him, a boy; nor did he try to force his own interpretation on that Voice. His great care was to put Samuel in direct communication with God; to make him listen to God; nay, and that independently of him, Eli. Not to rule him; not to *direct* his feelings and belief; not to keep him in the leading-strings of spiritual childhood, but to teach him to walk alone.

There are two sorts of men who exercise influence. The first are those who perpetuate their own opinions, bequeath their own names, form a sect, gather a party round them who speak their words, believe their belief. Such men were the ancient Rabbis. And of such men, in and out of the Church, we have abundance now. It is the influence most aimed at and most loved. The second class is composed of those who stir up faith, conscience, thought, to do their own work. They are not anxious that those they teach should think as they do, but that they should *think*. Nor that they should take this or that rule of right or wrong, but that they should be conscientious. Nor that they should adopt their own views, of God, but that faith in God should be roused in earnest. Such men propagate not many *views;* but they propagate Life itself in inquiring minds and earnest hearts.

Now this is God's real best work. Men do not think so. They like to be guided. They ask, what am I to think? and what am I to believe? and what am I to feel? Make it easy for me. Save me the trouble of reflecting and the anguish of inquiring. It is very easy to do this for them; but from what minds, and from what books, do we really gain most of that which we can really call our own? From those that are suggestive, from those that kindle life within us, and set us thinking, and call conscience into action—not from those that exhaust a subject and seem to leave it threadbare, but from those that make us feel there is a vast deal more in that subject yet, and send us as Eli sent Samuel, into the dark Infinite to listen for ourselves.

And this is the Ministry and its work—not to drill hearts,

4*

and minds, and consciences, into right forms of thought and
mental postures, but to guide to the Living God who speaks.
It is a thankless work; for as I have said, men love to have all
their religion done out for them. They want something
definite, and sharp, and clear—words—not the life of God in
the soul; and, indeed, it is far more flattering to our vanity to
have men take our views, represent us, be led by us. Rule is
dear to all. To rule men's spirit is the work of every *true* priest
of God, to lead men to think and feel for themselves—to open
their ears that God may speak. Eli did this part of his work
in a true spirit. He guided Samuel, trained his character,
"But God's spirit," Eli says, " I cannot give that. God's voice!
I am not God's voice. I am only God's witness, erring, listening for myself. I am here, God's witness, to say—God
speaks. I may err—let God be true. Let me be a liar if you
will. My mission is done when your ear is opened for God to
whisper into." Very true, Eli was superseded. Very true, his
work was done. A new set of views, not his, respecting Israel's
policy and national life, were to be propagated by his successor;
but it was Eli that guided that successor to God who gave the
views; and Eli had not lived in vain. My brethren, if any
man or any body of men stand between us and the living God,
saying, "Only through us—the Church—can you approach
God; only through my consecrated touch can you receive
grace; only through my ordained teaching can you hear God's
voice; and the voice which speaks in your soul in the still moments of existence is no revelation from God, but a delusion and
a fanaticism"—that man is a false priest. To bring the soul
face to face with God, and supersede ourselves, that is the work
of the Christian ministry.

There was in Eli a resolve to know the whole truth. "What
is the thing that the Lord hath said unto thee? I pray thee
hide it not from me; God do so to thee, and more also, if thou
hide anything from me of all the things that he said unto thee."
Eli asked in earnest to know the worst.

It would be a blessed thing to know what God thinks of us.
But next best to this would be to see ourselves in the light in
which we appear to others: other men's opinion is a mirror in

which we learn to see ourselves. It keeps us humble when bad and good alike are known to us. The worst slander has in it some truth from which we may learn a lesson which may make us wiser when the first smart is passed.

Therefore it is a blessing to have a friend like Samuel, who can tell us truth, judicious, candid, wise; one to whom we can say, "Now tell me what I am, and what I seem; hide nothing, but tell me the worst." But, observe, we are not to beg praise or invite censure—that were weak. We are not to ask for every malicious criticism or tormenting report—that were hypochondria, ever suspecting, and ever self-tormenting; and to that diseased sensibility it would be no man's duty to minister. True friendship will not retail tormenting trifles; but what we want is one friend at least, who will extenuate nothing, but with discretion tell the worst, using unflinchingly the sharp knife which is to cut away the fault.

In a very different style is the following paragraph upon the personal power of the Bible—a topic often treated, but upon which Mr. Robertson, of course, could not express himself as others had expressed themselves before.

This collection of books has been to the world what no other book has ever been to nation. States have been founded on its principles. Kings rule by a compact based on it. Men hold the Bible in their hands when they prepare to give solemn evidence affecting life, death, or property; the sick man is almost afraid to die unless the Book be within reach of his hands; the battle-ship goes into action with one on board whose office is to expound it; its prayers, its psalms are the language which we use when we speak to God; eighteen centuries have found no holier, no diviner language. If ever there has been a prayer or a hymn enshrined in the heart of a nation, you are sure to find its basis in the Bible. There is no new religious idea given to the world, but it is merely the development of something given in the Bible. The very translation of it has fixed language and settled the idioms of speech. Germany and England speak as they speak because the Bible was translated. It has made the most illiterate peasant more familiar with the history, customs, and geography of ancient

Palestine, than with the localities of his own country. Men
who know nothing of the Grampians, of Snowdon, or of Skid-
daw, are at home in Zion, the lake of Gennesaret, or among the
rills of Carmel. People who know little about London know
by heart the places in Jerusalem, where those blessed feet trod
which were nailed to the Cross. Men who know nothing of the
architecture of a Christian cathedral can yet tell you all about
the pattern of the Holy Temple. Even this shows us the influence of the Bible. The orator holds a thousand men for half-
an-hour breathless—a thousand men as one, listening to his
single word. But this Word of God has held a thousand
nations for thrice a thousand years spell-bound; held them by
an abiding power, even the universality of its truth; and we
feel it to be no more a collection of books, but *the* Book.

This paragraph occurs in a sermon on Inspiration,
which I have no hesitation in characterising as very incomplete and contradictory. He tells us, for instance, to "get
the habit—a glorious one—of referring all to Christ
throughout the Scriptures;" and of the Old Testament he
says, "Christ is perfectly, all that every saint was par-
tially;" yet of Christ in the Old Testament, he says,
"nothing is more miserable as specimens of perverted ingenuity, than the attempts of certain commentators and
preachers, to find remote, and recondite, and intended
allusions to Christ everywhere." I have referred to topics
like these, because I would not be supposed to be blind to
some points in the preacher's teaching, with which I have
no sympathy. But it is easier to trace the symmetry and
order in the nutshell we desiderate in the vast proportions
of some huge tropical tree, and a free mind must frequently
have phases very offensive to a narrow one. He was a
preacher little known beyond the circle of his own pulpit
influence in his life, but who held within his mind a power
of mystical and subtle insight—a free and glowing and un-
artificial eloquence—an eloquence of diction—a power of
expressing to men and women their manifold thoughts,

and meeting on simplest ground the cultured and educated classes, by the expression of sympathies—the common property of all, and uniting together the charms of goodness and greatness during the period of a brief ministry in such a manner as to make him, if not the first of all, yet one of the three or four really great English preachers of our time.

II.

On Arrangement of Texts by Division.

HAVE already said that sermons should have bones—should be structural, architectural, or rather anatomical—most certainly they should be this ; but, at the same time, how necessary to give to the skeleton muscles, flesh, blood, nerves, a heart, and lungs! No skeleton moves itself, or will affect any other way than unpleasantly if unclothed ; I come, therefore, to the method of sermons. Perhaps this lecture should have anticipated that of last week, and should have been preceded by that on texts. I surely need not say to you that to have any efficiency you must have method ; in fact this is the new life of logic, it is the science of arrangement ; if I ought not rather to say that all science is simply arrangement ; organization, order. You have heard, I dare say, that method is formal or cryptic—that is, visible and obvious, latent, hidden—effective for his purposes, but within the preacher's mind ; throughout the whole sermon, there should be the last, for your own benefit, that you know where to fall back, and where to find the topic of your thought ; for the benefit of your

(86)

hearers, there should be the first. I might refer you to
the *Morning Exercises** for some illustrations of the ridic-
ulous exercises of divisions. Among those exercises, most
of them, with all their excellences, lie open to this great
exception, that they confuse and tax the hearer's memory
with thirty, forty, or sixty particulars ; there is a sermon
by Thomas Lye, on 1 Cor. vi. 17, "the terms of which,"
he says, "I shall endeavor συν Θεω, clearly to explain."
This he does in *thirty particulars, for the fixing of it on a
right basis*, and then adds *fifty-six more to explain the subject*,
in all eighty-six. And what makes it the more astonishing,
is his introduction to all these, which is this, " Having thus
beaten up and levelled our way to the text, I shall not
stand to shred the words into any unnecessary parts, but
shall extract out of them such an observation as I conceive strikes a full eight to the mind of the Spirit of
God." And in the same volume Dr. Roger Drake intro-
duces into a discourse *above one hundred and seventy particulars*, and yet says, " he passed by sundry useful points,
pitching only on that which comprehended the marrow and
the substance." Well might Robinson remark upon this
style that, did any one adopt it, how it would be like the
goodly sight of the man of modern times dressed like a
Druid ; at any rate, we may say, the steel corslet, the buff
jerkin, or the slashed doublet of a later time.

I do not think you are at all in danger of running into
these absurd extremes, but there are others. John Edwards says :—†

They are people that rack their fancies and the texts together,
they stretch and scrue the words, they tease and worry, they

**Morning Exercises*, Vol. V. Nicholls' Edition. 1845.

†An Enquiry into Four Remarkable Texts of the New Testament, which contain some difficulty in them, with their probable
resolution. 1692.

torment and most unmercifully force and drag a text to their side. You may observe it, an arrant *critic* is a resolute sort of man generally, he is very earnest in his work, though in ever so light a matter, and pusheth it on to the utmost extremity. I could mention several professors of criticism who are guilty of this miscarriage, who make it their business to force their way. You shall see them set down before a text, and raise their batteries against it, and play their cannon and mortars upon it. If this will not do, they come with greater force and make a fresh assault with stronger Detachments from poets, orators, historians, philosophers, etc., and fall on with greater fury, thinking by this means to bring it to a parley, and then a surrender: or rather, by their furious attacks we may guess they intend no other thing than to take us by storm. And truly in this imaginary romantic adventure they think they have done it, they persuade themselves they have taken possession of the fort, and so the campaign is at an end, and there is a period to their doughty attempts. But I hate these violent courses, this besieging of a chapter and verse, this investing of a place of scripture. I abhor the common practice of ravaging and preying upon the Bible: I do not like the bombarding of Scripture, I approve not of the storming of a text, and taking it by force. It is very unchristian and unbecoming employment to extort a sense from any place of Holy Writ, and by little critical arts and fetches to bring over the words to a compliance with us, *i.e.* to the meaning which we design.

Our divisions should be simple, but simple as they may be, and should be, there is no reason why they should so naturally divide themselves that each division is anticipated by the hearer; while we must cheerfully admit, too, that there are some texts which furnish instantly such a series of topics that no insight of the preacher, or ingenuity upon his part, can at all reform. There are two ideas of division —one synthetic, this is comprehensive, going up the hill, it is inductive, and conducts one to unity of vision; the other, analytic, apprehensive, the going down the hill, and it is deductive, and takes a text in pieces. Method in the pulpit, of course including division, has been said to be all included in this, "Keep moving toward a given point."*

I told you some time since, when Rowland Hill was examining a young man for the ministry, he said, "Well, the Gospel is a good milch cow, she gives plenty of milk; I never write my sermons. I first give a pull at justification, then a plug at adoption, and afterwards a bit at sanctification, and so, in one way or the other, I fill my pail with the Gospel milk." And although this was said with all Rowland Hill's accustomed coarseness and drollery, yet it is full of truth; there is no doubt that a sermon should contain these three as the great elementary truths. The earth has a vesture of flowers and trees, gloriously green, and her fields and rivers; but what kind of world would it be without granite and limestone? and so you may have in your ministry multitudinous truths and illustrations, but out of every text should rise those mountain peaks : I mix my figures, but you will forgive me ; out of every text and passage you should press those three : *justification*, *i. e.*, the righteousness of God through Jesus Christ our Lord ; *adoption*, the family principle of God's church, His people ; and *sanctification*, a renewed nature, "walking in the midst of a crooked and perverse generation as lights in the world."

The usages of many ages and countries have decided that the text is a wise limitation and fence, and guide. The discourse in the pulpit, whether necessarily so or not, has been the subject of very considerable discussion. Vinet gives his weighty and admirable name against the constant use of the text, and he says that men of every different character and quite opposite doctrines have agreed in opinion that the use of texts is an abuse. VOLTAIRE, perhaps, will not command any great deference, but we may listen to him when he says :—" It were to be wished that

* Dr. L. Whithington, Art. " Method in Sermons," *Bib. Sac.*, 1861.

Bourdaloue, in banishing from the pulpit the bad taste which debased it, had banished from it also the custom of preaching from a text. Indeed, to speak long upon a quotation of a line or two, to labor to bring his whole discourse to bear upon this line, such a labor appears a trifling little worthy the dignity of the ministry. The text becomes a kind of motto, or rather enigma, which the discourse develops." So says Voltaire in his great work on *The Age of Louis XIV.* We can have nothing to take exception to in the manner in which the objection is urged, only that we regard the whole matter from altogether another standpoint. But the standpoint of Vinet may be supposed to be also identical with our own, yet he remarks that the use of iso·lated texts, joined to the necessity of never preaching without a text, has certainly in its rigor and in its absolute, something false, something servile, which narrows the mind, confines the thought, puts restraint upon the individuality of the preacher ; although this distinguished man admits, " that the liberty of preaching without a text would possibly have still more inconveniences, if the abuses which have resulted from it would not be more serious."

This is true, but it only meets a portion of our position. Should any one demand of me why I invariably take a text, I would say this arises from the nature of the Bible, the Book itself, and the nature of the message of which I am the channel, the ambassador from God to souls.

Yes, I own that I am amazed that any man should dispute the matter with us, for it seems clear to me that each pulpit service is to partake of the character of a demonstration ; a demonstration, either of a *truth*, or demonstration to the conscience ; the demonstration of the Spirit. You go into the lecture hall of the anatomist, or the chemist, or the astronomer, and upon a very small segment of truth you listen a long time to what is a demonstration from the chair of mental and moral science ; or from the chair of criticism. The minister is very frequently in the pulpit to *demonstrate* the truth ; a passage is, perhaps, isolated from its contextual relations, not unfairly or unrighteously, but because it is the key-stone of an argument, but it especially furnishes the very point, standing on which the whole region of the truth round about may be seen ; or it may be a text making a direct aim to the conscience—a text which the preacher may use like a flail ; while, further, the objection supposes that the text must always be a mere proverbial word of a few syllables. It may be a parable, it may be the whole of an argument, but, in any case, we may hold that for the upholding the authority of sacred Scripture, and for pressing home the truth, there is no method so advisable, so likely to fasten on the mind, and to pierce the conscience, as the judiciously-chosen text. "*Bring hither the ephod,*" said the priest in olden times. There is a story of a young man in a Scotch family, uttering a string of more than doubtful opinions, when he was stopped by the stern voice of the father or the grandfather, "*Rax me yon Bible,*" and no doubt in all matters of doctrine or of duty the Bible is our ephod ; nor, I believe, can any one say "I was distressed about my path of faith and obedience, and I sought the Bible in vain." No! and it is thus to be maintained by this daily use. Nothing is more striking in Popish Continental churches than the pulpit without the Bible. The Papist goes into our churches, and says he sees the Bible, and Bibliolatry, the "one man," the voice of the Church and no divine guide ; but in the Papal building what have we ?

And here let me offer this remark, that for the work of the permanent pastorate nothing will avail but keeping your own mind constantly at work upon the stores of Biblical knowledge and truth. You must not have to seek

your subjects week by week, or you will be often stranded
and never find them ; while, if you read the Scriptures
thoughtfully day by day, you will find every day light break
forth from the word, and from every part of it.   Only thus
can you be fitted for the permanent pastorate ; it is not
surely so difficult ; Monastic men have preached every day,
and there are men who still can preach every day without
a diminution of freshness ; but only in the way I suggest
to you, the placing yourself where every day the truth of
God may grapple with your own consciences.   There is a
preaching which has been called brushwood preaching, as
it is said the genius of some preachers is of the very nature of brushwood, which blazes and burns out with a
transient splendor.   There is need for method in the arrangement of your subjects, not less than in the introduction of them, and what a world of topics lies before you.
On you devolves, each in your separate sphere, the task of
presenting the Christian cosmos to the view ; all the whole
Christian zodiac of truth ; all the firmament of doctrine
and emotion.   The heavens are crowded with stars, but
they need the eye and mind of the spiritual astronomer to
group and to illustrate their plan.

But texts and divisions—some sermons have a very happy
and apt conjunction between text, and divisions, and treatment.

A young man not very many years since—the circumstance is given in the life of Dr. Waugh,* was sent for to
preach before the Prince of Orange at the Hague.   He had
indicated great talent and promise, and the Prince wished
to hear him.   The young man's father was also a preacher
at the court, and he was commanded by the Prince to push
his son at a moment's warning into the pulpit, that he
might give a fair specimen of his powers ; also the text was
given to him from Acts viii. 26–40.   You remember the

* *Life of Dr. Alexander Waugh.*

passage—the story of the courtier and his meeting with Philip. The young preacher was confounded, but there was no time to hesitate. After a suitable introduction he told his noble and crowded audience that his subject contained four wonders, four marvels, *(quatre merveilles)* which he should make the four heads of his sermon, and if he should say anything to which their ears had not been accustomed in that place, he hoped that his unprepared state of mind from his sudden call would plead his apology, and ·that they would consider the things he might speak as according to our Lord's promise, "given to him in that hour."

Marvel the first. A courtier READS. Here he deplored the sad neglect in the education of great men in modern times, and the little attention paid by them to books.

Marvel the second. A courtier reads the BIBLE. Here he deplored the melancholy condition of religious sentiments and feelings in the great, and the impoverished state of a mind so destitute.

Marvel the third. A courtier owns *himself ignorant of his subject.* Here he exposed the conceit and presumption of petulant ignorance in high places.

Marvel the fourth. A courtier applies to a *minister of Christ for information*, and follows his counsel. The Prince was famous for sleeping during the service, but he did not sleep during that sermon.

But our young friend was never asked to preach in the palace again. The Prince and the preacher took their revenge upon each other.

I suppose every one will agree with me that for that suggestiveness which pierces down to the centre of texts and subjects, sometime, it may be admitted, in a questionable manner, but more usually with great and most pertinent skill, we have some of the finest illustrations in MATTHEW HENRY. Turn for an illustration to Jeremiah xxxviii, where we have the account of Ebedmelech, the Ethiopian, drawing Jeremiah out of a dungeon, with cords, old cast clouts and rotten rags; the expositor draws many lessons in the way of fact and observation.

I. *Fact.* A prophet is in a dungeon. Whence observe it is common for wicked people to look on God's faithful servants as their enemies.

II. *Fact.* The king could not help him; whence observe those will have a great deal to answer for, though they have a secret kindness for good people, yet dare not own it in a time of need.

III. *Fact.* Ebedmelech was an Ethiopian. Whence observe some Gentiles had more equity and piety than some Jews.

IV. *Fact.* Ebedmelech was a courtier. Whence observe God has a remnant in all places, among all sorts. There were saints even in Cæsar's household.

V. *Fact.* The king was sitting in the gate on public business, when Ebedmelech applied to him for the release of Jeremiah. Whence observe whither should oppressed innocency flee for protection but to the throne? No time must be lost when life is in danger, especially valuable life. God can raise up friends for His people in distress where they little thought of them.

VI. *Fact.* The king orders his release. Observe, the hearts of kings are in God's hands; let this encourage us to appear boldly before God; we may succeed better than we thought.

VII. *Fact.* That Ebedmelech took old clouts and rags from under the treasury in the king's house. Observe, no waste should be made even in kings' palaces. Broken linen, like broken meat, should be preserved for the use of the poor.

VIII. *Fact.* Ebedmelech directed Jeremiah to put the soft rags under his arm-holes. Observe, distressed people should be. treated with tenderness.

IX. *Fact.* Ebedmelech did not throw the rags down, but let them down by cords. Observe, the poor should be relieved with respec'.

All this is very ingenious and not very far-fetched; there are lessons which should be brought out from the biographical and historical portions of Scripture constantly, since they arrest, and instruct, and abide.

The method of handling texts by division has recently fallen into disuse, but if many divisions have been un-wise, much more unwise is the disuse ; of old when the text was chosen, the next thing was to secure happy divisions, they were marked, and they were rememberable. True, some divisions may, in their mere unmeaning plat-itude-like character, be as good as none, and very often good preachers have been able to strike out such an out-line as to make it rememberable and happy. The divisions obtained by the old men, the sermon was almost completed. It became fixed and rememberable in the preacher's mind, and as fixed and rememberable in the mind and memory of the hearer. I do not say that divisions should not be obvi-ous ; on the contrary, to be useful they should, they must be obvious, but not so merely obvious that any hearer can anti-cipate and strike out such a method by merely glancing at the text himself ; but, on the contrary, there has come into vogue another style, still more absurd, the seeking about for modes of division, straining after intellectual effect, and I could present many magnificent receipts of this kind, for diluting wine into water, and thickening milk into mud. Fancy a man dividing a text after this fashion. " God is a Spirit," etc., here we have *first*, the transcendental prop-erties of the divine nature. " God is," etc. ; *second*, we have the anthropomorphic relations under which those transcendental properties are revealed, spirit and truth ; *third*, we have the symbolism under which those transcend-ental properties in the anthropomorphic relations become worship. They that worship " *must worship*, etc." This pretty little thing is a fair illustration of the "House-that-Jack-built" kind of style, beneath which "the hungry sheep look up, but are not fed." It is most vain work to float out upon a sea of generalities ; the text should speak,

and yet it is possible without any of such sinful folly to
permit a fair portion of human ingenuity to illustrate, and
to open without torturing it. The old Puritan preachers,
dealing as they did in interminable divisions, will be found
valuable in this : while their sermons can never be preached, they do often yet furnish very helpful methods of the
way in which a text may be made to yield up divisions,
which are as mile-stones to the thought, boundary lines of
definition ; or suggestive variations of idea. In Obadiah
Sedgewick's *Shepherd of Israel*, in the Sermons of Thomas
Watson, and in the less known but especially suggestive
works of John Smith, of Clavering, in Essex, called the
Essex Dove,* will be found especially illustrations of this.
The outline of THOMAS WATSON's Sermon, *Keep thy Heart*,
is illustrative of this comprehensive suggestive character.

I. Keep thy heart. 1. As thou wouldst a temple; 2. As a
treasure; 3. As a garden ; 4. As a garrison ; 5. As a prisoner;
6. As a watch.

II. The frame and posture in which it should be kept. 1.
Awake; 2. Jealous; 3. Serious ; 4 Humble ; 5. Sublime.

III. Keep the passages and forts and outworks of the heart.
1 The senses ; 2. The thoughts, motion, and application : If
we do not keep our hearts the Devil will.

But I cannot quote at length from these volumes, but I
may express my belief, that which I believe in all instances,
the modern sketches and skeletons of sermons are very
poor things for any real and adequate help to the preacher ;
a collection of the old outlines with brief extracts, showing
the methods of filling out and illuminating a division would
be invaluable and useful. I remember to have heard of an

---

* See his *Exposition of the Creed*, 1632, most fertile in simple,
happy similes, and happy textual divisions, and his *Exposition of the
Lord's Prayer*, and *Nature of Repentance*, in the *Essex Dove*, I presume posthumous ; these works are very easy and simple, but very
useful.

Antinomian preacher who, taking for his text, "Walk in love," accented the adverb *in,* "Walk *in* love." "This," said he, "is not to be taken as Arminians take it, as a call to works and to a disposition of mind, but a gracious invitation to the Church to enter." "Walk in Love." Thomas Adams treated it differently. "Walk in Love as Christ loved us." The text of course furnished him with several sermons I need not cite, but Adams is rich and suggestive in divisions, sometimes fanciful, but always self-evident but striking truths were gained.

In the sermons of Daniel Featly,* are several of these more happy and comprehensive methods of textual divisions; I will select a few. Thus, on the text in Rev. ii. 7, on the *Hidden Manna*—"to him that overcometh will I give to eat of the hidden manna, and I will give him a white stone, and in the stone a new name written, which no man knoweth saving he that receiveth it."

1. No man knoweth the new name, save he that receiveth it; 2. No man receiveth it, but he that hath the white stone; 3. No man hath the white stone, but he that eateth the manna; 4. No man eateth the hidden manna, but he to whom it is given; 5. It is given to none to eat thereof, but to him that overcometh.

In a second sermon on the same text the following divisions occur :—

The new name. We receive many things from our Saviour; 1. A *new testament* signed with His blood; 2. In this new testament a *new covenant ;* 3. In this *new* covenant a *new commandment ;* 4. To obey this new commandment a *new heart ;* 5. And answerable to this new heart *new tongues ;* 6. And consonant to these new tongues, *new songs.*

Again, on the text in 2 Cor. vi. 16, "For ye are the Temple of the living God," we find the following :

* *Clavis Mystica ; a Key opening divers Difficult and Mysterious Texts.* 1636.

1. There are many who deserve to be called cages of unclean birds, or rather sties of unclean beasts than temples, *ye* are the *temples*, etc.; 2. There are temples of idols, or rather devils, not of God, ye are the *temples of God ;* 3. There are gods not living, ye are the temples of *the living God.*

In the sermon on the words, "Blessed are the poor in spirit, for theirs is the kingdom of heaven," Matt. v. 3, we have the following singularly characteristic divisions: "I. *Re ;* II. *Spe.* I. *Re*, in the *present possession* of the kingdom of grace. 2. *Spe*, in the *certain expectation* of the kingdom of glory."

Again, in the sermon on *The Faithful Shepherd*, from the text "Feed the flock of God which is among you, taking the oversight *thereof*, not by constraint, but willingly ; not for filthy lucre, but of a ready mind ; neither as being lords over God's heritage, but being ensamples to the flock. And when the chief shepherd shall appear, ye shall receive a crown of glory that fadeth not away." 1 Peter, v. 2, 3, 4—occurs the following :—

Thus I have numbered unto you the several links of the apostle's golden chain of instructions for pastors ; now let us gather them together in a narrow room :—1. Be not such as need to be fed, but are able and willing to feed ; 2. Feed not yourselves, but the flock ; 3. Feed not the flock or droves of Antichrist, but the flock of God ; 4. Feed the flock of God, not out of your charge, or without you, but the flock of God which is among you ; 5. Content not yourself with feeding them only with the bread and sacrament, but overlook them also, have an eye to their manners : 6. Do this not constrainedly, but willingly ; 7. Not out of private respects, but freely ; 8. Not proudly but humbly ; not to show your authority over the flock, but to set them an example in yourselves of humility, meekness, temperance, patience, and all other virtues.

Coming from these old illustrations to modern times, I take one strong element of Mr. Spurgeon's success to have been his adhesion to the old method of breaking his subject up into parts, what are called heads and divisions ; and that, while this is invariable with him, there are not too many of them. They always assist the memory with-out distracting it. I should think most of his sermons, when heard, could be pretty well remembered and recited again. For a sermon, to be a sermon, must be neither like a leader in a newspaper nor an essay ; it must have its succession of pegs and points. The figure is true, and yet it scarcely represents the thing. A sermon should be arranged like a house, into different compartments and rooms. There may be the hall or vestibule for introduc-tion, dining-room and parlor, the chamber in which the heart finds rest ; and then in closing a step out into the garden, and a farewell in pleasure. I am persuaded that the modern method, which has refused to concede any-thing to the hearers in aptitude or ignorance, which has • treated texts, for the most part, as mere themes, has usually ended—it must always end, if the congregation be very large—in turning the memory into a jungle, or *olla podrida*, or lumber room, a something where nothing is arranged, and where the hearer usually finds himself too lazy and inert to attempt the task. Of course the power to marshal all the matters suggested by a text into order and archi-tecture, and to give to that order newness and impres-siveness, must depend on the freshness in the preacher's own mind. A sermon with the most admirable and sym-metrical skeleton of arrangement, may be a dry and bony business after all. But let us look at some of Mr. Spur-geon's texts, and his mode of treating them.

"In that day there shall be upon the bells of the horses holiness unto the Lord." The title of this sermon is *A Peal of Bells*. Three heads :—

I. Let us hear the horses' bells.
II. Let us commend their music.
III. Let us go home and tune our bells.

1. The bells of the horses speak of power, holiness, pleasure, journeying, merchandise, toil; such are the uses of horses. These are the things of which their bells speak.

2. Their music is commended for loudness, clearness, constancy, universality, divinely *long*.

Then comes the application:—

3. Go home and tune your bells. There is the Chamber-Bell; —the Kitchen-Bell;—the Shop-Bell;—The Visiting-Bell.

All plain and broken with pithy and sweet remarking which must have made the sermon very pleasant and good, we should think, to the listeners.

Another striking sermon, *The Cedars of Lebanon.* The text, " The trees of the Lord are full of sap, the cedars of Lebanon, which he hath planted.." We have :

I. The absence of all human culture. 1. The Lord's trees owe their planting entirely to Him; 2. They are not dependent upon man for their watering; 3. No mortal might protects them; 4. They preserve a sublime indifference to human gaze; 5. Their exaltations is all for God, not for man ; 6. The cedars of Lebanon are independent of man in their expectations.

II. The cedars of Lebanon are a glorious display of divine care 1. In the abundance of their supply ; 2. They are always green; 3. Observe the grandeur and size of these trees, and note next their fragrance ; 4. Attentively think upon the perpetuity of these cedars; 5. Notice these cedars are very venerable.

III. The fullness of the living principle. 1. Full of sap— this is vitally necessary; 2. Essentially mysterious: 3. Radically secret; 4. Permanently active; 5. Externally operative; 6. Abundantly to be desired.

The genius of THOMAS TOLLER, of Kettering, was shown in this happy dealing with texts in a wise and simple accommodation to circumstances. Thus upon an occasion of a great annual festivity, which for several days created a season of relaxation and festivity, he fell into the usual custom of delivering a discourse of an admonitory character, guarding the young against the dangers, but showing how the season might be made honorable to the Author of all blessings. He took for his text, "What think ye, that He will not come to the feast?" The following were his divisions:—

I. *He may be here.* There is nothing in such a feast inconsistent with Christ's practice.

II. *Suppose he should be here,* how different is this feast from all former feasts, 1. If Christ should come, no good man need be ashamed to be seen here. 2. If Christ should come, what a damp it will be to many people's pleasure. 3. If Christ should come, would not some be ashamed to behave as there is too much reason to believe they will. 4. If Christ should come a welcome guest, how gratefully and happily will everybody go away.

III. *Suppose Jesus Christ should not come to the feast,* then it will not be worth coming to. 1. If He is not there, then you know who will be—the devil will. 2. If He is not there, no good man has any business there. 3. If He is not there, it will be because He is not invited. 4. If He is not here, then you had better all have remained at home.

IV. *He will, He will be here.*

But I am too much forgetting, in my desire that the people should be interested and that you should be especially textual in your divisions and arrangement, that there may be many orders of division; so that first of all it is necessary to clear the subject in your own mind, and to determine on what you are going to treat, and how. There must be sometimes, and often, topical preaching in the unfolding of a subject, in which you will have to instruct your hearers by defining it; by fixing the limitations of it; by illustrating it; and this is perhaps the order of discourse which mostly suggests the concealed method. Now I would say, set forth an order and succession of thoughts which your hearers may carry in their memory. This textual preaching is closely related to exposition, and

for this mode of ministration I must confess my especial
fondness. It is comprehensive—it is exhaustive—and the
preacher may avail himself of everything in it. It should
not exclude the sermon, but it may be made most useful to
include the sermon. James Stratton had great power and
happiness in expounding, and some of the published
pieces of Dr. Candlish are admirable as guides to this
method, especially his *Life in a Risen Saviour.* It is a style
pre-eminently useful, as it is the most difficult to use with
ease. In becoming an expositor you are indeed the true
minister and teacher. The expositor is the man who fixes
the posts, who establishes the meaning, and puts it *there.*
Then, for this purpose, you may avail yourself of all helps,
etymological, or other. Far would I be from the recom-
mendation of a pedantic use of Greek or Hebrew words ;
but apart from the pleasure of reading the languages for
yourself—here is one value in any knowledge you possess of either—the glance at the word will be a light
to the text. I saw much of this by the fireside of my beloved friend, Benjamin Parsons ; and of all men I have
ever known he possessed most power at legitimately opening a text.

We must utterly despair of being able to present any graphic
picture of the fireside where with him, we have so frequently
worshipped. But let the reader try to conceive the pleasant
Domestic Scene. The husband and father at perfect ease in his
arm chair; the wife, the children, the servants, and any occasional visitors, each with a Bible, sitting in a large and happy
circle—every one reading a verse. *This* morning we are reading in Timothy, the second epistle, the first chapter. We have
read to the sixth verse, when his voice interrupts the reading—
" What is Timothy reminded by Paul that he is to do, Ben ?
—the youngest boy. " To stir up the gift that is in him."
" What Greek word have we, Melly, for that ' stir up ' ? "
"Αναζωπυρειν." " There are three words there, Richard ; what
are they ? " "Δια, signifying ' up '; ζωη, signifying ' life '; and

πυρ, signifying 'fire.'" "So that you see they mean literally, 'Give life to the fire,' or 'Stir up the fire.' What a forcible word! We have no single word in our language that can express it." Even while we were reading the fire was becoming dull. It was too good and apt an illustration to be allowed to slip; and he pointed to it: "See," he said, "this fire needs the poker; if we did not take the poker and stir, it would go quickly out. Although there are all the materials for a good fire there, I must stir the fire to make it burn brightly, and I must take care how I stir it. Mental materials are not only necessary, but activity to give them life and ventilation. We all have gifts and fires within us; but they all need stirring, or they will never burn. Little heathen boys have minds; little beggar boys have minds; they have no friends to help them to stir them, and cannot themselves do it. Anna, what gift does God bestow on his people?" "The gift of the Holy Ghost." "Yes; God giveth his Holy Spirit to them that ask Him, and seek it. There is a text which says, 'The spirit of the prophets is subject to the prophets.' God's gift does not move and propel us as that steam carriage is moved by the fire and steam, without its knowing anything about it. We can resist God's gift. We can quench God's gift. If Christians are cold it is because they do not stir up the fire in them. If preachers are cold it is because they do not stir up the fire in them. God answers by fire to His people; and if we cannot impart fire to others, it is a proof that we have not stirred up our own fire. Don't forget you have a fire within you, but it will only burn as you stir it." *

I have a great affection for etymological elucidation. Even many English words escape us because the meaning and sense of the old word is lost. Etymology is the great nut-cracker of textual meanings, and it often gives the true value of what is within. In exposition you can avail yourself of anecdote, historical allusion—every kind of illustrative allusion. More important still, I believe, few people

* The Earnest Minister: A Record of the Life, and Selections from Posthumous and other writings, of the Rev. Benjamin Parsons. Edited by Edwin Paxton Hood.

read the Scriptures as a continued argument or history; yet all the epistles are a continued argument—Romans or Hebrews, Ephesians or Colossians.   The divine intention— the magnificence of the many chapters—is seen when its proportions are more clearly seen, and you will best be able then to open the matter, and make it impressive when you see the scope of the whole, and so make it most effective over your audience.   It is wonderful how, without doing any injustice to the whole, what myriads of texts are a kind of microcosm-like dew-drops—perfect, pendent worlds, containing the whole globe and cosmos of truth, of faith and life.   Myriads of what Luther called little Bibles, the whole Bible is in many a single text; and there are innumerable chapters like a geometrical staircase, self poised and self contained.   The whole Bible and revelation, with all its processes, and all its results, is in them.   I would recommend you often, after the period of your settlement, to prepare an expositorial sermon.   Those hearers you would most desire to retain will be among those most thankful and most edified.

III.

Concerning Written and Extemporary Sermons.

AM to make a few remarks upon the relative merits of the two methods of preaching. We live in the age of written sermons, but it is satisfactory to me to know that I am addressing students who believe in, and practice the art of extemporaneous discourse, these two methods are put upon their trial, and I conceive that we shall only improve the effectiveness of our own ministration as we analyse the relative merits of the two. Usually the debate •between the two methods has been conducted with a good deal of mere passibility. Some have declared that all sermons not written must be rapid and ignorant; and others that all not extemporaneous must be cold and unimpressive; yet really something very considerable may be said on both sides modifying each theory. Many of the greatest pulpit masters we know, such as South, Taylor, and Barrow, wrote and read their sermons, the same is also true of Dr. Chalmers and Dr. Harris; on the other hand the elder fathers of the

pulpit, and the great preachers of the middle ages, and many of our most distinguished moderns, Robert Hall, and Edward Irving, and Dr. M'All, and Winter Hamilton, and James Parsons, have delivered extemporaneously or from memory their discourses.

The Wykehamist says well, in his *Papers on Preaching,* referring to the dispute between written and extemporaneous discourses :—

Nor, as we humbly conceive, neither *yes* nor *no* will stand the test of "semper, ubique, ab omnibus." *Sometimes each* will be true, according as a man is in nerve or not ; or with *some preachers,* according as a man has sufficient clearness to keep his subject from confusion ; or with *some subjects,* as whether a man is preaching on doctrine or a hortatory appeal ; whether he is preaching upon a text which admits of little scope, or on a parable or history where, if his memory should not be retentive, there will still be plenty of matter to suggest topics ; or to *some congregations,* to a university audience, or in a village church. Perhaps, also, there may be a style of sermon between the two, which unites some of the excellencies of each ; as, for instance, an extempore sermon having been written first, inasmuch as "*writing makes an exact man,*" and then delivered from notes ; in conversation at the family prayer, or the sick bedside, or the cottage and schoolroom lecture, inasmuch as "*conversation makes a ready man*"—always the subject having been previously studied and read up for, inasmuch as "*reading makes a full man.*" *

And I think we must draw a great distinction between the ordinary sermon and that performance which may be called an *oration ;* a sort of thing upon which I really do not feel that I have any advice to offer ; utterly incapable of it myself, I am unable to give receipts for the preparation of it ; it is produced by a kind of sweating process—to speak respectfully of it—it is a sort of spoken poem into which the man puts all and every power he possesses for, perhaps, a period of six months during its preparation.

* *Papers on Preaching and Public Speaking.* By a Wykehamist.

The mistake many people make, is in the supposition that it is to be produced once or twice, or three or four times in the course of a week. Of this performance, we may say at once, it is more likely impossible that it could be the effective thing it is if read. What would be the effect if Mr. Morley Punshon read his lectures instead of declaiming them? all things then being equal, I have no hesitation at once in saying that, of course, the discourse delivered—not read—must be the more telling, the more effective and powerful for the purposes of fashion, movement, and action ; there are things which cannot be done while the eye is slavishly fixed upon paper, and the whole body and being is restricted and restrained by the consideration of what comes next.

Nothing in the history of the pulpit surprises me more than the labor attaching to the composition and the delivery of sermons, especially in the Church of England. There is a book full of anecdotes of the pulpit of the Church of England. It is not too much to call it a *shameful book* ; it has only been published a year or two, in it the whole affairs of preaching are treated as a joke, or an affliction ; it is called *A Voice from a Mask.* It is written by a clergyman, and it sets forth the poverty of the Church of England pulpit in a most amusing light. The writer says, "It is no wonder, considering how much labor the composition of a sermon costs most of us, that we are chary of them. Some of my friends entertain an affection quite parental for these offsprings of their brain. A parson of this character, who kept his pulpit manuscripts in a box in his library, was roused from his slumber early one morning by his servant who informed him that his house had been broken into and the lower rooms ransacked. 'John!' cried the startled divine, jumping up in the bed, 'Have they, have they stolen my sermon-box?' 'No, 'tis only broken open.' 'Then bring up my shaving water at the usual time.'"

We laugh at these things, but they are *very shocking* to my mind. *A man professing to be a minister of God and of His truth, and having nothing to say!* no doubt vanity often rushes out into speech when it had better hold its tongue, but even this is better than the *sermon case, the black book,* which it has been said truly puts up a barrier between the preacher and the mind, and heart, and affections of his audience ; and with this goes another thing, that they are usually supposed to be dishonest. A man who gives forth evidently with no feeling at all words from a paper for twenty minutes or half an hour, why, I think the multitude may be pardoned for thinking that very likely they are not his own, and indeed, many are the sermons over which that prophetic exclamation may be raised, " Alas, master for it was borrowed." This I know you will scorn to do except in the righteous way in which I have in past lectures prescribed.

I believe we shall simplify matters very much, however, if we first of all lay down this especial canon—that excellence is not to be expected in either department of public speech and service, except as there is *labor* and *industry.**

The history of the world is full of testimony to prove how much depends upon industry ; not an eminent orator has lived, but he is an example of it. Yet, in contradiction to all this, the almost universal feeling appears to be, that industry can effect nothing, that eminence is the result of accident, and that every one must be content to remain just what he may happen to be. Thus, multitudes who come forward as teachers and guides, suffer themselves to be satisfied with the most indifferent attainments and a miserable mediocrity, without so much as inquiring how they might rise higher, much less making any attempt to rise. For any other art they would have served an apprenticeship, and would be ashamed to practise it in public before they had learned it. If any one would sing, he attends a master, and is drilled in the very elementary principles ; and only after the

* *Sacred Rhetoric : or, Composition and Delivery of Sermons.* By Henry J. Ripley. *To which are added Hints on Extemporaneous Preaching,* by Henry Ware, Jr., D.D.

most laborious process dares to exercise his voice in public. This he does, though he has scarce anything to learn but the mechanical execution of what lies in sensible forms before his eye. But the extemporaneous speaker, who is to invent as well as to utter, to carry on an operation of the mind as well as to produce sound, enters upon the work without preparatory discipline, and then wonders that he fails! If he were learning to play on the flute for public exhibition, what hours and days would he spend in giving facility to his fingers, and attaining the power of the sweetest and most impressive execution. If he were devoting himself to the organ, what months and years would he labor, that he might know its compass, and be able to draw out, at will, all its various combinations of harmonious sound, and its full richness and delicacy of expression. And yet he will fancy that the grandest, the most various, the most expressive of all instruments, which the infinite Creator has fashioned by the union of an intellectual soul with the powers of speech, may be played upon without study or practice; he comes to it, a mere uninstructed tyro, and thinks to manage all its stops, and command the whole compass of its varied and comprehensive power! He finds himself a bungler in the attempt, is mortified at his failure, and settles in his mind forever that the attempt is vain.

Labor which does not terminate with the arrangement of the subject, and the grouping of the thoughts, and the materials, and the images in their various compartments, but which also, and further, resolves the whole into the mind, the heart, and the memory. The man writes his sermon—his pen travels over his paper as if he were writing a letter to a friend. The length of his sentences, the piercingness, and the aptness of his words have not been thought upon; being written too, there is no danger of failure; the thing is before his eye—he cannot lose the chain of his connection; there can be no breakdown. So he goes into the pulpit—is it wonderful that it does not tell—that it seems to be a thing distant from himself? It is not wonderful if written, and to be read. Should it not have been made

completely his own by pondering and meditation, and by
fixing its distinct place in the memory.

But if, on the contrary, the preacher determines to deliver
his discourse extemporaneously, is this to exempt him from
preparation, from arrangement, from the selection of those
words which will most happily and comprehensively convey
his meaning.   In this case also is there not to be labor—
labor, the text burns in your soul, does it ? it is like a fire
in the bones, is it ? the question I know is proposed often,
how far is extempore address within the reach of the ma-
jority of preachers, and it is quite true that it requires more
study to do justice to unwritten than to written sermons.
One of the most perilous gifts is the gift of fluency, the
power of easy speech ; speech to which we listen, but which
produces little impression ; which will increase greatly with
all men ; fluency, the power of speech, weakening the necessity felt for conversation and thought.

Whence springs this feeling of the necessity of a slavish
committal to paper.   Partly no doubt it arises from the
variety of topics to which a preacher must attend ; an
average man with no more ability than any of the people
about him, has got to deliver himself upon many subjects
in the course of the week.   How can this be without running into a wasteful sameness.   But there is a deeper reason
than this, self-consciousness is the curse of the pulpit, and
it paralyses all genuine effort ; this is, you perceive, another
name for vanity, and is it not greatly to be feared that the
sense of personal vanity sadly over-rates the effort in the
pulpit.   I am afraid ministers, as a rule, are vainer than
other men ; fastidiousness, I know, is not a proof of this,
but it often illustrates it ; they are vainer than artists, tradesmen, professional men ; even than musicians and poets.   A
finickal fear of not hitting the exact shades of expression—
a tremulous shivering in the presence of the audience—frequently, perhaps, also an uncertainty about the thing said

itself. All these enter into the "fear of man that brings
the snare," we often pray against that fear, but few perhaps have practically realized how perpetually it haunts
the speaker, and enfeebles all discourse ; there is only one
fear which can give strength in the pulpit : fear for the Ark
of the Lord ; fear of God, fear in the presence of the felt, but
invisible, truth. A man would not be very courageous with
a ghost in the room. A trembling hesitating soul scarified
by a multitude, it could not be expected to clothe itself
with power ; it is the victim of its own fear, it is not merely
the fear of the green-baized and red-curtained pew where
Mr. Rigsby sits, who pays £20 a year for it ; or that highly
intelligent young man, Mr. Crumpit, with the cold eye behind his spectacles, who has studied at Gottingen or Tub-
ingen, had an article in the last number of *The Transcendental Bagman*, and takes in the *Saturday* and *Westminister
Reviews*. It is not merely the fear of that still more terrible
array of old Billys and Peggys who sit beneath the pulpit,
and shrink their shoulders, very much to the young brother's terror, when anything goes wrong, and nod their dear
old heads approvingly when anything bites them and goes
right. It is not even the fear of those more dreadful institutions, the churchwardens or the deacons—but it is a fear
composed of all these things put together, and no doubt
the first thing towards pulpit efficiency is, get rid of your
fears—only get rid of them legitimately, not by impudence,
not by mere boldness, but by sound-hearted piousness, by
true knowledge, by reliance, not upon your method, but
your truth. Especially by ability to say, Lord, I have done
all I can, and now I leave the result to thee.

This alone will save from that literary vanity which is
often at the foundation of the read discourse. Almost all
that foliage of flowery bewilderment in which some writers
indulge is of this kind, literary vanity, which must be put
on paper. "I caution you," says the great Herder, "against

committing to memory beautiful expressions and flowery sentences, they entice a person from the right path ; and the young man who follows such false lights is lost. A man who seizes on beautiful words, and for the sake of them, write out pages of fine sentences, I cannot regard with confidence ; he is doing a senseless childish piece of work. All florid language should spring out of the subject itself, just as natural flowers spring out of the earth. Images and figures should be naturally connected with the subject, as a bough and its twig, or as a blossom and its leaf spring necessarily, as it were, from such particular root or such a stem." And to the same effect, John Foster : "A gaudy verbosity is always eloquence in the opinion of him that writes it, but what is its effect upon the reader ? Real eloquence strikes upon the mind with irresistible force, and leaves you not the possibility of asking or thinking whether it be eloquence, but the sounding sentences of these writers leave you cool enough to examine with doubtful curiosity, a language that seems threatening to move or astonish you, without actually doing it, it is something like the false alarm of thunder ; where a sober man that is not apt to startle at sounds looks out to see whether it be not the rumbling of a cart ?" Among the great reasons of the aversion of men of taste to Evangelical religion, I think we may include fine preaching—the attempt, so disgusting, to say fine things—which really produce the effect on the cultivated taste, exactly like that of the young preacher describing the expansive character of the human mind. "Yes, my friends, the mind of man is so expansive that it can soar from star to star, and from satchelite to satchelite, and from seraphcem to seraphcem, and from cherrybeam to cherrybeam, and from thence to the centre of the doom of heaven."

But there are other preachers *who read their sermons from a godly fear*—the paper before the eyes, the exact word leads to a subdued manner of discourse, which is also one of the most effective and powerful ; the paper pulls the too impulsive speaker back, reins him in wisely, where other-wise he might trip or stumble or where he might rush in-to too bold and irreverent a style of speech. For this same reason also, some men, who have never lacked language, have yet chained their memories to a written form of words, and it must be remembered that all which passes for extemporaneous has often this qualification, a very im-portant one, and adding, we might suppose, much to the nervousness of the preacher. The great condition I would make is this—the mind and heart should be alive and at work in the pulpit. I believe if they are they will not fail to win. *I see no objection to the use of corks in learning to swim,* but you see those who use corks, they plunge and use their arms, and in fact they are alive in the water. I daresay with many preachers it is like swimming, like tak-ing a fatal plunge, and for such the notes are a kind of cork. When Sims Reeves declaims in Exeter Hall, he has his notes before him, the word and the bar. I would not have you cast off from a like help, but the words and the bar would be of little use without the skill, the knowledge, and the soul of music. These in any case must go as con-ditions with you into the pulpit—a mind above the fear of man, strong in the confidence of your own truth, subdued by that truth, and not pragmatically bold, and as much alive, and impressed, and at work there, as in your own study. I think if you remember and act upon these con-ditions, you will, with your notes or without, be beyond the condemnation implied in the words of Cotton Mather, " How can you expect your hearers to remember what, but for your book, you are afraid you should yourself forget "?

Referring to the advantages of written sermons, I know it will be said, that they give *compression to thought,* and compactness to style. *Remember, then, that this is not ordi-*

narily the thing you are to cultivate for the pulpit. This may
do for an occasional sermon, perhaps. You ought to set
aside some service in the month when you will aim at this,
but ordinarily you must diffuse—diffuse, beat out the gold
—not one person in a thousand of your hearers will be
good gold-beaters ; unwind the skein of silk, not one person in a thousand will do this—they pay you to do it for
them. Your audience will not forgive you if you give
them too much to think about, and I believe this would be
found to be the reason of the popularity of those men
who wrote their sermons. Dr. Chalmers was very diffusive
—far too diffusive, thought Robert Hall—"all very excellent, but why not go on, sir, why not go on? It's all
round the apple, all round the apple." Well, that is what
the people generally need—all round the apple, all round
the apple. *Dilate—diffuse;* this is the great business of
the preacher, to present the same subject in many aspects,
in many lights, enforced by many considerations, and
usually extemporaneous preaching is more favorable to
this. The proverbial style, therefore, is difficult, almost
unsuitable perhaps, for the unwritten speech ; but on the
contrary, who would write a parable, an allegory, or anecdote? Very true are the sayings of Owen Feltham, "I
never yet knew a good tongue that wanted ears to hear it."
But it is a difficult thing to bring about a perfect harmony
between the memory and feeling, especially if the delivery
is to be saved from the appearance of mere recitation. It
is true also, as the same quaint writer has said, "It is a
wonder to me how men can preach so little and so long ;
so long a time, and so little matter. As if they thought
to please by the inculcation of their vain tautologies. Yet
if we, out of copper, lead, or pewter preaching, can extract pure gold, 'tis no impeachment to our wise philosophy."

There is one great *advantage* and one great *danger* in extempore
preaching, with which we will conclude.

The *advantage* is this, which, in a late article of the *Quarterly Review*, on " The Parish Priest," is described in some such words as these—but we quote only from memory—" To those who do not repeat *memoriter*, but are masters of their subject, there is the advantage that they can watch the effect of their words upon their audience, and consequently contract or expand their arguments, and vary their illustrations according to the pulse of their audience, and the impression which they see to be produced ; and this, in St. Augustine's opinion, was the essential element of pulpit success. The happiest flights are those which are born of the occasion, the warmth of which will atone for many defects of style." If we made up our conversation before we went to a party, how flat it would fall compared with that which arises out of the occasion ; now something analogous to this occurs in preaching—at least sufficiently analogous to bear comparison. True, the audience at sermons cannot enter into a conversation with their tongues, but they can make the response to the preacher with the intelligence of their eyes and features. The preacher gazing into their countenances can see how far they appreciate, approve, or understand. In lecturing on science, Arago picked out a dull type of humanity among his hearers, with a low forehead. On him he kept his eye fixed —he addressed himself to him as if there were no other present, and by the effect of his explanations, as reflected in this man's countenance, he judged of their influence upon the rest of his audience. When this pupil remained unconvinced, the orator tried new arguments and illustrations till light beamed on his countenance. " We often see," says a modern preacher, " as we go on in our discourse, from the straining attention of some in the crowd, that we have not yet succeeded in what we have spoken. Are we, then, to go forward without making another attempt with some change of address or variation of imagery ? " The extempore preacher will, then, in this point, stand at a manifest advantage, because he has more freedom ; he can strike as he sees his blows tell ; if he sees his argument is beyond his audience, he can refrain. We will suppose his notes to be certain algebraic symbols, or natural contractions and signs, leaving the subordinate fillings up to the impressiveness and excita-

tions of the moment. Around these algebraic symbols the ex-
temporist can swing at leisure, anchoring the head of his ship
to them to avoid losing his course, while he has sufficient elas-
ticity to swing gracefully, expanding or contracting at will.
What would look like repetition upon paper does not sound like
repetition when spoken ; and repetition, with slight variations,
is necessary for the full understanding of many things.   To
the preacher from notes, we may say what Dr. Johnson said to
Boswell, when he handed him notes for a speech to an election
committee in the House of Commons,—" This, sir, you must enlarge on; you must not argue there as if you were arguing to
the schools.   You must say the same thing over and over again
in different words.   If you say it but once they miss it in a
moment of inattention."   Fox advised Sir Samuel Romilly, when
about to sum up the evidence in Lord Melville's trial, "not to
be afraid of repeating observations which were material."   Pitt
urged a similar defence for that amplification which was thought
a defect in his style.   " Every person," he said, " who addressed
a public assembly, and was anxious to make an impression on
particular points, must either be copious upon some points or else
repeat them, and copiousness is to be preferred to repetition."
Lord Brougham gives his testimony on the same side,—" The
orator often feels that he could add strength to his composition
by *compression*, but his hearers would then be unable to keep
pace with him, and he is compelled to sacrifice *conciseness* to
clearness.   The expansion, which is a merit at the moment of
delivery, is turned into a defect when a speech is *printed*.   What
before was impressive seems now to be verbose, and the effect
is diminished in much the same proportion as originally it was
increased.   It was for some such reason that Fox asserted, that
if a speech was read well it was a bad speech.   No Athenian
audience could have followed Demosthenes in the condensed
form in which his speeches are printed."—*Quarterly Review*,
No. 206.   Fuller reminds us that to the *uneducated* listener, the
intellectual food should not be presented in too *solid* a form,
saying, in his inimitable way, " without a fair proportion of chaff
a horse is apt to bolt his oats." *

* Papers on Preaching, etc.

But it is important to notice that when extemporaneous preaching is determined on, there should also be determined on some method to give effect to the determination. One of these determinations is, perhaps, as to the length of the sermon. It might be wise to learn the lesson taught by the fate of Eutychus. A Sunday-school teacher examining his class, asked, "Who was Eutychus?" "A young man who heard Paul preach, and falling down, was taken up dead." "And from this circumstance what do we learn?" "Please sir, we learn that ministers should not preach long sermons."

When Judge Jenkins expected to be hung by the Parliament for his zeal as a Royalist in the civil wars of England, he manifested a great desire for his political martyrdom, and resolved to go to the gallows with Bracton on his left shoulder, the statutes at large on his right, and the Bible round his neck, that these books, he said, as having been his counsellors, should hang with him. "And first," said he, "I will eat much liquorice and gingerbread, thereby to strengthen my lungs, that I may speak the louder, and be heard far and near." Stiff determination this, and so I may say, if you determine on extemporary speech some preparation is needed. There are natural qualities needed. You may with profit refer to and read the essay of the *Abbé Bautain* on this very topic.* I will not dwell upon these here, because they have already in a measure engaged us, excepting that I notice for the extemporary power, the necessity of a firm and decisive will. That is the power which will hold and modify the imagination ; will control the resources already prepared—will also guide the mind to the employment of that grand necessity of all successful public speech—*good sense*, right reason, the salvation of the

* The Art of Extempore Preaching. Hints for the Pulpit, the Senate, and the Bar. By. M. Bautain, Vicar-General and Professor at the Sorbonne, etc., etc.

mind from mere evaporating details. *Good sense is the great fitness for the speech of the orator.* Then for this speech there are acquired qualities and habits of the mind needed : *have a fund*, an exchequer, have a stock and store to fall upon. "That you know how to speak—first know how to think!" Is it not true that our self-respect may be raised by the furnishing of our minds, by the feeling that we have indeed a right to be heard? Then may not our self-possession be educated, and we made more collected, and steady, and calm? And shall we not especially educate this faculty by a principle of order ? it may be hidden, but not the less there, manifest. Then by the arrangement of every part—the illustrative texts, and the illustrative images, the quaint proverb, and the relieving anecdote. We have indeed no right to think that all this will be worked quite easily and happily at first. But order, order, makes an extemporaneous effort easy, and without order I do not wonder if it is thought by many impossible. Clear and arrange the things in your own mind ; throw yourself in a path of light, and you will move easily and happily, and you will not fail to carry those whom you address in that path with you.

And for successful extempore speaking there are two or three little maxims of common sense, almost you will per-haps think beneath the notice of a learned lecturer, but they very materially affect the discourse. When you begin to preach do as you do also when you begin to drive—*not at the rate of ten miles an hour at starting.* No, a very good horse, perhaps, but for the first five or ten minutes even two miles an hour may be best. "*Begin low*," said old Dr. Leifchild, "*and Proceed slow.*" Very much has this to do with the preservation of your own mind in a state of cool and self-possessed equability and firmness. Thousands of good sermons have been lost because they have been begun in a hurry. All things are badly done, done in a hurry, but especially sermons. *Take it coolly* at first ; be very still within yourself. Your remarks may be common-place—or if impressive, still then very clear and calm.

Begin low ; very few sermons or preachers can stand the test of a lofty, or inflamed, or impassioned exordium, or, for that matter, few audiences either. It should be the preach-er's aim to put himself on good terms with his hearers—to rest himself in and on his subject, and to be at rest with them, and to soothe them to quiet rest in and on him. There are some instances of even the noble and magnificent exordium ; but the wisdom of the preacher will be usually shown in using language and ideas, which shall be simply statement, explanation, and verbal elucidation. The occa-sional sermon may perhaps forcibly seize and command the attention at once ; but this will be always perilous un-less the preacher is perfectly at home in his subject, in himself, and with his hearers, and is conscious of his ability to hold in the same manner the attention to the close. It is one of the arts of pulpit eloquence, the introduction, surely it should never be careless ; on the contrary, always simple, never imaginative, never on any account highly wrought. So also the following of Hare's *Sermons for Easter*, "He is risen," seems to me also for the purpose of introduc-tion perfect.

"Christ is risen !" Such is the greeting in Russia on the morning of Easter-day. In the great city of Moscow, and throughout the whole country, when two friends meet on this morning, one of them says to the other, "Christ is risen !" Among all the customs I ever read of, this to my mind is one of the most Christian and most beautiful. It is seeing the resur-rection of Jesus Christ in its true light, not as a fact which we are merely to believe, because it is written in the New Testa-ment, without thinking or caring much about it, but as a piece of good news to ourselves, which we cannot help speaking of for joy. What the Russians then have said to each other on Easter

Day for hundreds of years, let me now say to you, let me say to you with a joyful and thankful heart, "Christ is risen!" The battle is over. The great contest between God, the incarnate Son, fighting for us, and sin and death fighting against us, is decided. Sin, having first been baffled by the life of blameless holiness, and unwearied active goodness, which the Man Jesus so long led, was conquered on Good Friday on the Cross. Death, the last and only remaining enemy, was conquered this morning by the Resurrection. The victory is complete, their yoke is broken, their sting is taken away; we have nothing more to fear from either. For Christ has risen, and by His rising has assured us that we shall rise also.

It has often been the case that preachers have adopted a quite hysterical style in the commencement of their sermons—a sort of attention-at-any-price kind of style—well illustrated in the sermons of LAURENCE STERNE ; a strange man to find in the pulpit at all ; but his sermons, principally from the wide fame of the wit, attained to a large celebrity, nor are they without some excellences, but chiefly of the sentimental and satiric kind ; jerks and artifices abound through them all, but especially in the commencements. Thus from Eccles. vii. 2, 3 :—

" IT IS BETTER TO GO TO THE HOUSE OF MOURNING THAN TO THE HOUSE OF FEASTING."

That I deny ;—but let us hear the wise man's reasoning upon it,—" for that *is* the end of all men, and the living *will* lay it to *his* heart: sorrow is better than laughter:"—*for a crack-brained order of Carthusian monks, I grant, but not for men of the world.* For what purpose, do you imagine, has God made us ? for the social sweets of the well-watered valleys, where He has planted us, or for the dry and dismal desert of a Sierra Morena ? Are the sad accidents of life, and the uncheery hours which perpetually overtake us, are they not enough, but we must sally forth in quest of them,—belie our own hearts, and say, as your text would have us, that they are better than those of joy ? Did the Best of Beings send us into the world for this end,—to go weeping through it,—to vex and shorten a life short and vexatious enough already? Do you think, my good preacher, that He who is infinitely happy, can envy us our enjoyments? or that a Being so infinitely kind, would grudge a mournful traveller the short rest and refreshments necessary to support his spirits through the stages of a weary pilgrimage? or that He would call him to a severe reckoning, because in his way he had hastily snatched at some little fugacious pleasures, merely to sweeten this uneasy journey of life, and reconcile him to the ruggedness of the road, and the many hard jostlings he is sure to meet with?

Surely a most unwise and irreverent mode of opening up a subject. Again, in his sermon on the character of Shimei —one of the best illustrations of Sterne's style—in which he shows how Shimei reflects all the features of David, according to the true temper of the world—as David is prospered, he honors him ; as he is unlucky, he reviles him.

" But Abishai said, Shall not Shimei be put to death for this ?"

—*It has not a good aspect.*—This is the second time Abishai has proposed Shimei's destruction.

The following passage illustrates Sterne's better, but wholly ethical and unevangelical, style :—

In all David's prosperity, there is no mention made of him ;— he thrust himself forward into the circle, and, possibly, was number'd amongst friends and well-wishers.

When the scene changes, and David's troubles force him to leave his house in despair,—Shimei is the first man we hear of who comes out against him.

The wheel turns round once more ; Absalom is cast down, and David returns in peace :—Shimei suits his behavior to the occasion, and is the first man also who hastes to greet him ;— and, had the wheel turn'd round a hundred times, Shimei, I dare say, in every period of its rotation, would have been uppermost.

O Shimei ! would to Heaven, when thou wast slain, that all

thy family had been slain with thee, and not one of thy resemblance left! but ye have multiplied exceedingly, and replenished
the earth; and, if I prophesy rightly,—ye will in the end *subdue* it!

There is not a character in the world which has so had an influence upon the affairs of it, as this of Shimei. Whilst power
meets with honest checks, and the evils of life with honest refuge, the world will never be undone: but thou, Shimei, hast
snapp'd it at both extremes; for thou corruptest prosperity,—
and 'tis thou who hast broken the heart of poverty; and, so
long as worthless spirits can be ambitious ones, 'tis a character
we shall never want. O! it infects the court,—the camp,
the cabinet!—it infects the church!—go where you will,—
in every quarter, in every profession, you see a Shimei following the wheels of the fortunate through thick mire and clay!—

—Haste, Shimei—haste, or thou wilt be undone for ever.
Shimei girdeth up his loins and speedeth after him. Behold
the hand which governs everything,—takes the wheels from off
his chariot, so that he who driveth, driveth on heavily. Shimei
doubles his speed,—but 'tis the contrary way; he flies like the
wind over a sandy desert, and the place thereof shall know it
no more:— stay, Shimei! 'tis your patron,—your friend,—your
benefactor: 'tis the man who has raised you from the dunghill!
'Tis all one to Shimei; Shimei is a barometer of every man's
fortune; marks the rise and fall of it, with all the variations
from scorching hot to freezing cold upon his countenance, that
the smile will admit of. Is a cloud upon thy affairs?—see,—it
hangs over Shimei's brow. Hast thou been spoken for to the
king or the captain of the host without success? Look not
into the court-calendar;—the vacancy is filled up in Shimei's
face. Art thou in debt?—though not to Shimei,—no matter;—
the worst officer of the law shall not be more insolent.

But I speak of Sterne's exordiums, thus in the case of
Hezekiah and the messengers:—

"And he said, what have they seen in thine house? and Hezekiah
answered, All the things that are in my house have they seen;
there is nothing amongst all my treasure that I have not shewn
them."

. —And where is the harm, you'll say, in all this?

Again :—

"—For we trust we have a good conscience.—"

Trust ! Trust we have a good conscience ! Surely, you will say, if there is anything in this life which a man may depend upon, and to the knowledge of which he is capable of arriving upon the most indisputable evidence, it must be this very thing : Whether he has a good conscience, or no.

If a man thinks at all, he cannot well be a stranger to the true state of this account. He must be privy to his own thoughts and desires. He must remember his past pursuits, and know certainly the true springs and motives which, in general, have governed the actions of his life.

Again :—

" Despiseth thou the riches of his goodness, and forbearance, and long suffering,—not knowing that the goodness of God leadeth thee to repentance ?

So says St. Paul. And Eccles. viii. 11 :

'· Because sentence against an evil work is not executed speedily, therefore the heart of the sons of men is fully set in them to do evil."

Take either as you like it, you will get nothing by the bargain.

The man had little regard for the delicacy of anything he chose to say in the pulpit or elsewhere ; he had a courageous familiarity, which must have been confounding to rustic hearers—and such for the most part his hearers always were. Mr. Gladstone has attempted to do a kindly justice to Laurence Sterne ; but read a sermon on the *Levite and his Concubine*, and notice what sad rubbish the Rabelais of the English pulpit could not only talk but print :—

" And it came pass in those days, when there was no king in Israel, that there was a certain Levite sojourning on the side of Mount Ephraim, who took unto him a concubine."

—*A concubine !*—but the text accounts for it ; "for in those days there was no king in Israel," and the Levite, you will say, like every other man in it, did what was right in his own eyes ;

—and so, you may add, did his concubine too,—" for she played the whore against him, and went away."

—Then shame and grief go with her : and wherever she seeks a shelter, may the hand of justice shut the door against her.

Not so ; for she went unto her father's house in Bethlehem-judah, and was with him four whole months. Blessed interval for meditation upon the fickleness and vanity of this world and its pleasures ! I see the holy man upon his knees,—with hands compressed to his bosom, and with uplifted eyes, thanking Heaven that the object which had so long shared his affection was fled !

The text gives a different picture of his situation "for he arose and went after her, to speak friendly to her, and to bring her back again, having his servant with him, and a couple of asses : and she brought him unto her father's house ; and when the father of the damsel saw him, he rejoiced to meet him."

—A most sentimental group ! you'll say : and so it is, my good commentator, but the world talks of every thing. Give but the outlines of a story,—let Spleen or Prudery snatch the pencil, and they will finish it with so many hard strokes, and with so dirty a coloring, that Candour and Courtesy will sit in torture as they look at it. Gentle and virtuous spirits ! ye who know not what it is to be rigid interpreters, but of your own failings,—to you I address myself, the unhired advocates for the conduct of the misguided. Whence is it that the world is more jealous of your office. How often must ye repeat it, " That such a one's doing so or so," is not sufficient evidence by itself to overthrow the accused !—that our actions stand surrounded with a thousand circumstances which do not present themselves at first sight !—that the first springs and motives which impell'd the unfortunate, lie deeper still !—and, that of the millions which every hour are arraign'd, thousands of them may have err'd merely from the *head*, and been actually outwitted into evil ! and, when from the *heart*,—that the difficulties and temptations under which they acted,—the force of the passions,—the suitableness of the object, and the many struggles of Virtue before she fell,—may be so many appeals from Justice to the judgment-seat of Pity !

Here then let us s'op a moment and give the story of the Levite and his concubine a second hearing.

How different is all this levity to a singular exordium I remember of Bishop Andrews, to a sermon on the text, "Remember Lot's wife," Luke xvii. 32 :—

The words are few and the sentence short ; no one in Scripture so short. But it fareth with sentences as with coins ; in coins they that are in smallest compass contain greatest value, are best esteemed ; and in sentences, those that in fewest words comprise most matters, are most praised. Which as, of all sentences, it is true ; so especially with those that are marked with *memento*. In them the shorter the better ; the better, and the better carried away ; and the better kept ; and the better called for when we need it. And such is this here of rich contents, and withal exceeding compendious. So that we must needs be without all excuse (it being but three words and five syllables) if we do not remember it.

As you advance you will *take fire, rise higher,* and the sermon will be an enjoyment to you ; but, if you make a mistake in the starting you will not most likely recover yourself for the whole sermon, and let this same advice rule you in the discourse. Even if all goes well, pause, look about you, wait, and take breath ; if a slight embarrassment seizes you—if a word trips, again be cool. If you are cool the audience will not notice it ; if you are hurried they will imagine a trip where there is none at all ; when most impressed be self-possessed, I know, also, how much this is a matter of temperament ; but surely temperament may be modified—the melancholy may be made sanguine, and the sanguine made wise ! These are of those acquired things which give success to the spontaneous speech and discourse.

Beside which you may call other and higher powers to your aid, as in the following interesting anecdote of the Abbé Bautain of Paris.

One day I had to preach in one of the principal churches in Paris. It was a solemn festival, and there was an immense audience, including part of the Court then reigning. As I was ascending the pulpit I perceived a person whom I had supposed absent, and my mind was carried away suddenly by a train of recollections. I reached the pulpit-landing, knelt down as usual, and when I should have risen to speak, I had forgotten not only my text, but even the subject of my sermon. I literally knew no longer what I had come to speak upon, and, despite of all my efforts to remember it, I could see nothing but one complete blank. My embarrassment and anguish may be conceived. I remained on my knees a little longer than was customary, not knowing what to do. Nevertheless, not losing head or heart, I looked full at my danger without being scared by it, yet without seeing how I was to get out of it. At last, unable to recover anything by my own proper strength,—neither subject nor text,—I had recourse to God, and I said to Him, from the very bottom of my heart and with all the fervor of my anxiety,—"Lord, if it be Thy will that I preach, give me back my plan ; " and at that instant, my text came back into my mind, and with my text the subject. I think that never in my life have I experienced anything more astonishing, nor a more lively emotion of gratitude.

I avail myself of an interesting illustration from a forgotten, indeed, never well known although very excellent book.*

It seems surprising, no doubt, that such a variety of forces and equipments should be employed for this work of the ministry. I conceive a neighbor who has a son tenderly loved, who in the season of youth is enticed by sinners, and allured by pleasures and offended by his father's councils and reproofs. I visit the father sitting beneath some soli-tary tree, or by some sorrowful fireside. He tells me the cause of his grief, and I offer to use my endeavors to bring back his son ; he bids me go, and God be with me ; but in

* *Lectures on the Nature and End of the Sacred Office, and on the Dignity, Duty, Qualifications and Character of the Sacred Order,* by John Smith, D.D., one of the Ministers of Campbleton. Glasgow, 1798.

order to accomplish the object what further directions I
wonder would he give me ; would he say, Have a care that
you arrange all your arguments properly, and that you
speak to my son in mood and figure, for I taught him *logic* ;
have a care also that you put your words in the best order,
and that you turn your periods artificially and nicely, for I
taught my boy *rhetoric ;* and take care especially that you
pronounce your words aright and commit no slip in grammar, lest you offend his ear, for my boy is a *grammarian.*
No ; instead of speaking in this unnatural manner, he only
says, "Go and bring back my child, set your heart and
soul on this important business as you wish to please me,"
and this is the commission our Master gives to us ; be in
earnest, be in earnest, the hearers cannot be unconcerned.
This then will be that state to which the great Chrysostom refers, "I have been told," says he, "and I can well
believe it, by a certain person, that he had seen a glorious
vision of an innumerable company of angels bending forward at the altar, and listening as soldiers around their
general." And what a consideration is this to a Christian
preacher, the Host of Heaven surrounding him, and thus,
while he improves one order of beings, he regales another,
he improves men, and he gives joy to angels. A man who
believes this how can he be indifferent, how can he be cold,
how can he confine his thoughts to the mere reading a paper, or to the repetition of words previously committed to
memory? On our theory of what the Christian ministry
is, it seems impossible that any one should perform the office of the ministry without lifting the thoughts heaven-
wards and being transported to the invisible, but more actual worlds of light. This is the mood of spirit which compels the preacher to weep and to fret ; his own feelings
command the feelings of his audience. And "Oh! how
deep into the heart go those periods," says Robinson,
"which are sown in the unforced, undescribed tears of the

preacher ; our inward concern should break forth through every pore, and without anything legal, theatrical, or extravagant, give life and animation to every tone of the voice to every feature of the countenance. If you wish me to weep, you must weep first yourself. If we thus plant and arrange the forces of our soul I conceive we are very much in the same case at which the first preachers of the Gospel were, fronting a wild and indifferent, a cultivated race of selfish people, but they had no mean, not a base amount of intelligence, and no wealth, but they believed and they succeeded.

Hence, when most impressed be self-possessed. *When most impressed?* it is not unnatural to suppose that it will be at the close, when the feelings are most excited, either in the preparation or the delivery of the sermon that the impression will be deepest in the mind and most alive in the breast of the preacher. Yet then, it will not be by the noisy and declamatory manner this will be most evinced ; power is reticent, emotion trembles along the speech. I apprehend this will not be known by the labored elaboration of what is called the peroration ; sometimes I know it will assume a passionate and rapt form of appeal, as in the following, which I remember to have heard from JAMES PARSONS, on the text :—

" THOU RESTRAINEST PRAYER BEFORE GOD."

I speak to men who have restrained prayer by omitting it altogether; and I tell them, as the great evil now impending over their condition, that if they live and die without the spirit of prayer, they will descend into a state of unchanging existence, where it will be found one of the worst and most agonizing torments, that they will pray, and pray *in vain.*

It is but seldom that the revelation of the Word of God draws aside the curtain that conceals the habitation of lost spirits in hell ; but there is one instance where that curtain is drawn aside, not by the hands of prophets or apostles, but by the hand of

Him who was the Master of both; and He expounds, my brethern, the following awful fact for the warning and the alarm of others. A rich man, who was clothed in purple and fine linen, and who fared sumptuously every day, died, and was buried; and in hell he lifted up his eyes, being in torment. He saw Lazarus, a beggar he had once despised, in the bosom of Abraham, in the Paradise of God. He prayed—and it was for *himself.* "Father Abraham, I beseech thee, send Lazarus, that he may dip the tip of his finger in water, and cool my tongue; for I am tormented in this flame:" and the poor request was denied He prayed again—and it was for *others.* "I pray thee, therefore, father, that thou wouldest send him to my father's house, for I have five brethren, that he may testify to them, lest they also come into this place of torment: "They have Moses and the prophets; let them hear them." Nay, father Abraham,"—as if rising to a maddening agony—Nay, father Abraham; but if one went unto them from the dead, they *will* repent." "Verily, I say unto thee, If they hear not Moses and the prophets, neither will they be persuaded though one rise from the dead." It was denied—and the spirit was lost forever. Ah, in this vast assembly, how many are to be found in danger of encountering the horrors of that world, of the inhabitants of which, it will be said, that they do pray *va.*

My brethren, we have now attempted to exhibit to you those general principles to which we have adverted, as legitimately to be deduced from the statement of this portion of the Word of God. We have reminded you that the employment of prayer is to be directed to God, as its only exclusive object; and that God has rendered it a matter of positive and universal obligation. We have reminded you that he is guilty of restraining prayer before God, who altogether omits prayer—who engages but seldom in prayer—who excludes from supplication those matters which are properly the objects of prayer—and who does not cherish the spirit of importunity in prayer. And we have reminded you, that the habit of restraining prayer before Him, cannot be indulged with impunity, that it prevents always the enjoyments of spiritual blessings both by ourselves and by others; and that it exposes especially to the judicial wrath of God.

I trust, my Christian brethren, to whom I would address u ;-
6*

self once more in approaching the conclusion of our address, that the subject which has been dedicated to your welfare, will not be offered to you in vain; and as, without exception, shame and confusion of face belong to us, because, to some extent, at least, we have restrained prayer before God, that to-night we will renew our vows, and retire to our chambers, and there beseech God, as His best boon to us, to pour upon us the spirit of prayer; and resolve, my brethren, in the language of the prophet that, "for Zion's sake we will not hold our peace," in prayer—that "for Jerusalem's sake we will not hold our peace," in prayer, "until the righteousness thereof go forth as the brightness, and his salvation as a lamp that burneth." No; we will take the censer that contains the blood of propitiation; we will draw aside the veil that separates us from the holiest of all; we will enter and stand in the presence of the shekinah, before the burning glory of Jehovah, and there sprinkling that blood upon the mercy-seat, and holding it before us that we die not, stand with an unwearied and with an unfainting cry, "*we will not, we will not, we will not* let thee go except thou bless us;" waiting until, from that shrine and that pavilion of glory, the voice shall answer, "Ye have prevailed; as I live, the whole earth shall be filled with my glory; the mystery of God which he spake to His prophets, soon, soon shall be finished."

And yet, my hearers, there are many now present, who have no title to the character of Christians, and to whom I would dedicate another word of exhortation before I close. My hearers, I tremble to think that I am now in the presence of a person who never prayed; a sinner born to die; a sinner whose breath is in his nostrils; a sinner who, by one stroke of his Judge, might be swept from probation to eternal doom. *A sinner who never prayed!* *Where is he?* Is it *you*—is it *you*—is it *you*, who never prayed? Suppose *you* were to stand forth; what a sight would it be! O sinner, we call upon you to pray *now*; go to the footstool and say, "God be merciful to me a sinner." *Is it uttered?* *Then utter it again,* "God be merciful to me a sinner." *Is it repeated?* *Then repeat it again*—God be merciful to me a sinner." *Saints pray for the praying sinner*—" God be merciful unto him a sinner." And the voice of united supplication will be heard; joy will be felt in the bosoms of the an-

gels; a greater than the angels will look down, as he did upon
Saul of Tarsus, and with the ecstacy of a satisfied travail, will
exclaim, " Behold he prayeth;" and the sigh of that sinner's
petition will be heard ; that sinner's transgressions shall be pardoned; that sinner's person shall be accepted; that sinner's soul
shall be accepted. Thus may God, by His spirit descend, and
preserve us from the habit of restraining prayer before Him.

Suffer me to cite another instance of the peroration of
another order, but equally impressive, from a great master
of pulpit speech, JAMES STRATTEN—the close of a sermon
from the text, "Hold fast till I come."

I confess myself to be filled often with delight and joy, when
I contemplate aged excellence, and think of longevity in connection with eminent services to the Church of God, and great
devotedness to the cause of truth and virtue and religion among
men. Abraham died "old, and full of years;" ripe in faith,
mellow in his principles, perfectly prepared to awake up in
righteousness, and to behold God's face in heaven. Jacob said,
" I have waited for Thy salvation, O Lord," amid the infirmities
and weakness which belonged to his condition. Moses " was
a hundred and twenty years old when he died; his eye was not
dim, nor his natural force abated;" God came and took him,
as a tree, with all its clusters hanging ripe, copious, luscious,
beautiful, abundant, transplanted at once, as by a stroke or by a
miracle, to the celestial Paradise. Then comes Caleb? " Lo, I
am this day, fourscore and five years old," he says, "and I am
as strong as I was in the day that Moses sent me ; " " I am competent to go out to war; I can do valiantly for God and for
His truth now, as I did in the days of my youth." Then there
is Barzillai, not so bold, not so champion-like : " I am, this day,
fourscore years old : and can thy servant taste what I eat or what
I drink? can I hear any more the voice of singing-men and
singing-women?" "the acuteness of my senses is departed
from me; all that I want is to go down to my grave in peace,
and to be buried in the sepulchre of my fathers. by the grave of
my father and of my mother "—of course, connecting his burial
as it respects His body, with the peace and rest of his soul in

Abraham's bosom. Then Simeon; " Lord, now lettest Thou
Thy servant depart in peace, for mine eyes have seen Thy salvation." Last, not least—in some respects greatest among those
whom we have named—is the inspired writer of this book—
John—the beloved apostle. Ninety, as it is supposed, now that
in Patmos he received " visions and revelations of the Lord ; "
living to be a hundred ; and, in his righteousness, steadfastness,
perseverance, in the depth of his love, and the transparency of
his knowledge, and the confidence of his faith, ripening, to rest
again a second time with Peter and with James, and not transi-
ently, for half an hour, but to rest for eternity, on the bosom of
his Lord. Oh ! let these examples help us. Hold fast that which
you have, until He shall come ; " let no man take your crown."

" *Till I come.*"

Then *Christ will come.* He " will come in His own and His
Father's glory, come in like manner as He was seen going away ;
come upon His great white throne." And it amounts to the
same thing, whether we regard this coming as at *our* final day,
or at *His* final day ; for as we are found, in our moral and spiritual condition, at our final day, when we die, so shall we be
found at His final day, when He shall make His personal appearance among us again.

He will come certainly. As surely as I am here and have
spoken these words, as sure as this Book is upon this sacred
desk, as sure as you are listening to the voice and do behold the
countenance of a fellow-man, so surely shall you hear the voice
of the trumpet of the great archangel, and see the face of Jesus
Christ.

He will come, and then will be revelation and disclosure of every man's state. Our words and principles will be tried, " so as
by fire." All books will be opened, the Book of God's remembrance, the Book of God's inspiration, the book of man's memory, the book of man's conscience. Clearest, intensest light will
be shed upon all, in order to the revelation and discovery of
what we really are. And then will come the verdict, sentence,
and destination, according to every man's condition.

Have we obtained nothing ? Is there no oil in the lamp at all ?
Has there never been any ?—mercy not sought, grace not applied

for, God not known, Christ not believed in, experience of the power of religion upon the heart never realized? No oil? No entrance then, " The door will be shut and they who have no oil in their lamps will be shut out."

Is there oil? Have we obtained mercy?—sought for grace, got the pardon, in possession of the righteousness and sanctification? Is there oil in the lamp? " Behold, the Bridegroom cometh, go ye out to meet Him." The lamp burns; the light is bright. Go ye in.

Not ready, " that wicked servant" not ready; " smiting his fellow-servants, eating and drinking with the drunken." The Lord comes, "cuts him asunder, and appoints him his portion with the hypocrites." *Ready;* loins girt, lights burning. " Blessed is that servant;" the Lord Himself " will gird Himself, and come forth " and wait upon those servants—will minister to their joy, will replenish them with satisfaction, will lift up their heads in everlasting honor.

Then " *hold fast, until I come.*"

I have intimated, *that some have nothing.* Is there any one of *you that has nothing*—that never thought about it, never prayed about it, never read the Scriptures for the purpose? " Now is the accepted time ; now is the day of salvation." You may gain the blessing. If you have never prayed before will you not pray now? Will you not turn to God to-night? Will you not seek mercy? Will you not examine this matter of the method in which a sinner is to be saved? Will you not say, " I will arise and go to my Father? Arise and go. Take the first step; gain the first blessing—the absolution and remission of your sins; and all the rest may follow in its train.

And if you have the thing, do not even look back. " Remember Lot's wife. No man having put his hand to the plough and looking back, is fit for the kingdom of God." Very memorable are the words of Christ in two places, respecting those who depart and decline. *The salt that has lost its savor,* is " good for nothing," not even for the dunghill; only to be "cast out and trodden under foot of men." *The branch broken off from the vine,* is utterly and absolutely worthless ; " withered ;" to be " gathered and cast into the fire and burned." *Hold fast.* Say with Paul, "I have not already attained, but I press on;" and you shall say with him at last—"I have fought a good fight, I have finished my course," I have attained unto perfection.

"He that hath ears to hear, let him hear," these plain, but most momentous things, which "the Spirit saith unto the Churches." And "now unto Him that is able to keep us from falling, and to present us faultless before the presence of His glory with exceeding joy; to the only wise God our Saviour, be glory and majesty, dominion and power both now and ever. Amen."

These illustrations, if wanting in that perfection of art which rhetoricians are fond of commending, are models of earnestness and intensity, aiming at usefulness in the last word or stroke of speech.

Methods, such as I have quoted, such as pressing home personally spiritual truth upon the conscience, seem to me far more in harmony with the intention and work of the Christian ministry, than the artificial corruscations and flames of genius so often admired. Take for an instance the following from a sermon preached by WILLIAM JOHNSON FOX, whose eloquence indeed, simply regarded as eloquence, was of the highest order : he was educated for the Independent Ministry, left that for the Unitarian, and exercised his latest powers in the House of Commons : the sermon from which the following is an extract was preached in 1819.

THE GREATNESS OF ENGLAND INDEPENDENT OF STATE CHURCHES.

To conclude: designing men, even in the present day, have dared to represent dissent from the church as synonymous with disaffection to the State. It is a foul calumny. The sternest and sturdiest protest against the one may co-exist with the most enthusiastic devotion to the other. England was great and glorious while her religion was Popery. She *then* reared her head above the nations, outstripped them all in the career of improvement, and soared above them towards the heaven of liberty. The great charter of *her* freedom was then wrested from unwilling power; commerce and manufactures were raising her citizens, burgesses, and merchants to wealth and intelligence, and placing them side by side with her barons ; while from contending elements arose the harmony of representative government. *She* was great while that change called Reformation was proceeding, or retarded, or subsiding into fixedness, through successive reigns. She then began to wave her flag of sovereignty over the sea ; *her* laws were framed in wisdom ; and her literature, splendid in genius, profound in learning, and mighty in originality, advanced with a giant step. *She was great* at that tremendous period when the crown was trampled in the dust, a regal head fell on the scaffold, and Cromwell sat on an ungarnished throne. Episcopacy was not the religion then. The Church of England fled to the wilderness ; the mitre was crushed under sectarian feet, and the crosier snapped asunder by unconsecrated hands : *yet then she was great ;* not a nation but cringed for her friendship, and trembled at her frown. Was there persecution, oppression, or insult on the continent ?—she lifted her voice of thunder, and Europe's hills were moved ; her mountains quaked and trembled to their foundations. And while Episcopacy has been Church-of-Englandism, our country has been great and glorious still ;—*yes*, through vicissitude, great ; in adversity and disappointment, in privation and suffering, in all changes and chances, in arms and arts, in literature and benevolence. The monuments of *her* majesty reflect the glittering of every star of heaven ; and not a wind can blow that has not wafted from her shores some freight of charity. And she would be great, were this assuming sect lost in oblivion with all its robes and forms, and wealth and creeds ; still to her would the nations look as to an elder sister of the earth, preeminent in wisdom, grace, and majesty.

Yes ; England, independently of adventitious circumstances or predominant sects, must be admired and loved by all who can rightly think and feel ; nor would the hand that might not object to pull down the clustering ivy from the oak, whose strength it wasted, and whose beauty it impaired, touch profanely one leaf of the hallowed tree. Oh, my country ! land of my birth, my love, and my pride : land of freedom and of glory ; land of bards and heroes, of statesmen, philosophers and patriots ; land of Alfred and of Sydney, of Hampden and of Russell, of Newton, Locke, and Milton; may thy security, liberty, generosity, peace, and pre-eminence be eternal! May thy children prize their birthright, and well guard and extend their privileges! From the annals of thy renown, the deeds of thy worthies, the precious volumes of thy sages, may they imbibe the love of freedom, of virtue, of their country! May the pure Gospel be their portion! Through every future age may they arise, as of yore, the protectors of the oppressed, the terror of tyrants, the guardians of the rights and peace of nations, the champions of civil and religious liberty; and may they be the possessors and diffusers of genuine Christianity to all countries, through all generations! Amen.

This is a magnificent passage, and such passages, no doubt, in their delivery, have a splendid effect upon cultivated minds, and the glowing language of perfectly formed sentences, elegant and eloquent, assisted by the graces of manner, often, as in the case of the orator I have quoted, overcoming and rising matchlessly triumphant over what might seem insuperable physical defects, moves an audience to noble excitements of feeling; but I should not desire to see even many Robert Halls in the pulpit. It is not in the pulpit we are to expect or to aim after those triumphs of style which charm in the pages of Macaulay; the polished period, the labored antithesis, the startling paradox, are out of place there, where "not many wise, not many great, not many noble," can be among the number of the called; there the weak things of the world are to confound, as of old, the things of the wise and the mighty; still, as of old, it is true, "Where is the wise? where is the scribe? where is the disputer of this world;" still, as of old, "The world, by its wisdom, knows not God;" and still, "it pleases God, by the foolishness of preaching" (which need not, however, be foolish preaching) "to save them that believe."

PULPIT MONOGRAPHS.

II.—Pusey, Manning and Newman.

THE Church of England has been more remarkable in the history of the literature of the pulpit, for the introduction of sermons suitable for the study and the oratory than the church. This must be very greatly the case when sermons are prepared by thoroughly educated men, who are more interested in perceiving and following out for their own edification the thoughts in their own mind, than in reducing them to the level of the attainments of a popular audience. The sermons of the illustrious Barrow were confessedly not intended for delivery, and when he appeared in the pulpit he was always tedious, and his noble and magnificent productions would not be listened to now, not merely with edification or patience, they would not be listened to at all. The same remark applies in a less, but equally certain, degree to the sermons of South and Taylor, and to those of John Howe and Charnock. We ridicule, and are angry with sensational preaching, but some measure of light and fancy and appropriate condensation and diffusion in style is necessary for all large and popular audiences ; this is the art of preaching. The elaborate and well-informed essay, the scholastic dissertation, are unfitted for public and ordinary service and worship; so also for the most part are those productions in which the man of extraordinary powers of subtilty, insight, thought, and even felicity of expression, utters truths far beyond the possible attainment of the ordinary mind. Our Lord could, indeed, combine the very different methods of speech contained in the seventeenth chapter of Luke, and the fourteenth chapter of John; but they were delivered in very different circumstances, and to very different audiences. Some men can attempt to follow the teaching of the Lord in one who cannot at all use or follow Him in the other. Are those more select sermons, then, which only found a very small and select audience in their delivery, to be cast aside? Certainly not; these may yet inform the ministers how to preach; he needs their instruction, and the humbler man may use and make more general their power of insight—their illustration and even their methods. Nor ought it to be forgotten that attention is needed for all real and great teaching; without this, vain is the power of any teacher; he, indeed, should lend himself in the most easy and happy manner to convey, but not the less should the hearer strive to receive. For the want of this, quite as much as for the want of aptitude in the ministry, it is that hearers cry for tropes and figures, glowing language and pathetic addresses. "Why do not our ministers," people say, "preach like the great divines of the French nation, and why do not they manifest the life and pathos of a Whitefield?" Alas! they have probably to preach to the same people about one hundred and fifty sermons every year, the great sermons to which they allude were delivered on great occasions after immense study and preparation—or they had been delivered many times by men like Whitefield, who appeared for a day, for a few weeks, and were gone; the animated style of eloquence is a luxury—and its elegancies and artifices cannot grow on every tree—but there is that which is better than all this—that moderate but yet more living warmth, which assists the whole life to live, which will bear pondering, and which may be turned to again and again. Dissenting congregations have been too neglectful and too impatient of this ; it is painful to think that the orator is most heard and more esteemed, and we lay our hands on innumerable volumes of sermons, many of them posthumous—most of them unknown, clear, and light-bringing, but their authors either had not condescended, or could not condescend to the popular method ; and therefore, they lived without reputation beyond the narrow existence, and if dead it may be said, " the place of their sepulchre knoweth no man."

There are three living preachers whose names are not known much, nor loved much in those circles in which excellence is estimated by the ovations of noise which greet it, and persuade it to believe that passions and tumults and notoriety are fame ; but to those who test the value of praise by the depth and tenderness of its accent rather than the tumultuousness of its expression, the sermons of Dr. Pusey, and of Dr. John Henry Newman, and of Dr. Manning, will seem among the most beautiful which have at any time been delivered from the pulpit. They, none of them, read to me like productions of the nineteenth century, and Pusey's, especially, have the quaint sweetness and fervor of an old cloistered monk of the mediæval ages. The greatest of these three modern models of sacred and gifted speech is John Henry Newman ; his genius, while the most subtle in its insight, and gifted with those views of truth which, in their mystical charm, are like revealing lamps shining on landing-places, higher than those usually attained in the turrets of thought and knowledge, or like the rich light in the west, bringing out into plain and distinctive outline the country beyond, with all its far-stretching region of hill or moorland, while yet the eye cannot discover the paths and roads, while it plainly discovers the affirmation of the infinite country lying there. Dr. Pusey's tenderness and pathos of expression are great, and his language has more of the measured march of that studied expression which seems like the gift of oratory and rhetoric. Yet the sermons of Pusey, while read slowly, and firmly, and feelingly, pour along a stream of meditation, they read as though rather fitted for the oratory than the pulpit; his sermons are bathed in the past, and formed in the language of the past; they may arrest and hold, but it is as if some monk moved us at his devotions, a real and pensive power subdues us; but it is a power out of the past rather than the present; and the words are quiet, and seize us as when we read pages of the Fathers to whom in their cloistered serenity the world was a thing lost sight of and forgotten. While Manning, again, has a style more sharp and clear and incisive than either, there is more orderly speech; language and ideas run more evenly in the grooves of dogma and of settled faith. A soft but steady light, like that which the fine summer sun leaves behind him over distant scenes, when he has set, is shed from Newman's magical pages. The light which as certainly shines in Manning's sermons is rather the light of a flash, arresting while abiding, and never unrelated to something of terror and awe. All these sermons are of the order, only to be appreciated by persons of culture—I do not mean the culture of the mind, the information of philology, and grammars, and histories, and sciences—but that other and profounder culture which it seems impossible for the tradesman intelligence ever to attain, which is scarcely compatible with a life in the office and the shop, with a life in which the mind must be occupied with the little selfishnesses, and fortune-makings, and interested aims of men of bustle and intrigue; they speak to the state in which the mind and heart are perpetually proving themselves, and asking questions of themselves ; or, perhaps, those natures who, having done this—natures, in which the hard doubts have been washed down by the rains of grief and tears into an alluvial and fruitful soil for the soul—are prepared to find the teacher and to receive his instructions through whom they may understand something of the mystery of a past experience, and make it the garden and the vintage of the soul : for we seldom can understand our own grief while we stand beneath the shadow of it ; but autumn harvests and vintages explain the gales and storms, the snows and dark nights of winter.   An intense, but not, I think, uncheerful gravity pervades the teaching of all these men.   Seriousness! why, many preachers are serious ; but there is a seriousness of deportment, and their is a seriousness of life, there is the seriousness of decorum and decency, like mourning weeds and slow steps assumed for the occasion, and taught by art and by rule ; and there is seriousness which sheds itself habitually over the face, real and not sentimental depth of expression, derived from the perpetual residence of the spirit in the neighborhood of visionary or intro-visionary scenes.

I do not think Pusey indeed reaches this depth of feeling ; his words read to me like those of a man who has settled his faith and convictions, and takes ideas and expressions rather as they come.   He is neither an Augustine nor a Gregory, nor Ephrem Syrus.   I cannot get away from my first impression, he is a monk ; and of these neither a Dominican, nor a Franciscan, nor a Carthusian, a good plain monk.   All his lessons and his lore are of the monastery ; Scripture and the Fathers are quite sufficient for him, without the lore of souls ; no raptures overtake him, no metaphysics disturb him.   His language is indeed more ardent than either of those I have mentioned with him, but it does not move so much, the light has more of the rich glow of church windows, when on fire beneath the dying sun they pour their prismatic hues with innumerable stains and splendid dyes, and dim emblazonings over the carven imageries, and the twilight saints and splendid scutcheons ; this, or tall tapers in the lonely church ; not that his style, any more than Newman's or Manning's, glows or pants with poetry or illustration. There is scarce an image or an expression that would be claimed by poetry in the ordinary and more vulgar conception of poetry in either of the writers ; they produce the effects of poetry without its rhythm and its imagery ; but Pusey uses a more sensational appeal, and, perhaps unconsciously to himself, he is more artificial, simple ; and yet like some Thomas à Kempis of our times, he indulges in that close and affectionate colloquy with souls, in which the soul must be very much subdued to listen, and must hush its breath while the stream of speech flows on. Here is such a passage on—

LIFE CONSIDERED AS A WARFARE.

But does the whole strife seem to you long and weary ? Look to eternity. It is nothing to look on to endless time. Time is no measure for eternity. For when eternity comes, time will no longer be. Yet even thus, look on to eternity. Look on to it, if but as countless, endless time, no nearer to any end, when thousands of thousands of years such as we now count them, yea, if each of these thousands of thousands of years were told over as often as there are grains of the dust of the earth or sand on the sea-shore, shall have rolled by, still thou must begin again, and again, and again, and when time and thought have failed thee, thou art still no nearer. And then say, what is the longest life on earth ? Shrivelled into nothing. In the presence of eternity, or of that countless time, not thy life only, but the whole being of this world is as nothing. But look on again in that eternity. I ask not where God hath said, Thou shalt be ; but, What shalt thou be ? Unchangeable as the unchangeableness of God, what thou hast become in this world good or bad? And where, then, is this weary strife which now seems to thee so long, so hard, so unendurable? Shrivelled up into nothing, past and gone. And what is there besides? One unchanging, unchangeable state. In all eternity, thou wilt be one and the same, even as God Himself is One and the Same. Here we may ever hope for change. We hope ever to be other, better, than we are. But change, growth, amendment, enlargement of the heart, is *here* alone. *There* our state is fixed. It is an awful thing in itself to think of our state being fixed: of all power of amending it, by God's grace, being gone. Who of us could endure the thought of being in all eternity what they are now, of having no more power to love than they have now? But think for one moment what that unchangeable eternity would be in woe, an eternity "in the fire which never shall be quenched, where their worm dieth not, and their fire is not quenched!" And what will it be to you, my brethren, if ye, by the grace of God, hold on for this little while? What is Eternity? Eternity to the blessed, is God's unchangeable love, shedding upon the countless hosts of Heaven, Angels and Archangels, Cherubim and Seraphim, Martyrs, Prophets, Patriarchs and the whole glorious company of the redeemed, and, if thou willest, by His Grace, on *thee*, the fullness of His infinite love, opening to them the treasures of His infinite wisdom, encompassing them round and round with His infinite bliss, satisfying their souls with His infinite beauty, and awakening in them a continual longing which shall ever be filled, never be cloyed.

He saith to *thee*, "All which I have is thine," *thine*, according to thy power to contain it. Now he bids thee with one earnest strife, cast out of thyself what chokes thy heart, that thou canst not contain everlastingly His Love. He bids *thee*, by His grace, enlarge thy heart, that He may fill thee more largely. All of this world will soon have passed away. But God will remain, and *thou*, whatever thou hast become, good or bad. Thy deeds now are the seed-corn of eternity. Each single act, in each several day, good or bad, is a portion of that seed. Each day adds some line, making thee more or less like Him, more or less capable of His Love, fitter for greater or less glory, to be nearer to Him, or to be less near, or to be away from Him for ever.

It is the strife long and hard ? Long and hard it would be to be ever defeated. But Christ shall lighten it for *thee.* He will bear it in *thee ;* He will bear thee over it, as He will bear thee over the molten surges of this burning world. Christ will go before thee. He saith unto *thee,* " Follow Me, and where I am, there shall *thou* be with Me. Follow *thou* me." " Be of good cheer, I have overcome the world." " If Christ be for us, who shall be against us !" Safely mayest thou fight, who art secure of victory. And thou *art* safe, if thou fight for Christ, and with Christ. Only give not way. If defeated, be the humbler, and rise again ; begin again, and pray to persevere. If thou succeed, give " thanks to Him who giveth us the victory, through Jesus Christ our Lord." And He will, by His blood, intercede *for* thee ; He will, by His grace, fight *in* thee ; He will keep thee unto the end, who himself crowneth, and is crowned, in all who are faithful to His grace.

What soul, being awakened, could listen unmoved to words like these ? Yet even these, if the preacher is more interested in his own words than the states of his hearers, will fall—as I suppose they do fall—very unimpressive, for it is so, there may be, it would seem, conviction without the accent of conviction, because the truth is held rather in solution in the mind than giving intensity to it. Another of these passages is the following :

THE CHRISTIAN LIFE.

Thou canst not have victory unless thou be assaulted. The thickening of thy temptations may be the very favor of God, who permits Satan to try and " sift thee like wheat," yet wills that thou shouldest not fall. Even then, though fierce temptation should come on thee in thy holiest moments, when thou art most earnest in prayer, or after thou hast received thy Lord in Holy Communion, or when thy will is strongest, thy soul humblest, thy love most self-forgetful, fear not. Rather thou mayest take it as a token of God's love, who sets thee in conflict. He will uphold thee by His Hand when the waves are boisterous. So shalt thou have the victory through His Spirit ; thou shalt, in His might, trample on the Evil One, the more he assaults thee. So shalt thou hate sin the more, the more thou art tormented by the sinfulness of thy mortal nature; and be a good soldier of Jesus Christ, who willeth to crown thee, and to be crowned in thee. Only hold fast to Him; grasp His Hand the tighter, by whom thou art held. He will refresh thee when wearied; He will meet thee, as the King of Righteousness, and will recruit thee with spiritual Food, His Body and Blood; He will forgive thy sins; He will heal thine infirmities; He will renew thy decays. He will hear thee when thou criest; He will answer thee when thou prayest; He will have compassion on thy afflictions; He will loose thy bands; He will uphold thy feeble knees; He will make straight paths for thy feet; He Himself, thy Redeemer, will be thy Way unto Himself, thy God.

Resist the very first motions. It is *then* that thou art most in thy own power. Be not weary of resisting, although the temptation come again and again. Be not off thy guard, although it go away for a time in order to come again. Each such resistance is an act of obedience to God; each, done by His grace, draws down more of His grace to thee; in each, His good pleasure will the more rest upon thee; by each, thou wilt become more a vessel of His grace and love, more fitted and enlarged for His everlasting love. Christ, who is the Power of God and the Wisdom of God, will dwell in thy soul, as in His own abode. He will rule thee, He will teach thee, He will speak with thee, He will fence thee from the assaults of the enemy, with the helmet of salvation. He will direct thy senses within, He will guard thee without.

And through all this conflict, the more thou art tossed here, the more thou wilt learn to long for thy heavenly home, the home of His rest and love. Thou shalt learn to long lovingly for that day when the remaining corruption shall be put off, and this body of sin have died through the body's death, but the body itself shall be instinct with new life, and conformed to the glorious Body of thy Lord. Death shall be to thee the gate of life, the end of woe and conflict, the beginning of eternal refreshment, the entrance into thine eternal dwelling-place, where thou shalt have all thou now longest for, shalt rest in the sight of God, joy in His love, be enriched by His imparting of Himself. Thou shalt then see what thou now believest; thou shalt have what thou now hopest for; thou shalt attain to what thou now canst not conceive. For thou shalt be one spirit with God, united with Him, dwelling in Him, beholding Him, encircled with His love, share His, and what is His shall be thine for evermore.

Pusey's sermons are calls to the soul—voices earnest and beseeching, while sometimes they rise to tones of rapture and of vision. But the sermons of Manning are of a much higher order; of their kind, I know not how to think there can be higher sermons; true they are intensely ascetic. All three of these preachers belong to the order of ascetic teachers, but they are wonderful sermons, and as we turn back to the memories with which we first read them, and as we turn their pages again, it is no figure of speech to say, the heart aches and the eyes almost weep, to think that the author of these extraordinary meditations has fallen into the hard, cruel, intolerant bigot—the very type of an ancient Dominican weaving his words into eulogies upon the Inquisition. One's own heart trembles for its steadfastness and wonders what secret sin it was that can have had power to issue in such a fall; for he is not merely a Romanist—but a Romanist intense in hatred to England, to Protestantism, and to all the interests of mind. Not so in these words and volumes, of which I know not whether to speak with most admiration, of the method and consecutiveness of every plan, of its grave sobriety, of chastened and yet richly-cultured thought, or of the rich revealing powers of genius and holy sanctity everywhere evident—subdued, calmed like the words of those to whom suffering and experience are very old; no strained expressions, no pomp, no glow of language, no attempt either at any great or chosen fitness of expression; no passion, no art, but that great knowledge of the ways of human souls which no metaphysics can teach, and which yet seems to be the intention of the teaching of all metaphysics. There is no attempt to untwist—to untie, or to cut the knot of life and its mystery ; there is no mental revolt as in Robertson ; there is only the patient submission of the will and the thought to that which is. The truths, too, taught have no light of novelty in their setting ; they are old, but their presentation calls up a chain of associated impressions and reflected lights. All these preachers, and Manning in a very distinct manner, are reverently Scriptural ; they press everywhere the service of texts and illustrations to sustain and support all their thoughts. They hold up the text and seem to say, "I stand still and watch what the light will reveal!" and here seem to be no rhetorical arts. If they were used they are all out of sight ; no impassioned prosopopœia or labored climax ; no pendulous antithesis or ambitious character sketch ; so modest, yet so powerful—so apparently characterless, yet impressively alive with character. As we remember Dr. Manning before these sermons were preached—full of action, passionate, glowing, rapid and even vehement—it is almost impossible to identify in this memory, powerful as the impression is, their delivery ; yet it is again impossible to conceive them other than penetrating ; but then they depend, as we have already said, on their audience, and there are lines and sentences which arrest and strike, but they especially lose by being dislocated from their context ; as when the sins of Christendom, as compared with the heathen world, are defined as probably " having less that is akin to the unreasonable creatures of God, but a nearer fellowship with Satan ;" or, when he relieves us by saying, "Who can tell what has ever been the ineffable yearnings of the heathen world—what tumultuous cries of spiritual sorrow have been heard in the ears of God?" "Sin can hide itself from the conscience—it is most concealed at its highest pitch of strength.

It is cold to us and we suppose it cold in itself. Fire has no heat to the dead—Christ did no mighty work among the unbelieving."

GRACE, AND THE WILL.

Such is the mysterious nature of the human spirit, of its affections, and will, such its energies and intensity, that it may, at any time, be so renewed by the Spirit of the new creation, as to expel with the most perfect rejection, all the powers, qualities, visions, and thoughts of evil. We know so little of spiritual natures, that we are compelled to use metaphors; and often our illustrations become our snares, and we turn them into arguments, and reason from visible things to the inscrutable conditions of our spiritual being. For instance, we speak of the stains of sin, the soils of lust, the scars and wounds made by transgression in the soul: and it is true, that what stains, soils, scars, wounds, are to the body, such are lusts, in deed, desire and thought, to the soul. But we cannot therefore say that the spiritual nature is not susceptible of a healing and purgation which is absolutely perfect, to which the cleansing or health of the body is no true analogy. For instance, the very life of sin is the will. By sin it is a corrupt and unclean will; by conversion it becomes cleansed and pure. So long as it is here subjected to the action of the flesh, it is imperfect; but when disembodied what shall hinder its being as pure as if it had never sinned? What is the substance of the will? What is sin? And in what does sin inhere but in the inclination of the will? When this is restored to perfect holiness, what effect of the fall will remain? We are greatly ignorant of all these things; but it is evident that, be we what we may, if our repentance and conversion be true, there is no height of sanctification, no approximation to the Divine Image, that we may not make in this world, and in the world to come be made sinless in the kingdom of God. And if our spiritual nature may be made sinless in the life to come, how can we limit its purification in this world? How can we say that it may not be brought out from the effects of any sin, or habit of sinning, as intensely and energetically pure as if it had never been bribed or corrupted by evil; and, moreover, sharpened with a peculiar abhorrence of the defilement from which it has been delivered? Such is the mysterious complexion of a spiritual nature, that it may, in a moment, and by an act of volition, virtually and truly anticipate an habitual condition of the soul; as, for instance, in a true death-bed repentance there is contained a life of penance and purity, though it be never here developed into act. And this may throw light on many questions; such as the condition of the heathen, and of those that are born in separation from the unity of the Church, and on the state of those who, after baptism, by falling into sin, have resisted the grace of regeneration. Of these last, it would appear that their condition is changed for the worse, in the point of having sinned with greater guilt, and done despite to that which should have been their salvation. By consent to sin, they have made the work of repentance more difficult and doubtful. The blood of Christ, and the grace of the Holy Ghost, have yet the power of a perfect healing and purification; but repentance, which, on their side, is the condition, it is harder to fulfil. Still, wheresoever there are the lingering remains of grace, or the least beginnings of contrition, there is hope of a perfect repentance, and of a perfect sanctity. It seems, then, that it was for this reason that our blessed Lord, the sinless One, suffered publicans, sinners, and even the adulteress, to draw near to Him; because, in them, under the foul gatherings of sin, which spread like a crust of leprosy upon them, and in the darkness and death of their inmost soul, He could see the faint strength of a living pulse, the dim spark of sorrow, fear, remorse, and desire to be redeemed from the bondage of the devil, and therefore the susceptibity of perfect holiness, the unextinguished capacity of an inheritance with the saints in light.

"Life does not hang on matter, nor on the organization of matter." "It is not as the harmony which rings out of a cunning instrument; but it is a breath—a spirit; a ray of the eternal Being—pure, immaterial, above all grosser compounds simple and indissoluble." "A riven heart is the best expositor of God's teaching about the saints asleep." "Men are already half reconciled when they have agreed to honor one and the same spiritual lineage." Such sayings, which, suggestive and tender as they are, look cold when taken from their connection, shed a softened effulgence through all these volumes. The grief of sin, the grief of life, the grief of thought throng like solemn-robed processions over these pages. They all weigh down with the overwhelming sense of the intolerable burden of life, sin, and time. Life is a purgatory of dreadful pain to the children of this kingdom, and beyond it are the terrible torments of hell, and the ineffable beauties and splendors of paradise. The following is beautiful on the

MORAL AND SPIRITUAL POWER OF WORK.

Next to prayer and a life of devotional habits, there is nothing that keeps the heart so pure, and the will so strong and steadfast, as a live of active duty. This is no doubt one peculiar blessing of those who live hard and laborious lives, and accounts, in great measure, for the singular simplicity, straightforwardness, unconsciousness of evil, which is to be found among the laboring poor. Their poverty, and daily intentness of mind upon the pure and simple tillage of the earth, shields them from a thousand assaults of evil, and a whole world of dangerous thoughts, schemes, desires, and designs which throng upon the idle or unemployed. Compare the open and natural character of a poor man with the complex, suppressed, inward mind of those who live in the world with much time at their disposal, and little or no laborious work. It is like the transparency of a child by the side of a darkened and deteriorated manhood. A lawful and regular employment, somewhat laborious, and even absorbing (so that it does not estrange a man's mind from God), is a great security against the temptations of the world and of our own hearts. It shuts out the approaches of temptations without number; and keeps the mind in perfect ignorance that such allurements exist in the world. It is the want of some fixed and regular course of duty that makes even good people inconsistent, uncertain, wavering and sometimes listless, unwary and infirm. Unsettled thoughts, roving imaginations, idle fancies, vacant hearts, wandering eyes, open ears, busy tongues, are the inseparable companions of a man who has little to do, or no rule and order of daily employment. From all this, steady labor would be his protection. Work is the very salt of our fallen nature, and keeps it from corrupting.

THE DEAD.

O fearful death! It has a lure which thrills in my soul, and seems to draw me to itself; it fixes me by the fascination of its eye. Death is coming towards me. I must one day die, and "how am I straitened till it be accomplished!" Blessed and happy dead! great mighty dead! In them the work of the creation is well nigh accomplished. What feebly stirs in us, in them is well nigh full. They have passed within the veil, and there remaineth only one more change for them—a change full of a foreseen, foretasted bliss. How calm, how pure, how sainted are they now! A few short years ago, and they were almost as weak and poor as we: burdened with the dying body we now bear about; harrassed by temptations, often overcome, weeping in bitterness of soul, struggling, with faithful though fearful hearts, towards that dark shadow from which they shrank as we shrink now.

THE CHURCH VISIBLE AND INVISIBLE—ONE PROCESSION.

Nothing was changed but the relation of sight; like as when the head of a far-stretching procession, winding through a broken hollow land, hides itself in some bending vale: it is still all one; all advancing together; they that are farthest onward in the way are conscious of their lengthened following; they that linger with the last are drawn forward, as it were, by the attraction of the advancing multitude. Even so they knew themselves to be ever moving on; they were ever pressing on beyond the bounds of its material world. They knew the life of the Church to be one, and indivisible; that, seen or unseen, there was but one energy of spiritual being, in which all were united: that all were nourished by the same hidden manna, and slaked their thirst in the same waters of life. They were one in the personality of Christ's mystical body; and all their acts of love and adoration were shared in full by each several member.

All the strength of Dr. Manning is in these volumes of

sermons ; perhaps Dr. Newman's sermons are equally
strong, but all his strength is not in them, he has put himself into fifty other volumes, extending over every variety
of mental exploit ; great everywhere, and in everything
great, with a Michael Angelo-like greatness, struggling,
massive, earnest hurling his books about like thunderbolts.
Manning has none of this power, his is aerial or ethereal
without being especially subtle, he makes his words persuasive as the air, sometimes terrible as the air alive with
lightnings, or auroras, or spectral armies fighting in the
clouds.   Newman's words are even yet more quiet, yet they
seem, like wondrous chloroform, to penetrate further, and
more internally to possess the mind.   To say that JOHN
HENRY NEWMAN is one of the greatest Christian sages
of our country in these times, would only expose me to
your suspicions, and it is only with his sermons I have to
do ; they are very much in the style of little homilies, and
yet every one contains some great thesis ; these, in a more
eminent sense than Dr. Manning's, seem to me, amazing
productions ; such charming and venerable simplicity, such
conciseness, such a vivid perception of the whole outbranch-
ing, such a firm grasp of the central stem.   Thus, in the
introduction of

THE CROSS OF CHRIST THE MEASURE OF THE WORLD.

Now, let me ask, what is the real key, what is the Christian
interpretation of this world ?   What is given us by revelation
to estimate and measure this world by ?   The event of this
season,—the crucifixion of the Son of God.

It is the death of the Eternal Word of God, made flesh, which
is our great lesson how to think and how to speak of this world.
His Cross has put its due value upon everything which we see,
upon all fortunes, all advantages, all ranks, all dignities, all
pleasures ; upon the lust of the flesh, and the lust of the eyes,
and the pride of life.   It has set a price upon the excitements,
the rivalries, the hopes, the fears, the desires, the efforts, the
triumphs of mortal man.   It has given a meaning to the various,

shifting course, the trials, the temptations, the sufferings, of his earthly state. It has brought together and made consistent all that seemed discordant and aimless. It has taught us how to live, how to use this world, what to expect, what to desire, what to hope. It is the tone into which all the strains of this world's music are ultimately to be resolved.

Look around, and see what the world presents of high and low. Go to the court of princes. See the treasure and skill of all nations brought together to honor a child of man. Observe the prostration of the many before the few. Consider the form and ceremonial, the pomp, the state, the circumstance, the vainglory. Do you wish to know the worth of it all? look at the Cross of Christ.

Go to the political world : see nation jealous of nation, trade rivalling trade, armies and fleets matched against each other. Survey the various ranks of the community, its parties and their contests, the strivings of the ambitious, the intrigues of the crafty. What is the end of all this turmoil? the grave. What is the measure? the Cross.

Go, again, to the world of intellect and science : consider the wonderful discoveries which the human mind is making, the variety of arts to which its discoveries give rise, the all but miracles by which it shows its power ; the next, the pride and confidence of reason, and the absorbing devotion of transitory objects, which is the consequence. Would you form a right judgment of all this? look at the Cross.

Again : look at misery, look at poverty and destitution, look at oppression and captivity ; go where food is scanty, and lodging unhealthy. Consider pain and suffering, diseases long or violent, all that is frightful and revolting. Would you know how to rate all these? gaze upon the Cross.

Thus in the Cross, and Him who hung upon it, all things meet ; all things subserve it, all things need it. It is their centre and their interpretation. For He was lifted upon it, that he might draw all men and all things unto Him.

There is such a seizing of all the innermost truth, such a compendious and full rendering of all that the preacher judged it necessary to say ; that these sermons may well

7*

stand as illustrations for those who think the preacher should not tax his audience beyond twenty minutes, for, I suppose, few of them took more than that time to preach. And it does seem clear that, unlike Manning's, they are especially topical, some innermost thought struck the preacher's mind in reading a gospel or an epistle, and it branched out in his mind through successive unfoldings of one thought—"Except ye see signs and wonders, ye will not believe," gives the sermon on "*Faith without demonstration*," and leads him to unfold that life cannot be spent in proving things, that faith does not ask jealously and coldly for strict arguments, but follows generally what has fair evidence for it. Christ's direction to the man out of whom were cast seven devils, "Return to thine own house, and show how great things God hath done for thee," gives the natural subject of "*the religious use of excited feelings.*" The story of the man by the pool of Bethesda gives "*Scripture a Record of human sorrow.*" "*Self-denial, the test of religious earnestness,*" is founded on the simple text, "Now it is high time to awake out of sleep." Sometimes the text and the subject seem to be paradoxical, as in the sermon, "*Religious faith Rational,*" founded on, "He staggered not the promise of God through unbelief." Nor is it in the text alone, but throughout the whole of these sermons Dr. Newman shows an extraordinary affluence of scriptural knowledge, like some of the Middle-Age monks in this, that he seems equally at home in fetching the recondite Scriptural allusion or illustration or the more cogent Scripture proof. These sermons look as if wholly unprepared, they have a grand negligence about them, yet a perfect unity, often paradoxical, with always a hidden current of thought and reasoning running along. Sometimes the logician uses the fence which, evidently is the delight, perhaps, almost the vice of his mind. As in the following, from the sermon

WAITING FOR CHRIST.

So it is, undeterred by the failure of former anticipations, unbelievers are ever expecting that the Church and the religion of the Church are coming to an end. They thought so in the last century. They think so now. They ever think the light of truth is going out, and that their hour of victory is come. Now, I repeat, I do not see why it is reasonable to expect the overthrow of religion still, after so many failures; and yet unreasonable, because of previous disappointments, to expect the coming of Christ. Nay, Christians at least, over and above the aspect of things, can point to an express promise of Christ, that He will one day come; whereas unbelievers, I suppose, do not profess any grounds at all for expecting their own triumph, except the signs of the times. They are sanguine, because they seem so strong, and the Church of God seems so weak; yet they have not enlarged their minds enough by the contemplation of past history to know that such apparent strength on the one side, and such apparent weakness on the other, has ever been the state of the world and the Church; and that this has ever been one chief or rather the main reason, why Christians have expected the immediate end of all things, because the prospects of religion were so gloomy. So that, in fact Christians and unbelievers have taken precisely the same view of the facts of the case; only they have drawn distinct conclusions from them according to their creed. The Christian has said, "All looks so full of tumult that the world is coming to an end;" and the unbeliever has said, "All is so full of tumult that the Church is coming to an end;" and there is nothing, surely, more superstitious in the one opinion than in the other.

Ever and again, the language, beautiful in its lofty simplicity, its uncolored and unadorned majesty—glimpses which show how painfully the mind of the preacher has stood up demanding the reasons for things, and other hints of a mind lying open, and awake, it would seem to any and every wildness of belief and even superstition? Alas! what is wildness of belief? and what is superstition? Dr. Newman would quite rebut the charge of mysticism, but assuredly he is a mystic, his faith stands reflecting all the old lights of mediæval ideas. How a man can rise out of rationalism, and not be a mystic, I cannot tell. Sufficient to say that these quiet logical sermons shine with the tempered rays of a world invisible, but assuredly near a world, not only of powers, but of souls, persons, and events. Those live there who are able to believe and to preach such things. These are three of the most eminent men in England to-day ; men of power. Orators, in the usual sense in which that word is used, they are not, although Dr. Manning might have been this, and Dr. Newman was wont to hold beneath the spell of his speech young and ardent spirits, but they are all alike unfitted to minister to the ignorant and uninformed—the busy and the thoughtless, these are men in a special manner fitted in the works to which we have referred, to be the ministers ; ministers, fitted rather to meet and to aid pained and thoughtful natures, than to awaken careless and sleeping ones. Manning and Newman, especially, contain fountains for many sermons, for years of consolation and light, many a sermon or even page may be a consensus for the conscience, for the mind, for the faith. This said, we may freely express our grief that they are where they are, in Rome. Yet that became their legitimate abode, when tradition and the Church had to eke out the Bible, and when the rights of the individual judgment were renounced and denounced.

IV.

Effective Preaching and the Foundation of Legitimate Success.

IN the course of these lectures so many illustrations have been given of the great effects of pulpit power in many nations and ages, that I may well fear that I have created some false impressions of what effective preaching is; that in the development of the character of the minister of religion, I have set that which is striking above that which is luminous, and the aberrations of genius above the calm and steady ministrations of the word. The effect of striking pictures may sometimes be to drive those who contemplate them to despair when they become the exaltation of the rarest efforts of human power and influence. We must make every allowance too in this department of labor for extraordinary endowment, and extraordinary attainment, also for extraordinary supernatural gifts of the Holy Ghost, for there is no doubt that some even in the kingdom of nature lie very much nearer than others to the most constant refreshments of Divine influence. The man is as some rare and extraordinary vessel, but being such originally, what can follow, when very extraordinary powers come into the man, but extraordinary and marvellous results. We have seen that the history of the pulpit is full of instances of effective preaching from such causes. We fix our eyes too much on the transcendent, it is well, it is admirable, students usually err on the side of over-estimation, veneration is a quality that grows with years, but we shall err if we compare our poor efforts with transcendent gifts and powers ; yet on the other hand we should believe that the Gospel ensures its own success in preaching. It is guaranteed by the most hallowed assurances ; I know that there are periodicals, and there are writers, who never weary of casting scorn and indignity upon the pulpit. I know many young men turn away from the pulpit because it seems to demand the renunciation of mental excitement ; at any rate, it is said so. Ministers have been called "marrying and christening machines," and the phrase as "dull as a sermon" has passed into a proverb. The influence of the preacher has suffered great depreciation, and especially from preachers themselves.

Now, in order to rectify such impressions, I know not that I should seek to fix your attention upon the great instances of pulpit power, yet such may detain us for awhile. *Some sermons seem to have a secret in them* ; What is it? You remember, I dare say, that great sermon of Jonathan Edwards from that fearful text in Deuteronomy xxxii. 35. "Their feet shall slide in due time." It is a wonderful sermon, in what is its awful and electrical power : while repeating the words of the text some of the audience seized fast hold upon the pillars of the meeting house, they felt so sensibly their feet were sliding into ruin. During the delivery of the sermon some of the auditors shrieked and groaned aloud, their cries drowned the preacher's voice and forced him to make a long pause. The influence of this sermon alarmed numbers and brought them to decision ; and that sermon has often been preached by other tongues, it has been said, with the same results. Two of my own friends, both among the most eminent ministers of the denomination to which I have the honor to belong, have mentioned to me their uttering the sermon with like effect, and I have often thought of preaching it myself, but I have never felt I could dare do so. The sermon has in every reading so searched me that I felt that I could not with a pure heart be its channel for the awakening of others, for we must never utter the conviction of other men at second hand, we must make them first of all our own.

Very remarkable indeed are many of the illustrations of pulpit efficiency, sometimes a single sentence has seized the attention. We read of the tremendous excitement that seized on the hearers of Whitefield as he exclaimed, " Oh ! my hearers, the wrath to come ! the wrath to come !" And when Massilon commenced his celebrated sermon on the death of Louis XIV. with the well-known sentence, " God alone is great !" all the audience rose in the vast and magnificent temple and reverently bowed ; and so also when M. Bridaine exclaimed, " Oh ! eternity ! eternity !" at the close of his great discourse, it produced an extraordinary effect. Effective preaching ! why, the effects of a spoken word have sometimes continued and wrought with a marvellous power half a century afterwards. A phrase dropped into the mind of a lad on one continent has brought forth extraordinary fruit half a century afterwards on another. Dr. Park mentions an instances of an individual who heard the great and good John Flavel preach at Dartmouth, he had been a member of the train band of Charles I., he was present at the beheading of the monarch, he had some acquaintance with Cromwell, he heard Flavel preach when he was fifteen years old from the text, " If any man love not the Lord Jesus Christ, let him be Anathema Maranatha." He went to America, passed through many experiences, and at 100 years of age was a farmer at Middleborough in the new world ; there sitting in his field, he heard the words come back to him as he had listened to them eighty-five years before, he remem-

bered the appearance of the solemn preacher rising to pronounce the benediction before he dismissed the auditory
and exclaiming in piteous tones, "How shall I bless the
whole assembly when every person in it who loveth not the
Lord Jesus Christ is Anathema Maranatha?" He was
alarmed at the reminiscence, and particularly at the fact
that no minister had blessed him during all those years, he
pondered that closing remark of Flavel, and at the beginning of the second century of his life, he gave evidence that
he was worthy to be enrolled among the members of the
Church written in heaven, and bore his testimony for fifteen
years afterwards as to the power of the truth over his
mind.

Ah! what stories of the results of the ministry? Who
was the unpolished country clergyman who supplied the
pulpit of Edmund Calamy that Sabbath in 1642, when a
young man, long in mental distress, came to hear him?
In mind dark, weak, frail, the young man had no disposition to move abroad although he wished, as Mr. Calamy
was absent, to hear that great scholar, Mr. Jackson, he
preferred remaining to listen to the obscure, unknown, and
unnamed country minister, who announced his text,
"Why are ye so fearful, O ye of little faith," and it was
restorative medicine to the invalid ; he became a new man,
he commenced a new life of Christian activity, he rose to
great honor in Church and State, became Vice-Chancellor
of Oxford University, he numbered among his pupils John
Locke, William Penn, Dr. South, Dr. Whitby, Sir Chris-
topher Wren, and he is still revered as an oracle and a
prince among divines.—It was John Owen, but he was
never able to discover to whom he was indebted for that
health-giving word, and probably, if found, it would only
have been some frail but truthful creature, only remarkable
for faith in the great power of God.

These are the traditions of the pulpit ; but how is the

power such instances record to be attained ? and you will go with me when I quote the words of an ancient writer on the vanity of all mere knowledge, and all mere scholarship for this purpose. "Quarry," says he, "the granite rock with razors, or moor the vessel with a thread of silk, then, may you hope with such keen and delicate instruments as human knowledge and human reason to contend against those giants, the passions and the pride of man." No, we are to believe in the ministry, and we are to believe in the ministry as a divinely-appointed and instituted order of men, but the guarantee of the success of the ministry is to be found in the fitting nature surcharged with a Divine influence. We cannot indeed estimate the influence of the ministry in many particulars ; if the minister be a man, if he maintain the work of personal education, if he sustain himself before men, he will influence the intellect of his audience and of his neighborhood ; he will influence the taste as well as the intellect, he will influence and modify the literary character of a people ; a power, his power will be obvious upon the morals and business life of the community, he will give a religious character to the community, but I conceive of all this as over and above, but still not beneath, the actual depth of the preacher's work ; and he may do all this, and many do all this, and they still sink quite beneath the real design of the Christian ministry, and they may be successful in all these departments, and still we cannot speak of their works as sufficient and really successful. Preaching stands really related to the law of Divine means and operations as every ordinance of nature is an illustration of a decree of God. In this also, as much as the sun and the lightning, the magnet and the dewdrop. Dr. Phelps says well and wisely, "Divine truth is never preached when God meant that it should be withheld, it is never withheld when God means it should be preached. And when preached it goes forth upon its mission, bearing on every breath that

utters it, to every ear that listens to it, a purpose formed
before the world was ; that same eye which has worked its
will that each separate raindrop and snowflake should come
down from heaven, and that just so many should fall, and
should fall just here and there, casts the same imperial look
upon the transactions of every Christian sanctuary.   The
very atmosphere of such a sanctuary vibrates incessantly
beneath the giving forth of everlasting decrees. Such is the
theory which must lie at the foundation of every intelligent
view of the Divine sovereignty as applied to preaching,
and its results."

It is obvious that for purposes so divine and almighty as
these, many of the modern pulpit methods are altogether
insufficient.   A modern satirist gives a description of his
modern travels upon the line of route taken by Bunyan.
"A truthful man, but infected with, many very fantastic
notions !" In the course of his travels he found that in
Vanity Fair things were ordered very differently to the
proceedings of the ancient day ; so different that, so far
from the inhabitants of the fair persecuting preachers,
every street had its church, and the reverend clergy he testifies are nowhere held in higher respect than in Vanity
Fair.   Estimable men there he met with, the Rev. Mr.
Shallowdeep, the Rev. Mr. Humble-the-truth ; there he met
with that fine old clerical character, the Rev. Mr. This-to-day,
and his excellent successor, the Rev. Mr. That-to-morrow,
the Rev. Mr. Bewilderment, the Rev. Mr. Clog-the-Spirit,
and that eminent divine, the Rev. Mr. Windy-doctrine ; for
such teachers as these, and really they are legion, we cannot prophesy with certainty any considerable amount of
success.

Often has the pulpit presented to the eye of the satirist
men, true citizens of the city in which Vanity Fair is built ;
the following lines would seem to have been dictated from
some such vision :—

See where the famed Adonis passes by
The man of spotless life—and spotless tie ;
His reputation,—none the fact disputes,
Has ever been as brilliant as his—boots.
And all his flock believe exceptionless
    His points of doctrine—and his points of dress.
He makes the supercilious worldling feel
That e'en religion can be—quite genteel.
He lets the hesitating sceptic know,
A man may be a Christian and a—beau ;
And so combines, despite satiric railers,
A model for professors and for tailors.
And all his mighty energies are bent—
On being the Beau Brummell of dissent.

The ministry of Vanity Fair is only the ministry of the wind, and its only legitimate fruit will be the whirlwind, sweeping away the refuges of lies. But whoever has eyes to see will not fail to behold results which in any other matter would seem to the eye amazing.*

* We fear that the following letter, which was originally published in the *Smellfungus Gazette*, will seem to be very much out of place in a work such as the present. It may, however, suggest some hints from which some young preachers may profit. It might have been included in Punch's *Letters to his Son*. This, however, is not the case ; it seems to be really a letter addressed, in all seriousness, from an old and beloved minister to his son, upon his entrance upon the ministry :

MY DEAR BOY :—At last you have received the call to that well-known and much-honored charge of the old interest of the Cave of Adullam. I need not say how " my heart rejoices, even mine." You know I have so often talked with you upon the matters pertaining to the ministry, that I can say very little you will not anticipate. You have asked me, too, to give you the charge on the day of your ordination. I shall accede to your request ; but that will be an affair *ad populum*, although addressed to you. I should like to address some hints which may be regarded as *ad clerum*—words addressed to your deepest convictions, to your most secret thoughts—words which may be connected with your happiest

Effective preaching! why, of the effects of the pulpit it has been said, that many of the results of preaching which the world affects to despise would be received with uni-

interests and best hopes. Lay these to heart, my dear boy, and they will not fail, if you constantly keep them, as I may tell you, now, speaking—" as such an one as Paul the aged," " to mine own son Timothy"—I have ever done ; would that I had done so more—they will not fail to bear and bring forth fruit.

I. A very foremost word. You are not married ; I am not aware that you are likely to be yet, and therefore I do not suppose this will excite any smile. But, of course, you will be ; then *I charge you, marry well*—look out for a rich wife. Why not ? It is just as easy for you to do this, my dear lad, as to marry a poor one. If you look round the circles of the most eminent servants of God, who have adorned the pulpit in these latter times, you will find how they have all laid deep the foundations of their eminence and usefulness by marrying well. This will be influence to you. *God works by human means, and money is one of the greatest of human means.* Oh, what wrecks of men I have known ; some who stood far higher than I did at college, but they lost themselves, alas! in their marriage. This guided me when I married your own precious mother; it is true she was a woman of prayer and piety—but what a gratification it has been to me to know that her money made both her and myself independent. I heard of your attentions to Lydia Mason—a very nice girl and good ; but, my dear boy, she is a poor governess ; and let me tell you, that my friend Bigsby, the brewer I mean, has inquired most kindly after you—his daughter, Letitia, is a most delightful person.

II. There is a great prejudice against the use of other people's sermons, so much so, that I have known two or three who, by a very imprudent use of them, have forfeited their positions ; but I should say to you, *cultivate a wise use of other people's sermons : it will save you much trouble ;* it will familiarize your mind with the best efforts of the best men, and it will call into activity the constant exercise of that most wonderful power of the mind, the memory. How strange is the prejudice against this. Yet at concerts you invariably find the greatest singers do not sing their own, but other people's words ; and I am told that those who are called actors in our theatres, do not utter and act their own words. The other evening I was persuaded to go to the Mechanics' Institute, versal admiration, and would render immortal the name of the man who should be instrumental in achieving them, if they were only the fruit of a discovery in science, or an

to hear a celebrated person from London read. To my amazement, he read nothing of his own. Now, this usage ought to be sanctified by a judicious use of the sermons which precious men have preached.

III. *Have*, my dear boy, a *due regard to health*. Especially *take care of the sore throat and weak chest ;* remember who said, " Master, spare Thyself." Indeed, when I think of your naturally tender lungs, and the danger resulting from exposure to the air, after coming out of crowded rooms—a danger to which those who simply attend as hearers cannot be subject—my tenderest parental feelings have been excited, in the hope that your mind might be drawn to dear Letitia Bigsby ; in that case you might—(in the event of that sad pectoral weakness and pulmonary indisposition, which, alas ! lay aside annually so many of our brethren, *who are able to afford to be laid aside*—the noble race of our modern martyrs, " men who have hazarded their lives in the high places of the field "—O, my boy, what part of the chapel can be found much higher than the pulpit !)—I say, in such an event, you also might be able to retire early in life with a comfortable independence ; and what a thought to employ, not only your talents and learning, but even your retirement for such high aims and ends ; as our great Milton has it,—

" They also serve who only stand and wait."

IV. *Cultivate respectable society.* Do not regard yourself as a poor preaching friar or miserable curate. If you come to regard yourself so, you will be regarded so. Some of my brethren in the ministry have often shocked me ; they have had a tendency to low society, under the idea of doing good ; now I have long thought that few people do much good out of their own circle, and we ought to believe that if God intends to make us eminently useful, He will find the occasion for it. You have always, through mercy, been accustomed to good society, and to the ways and usages of good society. *I hope you will never, as the apostle says, " Condescend to men of low estate ;"* the case is different in rising, it is our duty to attempt to rise. Cultivate, as far as you have opportunity, the intelligent upper circles. Who knows what a word spoken there may do, or in what way your influence may extend ? While I am experiment in philosophy. The very efforts of this ministration are superhuman. More marvellous, the ministry is most successful, is only successful, when it aims at the

upon this point, let me also say, wear the gown. I do not know if you have one in Cave Adullam vestry, but if not, a word dropped in the ears of a sister or two, will soon bring you the present of one ; and be sure you wear the hood of your degree over it—it tells. Why should you go into the pulpit, like an auctioneer into his box ? and how delightful to recall to mind, while you are robing yourself, that you are making yourself look more like an apostle. I firmly believe, my dear boy, that *the gown is a means of grace.* I have no doubt there are souls in glory to whom the word came with power, because it came in a gown ; and I say to you, " *Do these things and thou shalt save thyself and them that hear thee.*"   •

V. Referring to matters less immediately connected with your own pastoral duties, I would say, *be active on committees.* Committees I regard as one of the most distinctly divine agencies appointed in the Church. All the immense amount of good performed in modern times may be traced to the action of committees. In the course of a long life I can speak of the many blessed seasons I have enjoyed round committee boards ; they do amazingly limit and dilute individual responsibility ; and things done by committees do not go on so feverishly and impetuously. I have known many a vehement enthusiast worn out, and worn down, by being placed on a committee. Oh, it is a fine refrigerator, and I have often thought that as ices and champagne are the luxuries of the dessert table in high society, so committees are the ices, and those sweet occasions, the annual meetings, with their rich foam of excitement, are the champagne. You will notice, my dear boy, that the way to all eminence is through the committee-room. You will observe that those men who are the most prominent, the most beloved and honored names, are not the greatest of preachers or writers ; but they are punctual in their attendance on committees. This counsel is most vital—be great in committees, you may rule your world, whatever that world may be ; on the contrary, dear boy, do not think I quote such words irreverently ; but it may be truly said of committees, " Them that honor me I will honor, but they that despise me, shall be lightly esteemed." And how can we more surely know and test a man's disposition for use-

superhuman, is only mighty when it claims to be superhuman ; if not so, the sarcasm of Sydney Smith becomes
a natural expression of the truth, when he described the

fulness than by his attendance upon those committees which are
the very means of usefulness? Moreover, committees give the
endorsement of decency to a desire to do good. A man who has
no sanction from a committee for the good he says he does, or attempts to do, will usually be found to run into many indecencies of
zeal ; and it is your duty, my dear lad, from the responsible place
you are called to fill, to attempt to interpose between any such
rude efforts. How can that expect the blessing of God which is
not in the order of His Church.

VI. And now, yet more confidentially, my lad, I say to you, keep
a watch over your brethren in the ministry ; they are very likely
to become inflated by pride and success; if, therefore, you can say
a word at all calculated to keep them humble, especially humble
in the opinion of others, say it ; and I say this also, remembering
that your brethren will keep a watch over your interests in this
way. Never in the course of a long life in this have I found my
brethren wanting ; and never, I can truly say, have I been wanting in rendering this work of faith and labor of love.

VII. Keep also a watchful eye on all likely persons, especially
wealthy or influential, who may come to your town ; call upon
them, and attempt to win them over by the devotions of the drawing-room to your cause. Thus, you may most efficiently serve the
Master's interests. People need looking after, and the result of a
long experience goes to confirm my conviction long cherished, that
the power of the pulpit is trifling compared with the power of the
parlor. We must imitate and sanctify, by the Word of God and of
prayer, the exercises of the Jesuits. They succeeded, not by the
pulpit so much as by the parlor. In the parlor you can whisper—
you can meet people on all their little personal, private ideas. The
pulpit is a very unpleasant place ; of course, it is the great power
of God, and so on ; but it is the parlor that tells, and a minister
has not the same chance of success if he be a good preacher, as if
he is a perfect gentleman ; nor in cultivated society has any man
a legitimate prospect of success if he is not, whatever else he may
be, a gentleman. I have always admired Lord Shaftesbury's character of St. Paul—in his characteristics—that he was a fine gentleman ; and I would say to you, be a gentleman : not that I need to

first missionaries to India—Careys and Marshmans—as a little detachment of maniacs sent out to command the allegiance of hundreds of millions of men ; if there is no supernatural power determining the salvation of the world, and giving force and conviction to the truth, as spoken by the minister—this, the dining-out language of divines, is none the less the language of common sense. It is to be feared that preaching is often a vanity, a mere vanity ; the foundation of success is first of all the apprehension that the Gospel is the great power of God, if it is this it will

say so, but am persuaded that only in this way can we hope for the conversion of our growing wealthy middle classes. We must show that our religion is the religion of good sense and good taste ; that we disapprove of strong excitements and stimulants ; and O, my dear boy, if you would be useful, often in your closet, make it a matter of earnest prayer that you may be proper. If I were asked what is your first duty—be proper ; and your second, be proper ; and your third, be proper.

VIII. I would also say it is your duty to keep the vigilance of your ministerial brethren constantly awake by finding expedients for calling upon any of the members of their flocks. How sad it is to think how often some excellent member is hungering after some word of life which his or her minister has not to give, and you have it. I know this has sometimes most vulgarly been called poaching on your neighbor's preserves ; the expression is horridly vulgar. You must only, without heeding it, attend to the sacred calls of duty—"instant in season, and out of season." Occasionally, you see the member of a neighboring congregation in yours. This may be well made the occasion of a call—a little natural inquiry and attention in case of illness or death in the family—or any restlessness in the church or congregation, should be watched, and a word or two, rightly disposed, will go a great way ; and you must remember the object of your life in the sweet hymn—

" We are a garden walled around,"

and your business must be to make as much as you can of your own garden. Never fear, your neighbor will make the most of his.

IX. Keep at home ! don't invite brother ministers from your own neighborhood to exchange with you, or to supply your pulpit ; it effect a lodgment in the conscience, and it will overcome. It is so—mysteriously and awfully—it is so, there is indeed no warrant for ministerial success without divine influence ; without this, let us assert it again and again, our work becomes that of the mere artist, and we become mere deists. Listen to the very stirring words of Charnock : " Can a well-composed oration, setting out all the advantages of life and health, raise a dead man or cure a diseased body ?" You may as well exhort a blind man to behold the sun, and prevail as much. No man ever yet

disturbs the minds of your own friends; and unless your pulpit power is of the highest, it assuredly invites dissatisfaction. In order that this may be done more effectively, decry what is called " intellectual preaching." No good can come out of it. The pulpit has never been good for anything since the rage for it set in. The people like " the pure milk of the word;" recollect the Gospel is milk for babes. I heard an old lady say, the' other day, " I do love our dear minister ; for Sunday after Sunday we have the same thing over and over again. It 's always the same old story. No matter what text he may take, we always know what's coming." Oh, how I loved that dear old lady ! and oh, how peaceful and prosperous should we be within the walls of our Jerusalem if all were like her.

X. And, finally, have a proper regard to your office ; magnify it by keeping up a proper distance and reserve between yourself and your people—few people can afford to come too closely together without mischief to each other. We want, my dear boy, a *vade mecum* of ministerial etiquette, and I have sometimes thought I should like to spend these last days of my life in the compilation of such a volume—a kind of ministerial looking-glass, which might be studied before going into company ; but say nothing, and you will say nothing amiss ; study deportment ; remember all eyes are upon you. Admit no one to your friendship, and then nobody will abuse it.

Many other hints are on my mind ; but here, for the present, I close. Only remember, as the Apostle says, " If these things be in you, and abound, they will make you that you be neither barren nor unfruitful." I am your affectionate father, imagined that the strewing a dead body with flowers could raise it to life, no man can. The hungering man, spiritually dead—will elegant motions ever make him to open his eyes and to stand upon his feet? " Have you never," continues this eloquent reasoner, " discoursed with some profane loose fellow so pressingly, that he seemed to be shaken out of his excuses for his sinful course, yet not shaken out of his sin, that you might as soon have persuaded the tide in full sea to retreat, or a lion to change its nature, as have overcome him by all your arguments. So that it is not the faint breath of man or the rational consideration of the mind, that are able to do this work, without the mighty pleadings and powerful operations of the great Persuader or Advocate, the Spirit, to alter the temple of the soul." And in a similar tone, John Howe says : " Alas, what could preaching do, if we could suppose it never so general, while the Spirit of the living God restrains and withholds His influence? we may as well attempt to batter strong walls with the breath of our mouths, as do good upon men's souls without the Spirit of God."

I have thus dwelt too lengthily, many of you may feel, upon what, after everything is said, must be regarded as the chief foundation of all usefulness and of every efficiency in the pulpit. This distinguishes the preacher from the lecturer, it matters not where others draw the distinction, do you draw it in this, that your pulpit work is no mere mental exercise or exegesis—it is work lying immediately in the relation of the divine decrees, and beneath the pledge of the Divine Influence and Blessing.

But again, Mr. Bridges has truly remarked in his excellent work on the Christian ministry, that the very symptoms of success are very frequently mistaken, they may be at best but wonderful signs ; if people crowd to hear it is well, but John did not treat with glowing compliments the Scribes and Pharisees when they thronged to his baptism,

and if they admire the discourse, it may be the admiration
of the spirit charmed beneath the spell of music; like those
who heard Ezekiel; and if there is a general confession of
sinfulness, there may be no warning to flee from the wrath
to come; and if there is a temporary interest, it may be
only like the rejoicing of those who heard John, the willingness for a season. And then again, let there not be on
the other hand an unnatural despondency. Ministerial
success must be viewed as extending beyond present ap-
pearances; the saying is true, "one soweth and another
reapeth," "some men labor, and others enter into their labors;" innumerable instances show work, which seemed
most unproductive, may be the seed-time of some further
harvest-field. Highest witnesses attest this, the pathway
of the Word is not in a straight line, it is not even in a
calculable circle; but it has "a free course and it is glorified," it is like the meteoric currents, and effective as they
are in its career. "If Whitefield had not visited Cambus-
lang in Scotland," it has been said, "Buchanan probably
never would have visited Malabar;" we often do very
wrong when we expect to see a word bear fruit exactly
upon the same spot where the labor was bestowed, it may
bear fruit in the soil, nay, with a wonderful compound interest, even like the bending sheaf of corn, from the one
grain. But the soil is not confined to a village or a town,
a country or a kingdom, and while despondency is in the
heart of the laborer, the Master of the harvest may be saying, "Thrust in thy sickle and reap, for the harvest is fully
ripe." Some day we may know the law by which the great
Master Husbandman works, at present, it is confessed, we
labor on in faith, we have to remember constantly, the diffusive character of truth, the inherent value of one mind,
especially the power of the renewed mind to reproduce in
others, by the grace of God, its own convictions. And we
may well fear our power. Mr. Jones, in his introduction

to the English edition of Porter's *Lectures on Preaching*,
says, and it staggered my faith as I read it, for the sentence at any rate puts a possibility with fearful strength,
"The faults of one sermon from the pulpit may produce
mischief through a century, nay, through eternity." I
thought it was strongly put, but I remembered instances
which even seemed to confirm this harsh, this terrible statement. John Murray was a very eminent Puritan preacher
of Boston. He preached from the text, "Though the number of the children of Israel shall be as the sand of the
sea, a remnant shall be saved." This was one of the first
texts from which he discoursed in Boston, and this was the
first sentence—"If one should buy a rich cloth and make
it into a garment, and then burn it, but save the remnant,
what must be thought of him?" It was clumsily put, but
it had a sad effect upon a young man who heard it; he
carried it to his home in an inland town, there he published and warped that one sad sentence, and produced a
large dissension from the churches. It is when we hear
such things that we feel how natural was the language of
Luther, "I am now an old man, and have been a long
time employed in the business of preaching, but I never
ascend the pulpit without trembling." It behoves us to be
fearful, for we work beneath mysterious laws; a word, we
know, may be a fatal offence; it behoves us to guard ourselves against the woe of those by whom the offence cometh. But so also often the mightiest effect is the result of
some simple word, some sermon of which we thought but
little; most of the sainted Payson's sermons are very
simple; a discourse he thought little of, and wrote at a sitting, was one of the most effective he ever preached. "I
could not but wonder to see God work by it," he says.
Among the most simple and unformed of modern preachers was James Sherman, of Surrey Chapel, but Mr. Allon
in his recently published biography, goes so far as to claim

for him the place of the most effective minister in results ever since the days of Whitefield. "Rarely," says he, "did he preach without some ascertained conversions; sometimes they were numbered by scores, and to one sermon alone, preached in Surrey Chapel, in 1857, eighty-four persons who joined the church there, attributed their conversion." If we look into the by-paths of ministerial biography, we shall find much to confirm us in the impression of the efficiency of the pulpit; not every biography is either wisely or worthily done, but there are few, I think, from which a young student may not receive encouragement and help.

There are inferior considerations which enter into the conditions of legitimate success. Rhetoric—which is the power of giving effect to all logic, all composition, need not be treated with contempt; yet it may be surely said, few preachers aim to deliver well and effectively what they have even prepared with immense labor and care. When, in a Turkish mosque, one with a very harsh voice was reading the Koran in a loud tone, a good and holy Mollah went to him and said—"What is your monthly stipend?" And he answered, "Nothing." Then said he, "Why give thyself so much trouble?" And he said, "I am reading for the sake of God." The good and holy Mollah replied— "For the God's sake do not read; for if you enunciate the Koran after this manner, thou wilt cast a shade over the glory of orthodoxy."

And it is said, when a man of letters was ill and near to death, a priest was attempting to unfold to him the joys of paradise, but the sick man interrupted him, saying, "Speak to me no more about it, father, however pleasant the place may be, your bad style would disgust me with it." This seems, no doubt, very blasphemous, but the satire is not without its justice; I know how many have disdained the learning to preach; I am, as I have said, quite aware that the truth and the life are of the first magnitude, but then, too, we remember and apply what the learned John Selden says of ceremony—"It keeps up all things; it is like a penny phial to some rich and valuable essence, how great the difference, but break your phial and where is the essence?" so "we have this treasure in earthen vessels." But because the thing of great value is the treasure, let us not make our vessel repulsive, uncouth, or coarse; nay, why not the reverse to this and these?

I have said, therefore, think of the legitimate means of awakening and sustaining the interest of your audience. The very wording of my text implies that there are *illegiti-mate* means. Everything that tends to lower the tone of devotion and sacredness is illegitimate; everything that stirs the passions, or excites the curiosity, or the passions without quickening the conscience is illegitimate; everything that is simply secular, and does not relate the hearer to the life to come, and to the Saviour, as the anchor and centre of the life to come, is illegitimate. All prettinesses, artificialities—a sort of paper floral wreath, not growing out of, but stuck on, to a subject—all these are illegitimate, and all illegitimate means will in the end be unsuccessful means. You are to look to the long run, and take courage and capital from thence. I have before said, first, let there be self-possession; yes, but not the self-possession of ignorance, but of conscious acquaintance with the place, and the souls in it, and your moral furniture and its fitness to the place and the people. I know how hard this is to gain; I sympathize with, and pay homage to, the tremulous nervousness which shrinks and recoils from its duty, and yet daringly goes forward to meet it; perhaps it is this temper which achieves the highest things. Best natures fall and fail sometimes—Robert Hall did. I am not disposed to think he was simply a fool, and despicable, who announced his text—to the amazement of his audience—

"Peter crew, and the cock went out and wept bitterly," and, trying to recover himself, only gave a repetition of the same wonderful text, "Peter crew," &c. And that other deliverance of a young brother was almost as bad; his text announced, "He maketh the dem to hear, and the duff to speak—no, no, I mean the deaf to speak, and the dumb to hear"—it was a new version of the deaf to hear, and the dumb to speak, entirely resulting from the nervousness of the brother. And, although not immediately in the train of my remarks, let me say, you must gain the confidence of your hearers; get them to trust you, that is the grand preliminary to the pastor's pulpit success. And, how hard this is! You will not rely on the power of a startling sermon; preaching, says one, is a good nail, but practice is the hammer that drives it straight home; that practice must be your sympathy with your audience, and theirs with you.

I do not speak of evil life, and the confidence to be gained by the negative virtue of ceasing to do evil, although you may profitably remember what Jeremy Taylor says:

"A minister of evil life cannot preach with that fervor and efficacy, with that life and spirit, as a good man does. For, besides that he does not himself understand the secrets of religion, and the private inducements of the Spirit, and the sweetness of internal joy, and the inexpressible advantages of holy peace; besides all this, he cannot heartily speak of all he knows. He hath a clog at his foot, and a gag in his teeth. There is a fear, and there is a shame, and there is a guilt, and a secret willingness that the things were not true, and some little private arts, to lessen his own consent, and to take off the asperities, and consequent trouble of a clear conviction."

But this is little—Gresley well says, with regard to your intercourse with the world and its amusements, "It matters not to the wolf what innocent recreation the shepherd is engaged in, if he is not tending to his flock." Oh, there is so much to be guarded against. But I have no time to note here on the temper and conduct of life, and on the whole mode and manner of the pulpit. "If we are desirous to do execution," says an old writer, "and to make our way through difficulties, we must pass through the Alps with fire and vinegar, we must make brisk and bold assaults upon sinners." I cannot say that this is much to my admiration ; the spirit of meekness I believe to be a powerful spirit and mighty teacher, and I admire much more the language of dear old Dr. Alexander Waugh.

"The Good Shepherd," he says, "mends—not breaks—his reeds, when they are bruised. I have seen a Highland shepherd, on a sunny brae, piping as if he could never get old, his flocks listening, and the rocks ringing around ; but when the reed of his pipe became hoarse, he had not patience to mend it, but broke it, and threw it away in anger, and made another. Not so our Shepherd ; He examines and tries, and mends and tunes the bruised spirit, until it sings sweetly of mercy and of judgment, as in the days of old."

And then as to the pulpit. Of course your sermons are to be your own ; honestly your own, wrought out, thought out, spoken out—your own. Short of this, your influence cannot be legitimate ; and next, being so, it must be the result of your own clear entrance into the mind of your audience by thought clearly expressed. I have already dwelt on these, which I only mention, desiring to take for granted that you have no desire to obtain entrance into the heart and mind in any other manner ; he, who does so, in a real and sad sense "climbs up some other way."

Many orations appear to be very striking, to have many striking passages which are quite useless. There are limitations to the striking ; there is the striking which is quite illegitimate. Fence all your pulpit efforts by these six rules, which should each be a law to you. 1st. Have a distinct aim. 2nd. Have thought. Words are but the dress of thought ; it is idle to spend time in setting forth costly clothes without a living body and limbs. Or, like the mere passing empty buckets from hand to hand, it must be a very profitless and tedious employment, hardly worth the effort of seeking to do elegantly. 3d. Have unity, not mechanical alone, moral, spiritual. 4th. Be earnest. 5th. Be natural. 6th. Be appropriate. If you regulate your speech beneath the light of these laws, I may leave to you the use of philosophy—rhetoric excludes philosophy—and I may leave to you the use of poetry, never to be used at all, the rhetorician says ; I will say never, unless when it overflows the soul, certainly not by learning little pieces of poetry as stucco-ornaments for your sermons.*

1. Again, it ought to be remembered with what power *a text* will sometimes strike the key to a chain of thoughts and meditations ; a well selected text may be the most considerable part of the sermon, and the Bible furnishes texts for all seasons, for every kind of festivity, warnings for every state, order of sin or sorrow. That was a happy text that the first James of England and sixth of Scotland heard on his arrival in London, " James 1st and sixth, a double-minded man is unstable in all his ways." But I believe he never heard the good brother who used it preach any more. The text was too happy, and I daresay the sermon was not less so. And this reminds me that some men have turned the Bible to sad account. Thus when the discussion about inoculation for the small-pox raged vehemently in 1722, a celebrated orator in London preached a sermon which had a very great fame here and in America ; the text was from Job xi. 7, " And Satan went forth and smote him with boils," the doctrine of which discourse was that

* I scarcely need refer for most valuable hints to that well-known and most excellent book, " Lectures on Homiletics and Preaching." By Ebenezer Porter, D.D., Andover.

8*

Satan was the first inoculator. Most ample are the illustrations of the foolishness of preaching. I could detain you a long time upon such topics, I have collected many pieces giving a rich furniture in this way. And have cited several in this small volume. It is not respectful to the Word of God to treat it thus. Should a subject be chosen for a text, or a text for a subject? True it has been said of some sermons that there is nothing in the sermon but the text to remind the hearer that there is a Bible. The text is chosen rather from homage to authority and usage of society than from respect to the sacred Word ; and as Dr. Porter says, the end would be answered as well if the preacher took no text ; or like him whom Melancthon heard preach in Paris, who took one from the Ethics of Aristotle.

2. I think you should avoid all *affectation and peculiarity in the text.* This surely seems unbecoming the dignity of the pulpit. A scrap, a word—vulgar minds indeed admire the sagacity which can elicit so much meaning from a text. Dr. CAMPBELL mentions one who chose the words, " A bell and a pomegranate, and a bell and a pomegranate," as the ground of a discourse on the subject that faith and holiness should ever accompany each other. STERNE recommends that when the preacher is much at a loss for a text he should take " Parthians, Medes, and Elamites," and we do know some who have ransacked the Bible for odd words and phrases. This is a glorying self-conceit rather than opening the truth.

3. Remark that a text *should contain complete sense in itself.* This is a rule often violated for the sake of point and brevity.

4. A text should express a complete sense of the sacred writers.

5. The text should express the particular sense which constitutes the subject of the discourse.

6. The important quality is simplicity.

I think you will permit me to remind you that there are a number of texts which Luther called "Little Bibles." "God so loved the world," etc. "This is a faithful saying," etc., and such like. It is good to take these, and what a number there are. I am often amazed at the number of texts in the Bible, which seem to include the whole Gospel, the whole Bible. I often, in the course of preparing for the pulpit, say, Ah, here is another of Luther's little Bibles. Well, so also I would remind you with Vinet that there are in the language of the Bible a certain number of words which may be called *Capital*, and the meaning of which, to apprehend, gives a master-key to the Bible. You must enter into the *words*, for they are the signs for things, which, to understand, give the whole key of the Christian system; such as *fear*, *flesh*, *soul*, *heart*, *faith*, *righteousness*, *understanding*, *foolish*, *light*, *just*, *good*, *man*, *wicked*, *virtue*, etc. And I do thus apologise for those who even take no more than one of these words, with the determination thoroughly to elucidate it to the people. You are to take this divine and spiritual nomenclature, and make it apprehensible to the philosophy of the people. You must get through the external sense of the text, as I have already intimated. The difficulty will often be in the breaking of the *external* sense, without really finding the true internal. As in Quesnel, on that text, "The wise men returned to their country by another way," observing that we shall never return to heaven but by another way than that by which we departed from it! It has been truly said that the Bible seems to have been trifled with in the very proportion in which it has been venerated; while at the same time I also admit that of the texts of the Bible many of them are of *great width*. We may deprecate any private interpretation, or loose and arbitrary significations, and at the same time permit the mind and heart to feel the power of suggestions and impressions which yet should scarcely be moulded into sermons.

And there are two dangers to which I wish to address some remarks, for the purpose of limiting the illegitimate influences which some speakers attain over their audiences ; they are both illustrations of the striking manner ; first, is humor in the pulpit ; second, is declamation in the pulpit. What are the limitations of humor ? The truthful and simple naturalness of Latimer, the drollery of South, and, perhaps, that of Rowland Hill, all show us that it will be used ; and, moreover, there is something about it frequently so charming, so fresh of hue, so adding to the light around a subject, that I am not at all disposed to denounce universally the use of humor. But, indeed, you will not be able to read the old writers, who thought their own thought in their own way, without meeting with these happy gleams of humor. An admirable instance too of the illustration of it for the purpose of use, is Tucker's *Light of Nature Pursued*—a most suggestive book, while I will caution you against the theology. But the last *thing* I would wish to see in the pulpit would be a mere declaimer. Declamation is most empty work, most unprofitable work. Yet a man may even make this useful ; but he must be more than a declaimer to be anything useful. Even in your declamation, which I think you will, and must, as young men, indulge, let there be thoughtfulness, which is more. Some preachers will, in the very heat and tempest of their declamation, dart in a sentence which arrests like lightning, and so they move on. DEAN YOUNG's sermons seem to me an illustration of this—I do not mean the poet Young—I remember he exclaims in one, "The soul of man, like common nature, admits no vacuum. If God be not there, mammon must be ; and it is as impossible to serve neither, as to serve both. If a man forsake the fountain of Living Waters, yet he cannot forsake his thirst, and there-

fore he lies under the necessity of hewing out broken cis-
terns to himself, and this makes the connection infallible
between indevotion and moral idolatry ; between the
neglecting God's worship and the worshipping the creature." Again, he stays himself in the heat of one of his fine
words, " Remember, that God is as near to our mouths
when we speak, as that man who leans his ear to our
whispers ; He is as near to actions when we are in secret,
as they are whom we admit into our confidence ; He is as
near to our thoughts when we purpose, wish, or design
anything, as is our own soul that conceives them." Put
things like these into your declamation, and your words
will be as effective as the lightning. Again, in declamation,
beware of sentiment. Audiences have a keen eye for sentiment, and to most men sentiment is not affecting, it is
ludicrous,—sentimental words are most ludicrous. There
is a great danger in all declamation, that is mere sentiment ;
that is, unrealized prettiness and tinselly verbiage. I again
say, that for any legitimate hold over your audiences, you
must obtain, by fair means, an entrance into the soul—
into the mind ; then, once there, you may kindle it, seek
to inflame it. You must not seek to obtain an unfair
mastery by tossing your fireworks around it before you
have entered it. Dr. Young's *Night Thoughts* is as fine a
piece of declamation as anything in our language—and
often there is more than declamatory fervor—but you
would not like to produce simply the impression he produced on Dr. Beattie. " When one begins," says Beattie,
" to find pleasure in sighing over Dr. Young's *Night Thoughts*
in a corner, it is time to shut the book, and return to the
company. I grant that while the mind is in a certain state,
those gloomy ideas give an exquisite delight ; but their
effect resembles that of intoxication upon the body ; they
may produce a temporary fit of feverish exultation, but
qualms, and weakened nerves, and depression of spirits,

are the consequence. I have great respect for Dr. Young, both as a man, and as a poet. I used to devour his *Night Thoughts* with a satisfaction not unlike that which, in my younger years, I have found in walking alone in a church-yard, or on a wild mountain by the moon at midnight. When I first read Young, my heart was broke to think of the poor man's afflictions. Afterwards I took into my head, that where there was so much lamentation, there could not be excessive suffering, and I could not help applying to him, sometimes, those lines of a song,

'Believe me the Shepherd but feigns :
He's wretched, to show he has wit.'

On talking with some of Dr. Young's friends, in England, I have since found that my conjectures were right, for that while he was composing the 'Night Thoughts,' he was really as cheerful as any man." This must always be the revenge the feelings take for an illegitimate mastery over them. Do your work so that those who are impressed shall not ever after be ashamed of the impressions you have produced. And yet, it is right that you should seek to move the feelings ; it is to be a matter of study with you *how* you may judiciously avail yourselves of those nice points of detail which, thrown into a picture, not merely heighten the effect, but, which will, as by the sudden stroke, cleave and arrest the mind. To this end the painters will teach you ; look at the paintings of Wilkie, or those of Hogarth ; the end of both may be legitimately yours, only one intends to rouse your tears, the other your scorn ; the detail does it, but then not detail for the sake of detail, and not one particular which does not give effect to the whole. And I have said much depends on style, too. Even Jeremy Taylor has a singularly disgusting passage—

We must needs die ; we must lie our heads down on the turf, and entertain creeping things in the cells and little chambers of our eyes. The beauty of the face, and dishonors of the belly, the discerning head, and the servile feet, the thinking heart, and working hand, the eyes and the guts together shall be crushed into the confusion of a heap, and dwell with creatures of an equivocal production, with worms and serpents, the sons and daughters of our bones, in a house of dirt and darkness.

And when all is done you will have occasion to watch over your gains in learning, lest that which might have been blessed and useful becomes a mischief and a snare. I have read, in a very old writer, of a company of apes that had gotten a glow-worm amongst them, upon which they heaped sticks and other combustible matter; and laying their heads together, blew with all their might, hoping to make the little shining particle to kindle into a flame; but they did not increase the flame, or warm, or enlighten themselves; they extinguished and killed the glow-worm. Perhaps we can all make the application. We are not all gifted, as was the blessed Saint Domingo, who, when the Devil teased him in the shape of a flea skipping upon his book, found himself fixed by the saint as a mark where he left off, and was so used through the volume. Or, as on that other occasion when the wicked Scratch came like a monkey to tease him and was cooly told by Domingo to hold the candle and let it burn down to the snuff, very much to Scratch's annoyance. But, one night the saint found the wicked one in the Dormitory reading a paper by the light of the lamp with great glee, and the following dialogue took place; said the saint—"Beast, what are you doing?" "I am doing my business," said the evil one, "laboring in my vocation in which I always gain." "Cursed be thy gain! what can you gain in the Dormitory, are not the religious all asleep? Is there a will in sleep that can aid thy malice?" "I gain much, I always disturb them by all manner of means; some I keep awake that they may lie a-bed and sleep when it is choir time, or go there so sleepy as to yawn over the service, and then, if they let me, I do worse there." "Why, what mischief dost thou do in the Church?" "More than in the Dormitory, I make them go late and against their inclination, and with a wish the job was over." "And in the Refectory?" "Oh, there are few whom I do not get at there, some I make eat too little, so that they weaken themselves till they are not able to do their duty; others too much." "And what in the room where conversation is allowed?" "Oh, that is my own room—there I make them talk about the news, and joke, and laugh, and grumble." "And in the Chapter House (where confession is made and penance done)?" "That is my Hell, there all I do is undone, half an hour loses me the labor of years," and so Scratch disappeared. Those old saints tell strange stories; and, perhaps, we do not think so much of confession cells and penances; but, we also, may try and watch our spirits so that with us our studies and apparatus do not hurt or hinder, instead of advancing us.

I think I may not inappropriately close by reminding you of a wise agricultural saying, which I have somewhere met with from a sage old farmer who recently remarked that "he fed his land before it was hungry, rested it before it was weary, and weeded it before it was foul." I have seldom, if ever, seen so much, I will not say of agricultural, wisdom condensed into a single sentence. I have seldom seen a sentence which so accurately expressed what, for the purposes of usefulness, every preacher should do.

PULPIT MONOGRAPHS.

III.—Charles Spurgeon.

THE Church has had great preachers, and we shall not suppose that the minister of the Metropolitan Tabernacle possesses the amazing splendor and pathetic eloquence of Chrysostom, or the subduing accents of Whitefield. The achievements of the great friars of the Middle Ages, Francis of Assisi, Bernardine of Montefeltro, and Bernardine of Sienna, and others, who preached in immense squares to twenty or fifty thousand people, for the honor of a visit from whom, to hear them preach, great cities contended; whose presence closed all the shops, and courts of justice, suspended all the functions of trade, and who usually, after their sermons, presided over the immense bonfires, into which their converted and panic-stricken auditors cast their dice-boxes and tables, impure books and pictures, their fashionable or licentious dresses, and who left on their departure often, some cross inscribed with the name of Jesus, or huge stone pulpit, erected by the city in grateful remembrance of the uses of the visit. Mr. Spurgeon has addressed his audiences of twenty and twenty-five thousand people, but we know of nothing in his instance, or in the history of the modern pulpit, bearing comparison with those old achievements; yet, from other aspects, the rise and progress of

the missions of the Metropolitan Tabernacle are even still
more remarkable, a fact quite unique in the whole history
of the Church. It may be safely affirmed that never, in
any period of the history of the Christian Church, did any
man rise and hold in sustained attention and active Christian useful labor a weekly congregation, certainly not numbering less than from five to six thousand persons, with no
popular prestige, no music to aid, no robes to give effect,
no ceremonials of service—plain, simple, unadorned. Then
the sermons, "seven hundred and twenty-seven," we perceive, is the last number of the last volume. These sermons, translated into the principal languages of Europe,
and some, we believe, into the dialects of Asia ; circulating
largely throughout the United States, throughout the English Colonies ; and the preacher, after all this extraordinary achievement, after having enrolled in his church up-
wards of three thousand members, having founded his college, and poured his young followers—themselves a sort of
rough, earnest, Protestant-preaching friars—over the whole
country : after having been abused and assailed on every
hand, and having received and worn the still more fatal and
dangerous commendations and flatteries of—perhaps it is
not too much to say—millions, still at this hour not far beyond the years of youth, still in the years of early manhood. We are not aware that the records of any church
or sect or of all Church history, furnish an analogous instance to such a phenomenon ; and the fact that he appeared at a time when the pulpit was fast asleep, and had
almost forgotten its mission, and the other fact that his
success may be greatly attributed to his appearance in an
age so thronged and crowded as ours is in this country,
are not so satisfactory as to the cause of his amazing popularity as to make it needless to inquire a little, with these
substantial volumes before us, into the origin of so great
a fame, and wide-spread usefulness.

"How do you account for it all?" said a minister to me the other day. And I replied, "Have you read the volumes of sermons?" "Who can wade through all those?" he said. And I replied, "True, but if you would wade through them—and such a task to a minister would be not a difficult, but a very instructive exercise—you would find in Mr. Spurgeon's sermons, that one of the striking elements of their greatness and strength is their average power; of course, some sermons are better than others, some are more eloquent, passionate, vehement, but there is an average of strength and raciness very delightful, also very astonishing, but which goes far to explain the staid and sustained attractiveness of the preacher." It has come about, from some cause or other, that *The Times* newspaper is scarcely a more acknowledged fact than Charles Spurgeon; and for myself, feeling it impossible that scores of thousands of people can go on being mistaken for long years together, I am disposed rather to look quietly at the fact, and to spend a little time in inquiring into its cause, how it is that the thousands throng week by week, and that those who hear the most constantly are the best satisfied?

There can be no doubt that perhaps first, and before all things, the voice accounts for much—a voice of astonishing compass, a voice, the waves from which roll with astonishing ease over the most immense company, full, sweet and clear—clear and ringing as a bell—a voice like the man and the matter, independent of most nervous impressions, all nervous agitations. It is a clarion of a voice; other voices of orators have pierced us more, have possessed more accent, have been able to whisper better, but we never knew nor conceived a voice with such thundrous faculty. I have called it a trumpet, and better still, a bell; it is not a perfect peal, but its tones roll on, there is no exhaustion; the tones are not many, but they are full and sweeping, and they give the idea of a great, fully-informed, and immensely capacious will and nature. Mr. Spurgeon might possess many of his mental attributes, but, manifestly, this power of being easily heard, of always striking the right pitch, so that he compasses immense assemblies, is one great element of success in holding the attention of masses of people. It is an old idea, and a very true one, we believe, that the voice is the man, as the voice is so the soul—a full voice is a full nature. The last achievement of Mr. Spurgeon will be regarded by many as the most wonderful of all in his early but extraordinary career. Whatever the capacities of the Agricultural Hall of Islington may be, and its minimum of 12,000, or its maximum of 20,000, auditors, unquestionably the Church notes, in its history, very few instances of preachers able to attract and hold in attention so mighty a mass. True, audiences grow like avalanches, and as fame grows, the means of sustaining fame also grow. But the greatest of the preachers the Church has known, such as Chrysostom, Augustine, Hall, Chalmers, or Irving, however the passion of their accents might have been desired, and the majesty or music of their eloquence would have found themselves as foiled by their own voice, as a silver bell on the mast of a vessel in the roar of a storm, in immense masses ; the measured cadences, the swing and toll, the melodious roar, if we may use the expression, of Mr. Spurgeon's voice, rises rather like the fabled Inchcape bell, tolling highest and deepest when the waves and winds were at their loudest. It may be, as I have implied it is, Mr. Spurgeon's least attribute, but it is that without which he would have possessed all his other attributes in vain, for the immense influence they possess and wield, We come to the sermons themselves.

The travelling over his twelve volumes of sermons astonished me ; and yet they are only, if they are, a decimal of his public talk. Richness of his own order is in them to profusion. They form but one weekly sermon. Of ex-

positions at Bible-classes, of Thursday and Sabbath evening discourses, of those delightful talkings about the chapter read in the service, never criticism, perhaps scarcely
expositions, but full of suggestive jets of speech ; of all
this we have no hint. Mr. Spurgeon is evidently a born
preacher—absorbs into his mind readily all that he sees,
reads, or hears, and talks it all forth again with amazing
fulness and freshness. His memory, that wondrous assim-
ilative power which, indeed, constitutes the soul, is something prodigious. It is not difficult to him to talk at any
time, to any length, although his wisdom has always been
shown in the moderation with which he has taxed the time
and patience of his audiences. This talking power is another reason of his great success. It has precluded, in his
case, the necessity of great preparation, which, however
splendid may have been its results in many eminent preachers, is always a token of, or a preparation to, remoteness
from an audience, where it is not a sign, as it more frequently is, of the poverty and shallowness of the stream
from which the preacher fills his vessel. Mr. Spurgeon's
sermons, printed or not, we know to be *comparatively* im-
promptu, *i. e.*, he is in fact always preparing ; texts and
thoughts are always coming ; and the opportunities with
them for binding them into sheaves. The waters of experience are always flowing, and he is always filling, There
are seasons, of course, hours—perhaps even on the Saturday—a day, for the receiving, remembering, and marshalling into order ; but it is in that infinite fulness of ready
talk, that copiousness of words reflecting moods, illustrations, homely proverbs, household usages, anecdotes, never
far removed from the knowledge and ordinary sense of the
people, that we find the second great cause of his fame.

No man can do a very extensive and world-wide mental
work to whom it is a hard and painful thing to prepare
and compose. Rapidity and facility, spontaneity and va-

riety have ever been the marks of genius. Socrates was
always ready; the fecundity of Plato is remarkable; the
works of Raphael and Michael Angelo would astonish us
by their innumerableness if we did not know that it is a
condition of the soul's perfection that it is always itself,
always at home; that to exist is to go forth, that to the
measure of its power, and its perfectness in its own region,
is its incessancy and activity. The stamp of genius always
bears this mark of infinite readiness and manifoldness; to
talk incessantly is not always to talk plainly; Coleridge,
we suppose, in his wonderful conversations, rolled along a
dreamy sea of sound. There is something attractive, and
even delightful, in hearing a full and resistless talker flowing on, even when we do not thoroughly comprehend, or,
perhaps, nearly comprehend what he means, or what he
says. A full soul is very charming and attractive, and when
the cadences of the voice are mystical and dreamy, and the
words are gorgeous and suggestive, we can listen even as
we listen to rich sopranoes, to the trill of nightingales and
larks, although no words reach us, and we have no present
idea beyond that of pleasure. This, however, would not
be sufficient to hold beneath its spell immense and uncul-
tured congregations, however refined taste and exquisite
sensibility might be delighted. Nor am I under the necessity of making any such concessions or explanations on
behalf of Mr. Spurgeon; for a third element of his power
I take to be that he is not more extensively heard than understood. His words have no peculiar selectness of subtle
and charming propriety like that which pleases so much in
the masters of melodious composition. Twelve years since,
in a paper I wrote upon him, I likened his style to that of
William Cobbett. The likeness would be still more apposite now; it is a level style on the whole, though, of course,
we are prepared to note great exceptions; it is a thoroughly English style, it rolls, yet the sentences are never long

—they never will be where the wheels of the mind are
running swiftly, and the furnace of the soul is hot. Quiet,
sweet, contemplative spirits, like Jeremy Taylor, who wrote
his sermons for drawing-rooms, and the private chapels of
country mansions ; thoughtful, but unearnest time-servers
like South—though he illustrates to us how striking and
telling he could make his sentences when he had any bul-
lying or coarseness to do with that renegade tongue of his
—preachers like Barrow, who did not write his sermons to
preach at all, but as exercises for the study, or if preached,
as we know, expected his audience to listen for three or
four hours ; preachers such as these, who are not especially
enkindled themselves in the pulpit and who have not upon
their souls the determination to keep their audiences alive
and awake, do not break up their words and sentences.
There is all the difference in their style and such a style as
that of William Cobbett or Charles Spurgeon as there is
between an Atlantic and a Pacific wave. The long, peaceful, measured roll of the one is very different to the sharp
and rocking surge and clash of the other. They are both
seas and waves; but for a strong excitement, for keeping a
soul alive, thoughtful, intense, and up to the listener's mark,
and as indicating the real life of the preacher himself
in the place where you expect him to be alive, in his
pulpit, and among the people, it seems an indispensable
requisite that his words should fall into rapid transforma-
tions. Perhaps in that case, he may not, like the great
names we have quoted, serve the brooding spirit so well in
its study; but it should be remembered that what constitutes a preacher is his power to gather, and to hold the
people interested while he speaks ; to use not select, but
average words ; to meet average and every-day moods. I
have heard of preachers who have addressed themselves to
the two or three, the half dozen cultivated and very thoughtful persons in their audience. It is a common, but a great

mistake ; Christ did not so ; it is a practice which must ensure the defeat of the preacher. Much wiser of the two was that preacher who always selected the man whom he thought the most stupid in his congregation, and determined to use such a variety of plain words, such a nimble recurrence of level, apposite, easily-understood illustrations, such a succession of appeals to his obtuse conscience, that he should be left no loop-hole of escape. A thoroughly well-informed and furnished nature, speaking to the lowest, will be sure to touch the highest ; millions who are not able to see and feel all the things in the 14th, 15th, and 16th chapters of John, drink in every word of the parable of the Prodigal Son, and it has long been noticed as a circumstance about the beautiful village sermons of Augustus Hare, that while admirably fitted in every sentence to instruct peasants to whom they were delivered, they informed men of culture and taste ; and of Mr. Spurgeon it is remarkable that while the masses of the rudest and most uninformed throng round him, he numbers in his church artists, men of the richest taste, and has had the personal friendship of, and a delighted listener in, the greatest master living of a glowing, gorgeous, and rich English style, John Ruskin. It arises from the reasons we have indicated ; for a conscience earnest, burning and impressed to aim at truth, at conscience, at what is supposed to be most ordinary in human nature, is to reach that which is common to all, and interesting to all the truly human in man. All this belongs to style, to the combination of words, their fitness, appositeness and power. Mr. Spurgeon illustrates the proverbial axiom of rhetoric, " The style is the man." Thus we have seen, we think, that the lower reasons for the immense following he has obtained are substantial and natural ; we are not surprised at it. Turning to the things we meet with in the sermons themselves, we find other reasons ; looking through his volume of sermons we meet with what, from what we have said, our readers will expect we should find ; a teeming mind will be a fresh mind, there is great originality here, originality in the selection of texts, and originality in their mode of treatment.

I have referred especially to Mr. Spurgeon's mode of division. Thus we have *The Lord the Liberator*, from the text, " The Lord looseth the prisoners." The text suggested to the preacher to go through the corridors of the great world-prison in which prisoners were confined.

I. The common prison—the ward of sin.

II. The solitary cell—the place of penitence, where was a secret spring, called faith, which, if a man could touch, he could go forth.

III. The silent cell, where he met with people who could not pray.

IV. The cell of ignorance.

V. The prison of habit.

VI. The hard-labor room.

VII. The low dungeon of despondency.

VIII. The inner prison, the hold of despair.

IX. The devil's torture-chamber

X. The condemned cell.

Ingeniousness is the characteristic of most of Mr. Spurgeon's divisions. Ingeniousness, which determines to travel through all the words or syllables of a text, and make each yield a variety of suggestions to his hearers.

Sometimes his mode of preaching has a special singularity. *I have sinned* is a sermon with seven texts—and yet but one. It repeats itself seven times in the Scriptures.

I. The hardened sinner—Pharaoh—says, " I have sinned."

II. The same confession is made by the double-minded man, Balaam—" I have sinned."

III. The insincere man, Saul—" I have sinned."

IV. The doubtful penitent—Achan.

V. It is the expression of the repentance of despair—Judas.

VI. Also of the repentance of the saint—Job.

VII. It is the blessed confession of the prodigal.

Such is the outline of the sermon with seven texts. One of his sermons is headed, *War! War! War!* The text, "Fight the Lord's Battles." The third head is devoted to the reading the articles of war, the regulations of the code martial—which are these :

Regulation I. No communication or union with the enemy.

II. No quarter to be given or taken.

III. No weapons or ammunition taken from the enemy are to be used by Emmanuel's soldiers, but are to be utterly burned by fire.

IV. No fear, trembling, or cowardice.

V. No slumbering, rest, ease, or surrender.

Then there follows seven postures for the Christian soldier.

I. Down upon both knees, hands up, and eyes up.

II. Feet fast, hands still, eyes up.

III. Quick march ; continually going forward.

IV. Going through Vanity Fair—eyes shut, ears shut, heart shut.

V. Feet firm, sword in hand, eyes open, watch every feint the enemy makes, and watch your opportunity to let fly at him, sword in hand.

VI. Hands wide open, heart wide open, helping our brethren.

VII. Patient waiting. Go home and put yourselves through this form of drill.

This mode of dividing texts, of course, will not commend itself to many readers and preachers. But, as I have said, Mr. Spurgeon's thought is to preach. He is what would be called a desultory preacher. In the course of his sermon, he seeks to hold up his text so that it is made to reflect many lights. Sometimes his sermons seem more topical, more the treatment of a subject. No sermon or text will give any idea of the whole preacher. In the volumes before us there is every variety; but it is plain that he does prefer the quaint old Puritan method. Many of his titles and treatments strike me exactly as the witty, pithy ways of thought of that greatly-beloved old Puritan, Thomas Brooks. The sermon entitled *A Bundle of Myrrh*: text, "A bundle of myrrh is my well-beloved unto me," is treated exactly as old Brooks would have treated it.

Jesus Christ is like a bundle of myrrh.
  I. Precious; a very valuable drug.
  II. Pleasant.
  III. Perfuming.
  IV. Preserving.
  V. A disinfectant
  VI. A cure.
  VII. A beautifier.
  VIII. It was connected with sacrifice, incense, etc.

Another sermon, entitled *Nothing but Leaves*, suggests—

  I. Those who follow the sign and know nothing of the substance.
  II. Those who have opinion without faith.
  III. Talk without feeling.
  IV. Regrets without repentance.
  V. Resolves without action.

The Broken Column is the title of a sermon on the text, "And another said, Lord I will follow Thee—But—" the broken text itself instantly preaches the sermon. It is interesting merely to run over the titles alone of very many of the sermons. 1 Corinthians, vii. 29–31, is *A Drama in Five Acts*, "So he paid the fare thereof," gives us, *Travelling Expenses on two Great Roads*. A text from Job gives a *Sermon from a Rush*. *Satan considering the Saints; The Barley-field on Fire; The Pierced One pierces the heart; Frost and Thaw; Secret sins driven out by stinging Hornets; The Root that beareth Wormwood; Have you forgotten Him?*

Am I sought out? Tell it all; A Bottle in the Smoke; Lions lacking—the Children satisfied; &c., &c. So, did space permit, I might note down very many, arresting in the text, strikingly suggestive in the mode of application, and running through many moods of tender and effective appeals to the conscience in their titles or designations.

But I should convey quite a wrong impression of the preacher if I implied by this that these sermons have only this varying mannerism. Mr. Spurgeon has a theological system; he knows what he believes, and many of his sermons have an accumulative breadth and height of theological building and furniture. Some of them may be called even massive presentations of religious truth and knowledge. I have before remarked upon the fact that from the time he began to preach, when almost a boy, the scheme of Christian truth presented itself before his eyes with singular distinctness. The later volumes of his sermons, of course, as might be expected, unfold this; still, in many instances, I might refer to many of these sermons as pieces of plain talk, yet dealing in a masterly manner with the reasonings of theology; exhibitions of truth which could not be listened to without revealing the depths and heights of argument and experience involved in the Christian system. Some amongst us who think that Christian truth is not so much a scientific and dogmatic form as a free and spiritual life, may be disposed to underrate, even depreciate and decry, this aspect in which the preacher presents himself. We may be sure, however, that a large amount of his power is in what may be called his dogmatism. The unhesitating certainty with which he expresses himself, whatever doubts, whatever casuistries or reasonings he ever may have been the subject of, he apparently never entertains his people with them. His spoken words are all firm as a rock; to himself his truth seems certain; and its various parts harmonious and consistent. The volumes before us run-

ning through twelve years of a young man's history, are
perfectly synthetic. It would not seem that he is ignorant
at all, at any rate of the popular forms of the thoughts and
theories which have disturbed the repose of faith in so many
minds during these eventful years. It would be a sin to
say of him that he is a preacher merely by rote. His peculiar moral qualities make it certain that he must see the
grounds of the earthquake which have shaken so many
houses of faith to their very foundations ; yet the shock
seems never to have come nigh him. This theology some,
regarding it at a distance, might perhaps call hard ; but
assuredly the traces of a hard and untender nature are not
in these volumes ; rather of a very tender and morally affectionate one. He always stands by the great truth of the
atonement, and cries, Believe ! With a certain order of refining and luxurious doubting and disbelieving, to which it
seems also certain too much deference has been paid by
preachers, he has no sympathy. I should expose him, I
am aware, to the contempt of many if I were to say of him-
he only has contempt for it. However that may be, it seems
certain that his theology is not reared from moods and feelings alone, but is wrought out on the strong anvil of a forcible and sagacious intelligence ; and it is perhaps true in
his instance that hard, incessant, and imperative work has
kept him from handling very closely those refining and fastidious fears of the intellectual nature which have stung
and wounded many so fearfully. I believe work has kept
him firmly to his principles, and has, no doubt, answered
to him those questions which must be answered to every
man, and answered in the affirmative, if he would be happy, and find a heart at rest, and a tongue entirely free.

I have referred to the manifoldness of this speech ; a
flow of talk, a happy arrangement, an impressive manner,
do not of themselves complete and constitute eloquence ;
eloquence in a great preacher, must be like a many-colored

garden, or it tires. Especially are there some kinds of more ordinary eloquence which surfeit and cloy. Mr. Spurgeon touches many strings ; aphorism and anecdote, coarse, quaint, outrageously grotesque ; then again, quiet, subjective, profoundly tender and subdued, snatches from unexpected poets, strains of household songs, come lilting along, with troops of quotations from all the sacred poets, versicles of hymns by wholesale, giving a chorus to his own feelings and a relief to the feelings of the people. Travels to and fro in England are always furnishing him with stories of persons and places. Anecdotes, humorous or pathetic ; gushes of rich poetic description, sometimes a sublime, sustained exordium ; vehement, passionate, overwhelming peroration. They must have strange scenes, one thinks, sometimes at the Tabernacle. It must have been a fine moment when preaching a new-year's sermon from the text, "To Him be glory both now and for ever, Amen," the invocations of the preacher were met and responded to by the massive thousands thundering back to him again, and again, and again, their loud Amens at the close of each passage.

Perhaps you will be pleased if I make a brief catena of passages illustrating the variety of style to which I have referred. Tenderness has not always been supposed to be a considerable attribute of the preacher, yet manifold pages contain tenderest expressions. The first extract is from a sermon on *Spring*, "The rain is over and gone," &c.

THE DYING DAY OF THE CHRISTIAN A SPRING DAY.

The time is coming to us all, when we shall lie upon our dying beds. Oh ! long-expected day, hasten and come ! The best thing a Christian can do is to die, and be with Christ, which is far better. Well, when we shall lie upon our beds panting out our life, we shall remember that then the winter is past for ever. No more now of this world's trials and troubles. "The rain is over and gone ;" no more stormy doubts, no more dark days of

affliction. "The flowers appear on the earth;" Christ is giving
to the dying saint some of the foretastes of heaven; the angels
are throwing over the walls some of the flowers of Paradise.
We have come to the land Beulah, we sit down on beds of spices
and can almost see the celestial city on the hill tops, on the other side of the narrow stream of death. "The time of the singing of the birds is come;" angelic songs are heard in the sick-
chamber. The heart sings too, and midnight melodies cheer the
quiet entrance of the grave. "Though I walk through the valley of the shadow of death I will fear no evil, for thou art with
me." Those are sweet birds which sing in the groves by the
river Jordan. Now it is that "the voice of the turtle is heard
in our land;" calm, peaceful and quiet, the soul rests in the consciousness that there is no condemnation to him that is in Christ
Jesus. Now does "the fig tree put forth her green figs;" the
first fruits of heaven are plucked and eaten while we are on earth.
Now do the very vines of heaven give forth a smell that can be
perceived by love. Look forward to your death, ye that are believers in Christ, with great joy. Expect it as your spring-tide
of life, the time when your real summer shall come, and your
winter shall be over for ever.

> One distant glimpse my eager passion fires!
> Jesus! to thee my longing soul aspires!
> When shall I hear thy voice divinely say,
> Rise up, my love, my fair one come away.
> Come meet thy Saviour bright and glorious,
> O'er sin, and death, and hell victorious.

HE BROUGHT ME UP.

I thought I saw just now before my eyes a dark and horrible
pit, and down deep below, where the eye could not reach, lay a
being broken in pieces, whose groans and howlings pierced the
awful darkness and amazed my ears. Methought I saw a bright
one fly from the highest heaven, and, in an instant, dive into
that black darkness till he was lost and buried in it. I waited
for a moment and to my mind's eye I saw two spirits rising
from the horrid deep, with arms entwined as though one was
bearing up the other. I saw them emerge from the gloom: I

heard the fairest of them say, as He mounted into light, "I have loved thee, and given myself for thee." And I heard the other, who was that poor broken one just now, say, "I was foolish and ignorant, I was as a beast before thee." Ere I could write the words both spirits had risen into mid-air, and I heard one of them say, "Thou shalt be with me in Paradise," and the other whispered, "Nevertheless I am continually with thee." As they mounted higher, I heard one say, "None shall pluck thee out of my hand," and I heard the other say, "Thou holdest me by my right hand." As still they arose they continued the loving dialogue. "I will guide thee with mine eye," said the bright one; the other answered, "Thou shalt guide me with thy counsel." They reached the bright clouds that separate earth from heaven, and as they parted to make way for the glorious One, he said, "I will give thee to sit upon my throne even as I have overcome, and sit upon my Father's throne," and the other answered, "And thou shalt afterward receive me to glory." Lo! the clouds closed their doors and they were gone. Methought again they opened and I saw those two spirits soaring onward beyond stars, and sun, and moon; right up beyond principalities and powers; on, beyond cherubim and seraphim; right up beyond every name that is named, until in that ineffable brightness, dark with unsufferable light, the awful glory of the Deity whom eye cannot see, both those spirits were lost, and there came the sound of joyous hallelujahs from the spirits which are before the throne. May it be your lot and mine thus to be brought up, for we are thus fallen; may it be ours to be thus caught up to the third heaven, for we are thus broken and cast down into the lowest hell by nature. God give us faith in Christ. Faith in Christ, that is the link, the bond, the tie, "Believe in the Lord Jesus Christ, and thou shalt be saved." "Lord, I believe, help thou mine unbelief."

THE PEN THAT WROTE "PARADISE LOST."

Oh! what poor little things we are, and yet we think we do so much. The pen might say, "I wrote Milton's *Paradise Lost.*" Ah? poor pen! thou couldst not have made a dot to an "i," or a cross to a "t," if Milton's hand had not moved thee. The preacher could do nothing if God had not helped him. The axe might cry, "I have felled forests; I have made the cedar bow its

head, and laid the stalwart oak in the dust." No, thou didst
not; for if it had not been for the arm which wielded thee, even
a bramble would have been too much for thee to cut down. Shall
the sword say, " I won the victory; I shed the blood of the mighty;
I caused the shield to be cast away ? " No, it was the warrior,
who with his courage and might made thee of service in the
battle, but apart from this thou art less than nothing. In all that
God doth by us, let us continue to give Him the praise, so shall
He continue His presence with our efforts, otherwise He will take
from us His smile, and so we shall be left as weak men.

THROUGH HIM WERE ALL THINGS.

Through Him were all things, from the high archangel who
sings His praises in celestial notes, down to the cricket chirp-
ing on the hearth. The same finger paints the rainbow and the
wing of the butterfly. He who dyes the garments of evening
in all the colors of heaven, has covered the king-cup with gold,
and lit up the glow-worm's lamp. From yonder ponderous
mountain, piercing the clouds, down to that minute grain of dust
in the summer's threshing-floor, all things through Him are.
Let but God withdraw the emanation of His divine power, and
everything would melt away as the foam upon the sea melts into
the wave which bore it. Nothing could stand an instant if the
divine foundation were removed. If He should shake the pillars of the world, the whole temple of creation falls to ruin, and
its very dust is blown away. A dreary waste, a silent emptiness,
a voiceless wilderness is all which remaineth if God withdraws
His power; nay, even so much as this were not if His power
should be withheld.

That nature is as it is is through the energy of the present God.
If the sun riseth every morning, and the moon walketh in her
brightness at night, it is through Him. Out upon those men
who think that God has wound up the world, as though it were
the clock, and has gone away, leaving it to work for itself apart
from His present hand. God is present everywhere—not merely
present when we tremble because His thunder shakes the solid
earth, and sets the heavens in a blaze with lightnings, but just
as much so in the calm summer's breeze, when the air so gently
fans the flowers, and gnats dance up and down in the last gleams
9*

of sunlight. Men try to forget the divine presence by calling its energy by strange names. They speak of the power of gravitation; but what is the power of gravitation? We know what it does, but what is it? Gravitation is God's own power. They tell us of mysterious laws—of electricity, and I know not what. We know the laws, and let them wear the names they have; but laws cannot operate without power. What is the force of nature? It is a constant emanation from the great Fountain of power, the constant outflowing of God himself, the perpetual going forth of beams of light from Him who is the " great Father of Lights, with whom is no variableness, neither shadow." Tread softly, be reverent, for God is here, O mortal, as truly as he is in heaven. Wherever thou art and whatever thou lookest upon, thou art in God's workshop, where every wheel is turned by His hand. Everything is not God, but God is in everything, and nothing worketh, or even existeth, except by His present power and might. "Of Him, and through Him are all things."

TALK OF SINNERS. (Close of a Sermon).

Talk of sinners! Walk the streets by moonlight if you dare, and you will see sinners then. Watch when the night is dark, and the wind is howling, and the picklock is grating in the door, and you will see sinners then. Go to yon jail, and walk through the wards and see the men with heavy, overhanging brows, men whom you would not like to meet out at night, and there are sinners there. Go to the Reformatories, and see those who have betrayed an early and a juvenile depravity, and you will see sinners there. Go across the seas to the place where a man will gnaw a bone reeking with human flesh, and there is a sinner there. Go you where you will, and ransack earth to find sinners, for they are common enough; you may find them in every lane and street, of every city and town, and village and hamlet. It is for such that Jesus died. If you will select me the grossest specimen of humanity, if he but born of woman, I will have hope of him yet, because the Gospel of Christ is come to sinners, and Jesus Christ is come to seek and to save sinners. Electing love has selected some of the worst to be made the best. Redeeming love has bought, specially bought, many of the worst to be the reward of the Saviour's passion. Effectual grace calls out and compels to come in many of the vilest of the vile; and it is, therefore, that I have tried to-night to preach my Master's love to sinners.

Oh! by that love looking out of those eyes in tears; oh! by that love streaming from those wounds flowing with blood; by that faithful love, that strong love, that pure, disinterested and abiding love; oh! by the heart and by the bowels of the Saviour's compassion, I do conjure you turn not away as though it were nothing to you; but believe on Him and you shall be saved. Trust your souls with Him and He will bring you to His Father's right hand in glory everlasting.

A VISTA VIEW OF THE PAST. (" Hitherto has the Lord helped us.")

I like, sometimes, to look down a long avenue of trees. It is very delightful to gaze from end to end of the long vista, a sort of leafy temple with its branching pillars and its arches of leaves. Can not you look down the long aisles of your years, look at the green boughs of mercy overhead, and the strong pillars of loving-kindness and faithfulness which bear your joys? Are there no birds in yonder branches singing? Surely, there must be many. And the bright sunshine and the blue sky are yonder; and, if you turn around in the far distance, you may see heaven's brightness and a throne of gold. " Hitherto! hitherto!"

EDDYSTONE LIGHTHOUSE.

You may have a very strong faith in everything else but Christ, and yet perish. There was an architect who had a plan for building a lighthouse on the Eddystone Rock. It quite satisfied his mind; and, as he sat by the fire looking at his plans he was quite sure that no storm that ever came could shake the building. He applied for the contract to build the lighthouse, and did build it, and a very singular looking place it was. There were a great many flags about it and ornaments, and it looked very promising. Some shook their heads a little, but he was very, very firm, and said he should like to be in it himself in the worst wind that ever blew. He was in it at the time he wanted to be, and he was never heard of again, nor was anything more ever seen of his lighthouse. The whole thing was swept away. He was a man of great faith, only it happened to be founded on ·

mistaken principles. Now, sometimes, because there is a way of talking which looks very much like assurance, you may say, " I am not afraid ; I never had a doubt or a fear ; I know it is all right with my soul ; I am not afraid of the test of the day of judgment." Well, whether you wish it or not, that test for the labor of your lighthouse will come, and if it should prove that you built it yourself, it will be swept away and you with it. But if your soul takes God's Word, and reads that Word, believing it, and being willing to be taught its inward meaning,—if you take that Word as it stands, and rest upon it, and act upon it with all your heart and soul, the worst storm that ever blew shall never shake your rock and refuge, nor you either ; but you shall be safe when earth's old columns bow, and all her wheels shall go to wreck and confusion.

Rest thou in the Lord Jehovah. Depend on the blood and righteousness of the Lord Jesus Christ for all thou needest, and rest wholly in Him with the whole weight of thy soul and spirit, and then there shall be no fear but what thou shalt see God's face with acceptance.

HEADS AND LEGS.

Oh ! I would that some Christians would pay a little attention to their legs, instead of paying it all to their heads. When children's heads grow too fast it is a sign of disease, and they get the rickets, or water on the brain. So, there are some very sound brethren, who seem to me to have got some kind of disease, and when they try to walk, they straightway make a tumble of it, because they have paid so much attention to perplexing doctrinal views, instead of looking, as they ought to have done, to the practical part of Christianity. By all means let us have doctrine, but by all means let us have precept too. By all means let us have inward experience, but by all means let us also have outward "holiness, without which no man can see the Lord."

THE POWER OF GOD.

What is there which he cannot do ? We see but little of God's power comparatively in our land. Now and then there comes a crash of thunder in a storm, and we look up with amazement when He sets the heavens on a blaze with His lightning. But

go and do business on the deep waters; let your vessel fly before the howling hurricane; mark how every staunch timber
seems to crack as though it were but match-board, and the steady
mast goes by the board, and snaps, and is broken to shivers.
Mark what God does when He stirs up the great deep, and seems
to bring heaven down and lift the earth up until the elements
mingle in a common mass of tempest. Then go to the Alps, and
listen to the thunder of the avalanche. Stand amazed, as you
look down some grim precipice, or peer with awe-struck wonder
into the blue mysteries of a crevasse; see the leaping cataracts,
and mark those frozen seas—the glaciers—as they come sweeping down the mountain side; stay awhile till a storm shall gather there, and Alp shall talk to Alp, and those white prophetic
heads shall seem to bow while the wings of tempest cover them!
There you may learn something of the power of God amidst the
crash of nature. If you could have stood by the side of Dr.
Woolf, when rising early one morning, he went out of Aleppo, and,
upon turning his head, saw that Aleppo was no more; it having
been in a single moment swallowed up by an earthquake, then
again you might see what God can do. But what need I feebly
recapitulate what you all know so well? Think of what that
Book records of His deeds of prowess, when He unloosed the
depths, and bade the fountains of the great deep be broken up,
that the whole world,—that then was,—might be covered with
water. Think of what he did at the Red Sea, when the depths
stood upright as a heap, for a time, while his people went
through, and, when afterwards with eager joy the floods clasped
their hands, and buried the foemen in the deep, never to rise
again! Let such names as Og, king of Bashan, Sihon, king of
the Amorites, and Sennacherib, the mighty, rise before your recollection, and mark what God has done! Who has ever dashed
upon the bosses of His buckler without being wounded? What
iron has He not broken? What spear has He not shivered?
Millions came against Him, but by the blast of the breath of his
nostrils they fell, or they flew like the chaff before the wind. Let
the sea roar, and the fullness thereof, but the rocks stand still and
hurl off the waves in flakes of foam, and so doth God, when
His foes are most enraged and passionate. He that sitteth in
the heavens doth laugh · the Lord doth have them in derision;

and He breaketh them in pieces without a stroke of His hand, or even the glance of the eye. Think, sinner, think of Him with whom thou contendest. Hast thou an arm like God's? Canst thou thunder with a voice like His? Canst thou stamp with thy foot, and shake the mountains? Canst thou touch the hills and make them smoke? Canst thou say to the sea, "Be stirred to thy depths," or canst thou call to the winds and bid the steeds of tempest be unloosed? If thou canst not, then think of the battle! Attempt to do no more, but hie thee back to thy bed, and there commune with thy own heart, and make thy peace with Him against whom thou canst not hope successfully to contend.

IMPRESSIONS OF TIME.

Only a few Sabbaths ago I was talking to you of Ruth in the harvest-fields, and of the heavily-laden wagon that was pressed down with sheaves; and now the leaves are almost all gone; but few remain upon the trees; these frosty nights and stong winds have swept the giants of the forest till their limbs are bare, and the hoar frosts plate them with silver. Then, before we shall have time to burn the winter's log, we shall see the snow-drops and the yellow crocuses heralding another spring! At what a rate we whirl along! Childhood seems to travel in a wagon, but manhood at express speed. As we grow older I am told that the speed increases, till the gray-headed old man looks back upon all his life as being but a day; and I suppose if we could live to be a hundred and thirty we should feel the same, till, like Jacob, we should say, "Few and evil have been the days of thy servant;" and, if we could live as long as Mathuselah, I doubt not our lives would appear shorter still. How time flies, not only by the measurement of the seasons but by *ourselves!* A few days ago I trudged with my satchel on my back to school, or joined in boyish sport. How lately was it when the boy became a youth, and must be doing something, and was teaching other boys as he had been taught in his day. It was but yesterday I came to Park Street to address some few of you, and yet how time has fled since then, till now some nine years of our ministry have passed. No weaver's shuttle, no arrow from a bow, no swift post, no meteor seems to fly at a rate

so wonderful as does our life! We heard of one the other day
that had seen Wesley preach, and so we find ourselves side-by-
side with the last century, and those old people have known
some others in their youth who told them of the yet older time,
and you find that going through the history of some ten or
twelve persons you are carried back to the days of William the
Conqueror, and you see our country taken by the Normans, and
then you fly back to ancient British times as with a thought.
You no longer say, "How long the nation has existed!" for it is
as a sleep. You stand by some old cliff and see a deposit of
shells, and as you remember that it may have taken a million
of years to have formed that bed, you think—"What is man?
and what is time? It is not here, but gone!" We have only to
think of what time is to conclude at once that time is not! It
is but a little interlude in the midst of the vast eternity; a narrow neck of land jutting out into the great, dread, and unfa-
thomable sea of everlastingness!

COLERIDGE'S "ANCIENT MARINER."

Have ye ever read Coleridge's "Ancient Mariner?" I dare say
you have thought it one of the strangest imaginations ever put
together, especially that part where the old mariner represents
the corpses of all the dead men rising up,—all of them dead,
yet rising up to manage the ship; dead men pulling the ropes,
dead men steering, dead men spreading the sails. I thought
what a strange idea that was. But do you know I have lived to
see that true: I have seen it done. I have gone into churches
and I have seen a dead man in the pulpit, and a dead man as a
deacon, and a dead man holding the plate at the door, and dead
men sitting to hear. You say, "Strange!" but I have. I have
gone into societies, and I have seen it all going on so regularly.
These dead men, you know, never outstep the bounds of prudence,—not they: they have not life enough to do that. They
always pull the rope orderly, "As it was in the beginning, is
now, and ever shall be, world without end, Amen." And the
dead man in the pulpit, is he not most regular and precise? He
systematically draws his handkerchief from his pocket, and
uses it at the regular period, in the middle of the sermon. He
would not think of violating a single rubric that has been laid

down by his old-fashioned church. Well, I have seen these churches—I know where to point them out—and have seen dead men doing everything. "No," says one, "you can't mean it?" Yes, I do; the men were spiritually dead. I have seen the minister preaching, without a particle of life, a sermon, which is only fresh in the sense in which a fish is fresh when it has been packed in ice. I have seen the people sit, and they have listened as if they had been a group of statues—the chiselled marble would have been as much affected by the sermon as they. I have seen the deacons go about their business just as orderly, and with as much precision as if they had been mere automatons, and not men with hearts and souls at all. Do you think God will ever bless a church that is like that? Are we ever to take the kingdom of heaven with a troop of dead men? Never! We want living ministers, living hearers, living deacons, living elders, and until we have such men who have got the very fire of life burning in their souls, who have got tongues of life, and eyes of life, and souls of life, we shall never see the kingdom of heaven taken by storm. "For the kingdom of heaven suffereth violence, and the violent take it by force."

THE MOUNTAIN ESTABLISHED ON THE TOP OF THE HILLS.

Transport yourselves for a moment to the foot of Mount Zion. As you stand there, you observe that it is but a very little hill. Bashan is far loftier, and Carmel and Sharon outvie it. As for Lebanon, Zion is but a little hillock compared with it. If you think for a moment of the Alps, or of the loftier Andes, or of the yet mightier Himalayas, this Mount Zion seems to be a very little hill, a mere mole-hill, insignificant, despicable, and obscure. Stand there for a moment, until the Spirit of God touches your eye, and you shall see this hill begin to grow. Up it mounts, with the temple on its summit, till it outreaches Tabor. Onward it grows, till Carmel, with its perpetual green, is left behind, and Salmon, with its everlasting snow, sinks before it. Onward still it grows, till the snowy peaks of Lebanon are eclipsed. Still onward mounts the hill, drawing with its mighty roots other mountains and hills into its fabric; and onward it rises, till piercing the clouds it reaches above the Alps; and onward still, till the Himalayas seem to be sucked into its

bowels, and the greatest mountains of the earth appear to be
but as the roots that strike out from the side of the eternal hill;
and there it rises till you can scarcely see the top, as infinitely
above all the higher mountains of the world as they are above
the valleys. Have you caught the idea, and do you see there
afar off upon the lofty top, not everlasting snows, but a pure
crystal table-land, crowned with a gorgeous city, the metropolis
of God, the royal palace of Jesus the King. The sun is eclipsed
by the light which shines from the top of this mountain; the
moon ceases from her brightness, for there is now no night;
but this one hill, lifted up on high, illuminates the atmosphere,
and the nations of them that are saved are walking in the light
thereof. The hill of Zion hath now outsoared all others, and
all the mountains and hills of the earth are become as nothing
before her. This is the magnificent picture of the text. I do
not know that in all the compass of poetry there is an idea so
massive and stupendous as this—a mountain heaving, expanding, swelling, growing, till all the high hills become absorbed,
and that which was but a little rising ground before, becomes a
hill the top whereof reacheth to the seventh heaven. Now we
have here a picture of what the church is to be.

*   *   *   *   *   *   *

It has never been my privilege to be able to leave this country
for any time, to stand at the foot of the loftier mountains of
Europe, but even the little hills of Scotland, where half way up
the mist is slumbering, struck me with some degree of awe.
These are some of God's old works, high and lofty, talking to
the stars, lifting up their heads above the clouds as though
they were ambassadors from earth ordained to speak to God in
silence far aloft. But poets tell us—and travellers who have but
little poetry say the same—that standing at the foot of some of
the stupendous mountains of Europe and Asia, the soul is subdued with the grandeur of the scene. There, upon the father
of mountains, lie the eternal snows glittering in the sun-light,
and the spirit wonders to see such mighty things as these, such
massive ramparts garrisoned with storms. We seem to be but
as insects crawling at their base, while they appear to stand like
cherubims before the throne of God, sometimes covering their
face with clouds of mist, or at other times lifting up their white

heads, and singing their silent and eternal hymn before the throne of the Most High. There is something awfully grand in a mountain, but how much more so in such a mountain as is described in our text, which is to be exalted above all hills, and above all the highest mountains of the earth.

KILLING THE WATCH-DOG, CONSCIENCE.

Whenever you have heard an earnest powerful sermon, you have gone home and labored to get rid of it. A tear has stolen down your cheek now and then, and you have despised yourself for it. "Oh !" you say, "it is not manly for me to think of these things." There have been a few twitches at times which you could not help, but the moment after you have your heart like a flint, impenetrably hard and stony. Well, sir, I will give a picture of yourself. There is a foolish farmer yonder in his house. It is the dead of night; the burglars are breaking in— men who will neither spare his life nor his treasure. There is a dog down below chained in the yard; it barks and barks, and howls again. "I cannot be quiet," says the farmer, "my dog makes too much noise." Another howl, and yet another yell. He creeps out of bed, gets his loaded gun, opens the window, fires it, and kills the dog. "Ah ! it is all right now," he mutters, he goes to bed, lies down, and quietly rests. "No hurt will come," he says, " now; for I have made that dog quiet." Ah ! but would that he could have listened to the warning of the faithful creature. Ere long he shall feel the knife and rue his fatal folly. So you, when God is warning you—when your faithful conscience is doing its best to save you—you try to kill your only friend, while Satan and Sin are stealing up to the bedside of your slothfulness, and are ready to destroy your soul for ever and ever. What should we think of the sailor at sea who should seek to kill all the stormy petrels, that there might be an end to all storms ? Would you not say, "Poor foolish man ; why, those birds are sent by a kind Providence to warn him of the tempest. Why needs he injure them ? They cause not the tumult; it is the raging sea." So it is not your conscience that is guilty of the disturbance in your heart, it is your sin; and your conscience, acting true to its character as God's index in your soul, tells you that all is wrong.

THE UNCONSCIOUSNESS OF NATURE.

When I look abroad upon nature, it is true I do not see nature fussily trying to make itself tidy for a visitor, as some professors do, who, the moment they think they are going to be looked at, trim up their godliness to make it look smart. But, on the other hand, nature is never bashful. She never tries to hide her beauties from the gazer's eye. You walk the valley; the sun is shining and a few rain-drops are falling; yonder is the rainbow; a thousand eyes gaze at it. Does it fold up all its lovely colors and retire? Oh, no! it shrinks not from the eye of man. In yonder garden all the flowers are opening their bejewelled cups, the birds are singing, and the insects humming amid the leaves. It is a place so beautiful that God himself might walk therein at eventide, as he did in Eden. I look without alarming the bashful beauties of the garden. Do all these insects fold their wings and hide beneath the leaves? do the flowers hang down their heads? does the sun draw a veil over his modest face? does nature blush until the leaves of the trees are scarlet? Oh, no! Nature cares not for gazers, and when any come to look upon her, she doth not hasten to wrap a mantle over her fair form, or throw a curtain before her grandeur. So the Christian is not to be always wishing to expose what is in him; that were to make himself a Pharisee; yet, on the other hand, if God has put anything that is lovely and beautiful, and of good repute, in you; anything that may glorify the cross of Christ, and make the angels happy before the eternal throne, who are you that you should cover it? who are you that you should rob God of His praise? What! would you have all nature's beauties hid? Why, then, hide the beauties of grace? Jesus Christ deserves to be confessed before men. He is not ashamed to own himself our friend amidst the splendors of His Father's court. Nor was He ashamed amidst the mockery and spitting of Pilate's hall. Why, then, should you find it a hardship or a difficulty to acknowledge *Him?*

THE NAME OF THE LORD A STRONG TOWER.

Strong towers were a greater security in a bygone age than they are now. Then, when troops of marauders invaded the land, strong castles were set upon the various hill-tops, and the inhabitants gathered up their little wealth and fled thither at once. Castles were looked upon as being very difficult places for attack; and ancient troops would rather fight a hundred battles than endure a single siege. Towns which would be taken by modern artillery in twelve hours held out for twelve years against the most potent forces of the ancient times. He that possessed a castle was lord of all the region round about, and made their inhabitants either his clients who sought his protection, or his dependents whom he ruled at will. He who owned a strong tower felt, however potent might be his adversary, his walls and bulwarks would be his sure salvation. Generous rulers provided strongholds for their people; mountain fastnesses, where the peasantry might be sheltered from marauders. Transfer your thoughts to a thousand years ago, and picture a people who, after ploughing and sowing, have gathered in their harvest, but when they are about to make merry with the harvest festival, a startling signal banishes their joy. A trumpet is blown from yonder mountain, the tocsin answers it from the village tower, hordes of ferocious robbers are approaching, their corn will be devoured by strangers; burying their corn and furniture, and gathering up the little portable wealth they have, they hasten with all their might to their tower of defence which stands on yonder ridge. The gates are shut; the drawbridge is pulled up; the portcullis is let down; the warders are on the battlements, and the inhabitants within feel that they are safe. * * * "The name of the Lord is a strong tower; the righteous runneth into it and is safe."

These are very fair illustrations of what the reader will find strewn with rich affluence over the many thousands of pages. I think that the course of remark I have made, and the illustrations I have given, are sufficient to show that it is not a mere unreasoning *furore* which has created the great popularity Mr. Spurgeon enjoys. It is founded on that which is quite real and worthy of him, and is not at all to be set aside by the fact that there may be minds desiderating in him the teaching they especially desire. It is a remarkable circumstance, that almost the only one of our higher order of reviews which has spoken of him with much respect, is the *Dublin*, the leading Roman Catholic review ; and its estimate, in substance kindly expressed, was formed in 1857, when he was in the first years of his great fame. It spoke of it then as quite inexplicable, and as worthy of some speculation and inquiry, for the purpose of reaching the cause.

Considering the quarter from whence those remarks came, they can only be regarded as respectful and kind. But, if Mr. Spurgeon was a marvel in 1857, how much more is he a marvel now? Unabated, his popularity has grown into such gigantic proportions, that, as I have said, the instances are very rare that at all resemble it in the whole history of the Church, I can conceive a cynic regarding it as one of those periodical fits of madness which surprise nations. It is the most sober and orderly madness the world or the Church has ever, on so great a scale, known. If we are to seek for causes beyond those we have noted, for the power and the success, then shall we not also remember one or two other things? I have already hinted at the amazing work wrought at the Tabernacle—a church, I believe, of about 3,000 members ; a college pouring its rough and ready-going preachers over the whole country ; chapels rising, evoked by some magic from Mr. Spurgeon and his band of workers. But there are triumphs of faith in all this. A little passage of autobiography, illustrating the temper of the preacher's mind, is in the following passage from one of his sermons.

You know how we, as a church, have been led to see mysteriously the hand of God. I recollect one night, when we resolved to build this house of prayer; we knew that we were poor, much too poor ever to be able to raise so large a sum as this house would cost, especially when the vow was registered that it should never be built with borrowed money, but should either be paid for or else not built at all ; I recollect preaching that evening from the text, "And the iron did swim," and saying that

the building of this house seemed as likely a thing to happen as
if the iron should swim; but I said I was glad it was twenty-
five thousand pounds which we wanted, for if it had been only
five thousand pounds, or ten thousand pounds, we might feel able
to raise it; but twenty-five thousand pounds was impossible, only
I believed that God could do impossibilities. It was one of the
most singular things that ever occurred, when a friend at a distance whom I never saw but once in my life, and who had no
connection with us, put down five thousand pounds himself towards it. We were encouraged; we went to work and the thing
was done; and, as it went on more and more singular helps were
sent. When the College of which I am President had been commenced for a year or so, all my means stayed; my purse was
dried up, and I had no other means of carrying it on. In this
very house, one Sunday evening, I had paid away all I had for
the support of my young men for the ministry. There is a dear
friend now sitting behind me who knows the truth of what I
am saying. I said to him, "There is nothing left whatever."
He said, "You have a good banker, sir." "Yes," I said, "and I
should like to draw upon him now, for I have nothing." "Well,"
said he, "how do you know? have you prayed about it?"
"Yes, I have." "Well, then, leave it with Him; have you opened your letters?" "No, I do not open my letters on Sun-
days." "Well," said he, "open them for once." I did so, and
in the first one I opened there was a banker's letter to this effect—"Dear Sir—We beg to inform you that a lady, totally unknown to us, has left with us two hundred pounds for you, to
use in the education of young men." Such a sum has never
come since, and it never came before; and I have no more idea
than the dead in their graves how it came then, nor who it came
from, but to me it seemed that it came directly from God. We
have gone on ever since with that work successfully, and are resolved to launch out into others; and I believe that we only
want as a church, and your pastor only wants as your pastor, to
have faith in God, and we shall find Him "wonderful in counsel and excellent in working." Wherever there is the hand of a
true man, there is the wing of an angel.

Then we read sometimes of the immense chapel—holding about 5, 000 people—crammed at prayer-meetings; and

we read of days set apart there for fasting and prayer. All this represents great spiritual power, intense faith, that belief in the Invisible, "Enduring, as seeing Him who is Invisible," which is the real fountain of all great spiritual energy; and such facts as these ought never to be separated in any estimate we may attempt to form of the preacher. It is evidently one of those consecrated lives which almost ignores the right very closely to criticise; and we are rejoiced to perceive throughout the prefaces to these volumes of sermons, a tone of genuine and unaffected modesty very delightful to notice. Mr. Spurgeon regards himself less as a great preacher than an evangelist. He seems to be amazed at his own success, and almost deprecates the idea of the possession of talent. He says:—

It is extraordinary grace, not talent, that wins the day. It is extraordinary spiritual power, not extraordinary mental power that we need. Mental power may fill a chapel; but spiritual power fills the church. Mental power may gather a congregation, but spiritual power will save souls. We want spiritual power. Oh! we know some before whom we shrink into nothing as to talent, but who have no spiritual power; and when they speak, they have not the Holy Spirit with them; but we know others—simple-hearted, worthy men, who speak their country dialect, and who stand up to preach; and whether it be in a barn, or a village green, the Spirit of God clothes every word with power. * * * *

This seems to explain very much; unfastidious boldness, intrepid certainty, indefatigable activity, resolved into "this one thing I do"—this seems to account for very much.

I am quite aware, Mr. Spurgeon himself evidently, by the modest words of the preface to one of his volumes, is aware of the points in which we must not compare him with some of the great preachers of our age—for instance, with the Dominican, Lacordaire, with Le Père Félix, or this moment's wonder of Paris, the Carmelite, Hyacinthe. These names suggest some resemblance, and as instantly forbid comparison ; these men, excellent and devoted, we have no doubt, in their order and in their lives, have thronged the immense and voluminous aisles of Notre Dame ; preachers with wonderful accents—saintly men we hope, we desire to believe ; from their monasteries, after their period of solitude and retreat, of introspection and thought, it has been their wont, I understand, to emerge like apparitions. With the harangues of Hyacinthe we are not so well acquainted. Those of Lacordaire and Felix are well known to us ; they are, and especially those of the first, grand and majestic flights ; wheeling sweeps of wings of astounding power, surveying from the air of the mid-heaven the tangled world, not only of sin, but the perplexed convolutions and folds, and coils of thought. What effect they have produced on Parisian society I have no means of knowing ; to what extent impressions are gathered up, and made the permanent furniture of the Church, I know not. We know what great, intellectual, and magnificently-artistic preaching usually is ; it is not likely that Lacordaire produced effects more profound than Bossuet, or that Hyacinthe is more successful in this way than Massillon. These men, great as we know, good as we hope they were or are, all seemed or seem to treasure up their aphorisms, impressions, apt illustrations, excursions of fancy, surprises of logic, attained grandeur of soul, by long, solitary, mental communion : then comes the annual occasion, and all the fashion of Paris throngs to listen to the orator who varies the amusements for the great city with the last opera of Meyerbeer. This is not untrue nor unkind ; but how different to the orator, the incessant talker, the plain, undignified unpriest-like youth of the tabernacle, who has reared for himself a church, for his weekly audiences, holding as many auditors as Notre Dame, and gathering up all the wares of his eloquence into a plain, resolute English working. What shall we say of the two, but, that the one is thoroughly French, and the other is thoroughly English.

V.

On the Mental Tools and Apparatus needful for the Pulpit.

FTER all that I have said, I am still reminded of old Cotton Mather's title to his "Manu ductio ad Ministerium;" he calls it "The Angels Preparing to Sound the Trumpet;" it is all only preparation to the end.* I have vindicated the dignity and necessity of the preacher's work, I believe in its reality, importance and power. I confess, while all or many of the vices and shortcomings of the modern pulpit have not been unapprehended by me, I cannot, with Frederick Robertson, believe "that

* I am sure I do well in commending to the attention of young preachers and students for the ministry, Dr. Mather's valuable, but now quite forgotten, although not outlived little books. In addition to that I have noticed above, his *Student and Preacher; or Directions for a Candidate for the Ministry*, there are his *Essays to do Good;* with these may be mentioned *The Student and Pastor; or, Directions how to attain to Eminence and Usefulness in those respective Characters: by John Mason.* These are vigorous and animated little books, and I think could not fail of usefulness and acceptance if they were reprinted; they have an anecdotal and aphoristic sprightliness about them, which commends them to young minds; and their seriousness of purpose, and height of standard for attainment are well calculated to promote a pious ambition.

it tends to make people worse instead of better," and that the excitement of the preparation "demoralizes and destroys the tone of the heart, and unfits for duty ;" there is a side of truth, no doubt, in these charges, but as the statement of a great fact they are not true, and where true, they ought not to be true : the work of the pulpit ought to be robust, healthful, and invigorating, a fountain of strength to the preacher himself, and to those who hear him ; look away from little aims and it will be so ; little sentimentalities in a poor little impoverished character may have the effect Mr. Robertson describes, and there is a strain upon the feelings that may enervate the preacher, even as the poet, or the artist ; the preacher must cultivate a moral health which shall rise above it. When a young man full of vanities and affectations came to Robert Hall desiring to be introduced into the ministry, saying, "You know, Mr. Hall, I must not hide my talents in a napkin," Mr. Hall said "Oh, never mind about a napkin, sir, your pocket-handkerchief will do very well for that purpose." And I want you to look away from a complacent regard of your talents ; whatever they may be, they will always need the spirit of prayer, and the life of culture, and they will always fall short of the grandeur of the work, which, if you be true ministers, you have set before you.

One of the first thoughts suggested by any vast pile of architecture is the sense of power it conveys—how lives now passed away wrought at this ; stand in imagination before many buildings, such as the Cathedrals of St. Paul's, Notre-Dame, Milan, or Cologne, the first impression is the marvellous sense of manifold power ; every part conveys the thought of power—it was reared by men—but spire or turret, the infinity of the nave, the mystery of the choir, the charm of the chapel, the fret, or the corbel, the pillars or the facade, the solemn gloom of crypt and cloister, the dangerous passages of the triforium, all these speak of power. Does a life convey less the idea of power? a human life, a life building or built, a noble life, a life with vast powers spent on vain purposes, a life dreaming, especially a life achieving, life winning battles, like a Wellington, a Marlborough, a Livingstone. Life writing poems, like a Tennyson, a Wordsworth, or a David. Life discovering, like a Columbus, a Watt, or a Newton. Is not the chief charm of such lives, after that which they have given us, the sense of power they convey, they rise like buildings, mighty fanes, vast and awful to the eye.

And has it not often occurred to you to notice the difference, the essential difference between what we call a Grecian building like St. Paul's, and a Gothic building like Westminster Abbey. St. Paul's and all like it, doric, ionic, or any such style. How smooth, how untroubled, it looks! how complete, how finished, how elegant, what a unity in it; it says, or seems to say, "I am at home, and I am content;" it is the very architecture of a well-to-do, optimistic citizen. Sometimes it is even grand in its repose of luxurious grace. But the gothic, on the contrary, with its huge shapelessness, its unfinished mysterious infinity of dark and shadowy recesses, where the light lingers, and the worshipper may hide himself from sight, and joy in harmony with the sound of worship. Crocket and wreathed pillars, and sharp acanthus, if found in the gothic, how it says, the whole gothic architecture, "I suffer and I struggle, but I aspire." I never think of it in contrast to the classical, but see how truly ideas write themselves in stone. The Grecian architecture is the very transcript of that mind which, in its sublime indifference and sceptic scorn, reared temples graceful, but irreverent. The gothic has the very imprint of that idea conveyed in those words,—"I came not to send peace on earth, but a sword," it is the offspring and representation of a struggling soul.

This then is the effect of the two architectures of life, this is the result of the two life buildings. " I am at home, I am content," on the contrary, "I suffer, I struggle, but I aspire."

But I have no design this morning to dwell upon those which are the first and most important preparations of all. As Jeremy Taylor says, in his admirable sermon before the University of Dublin, entitled, " Via Intelligentia : showing by what means the Scholar shall become most learned and useful : "—" In this inquiry I must take one thing for a pre-cognitum, that every good man is Theodidaktos—he is taught of God, and, indeed, unless He teach us, we shall make ill scholars ourselves, and worse guides to others. If God teaches, then all is well ; but, if we do not learn wis-dom at His feet, from whence should we have it ? It can come from no other spring ; and, therefore, it naturally fol-lows that, by how much nearer we are to God, by so much shall we be better instructed." On all this it does not need that I dwell at all ; it is by love to God, and the truth of God that we shall become the most able ministers of the New Testament. True ever is it, "Knowledge puffeth up, but love buildeth up ; " and no sermons can edify, and no Scriptures rear up a holy building, except as the love of God is shed abroad in the heart. Let me beg you not to take these words as words of course. Coleridge has well said, "An hour of solitude passed in sincere and earnest prayer, or the conflict with, and conquest over a single pas-sion or subtle bosom sin, will teach us more of thought, will more effectually awaken the faculty, and form the habit of reflection, than a year's study in the schools without them." * Holiness is the best wisdom, and holiness is the surest way of understanding ; and if it be inquired, Is a godly man better able to determine the questions of trans-substantiation or purgatory ? or the chaste man better able to reconcile the casuistries of Hamilton, Cousin, or Kant ?

* Aids to Reflection. Vol. I., 5.

or, is a temperate man a better scholar than a drunkard? I reply, that holiness of life clarifies the instrument of knowledge, and that principle of spiritual discernment by which truths are really known ; this is not always done by what we call helps and aids. Erasmus testifies, that when he first read the New Testament with fear, and a good mind and a purpose to understand it and obey it, he found it very useful and very pleasant ; but, when afterwards he fell on reading the vast differences of commentaries, then he understood it less than he did before, and began not to understand it ; and we ought to remember what Plutarch tells us, that when Eudamidas, the son of Archidamus, heard old Xenocrates disputing about wisdom, he asked very soberly, "If the old man be yet disputing and inquiring concerning wisdom, what time will he have to make use of it ? " This then, is the first thing to attain—a holy wisdom, a wise holiness. Yet, of course, there is a mechanical and material apparatus, with which you should provide yourselves. The chemist has his apparatus, his furnace, his allembics, his phials for the preservation of his essences. He cannot work without them ; he needs his laboratory and the furniture of his laboratory, and the surgeon has his apparatus—he cannot effect his cure without—bright, shining, cruel instruments they are, too ; but the secrets of life and disease would not be laid bare, nor would the disease be arrested without them. Every profession has its apparatus and its tools, more or less simple or complicated— the geologist his little iron mallet ; the bell-founder, his furnace and his fire. The apparatus differs with the work ; the blasting of a mine ; the amputation of an arm ; the grafting of a tree or plant ; the evolution of an essence. What do you seek to do ? In all things this, perhaps, determines the tools and the quantity of them, and we may remember that, "the number of the tools does not give the quality of the work, but the hand and the eye of the workman does." I believe one of the great mistakes of our modern student-life is, that we devote more time and preparation to the tools than to the work. Some foreigner asked Wollaston, the great chemist, to show him his laboratory. He rung the bell, and his servant brought in a common round tray, on which "were a few glasses and a retort or two." "That," said Wollaston, "is my laboratory!" On the contrary, we become confused with the superfluity of our tools. What is all this bathos and cant we hear often, for it is little more, about the "artist"—the artist age. Preachers must be artists! I do declare, I am disposed some times to say with Thomas Carlyle, "May the Devil fly away with the fine arts." We may be sure of this whenever we aim at diction, for its own sake, for instance, we surely miss that for which we aim, and, of course, we miss that to which that aim should be dedicated. Can it be believed that Homer, or Shakespeare, or Milton, or Walter Scott could ever have aimed chiefly and especially at style—style for its own sake? Never! Thought fused their words; thought burnt along their soul; their object was within, beautiful words came inspired by beautiful emotions and beautiful thoughts. So must it ever be; but we, many of us, we are like men troubled about so many things in our serving, that we forget the chief end of our serving. Diction, Elocution, Rhetorical power! We are like men who, before a besieged city, act as if on the parade-ground; a real life and death business is before us, and we are attending to the shape of our epaulettes, the crease of our coat, the glitter of our adornments; and we have our holiday displays, and mock engagements, and trials of skill. We dissipate our energy in our display, and we expect a divine blessing upon our pretty human accomplishments, and our tools seem to be the words of wisdom as man teacheth.* There is danger that these are regarded as our tools then; the expectations

* Dr. Newman's *Lectures on University Subjects,* 190.

of the churches from the ministry are extravagant and pre-
posterous. "Are all pastors and teachers?" said the apostles. "Well," say the churches, "we must have it so.
Every man a pastor and teacher; every man an apostle and
a prophet; every man to do the work of an evangelist,
helps and governments, and diversities of tongues, and
gifts and healings, too, if possible." Although about this
last there may be a little matter of doubt; it must be admitted, for all this a large chest of tools is required.

It follows from this almost of course, that men have come
to believe too much in tools—too exclusively in tools, as if
the tool could do it. Many students act as wisely as he
should who supposed, that having acquired his chest of
tools, and having placed it by the side of the plank of wood
—the wood would start up a table or a chair. No; tools
need hand and eye, force and perception. It is also note-
worthy that often the pulpit artist—if I am to speak of
him thus—deals, almost necessarily, very differently with
his tools, to the way in which other artists deal with theirs.
The young painter is really at his work; his knowledge of
colors, and the effect of form, of light, of shade; his easel,
his palette, his canvas—these are his tools, and he is at work
for the end at which he aims with these. It is so with the
young sculptor; each stroke of his chisel, each mould he
takes—the plaster and the stone, these are all real tools
tending to real effects. Something is done with every lesson; even the little smith or the little carpenter, he is
learning to drive a nail; a grand feat that; to hold and to
use a saw; he has done something to make his work easier, he has real knowledge. Now with the student for the
ministry, this by no means follows, except as he internal-
ises his work. Usually, the student makes the great mistake of supposing that, acquiring the use of tools, he has
acquired his work. Now it is done. No; all has to be
done: he has everything to do; knowledge of languages,

knowledge of history, knowledge of physical science. All these are to be received into a deeper consciousness; they are to lie there, they are to die there, that they may bring forth fruit. It is true of knowledge in the soul, as of many things in the deep words of our Lord, "it is not quickened except it die." As the hills are, on their summits, bleak, and hard, and lifeless, and bare, but washed down by the attritive force of rains and winds; they turn into an alluvial earth and feed the seeds and become the soil over which waves the harvest crop. So facts and truths are dead in themselves; they are hard and stony as mountain chains; but resolved into the soul how different! they become the earth of the soul—they become the soil, nay, they become the very harvest and vintage of the soul. Generally, I expect to find M.A., and B.A., and LL.B.'s, especial dunces to all the higher forms of truth or reading; they have the wood and the tools, and they marvel they do not become tables; perhaps they have used them to make coffins.

Do you know Voltaire's definition of a doctor or physician? "One who pours drugs of which he knows little, into a body of which he knows less." But how often this also might be the definition of a preacher, and how shocking if it should be so; one who pours truths of which he knows little into the souls of which he knows less. We may surely say, this will be the case always, where the tools are regarded more than the work; and yet, let me now say a word from the other side. It is most necessary that we have tools; scholarship, if not our own, then other men's, and that we know how to use other men's. With us, indeed, the relation of the scholar to the preacher is not at all defined. Independents and Baptists have no place for the scholars; we have no foundations, no fellowships, no halls of learning; we have no place of learned leisure to examine. If a man cannot preach, and yet is poor, what can we do with him ? He may be a very Cuvier in his piercing intuitions of insight and wisdom, but he must get his bread in some way, and be distracted with these many cares, and be soured and embittered by the hard crusts of life. Have we not many such, whose accomplishments and genius would have adorned us, but whom we have left to starve without books, without literary society, because they could not preach in such a way as to command a ,congregation able to enable them to live. Yet from such men you will have to derive much ; from their sagacity, from their learning they will furnish you with tools, criticisms, openings of texts, volumes, perhaps which they wrote while almost starving, and which never yielded them a penny. Humble men, some of these have produced books, the mere reading of which has inflated and inflamed the vanity of the talkers ; the men not able to make their own tools, but able admirably to use those placed in their hands. No, let us by no means despise tools and helps. It would be like the contempt Lord Kames expressed for manure. In a conversation with his gardener, he said one day : "George, the time will come when a man shall be able to carry all the manure for an acre of ground in one of his waistcoat pockets." "I believe it, sir," said the gardener, "but he will then be able to carry all the crop in the other." And the truest means is labor, labor, labor—industry, and this will conquer, and this nothing can supersede. I have heard of a bishop who always insisted on the Greek of those he ordained. "They may deceive me," he was wont to say, "when they talk of Christian experience and the divine call, but they cannot deceive me in Greek."

By tools and apparatus, then, I mean the mechanical appliances and helps—always remembering that to the preacher especially may be appropriated the language of the Welsh Triads on Genius. "The three foundations of

10*

genius are the gift of God, human exertion, and the events of life. The first three requisitions of genius are an eye to see nature, a heart to feel it, and a resolution that dares follow it. The three things indispensable to genius are understanding, meditation, and perseverance. The three tokens or proofs of genius are extraordinary understanding, extraordinary conduct, and extraordinary exertions. The three things that improve genius are proper exertion, frequent exertion, and successful exertion." There are things with which the richest, and the most accomplished, and thoroughly furnished mind cannot dispense. Can we do without books? I know the furniture of some noble minds has been in this way but small. I know also that the worth and the wealth of production depends, not upon the multitude of books, but upon the mind working, and the material wrought upon ; and it is sad to think how little any of us have to spend on books, the best of us— excepting one or two instances only—with the salary of a third-rate clerk, and a disposition to dip into all the scholarships beneath the heavens. But we must have books, and if we use them well, and arrange them well, we shall make a few go far, we must make all our books yield. And they will be among our most important tools. Ministers are neither to be bookworms nor librarians. But not to know books, not to have a taste for books, not to love books, not to group the study round with books, this is to cut ourselves off from our heritage in the past, in the distant, in the curious. Books do more ; they bring facts to us ; they draw our nature out of us ; they make us acquainted with ourselves ; they are hints, they are maps. I know how vain they are without a study of human nature too, as Mr. Pycroft says in his "Twenty Years in the Church, "Some country clergyman on being asked whether he studied the Fathers, said no, the fathers were generally at work in the fields, but he always studied the mothers. A mere bookman is not a very high type of being ; but a minister, I say, who does not love books, he cuts himself off from abounding means of instruction and edification, from many a soothing influence at the end of the weary day, and from much happy help and aid in the prosecution of all that work, ever, it is to be supposed, dearest to him. Remembering always that you are ever learning, you will never cease learning ; ages infinite will crowd to your feet with all their treasures, and heavens infinite pour down upon you all their wealth. Of the minister in his study, with holy volumes and meditations, it may especially be said to him are given "the precious things of heaven ; the dew and the deep that coucheth beneath ; the precious fruits brought forth by the sun ; the precious things put forth by the moon ; the chief things of the ancient mountains ; the precious things of the everlasting hills ; the precious things of the earth and the fullness thereof." And, over all, "the good-will of Him that dwelt in the bush."

But this I say of the love of books in general. I may also remark, I trust, with no risk of being misunderstood, that I think it is one of the most healthy, even desirable occupations, for the pastor occasionally to take a book and preach it. A book strikes you ; it holds and rivets you ; it is a powerful, strong, useful book ; the chain of the argument is very interesting to you. You have read it ; you feel that something is won by it. But you feel that something is defective in it. You see over a chapter, it may be ; you look beyond it. Now, if you were a reviewer, you would review that book. But being *only* a minister, you throw it by, and it is soon forgotten. But why not preach it? popularise it unconsciously to your audience? reply to it ; turn it into other language. See, appropriate, enlarge upon its illustrations and its arguments ; there will be no dishonesty here, and much profit. As your taste leads—

and your taste will be very much that of your audience, and that of your audience yours—do this occasionally with the old books and the new. Ah, if you would condense feelingly thus, John Howe's "Blessedness of the Righteous," or "The Vanity of Man as Mortal," or "The Dominion of Christ over the Invisible World," or "The Living Temple ;" or treat thus the essays of Alexander Knox, or the noble work of Edward Irving, on "The Incarnation ;" or to turn back, treat thus Culverwell's "Light of Nature." Suppose you put down, and put into sermons, the magnificent argument of my dear friend, Dr. John Young, "The Christ of History." Only be honest: let all be wrought into the texture of your own mind. Made all yours, and you will soon see how you are acquiring for yourself a large amount of mental furniture, and how you are also enriching your people. And saying this, it is like the same general remarks upon the love of the Scriptures, and the general reading them ; there must be a general love, and a particular love—a love for itself and for its own sake, a love also for its relation to the great and chief end we have in view. I do, undoubtedly, think that the two most valuable acquisitions of the mechanical sort for a minister, are a general love of books, and a good pair of eyes : the power in the first to see things with the eyes of other men ; the power second, to see things with his own. Undoubtedly, I should set the last even higher than the first, but why not both ? why not both ? This last power indeed— the power of a good pair of eyes, is that possessed in so large a measure by WARD BEECHER ; it is this which gives to his sermons that wonderful fulness of illustration which is their chief characteristic. We have this power evidenced in his last published volume, "Eyes and Ears." A charming book, but especially illustrating how sermons may be preached from everything, by a man who has his eyes open. In this volume all the pages are not, of course, of this description, but it is sufficiently illustrative of this, that the preacher is especially to be sure that he has a good pair of eyes. And what sharp-sighted people these masters of fiction are, masters and mistresses too ; how quickly they catch up things. How they see all the sides of things, and the insides of things—and why should not we ? and I have often thought that the very perfection of pulpit talk, when it does not rise above talk, would be the style in the "Recreations of the Country Parson." So homely, so pleasant and cheerful ; it is the talk of a man who has thought a good deal about common things ; and a very large amount of your power over your audience in dealing with the uncommon—the kingdom of distant truths, great truths which you would have your audience to perceive—will arise from your giving them to know that you have touched and handled little ones. Show them that you are well acquainted with the coast and bay, in order that they may trust you when they have with you to put out to the great and wide sea. The tools of your ministry lie all around you. Happy you, to be able to take the commonest thing, and to surround it with a glory, to give a lesson about it that shall abide. Every mean thing, every little thing, every obscure thing, and every human thing, may be a tool with which you work your way to a truth. And for this irresistible force what can be of sufficient power ? "Who," said the apostle, "is sufficient for these things ?" And Horace says, " *Can we expect words to be composed worthy to be preserved in Cedar or in Cypress when once the rust and care of wealth hath tainted the mind.*" Those men preached best who preached even at the stake and in the dungeon. None have transcended him in preaching who "suffered the loss of all things ;" but that which interferes with the settled calm of the mind ; the repose ; the elevation above Easter, and time—all this interferes with the true purchase and power, and is a non-conductor to that

influence which might be immortal leverage. I hope I
shall not touch too closely upon the province of those better able than I am to speak upon the other departments.
Biblical criticism is a tool you must of course make yours ;
it has done wonderful things within the last years, and you
have quite understood me to deprecate the general use of
criticism in the pulpit, but you should none the less use it
for yourselves in private. In this, as in other matters, let
results declare processes, and while you use some old
books, only conditioning their use by judiciousness, you
will not fail to use some new. The criticisms of Olshausen
are usually admirable and simple ; but as the guide to a
method for opening a chapter, I think I must give my
higher word to Lange. He has not, perhaps, the original
grammatical and etymological insight of Olshausen, but
he has a greater variety of useful excellencies, and especially for comparatively unfurnished minds ; and my com-
mendation of Lange to you is also founded on this, that
he, beyond any other critic of his order, combines the three
great departments of the preacher's thought, the critical,
the doctrinal, and the homiletical. Too much we use the
homiletical alone ; but for ourselves, we must use the critical method, and for our hearers we must use the doctrinal. And should there not be caution—*Keep it nine years.*
You have all heard that famous maxim of Horace—*Non-
umque prematur in annum*—"Let it be suppressed for nine
years," and we may act on the spirit of this cautious advice, so far that all new ideas, and strange ideas—all heretical ideas—thoughts and things which jeopardise our
usefulness ; which assault the opinions of ages ; which
seem to contravene the best experience of holy souls and
sainted men—they may possibly be true ; it may be your
duty to publish them ; but, probably, it may not ; therefore—"*Put it by for nine years.*" Another important piece
of apparatus is the close and distinct study of sacred geo-

graphy : this is also light and it is power. Surely, Stanley's *Sinai and Palestine* must be a hand-book to those, too, who have not visited the Holy Land, and this is a study as delightful as it is useful. Use sacred geography, so that in your hands the story lives again, and lives anew. This will give freshness to the history, and it will give vigor, and point, and reality to the picture. I would not have you to be in the pulpit a mere topographer ; but your knowledge may be given in a touch, a hint, setting the scene, as in a stereoscope, to the eye. Without this knowledge a good many references must be quite dark to you. Learn the localities of the tribes. Geography is one of the eyes of history ; the events were what they were because the scenes were also what they were. Realize for yourselves the heights and passes of Benjamin ; the great battle field of Israel ; the ground of Bethhoron ; the Maritime Plain ; the dispositions of the trans-Jordanic tribes, realize all these ; these should live in your eye as in a map. You cannot read with all the interest with which you might, even if you read with all the instruction, unless you use this as one of the tools of your ministry. I will not cite instances, I will simply say, take Stanley's *Sinai and Palestine*, and completely absorb it into your knowledge.

Consider again what are the ways and means of ministerial usefulness. Rather more than one hundred and fifty years have passed away since Dr. Cotton Mather published his *Essays to do Good*. That little valuable suggestive book occupies a place in the literature of benevolent activity similar to that occupied by Watts's *Improvement of the Mind*, in the literature of mental discipline. I suppose it is seldom read, and even not much known ; indeed, the suggestions of its pages have now been incorporated and framed into institutions, but it is still a book to set the right sort of soul on fire ; a noble stimulant to ministerial activity and zeal. Its singularly happy quotations, its anecdotes, its rapid and noble glances of appeal, should have saved it from the neglect into which it has fallen. But, of course, it is easy to perceive that such a book, with all its vivacity, is greatly superseded, and the receipts for the ways to do good now, in our vast populations especially, need at once a comprehensiveness and a concentrativeness to which our fathers, especially one hundred and fifty years since, were strangers. It is true, too, that in doing good in our day, more, perhaps, than at any previous period, the grace and gift of exceeding prudence is needed. There are many persons in our own day prepared to act upon the spirit, if not to use the language of the Ephesians, when they expelled the best of their citizens, "If they are determined to excel their neighbors, let them find another place to do it." Yet says the writer to whom I have referred, Dr. Cotton Mather, "of all the trees in the garden of the Lord, which is there that envies not the palm-tree—out of which alone, as Plutarch informs us, the Babylonians derived more than three hundred commodities—or the cocoa-tree, so beneficial to man that a vessel may be built, and rigged, and freighted, and victualled from that alone—who would not wish to be such trees of righteousness, so planted that 'God may be glorified.'"

Well, ministers are, no doubt, very generally and very eminently expected to be such ; the expectation is not unnatural, it is very natural ; and while it may be quite impossible to be all that the populace demand, it is very possible to be much. And here we cannot but think that we should be very thankful that we are ministers. Does not the office and the position clear the ground for much usefulness? True, we are not clergymen in the mechanical sense of the word ; that office is really imperial. We often envy the clergyman his power : in most instances he uses it, I believe, very badly ; but, how instantly to him all doors fly open, from the highest circle, which is not to be despised, to the lowest, which is to be prized ; all classes are accessible, and he has but to inaugurate any scheme of usefulness, and he meets, of course, with responses. With us it is wholly different ; and, in the more narrowed and confined districts and smaller churches, we have to fight our way through suspicion within, and neglect and contempt without ; this is true, but our ministers have done it, and are doing it.

If we attempted some classification of the ways and means of ministerial usefulness, we should probably find them three-fold—Personal, Pastoral, and Public. *Being* must precede all really efficient *doing.* It seems, no doubt most necessary that for any real measure of usefulness, we keep our own mind at work, the only way by which can be kept a fresh and natural mind ; but this is a great problem how to do this with such incessant taxation of our powers ; reading will not do it alone, and communion with our fellows will soon run us dry, and leave us an unfilled cistern. In order to usefulness, no doubt a very great necessity is health ; sickly people, as a rule, are not good companions for sickly people, and one of the very first conditions of ministration is health. We should aim to get robust souls, we shall find their power will tell in any circle. We can only account for some of the marvels we behold in the way of usefulness thus. We should be otherwise perplexed at it. Our brother, *Persalto* has often amazed us ; we believe there is little in him compared with the wealth of our brother *Tristis*, but Persalto is a healthy brother, and there is such an instinctive apprehension of health in a man ; people are charmed with it, and find it not only desirable, but delightful. Of course we are thinking of natural states ; sentiment delights to contemplate sickliness, just as all morbid people fall in love with deformities. Well, that we may be the ministers of health ourselves, it seems necessary first that we become healthy. Perhaps, as a general principle, it is our *duty* to be healthy, and this is a very necessary kind of word for towns like Brighton, Cheltenham, and fashionable watering-places in general. We believe one of the curses of the Church to be mere sickly sentimental priests—men who minister to, rather than minister to remove, the mental ailments of those who look to them. Many diseases arise from a weight of cares lying on the minds of men, or they are thereby increased ; and there is a mysterious power we know of in conversation—in agreeable, healthy conversation—by which they might be removed. Disorders of the mind first bring diseases of the stomach, and so the whole mass of blood gradually becomes infected, and as long as the mental cause continues, the diseases may, indeed change their forms, but they rarely quit their patients. It is true that a "cheerful heart doeth good like a medicine," and "the fear of the Lord tendeth to life."

Among the ways and means of ministerial usefulness of course, we purposely pass by many ; perhaps, we may say, one of the chief means would be—we speak from experience of the opposite—*the doing few things*, not many things ; we must not pray for the gift of a hundred arms, but for strength for two ; after all, we have only two feet, although a healthy body and a wise walking will make two feet go a great way ; and we have only two hands and ten fingers. My servant, the other day, tried to make them do the work of about four pair of hands, and we had a sad tragedy among plates and sauce : loose holding and management is one of the great causes of failure ; a tight grip is moral power. A good prayer might be, "Lord, I know Thou wilt never give me too much to do ; save me from picking up too many things from a mistaken idea of duty ; help me to narrow my circle, that I may fill it."

We suppose the whole problem of our ministerial life and labors may be expressed in this, how to get to people ; the whole pulpit work comes to that. Schools, classes, and lectures come to that—how to get to people. And it is quite sad to think how many thousands of people we see without ever getting to them. It is a theory of ours, not of course, without some limitations, that, if we were masters of the art and rhetoric of conversation, we should be masters in the pulpit. We are persuaded we do not study and work the mine of conversation as it might be worked ; not with a view to brilliant corruscations of table-talk ; not with a view to the retail of anecdotes ; or, even with a view to the provision of forced meat for the company. Nothing so puts a man upon himself as conversation, in the pulpit we have it all our own way, and we can fine people if they interrupt us ; but in company, if anywhere the opportunity is given to it, if we can avail ourselves of it to get near to people. Mr. Blunt says of pastoral conversation and its power—

That through the medium of such topics, and whilst never exalting them to an undue and dangerous importance, he will frequently be able to give conversation a profitable bias without force or violence ; he will convey to the mind of his more intelligent parishioners purely religious knowledge, without seeming to do so ; without obtruding the preacher on the drawing-room, which might make his good intentions miscarry ; he will leaven the society in which he mixes in private with something of a sober and unworldly spirit ; he will stop out imperceptibly many topics of discussion which, however innocent in themselves, might be frivolous, or which might impart somewhat too much of a secular character to the minister, who partook of them with eagerness ; he will add authority to the direct exercise of his functions as parish priest by such, this extra-official carriage, which will be in harmony with the other ; and last, but not least, he will thus save his pastoral speech from returning to him void, neither touching the heart or head of any man who hears it, for want of some timely angel, in the shape of some such topic as I have supposed, to step down and move the waters.*

* *The Duties of the Parish Priest, &c.* By Rev. J. J. Blunt, D.D.

It is a most strange thing that we can talk in pulpits, on platforms, at lecturers' desks ; we can address juries, and prime ministers, and even majesty itself, and fire off cannonades on the hustings, and would not hesitate even in the senate itself, if we had the chance ; but we cannot talk to each other by the fireside and at the table ; we are afraid of our children and our servants ; and, when we go out to the party, the soul of conversation is strangled in us by our cravat and M. B. waistcoats.

As painters and artists find their hints in every wandering—food for descriptive sketches or studies in every scene —so it is with the preacher ; he a student of human life and character, and he may find the subjects of his own sermons in every visit, in every walk, in every home ; it was so, that Dr. Doddridge used to say, when thoughts and criticism were too much for him, he went off and walked through the streets of Northampton, to talk to some of his old women or old members. There are volumes which are a rich repertory of this kind of pastoral experience— such as *Spencer's Pastoral Sketches*, or *Dr. M. Gavin's Scenes and Characters in a Scottish Pastorate*, or *Dr. Liefchild's Selection of Remarkable Facts*—instances selected from the visitations and results of his ministry. I have said that a sermon may be obtained from an intercourse with the very humblest mind ; and there is an illustration of this in Dr. Liefchild's interview with a poor lad he met among the mountains of Ireland—one eleven or twelve years of age— poorly clad, no covering for his head, no shoes or stockings —but with a mild and cheerful countenance, and with a New Testament in his hand, keeping the gate of entrance to one of the richest and more magnificent views. " Can you read ? " said the Doctor.

" To be sure I can."

" And do you understand what you read ? "

" A little."

" Let us hear you;" and I turned his attention to the third chapter of the Gospel of John, which he seemed readily to find, and said, " Now read." He did so with a clear unembarrassed voice—'There was a man of the Pharisees named Nicodemus a ruler of the Jews; the same came to Jesus by night and said unto Him,—Rabbi.'"

" What does that mean?"

" It means *Master.* 'We know Thou art a teacher come from God, for no man can do these miracles that Thou doest, except God be with him.'"

" What is a *miracle?*"

" It is a *great wonder.* 'Jesus answered and said unto him, Verily, verily, I say unto thee.'"

" What does 'verily' signify?"

" It means 'indeed.' 'Except a man be born again.'"

" What is that?"

" It means," he promptly replied, " a great change! 'Except a man be born again, he cannot see the Kingdom of God.'"

" And what is that Kingdom?"

He paused, and with an expression of seriousness and devotion which I shall never forget, placing his hand upon his bosom, he said, " It *is something here!*" And then raising his eyes he added, " And *something up yonder.*"

And who that has visited the homes of the people does not know how often such a happy kind of thought has struck a refreshing light into the heart of the pastor.*

* Scarcely impertinent to the matter of this lecture, and the remarks of this text will it be, if I print here some outlines of a sermon I preached some little time since on Table Talk,

"A GOOD CONVERSATION." JAMES iii. 13.

A rare thing, whether we interpret the words of that general and most comprehensive conversation, our neighborly civility and conduct among men; or, whether we interpret it of that life of words which flows on in intercourse with each other. I intend to use the words for the purpose of suggesting some hints upon the latter and

I am afraid our ideas are not very high. That was a high character Cranmer gave for a minister he designed for preferment. "He seeks for nothing, he longs for nothing, he dreams about nothing but Jesus Christ." Our aims are low ; we think of the visit, the sermon, the meeting, the reading ; we do not think of that which should consecrate and crown all, and so we fail in all, and we are not religious enough in our efforts. Is it not true that we are afraid, may we not all plead verily guilty to that? We are afraid of being charged with obtruding religion ; our business that to which we have been set apart, is to insinuate religion upon people's regard. We fear we do not root and ground people in the truth, our Sabbath-schools, and our

less regarded subject, for, indeed, a good conversation is one of the rarest luxuries, certainly now-a-days. Our fathers were our superiors in both the art of letter-writing and the art of conversation. "We hold our speech even from good," and this is bad.

We have surely, for many reasons, become more self-contained and reserved ; we do not freshen ourselves and each other with the spray of free speech. We do little with our speech compared to what we ought to do—it is stilted, narrow, and confined. We have little intercourse and communion with each other's souls, yet I suppose all the intercourse of this kind on the earth is to be found in the church for the church was greatly designed to aid the life of souls with this very mental communion. In the world, I say there is little or none of it ; some talk of actresses and hounds, a little talk of politicians and horses make up the life of the table. It should not be so with us. We may remember that speech is a divine gift, a channel for the dissemination of knowledge and goodness ; but it is difficult to elicit speech, for the most part we cannot talk at all, or one has to talk alone. Yet, what a true characteristic that is of the earnest heart or the earnest age, "They that feared the Lord spake often one to another." Our praying together springs from this sense of divine fellowship, this opening of the heart, the inauguration of all the great religious movements has began thus ; thus they maintained much of their earnestness and life ; thus they grew ; thus they kept the spirit healthy and fresh ; personal religion and denominational zeal are greatly dependent on "a good conversation."

families. When we were boys we learnt through several times the Assembly's catechism, with the proofs. We have now a morbid horror of catechisms ; they are never introduced into our Sabbath-schools. Is this wise ? In consequence of this, are not our instructions there inorganic, unrelated, incoherent ? In fact, do we not feel the need of discipline in our instruction altogether ? Would not the effect be good if we kept in our mind a course of sermons, on some such system as the Assembly's Catechism, keeping the organism out of sight? should we not find that we distributed a large amount of religious doctrine ? And, if our fathers err from too much of this, do we not err from too little ?

The highest efforts of the pulpit seem to me to be best described by the term, " a good conversation ;" not the remote and foreign talk of stately periods, and lofty Chatham-like harangues, in which the spirit stands astonished as in a thunderstorm, and the fright is the principal part of the impression, but a quiet stream of personal talk in which speaker and hearer realize their unity and nearness—how much better to insinuate oneself as by the fireside, than to create a marvel in the soul. " A good conversation has four characteristics " which make it good.

I. " The characters who engage in it." We should scarcely call that a good conversation in which worthless men engaged, or were introduced to each other, for conversation flows from the life. As we have read, " Out of the abundance of the mouth the heart speaketh "—true, a full heart does not always imply a fluent tongue —far from that—but the character of the tongue is in the heart. David said, " My heart is ' inditing,' and I will speak, my heart is boiling within me and I will speak ;" and, indeed, we know that evil character possesses the power to dry up the fountains of holy conversation, to check the stream of prayer at its bound and flow. " Every affection has its proper voice and dialect," and " we cannot but speak the things which we have both heard and seen," so the love of Christ constraineth us, this gives the character when the true people of God meet together, they may sit in silence neither singing nor praying, but there have been circumstances when even this has not prevented the sense of the good conversation. It is not

That is a healthy essay in the *Recreations of a Country Parson*, "concerning giving up and coming down." The great lesson he lays down for the wise and true man is the learning through life how to come down without giving up all. Our temptations lie in the direction of giving up if unsuccessful, if we don't succeed in effecting that piece of work, or reaching that character. We do not sufficiently remember that there is a way to reach everybody and to do everything; and because we *have* failed it is by no means certain that we *must* fail. He was a wise man who fixed his mind upon the most stupid of his auditors, and fixed his arguments and illustrations, his persuasions, and his intentions upon him. He was a lecturer upon chemistry, too;

to be thought that there was much conversation when the Lord and His Apostles met together in the bright cloud and on the hills, and Peter exclaimed, " It is good to be here.

II. The second characteristic of a good conversation is " the topic," and we have often felt that this will charm us even when the words do not move freely on the hinges and gates of ideas. How some subjects charm! how fresh they are! how good! how ever new and young! we recur to them again and again. The oldest topics are the best; those of which Moses talked with the shepherds of Jethro—those of which Abraham talked beneath the oak of Hebron —most conversations so called great, do not seem to me so. How poor, looked at thus, the talk of Sydney Smith; among talkers, he seems to me what Ingoldsy is to me among poets; it is a kind of nonsense conversation, scarcely worthy to be called innocent sheet-lightning of talk. Perhaps not useless, either. How different to Luther's talk or Coleridge's!

III. Characteristic, the conduct of it, when grace is poured into the lips, when as the Apostle says, " the speech is with grace seasoned with salt." This is even still more difficult, for we taint our speech with asperity, we fly from the main and central thought to our own little griefs, arrogancy, we become egotists. Matthew Henry says, "Our conversation need not always be of grace, but it can always be with grace."

IV. The " effect," what has been its effect? How has it found us, how left us ?

and he found that when he had succeeded with his stupid auditor he had not only won the perceptions, but the affections and the interests of his whole audience.

There are books to which I call your attention, written, of course, by clergymen for clergymen, but they may be read by Nonconformist ministers with profit. There is method, and scholarship, and grasp of thought, in Mr. Blunt's book, which render it a deeply interesting treatise. I do not know a more competent work upon the subject to which it refers. I believe the excellent author has gone to that kingdom where even Churchmen acquire in the new atmosphere large hearts, or we should have taken occasion to remark upon the singular impudence of those passages in which he refers to that odious thing—Dissent. Certainly, Congregationalists have never had to feel that they halt behind the ministers of the Establishment in power ; nay, but in a few rare instances, the Establishment has to feel that its power in the pulpit is poverty compared with that of ministers of the Baptist and Independent denominations. The following is an interesting passage :

And if there is one thing more than another that fosters Dissent, it is this that, practically, men see no great difference between the preacher in the church and the preacher in the chapel. The bulk of the people are not as yet in a condition to appreciate the argument of the Apostolical Succession ; to understand the commission of the clergy ; the power of binding and loosing conveyed to them ; the influence such prerogative may have upon the soundness or unsoundness of the sacraments administered. They observe the two divines dressed in the same way, both wearing black coats ; called both by the same name of reverend, and, sometimes, with the same or similar symbolical letters attached to it : both apparently acquainted, and, perhaps, equally so with the English of Macknight, Doddridge, or Matthew Henry ; both handling their sermons much after the same manner, suppressing by common consent, all allusions to a church or a schism from it ; and, on the whole, not feeding any hearer whatever to

11

despair, either from the attainments he would have to acquire or the barriers he would have to break through of being a preacher himself, if other resources failed him. What wonder then that the church and the chapel should be confounded by vast numbers of the people; or, what wonder that they should see a difference in their structure, steeple or no steeple, decorations, surplice or no surplice, and there stop?

But, let a minister have the knowledge I presume; let him be perceived to be drawing out of that stock; and it will at once be admitted by all who come into the Assembly, that worthy is that man to sit in Moses' chair, and "they will fall down and worship God, and report that God is in it of a truth." It will be seen by the simplest, that he has precious funds out of which he dispenses; that his Hebrew, Greek, and Latin, which he had spent the first and best twenty years of his life in acquiring, have not been lost upon him; but, that they are the safe scaffolding on which he has reared, and is still rearing, his knowledge of geology; and, that the structure is sound, substantial, and massive; such as the Dissenting minister in general, with no such framework at all to aid him, cannot attain unto or approach, be his zeal and talents what they may. Then will the people not fail to discover, and to remark it, that the grace accompanying the imposition of hands by the bishop, which they may have hitherto disputed (for they believed it not, because they could not see it, neither know it), is seconded and confirmed by what they *can* bear witness to—(though not in itself more real)—genuine knowledge in the man.

" What would many a Dissenting teacher give for the scholarly knowledge of languages, which numbers of our young clergy carry with them to their curacies from this place, and then, alas ! never turn to the slightest account all their days "—unconscious apparently of the treasury they possess (though one would think they might remember how long and how hard they had wrought for it), and, like the Æthiop, inconsiderately casting away a pearl. "How is the want of it manifest even in the most remarkable man the Dissenters have perhaps had amongst them, in later times at least,—Robert Hall ! "

A precious passage, truly, and much Mr. Blunt could have

known of Robert Hall and his life, his studies, and his attainments ; of whom, in his university it was said, he was the Plato, as his fellow-student Sir James Macintosh, was the Herodotus of his college, from their fondness for, and intimacy with, masters of old Grecian thought and narrative. But it pleases Churchmen to pat each other thus generously on the back, and it pleases us to laugh at it. For ourselves, we shall refuse to admit the vast superiority of these men. We have ourselves conversed with too many Greek dunces and Latin coxcombs not to know that a man may acquire a knowledge, a paltry knowledge of a few classical authors, at the expense of all the little common sense with which nature endowed him.

Mr. Blunt's book is very learned in the knowledge of the good things provided for his church ; but there is another side to the matter, which I may touch without, I hope, exposing myself to the charge of mere sectarianism.

I was so fortunate the other day in the course of a ramble into Yorkshire, as to alight upon one of the most remarkable, of the many remarkable sermons it has been my fatality to peruse. It appears to have been preached not very long since, in the parish church of Howden, by its then curate, who is, also, the master of its Grammar School, the Rev. Samuel Secretan, B.A., and the delectable little *brochure* carries the information upon its title-page that its treasures are to be obtained for the sum of six pennies. Those bishops who hold the pastoral crook over the sheep and shepherds of the Church of England, delegate the functions of the shepherd to strangely qualified characters. I have often had occasion to marvel at the wondrous teachers ordained and set apart to the task of instructing, but I never felt a disposition to marvel more loudly than when I read the performance of Mr. Secretan. What adds to the interest of the performance is, that several of his hearers, the parishioners had expressed dissatisfaction at the strange, obfuscatory character of his elucidations and emendations of Divine truth when, in simple self-defence, the good young man published the remarkable performance into which I have struck my fangs. In the sermon, Mr. Secretan boasts very loudly of his Greek and Hebrew ; and informs his hearers, that the meaning of Scripture depends upon a Hebrew or Greek dictionary. How far he is acquainted with the German lights we know not, but, before his astonished hearers, and in the pages of this astonishing sermon, he most certainly out-Hegels Hegel, out-Schellings Schelling, and out-Strausses Strausse ; in fact, the sermon—which seems to be on no subject or topic, or text either, in particular, *Genesis, chapter* i. being the somewhat liberal allowance of Scripture he sets before himself to open—the sermon, I say, is that veritable old hag, Atheism, dressed up in gown and bands, made sacerdotal, and led to bob about her old skeleton in all the gimcrackery of scholastic bathos. That I do not express myself too severely, may be seen by the following :

We are soon struck with the peculiar manner in which Moses speaks of the Elohim—the reverences. He speaks of those spiritualities as if they were a person. He supposes them to possess bodily organs ; such as the tongue and the eye. This appears in the words " Elohim said "—*Reverence said*. "Elohim saw that it was good."

I am not pretending to explain that spirit which, under the name of Elohim—reverences—is stated by Moses to have created the heavens and the earth. Far from it. But I only submit to you the necessity of remembering that as the Creator is a spirit, having no body, or parts, *He has no tongue, nor eye, and consequently cannot speak or see.*

I will not draw your attention to the words—the Spirit of the Elohim moved upon the waters. This I would attempt to explain thus :—That agency, of which Moses had so grand a conception, that he gave it the name of reverence, mysteriously operated in the formation of physical matter. In other words, the wind, the breath, the principle of life, which abstract qualities such as reverence must have, exerted itself in the work of creation. *The breath of abstract ideas—the life of the spirit consists of wisdom, excellence, power. These brooded over nothing—and lo! the heavens and the earth.**

I must, however, quote one other paragraph :—

I believe that the terms now used in reference to the Creator, whom we ought to reverence, worshiping the spirit of understanding, excellency, power ;—honoring, that is, whatsoever is spiritual, intellectual, pure, moral, noble—are the terms conveying best the idea which Moses had of the Creator. And, if we descend to later times, to those of the writers of the New Testament, I think we get another idea still of the Hebrew word Elohim. We get the idea of the Greek word Theos, which is supposed to come from the word *theo*, to set in order, to arrange. The three languages together—the Hebrew, the Greek, the Saxon—Elohim, Theos, God—Reverence, Arranger, Goodness—impress our minds with the high worth that the Creator Spirit has —of the indisputable claim which he has upon our sympathy and devotion !

Let us take a passage of St. Paul to the Corinthians, in which the Greek word Theos, Arranger, occurs, and let us substitute the Hebrew idea for that Greek idea, and notice how the passage reads. Let us select this passage—" Know ye not that ye are the temple of God, and that the Spirit of God dwelleth in you; if any man defile the temple of God, him shall God destroy: for the temple of God is holy, which temple ye are. Now, instead of the Saxon idea of Goodness attributed to the Spirit here referred to, substitute the Hebrew idea of Reverence—*i. e.*, high spiritual qualities, worthy of reverence ;—" Know ye not that ye are the temple of high spiritual qualities, worthy of reverence ; and that the spirit of these qualities dwelleth in you : ' if any man defile the temple of these high spiritual qualities,

---

* I of course plead guilty to the italicising the words in the foregoing quotation. I am desirous that the rich eloquence of so beautiful a paragraph should not be lost upon my readers.

him will these spiritual qualities destroy.'" To me this seems a deeply sensible reading of the passage. High spiritual qualities, worthy of reverence, dwell in man. If you defile your understandings, your excellence, your power, they will defile you. Privileges abused become their own Nemesis—avenger. Your spiritual qualities will become that two-edged sword—a remorseful conscience. These high spiritual qualities, worthy of reverence, that dwell in you in this gospel age, are the perfume of Christ. They are a sweet savour or perfume, though you abuse them. They are a sweet perfume in those that are being saved, and in those that are perishing. In you that are being saved is made manifest the savour or perfume of Christ's knowledge. In you that are perishing is still the perfume of Christ's knowledge—still there, hoping, and knocking, and warning, and assisting.

What more useful, and therefore I must think Scriptural, advice can I give than that we take care of " those high spiritual qualities, worthy of reverence, which dwell in us—created at first with a shadow of them—in their likeness—and renewed into them now by the sweet savour of Christ's knowledge. Taking this care of them because they are the representatives in us of that Great Unknown Creator Spirit, whose earliest name in the Scripture is Reverence."

Such are specimens of this astounding utterance, delivered in the venerable church of the small old town in the east riding of Yorkshire. An intelligent little town. I have had some knowledge of, and affection for it for nearly twenty years ; but whatever may be the mental calibre of the town in general, you may conceive the utter bewilderment of the upturned eyes and wide open mouths of farmers and laborers, and artizans, at these amazing discourses from the oracle of Mudfog. For myself, I may tremble lest Mr. Secretan should issue an injunction against me for printing the whole of his sermon ; the extracts will not seem to you lengthy, but I assure you that I have quoted the greater part of the published sermon. Mr. Secretan,

heretic as he is to his prayer-book and his creed, is ortho-
dox enough as to time ; to think of it, that a man cannot
talk for more than a quarter of an hour, and scarce a syllable of sense in the whole fifteen minutes ; and Mr. Secretan is an ordained clergyman and faithful watch-dog of
the Church of England, one who would receive Mr. Blunt's
commendations as "possessing a structure of knowledge
substantial and massive," such as no Dissenting minister,
"not even Robert Hall, can attain unto or approach."
Once more I say—What will these bishops ordain next?
I should like to know whose were the episcopal hands
whose fingers transferred power and light to that much-
thinking and penetrative brain. I should be curious to
know the name of the chaplain who examined him for ordination. Certainly he could not say, "Thine eyes shall
see thy teachers," here is "false doctrine, heresy, and
schism ;" and it will be well to recollect that, in Paul's
view, there was no schism like that of "not holding the
head." Yet it is probable that Mr. Secretan is not much
more heretical than many of that theological school he
represents.[*] I suppose he would pass muster with many a
clergyman better known, and occupying a far higher position in the establishment as a Broad Churchman. Many
of these gentlemen seem to allow for their theology a margin of uncommon breadth. Perhaps most of them would
be more at home in Mr. Secretan's region of "Abstract
ideas," than among explicit texts and statements. Like
our singular and eccentric Yorkshire curate, their minds
seem to be either possessed by, or in the possession of (it
really does not matter which), a vast number of incogniz-
able, inexplicable, and inexpressible ideas, not particularly
edifying to themselves, and utterly worthless, for all purposes of edification to their hearers. It really was a very
wise thing in the Church of the Establishment, when it
was first settled on something like a solid basis, to provide

for the exigencies of religious clerical ignorance, or egre-
gious clerical heresy, by the publication of the *Homilies*,
though this did not always avail, as you will very well recollect in the instance of the erudite clergyman of the last
century, who got hold of a volume of *Comedies* instead of
Homilies, and read one off for the practical edification of
his interested audience. I sometimes think, amidst the
entanglements of clerical wisdom or folly, it would be well
if the Bishops saw a little more vigilantly into the reading of these *Homilies*, or parts of them, to congregations.
It would appear that the Privy Council never had much
faith in the average gifts of the clergy. We poor Congregationalists have had strange people amongst our teachers
—blacksmiths and shoemakers—so at any rate say the
members of the Establishment—tinkers and sweeps ; but,
whatever may have been the depth of social ignorance
from which our preachers have emerged, it has never been
necessary to provide them with a volume of sermons, because they could not make a deliverance of some kind for
themselves ; not that we are disposed to harp too much
upon this as a very peculiar excellence. I have even sometimes thought it might be well to prepare, compile, and
publish some volumes of sermons, which might be recommended to the innumerable, incompetent heads we have
amongst us. I have long felt how great a calamity it is,
while our shelves are crowded with admirable sermons
suited to every capacity, with all the pith and power of
puritanism, or the music and majesty of the great masters
of mind and diction, our congregations should be compelled to listen to long discourses from that remarkable
preacher, Dr. Windy Doctrine, or his equally eminent
brother-in-law, the Rev. Cloudy Screech. It has occurred
to us, that it would sometimes be a good thing to call upon a brother, and put into his hands a piece of old Thomas
Watson, or Thomas Adams, or Brooks, or perhaps old

John Stoughton, and say to him—"It must be very clear to you, you have nothing very distinct to say to your people from yourself, this is Monday—now take this, read it over twice every day; here is material for two sermons" (for people were not only better preachers, but better listeners two hundred years ago), "drill this thoroughly into you, and then go you up next Sunday into your pulpit and give it to your people—they will thank you—the probability is they will understand you, or the stupidity will be on their part." Such reflections have passed through our minds as we have meditated the performance of Mr. Secretan.

But his words led us out upon another track of thinking —the Howden preacher is not the only one, nor does he belong to the only order of preachers who seem to conceive themselves set apart to form the "cloud" for the second advent. Many are they who do very little to prepare the way of the Lord, but who, whenever they begin to speak, instinctively stir upon our lips the exclamation, "*Behold, He cometh with clouds!*" We have come, at last, to that time when there has been created the church of involved meanings, the church in the clouds, yet distinct enunciation of meaning in prayer, and in preaching is the only means our people have of being reached in their consciousness. We live in a perfect whirlpool of opinion; on every hand we are met by cloudy expressions or cloudy sentiments, through which ordinary minds find difficulty in disentangling their way. Thus we have, on one side, Mr. Secretan and his whole school—*to whom, of course, God, the Saviour, the church, and the soul, are the only terms for abstract ideas;* and, on the other hand, that mountain of iron, that loadstone pillar, to which such writers as Dr. Newman and his church would conduct us, to be held there by the attraction of cohesion, with all and every kind of substance, servile enough to prostrate the will in obedience

11*

before its magnetic attraction. But too much of this—
only it singularly illustrates Mr. Blunt's "sound, substantial, and massive structure" of the average clerical mind.

We might feel that we shall increase our usefulness if
we keep out of the way of clergymen of all sorts. We
shall rarely meet them without a latent misprision of insult
being very present with them. As a rule we may say of
them as God said of Israel, "Your ways are not my ways,
nor your thoughts my thoughts." We should have no objection to continue the quotation, but we forbear. We
may be charged with sectarianism, but our communion
will grow; in fact, when we had less to do with the clergyman we were stronger than now. We ought to maintain
the essential distinction between the Establishment and
ourselves. The doctrine of apostolical succession and the
doctrine of baptismal regeneration are the badges upon a
superstitious livery which it should be our object not to
flatter and fawn upon, but to mark and distinguish as the
sign and token of unwaverings. During the last few years
we have had poured upon us a torrent of insolence of a
most remarkable character from the *Tracts for Priests and
People* from the Rev. Mr. Ryle, from Rev. Mr. Brooks, in
his prophetic interpretation, and from Archdeacon Sand-
ford and the Bishop of Oxford.

Mr. Monro's book* is very interesting; it seems also to
us to contain more spiritual freedom than the volume of
Mr. Blunt, as it certainly is more pleasantly written. It
really deals with the homely aspects of pastoral visitation.
It has not the dignified reticence of the Professor's chair.
It is too discursive, but it contains admirable hints to
preachers upon the desirableness of combining, with hints
for the method of accomplishing the combination of a
knowledge of life by the fireside with power in the pulpit.

* *Pastoral Life. The Clergyman at Home and in the Pulpit.* By
Rev. E. Monro.

The simple difference between the two books is, that Mr. Blunt writes like a professor bent on maintaining untouched the dignity of the Ecclesiastical office, while Mr. Monro, very likely quite as high in Church notions, writes like a man only desirous to reach people; he writes also like a man who, as a minister of some small village, has made himself acquainted with the inside of his parishioners' homes. Mr. Blunt's book is undoubtedly more systematic; has more breadth of acquaintance with the subject, while Mr. Monro's book overflows with geniality and sympathy, some readers will say with too poetic a cast of expression. Mr. Monro has not sufficiently guarded and informed some of his expressions. He refers at great length to the influence of natural scenery in forming the mind of the pastor and the preacher. We quite go with him as to its importance in forming a strong and perfect character. He illustrates his position thus :—

It is certainly true and remarkable, that one man who has the power of originality will go into a cottage, and with saying "very little," not "reading the Bible aloud," "doing" scarcely anything, not giving a penny, will come out having done a work and effected a result, which other men who have not that power, with an hour's hard work in the same cottage, reading half an Epistle through, lending tracts in large print fresh from the Christian Knowledge Society, talking, arguing, reasoning, and giving half a crown to boot, will not effect. What is this power?

First, there will be "pictorial" power in the person possessing the genius for parish work. You are called to a cottage. You have known it for years. A boy of sixteen is dying there. The cottage is one of two. It stands down a lane: a lane whose hedges offer homes for the birds in summer, and whose hawthorns the woodbine crowns in July. The ruts are deep, and on either side the green sward covered over with the weeds of June glows the sunshine, or repose the deepest shadows. There by a pond groups of children play the year round. The early light is greeted by their merry laugh: the hot June day finds them wading up the stream in the cool water: September knows the stretching out of eager hands to catch the berries for a Michaelmas crown: or in winter, the happy groups gather on the ice to slide away their brief holiday,—the same troop all the year round. And that dying boy was one of the little company: known in that lane, and known so well nowhere else in the village: he knew it from infancy, and knew no other. He is dying; and he loves the lane; and as he is propped up in bed his eye rests on the hedge opposite, and the sunset behind it, and he hears the shout of children through the open window, and he longs to be with them. But he smiles patiently, and is glad to see you; you come to pray with him, and speak of heaven; he knows he will not live, but he has been long getting ready. The furniture in the bedroom is all part of his history, known from childhood, no more and no less than what it is now; the stump bedstead, the two chairs, the table between the fireplace and the window, the white-washed wall, and the great spot of damp in the corner, which always has been there, only it gets a little larger; the oak chest by the side of the bed, with its odd quaint carvings, half pomegranate, half seraphim. You go on visiting him till he dies; and he dies, and you kneel with his sorrowing parent by the bed, and speak of heaven, and go out into the lane where he played; and then the funeral goes along it, and the coffin is carried under the hedge, and the children, old playmates, gaze in wonder. All is over, and whenever you go into that lane, you think of that boy.

Now I mean, the power to realize and grasp all this by the "pictorial power." Of course I have described a commonplace state of such things; such an event as any clergyman in Hertfordshire, Shropshire, Buckinghamshire, or any agricultural country, must well know occurs continually. But the power to "feel" it all, to see it in that way, to appreciate it, to be under its influence, *that* shows the pictorial mind of which I am speaking, and which I conceive to be a part of the "parochial genius."

Now, admirable as all this is, we should scarcely have called this pictorial power, and in calling it so, Mr. Monro puts the lesser for the greater ; he might as well say a poet is a man who used words ; he does so because he is a master of their meaning, and has a knowledge of things. Could not our writer have used the old words, sympathy, humanity. It is sympathy which gives this fellowship with nature, and scenery, and man, which is the source and secret of all pastoral power. It is, no doubt, true power, real power ; but probably for a hundred men able to preach, there is not one who is able to grasp the work of the pastor ; it is closer, deeper ; it cannot admit of mere generalities, and probably, as Mr. Monro intimates, every man profoundly affected by the moods and changes of nature, will be also as profoundly affected by the moods and changes of the human soul. Death and birth, sorrow and joy, will be very touching to such a heart; the one sympathy will aid, will illustrate, and set off the other. I have myself been very conscious of this on many occasions very impressive to me. I remember myself being called to a midnight death-bed. Among the solitary and wild hills, a member of my church was in her last moments. She died in my arms. I stepped out of the house ; the flickering light trembling through the window, the thought of what was behind that curtained window, then the tall black hills, the valleys, and the heavens, and the unreplying stars, gave to me a sense of power and awe I have not often realized. Once more, in one of the wild regions of Cumberland, I remember having, late in the afternoon, climbed one of the tallest of the hills. The sun was setting, I went down over the gloomy scenery, and I was alone with the evening and the night ; a sense of dreadful desolation overmastered me, until, looking over the crag, I saw beneath me the pathway which had been trodden that day by men and sheep, to be trodden also to-morrow ; and that pathway brought me back again to freshness and life. I have no doubt that man gives the key to nature. Nature is only significant by man ; and I believe this is what Mr. Monro really means by the pictorial power ; it is that sense of sympathy which takes in and relates itself to all particulars, and invests all tenderly with the consecrating charm of all.

But I must close, and my last words shall be words I love to think of, the last prayer of the great and good, the loving and beloved, Dr. Arnold, only written in his journal an hour or two before his death :—" Above all, let me mind my own personal work, keep myself pure, and zealous, and believing ; *laboring to do God's work, yet not anxious that it should be done by me rather than by others if God disapprove my doing it.*"

PULPIT MONOGRAPHS.

IV.—The Abbe Lacordaire and Thomas Binney.

MONG the great masters in the pulpit, such a man as Lacordaire presents very special claims to observation, and even to admiration. When he died, the *Saturday Review*, with a maliciousness all its own, tortured some of the words of the orator to pronounce its verdict upon him, as "one only not monstrous, because ludicrous;" it represented him as speaking of human reason as the "daughter of nothing." "A power which, originating in the demon, is incompatible with faith, which is of God." It is very pleasant and quite illustrative of the character of the *Saturday Review*, that these things were said by Lacordaire, not of human reason at all, but of rationalism, which is a very different thing. There are points in the character and work of Lacordaire which Protestant as well as Catholic may admire. When twenty thousand people gathered round his remains, in his monastic retreat at Soreze, a poor woman pronounced perhaps the finest funeral oration, when she said, "We had a king, and we have lost him." A great, eloquent, singularly impulsive and free nature, he filled for a considerable time a large space, especially in the thought

(255)

of the young intelligent mind of France, or of Paris, which is all that France seems to have of France. He was born the beginning of this century, about the year 1802. He was the son of a village doctor, brought up by a pious mother. He lost his faith at college, became a deist ; at the same time the passionate love for liberty and free institutions, especially characteristic of the mind of France at that time, hung round his soul those generous illusions, and penetrated him with those noble convictions, which perhaps assisted in the work of his salvation, and certainly never deserted him. In morals and in manners he seems to have been always pure, and at about the age of twenty he became the subject of conversion ; he used to say, that of it "neither man nor book was the instrument ; a sudden and secret stroke of grace opened his eyes to the nothingness of irreligion ;" in a single day he became a believer, and wished to become a priest, and he henceforth walked along a distinct and dignified path in harmony with the convictions of that day. Before this he had passed his college course, and qualified himself for a barrister,—a qualification of some importance to him before long. He became a Seminarist of St. Sulpice, was ordained a priest in 1827—Confessor of Nuns in 1828. Soon after this came the crisis of his life ; he became the intimate friend, companion and co-laborateur of the unhappy Abbé de la Mennais, a spirit who, with the best intentions, has done as much as any teacher to give vitality to the devils of infidelity in our day. At this time, however, his principles were not so distinctly marked ; it was not until Lacordaire had entirely separated from him, that De la Mennais published *The Words of a Believer*. At this time he was, perhaps, the most celebrated and venerated of the French clergy, Lacordaire, utterly obscure and unknown, and not more than half the age of De la Mennais ; together they started the *Avenir*, with the purpose of teach-

ing Catholics to look up to liberal institutions and ideas
for weapons by which their Church might become free.
The eloquence of the young priest soon made him remarkable. He also very soon came into contact with the func-
tionaries of the illiberal government; he was brought
several times before the Court of Correctional Police,
sometimes as a defendant, sometimes where his friends
and principles were involved as counsel.

Count de Montalembert says, he well remembers the
surprise of the President of the Court one day, on finding at the bar, dressed in his barrister's gown, the priest
named in the indictment; but this was prevented at last
by the Council of Discipline, although for some time he
made these occasional advents, in which he bothered counsel, and electrified his audience. One day a Crown lawyer
said, "Roman Catholic priests were the ministers of a
foreign power." Lacordaire started to his feet immediately, exclaiming, "We are the ministers of One who is a
foreigner nowhere—of God!" At that time no persons
were so unpopular in Paris as the clergy; but the Court
burst into a cheer, and one voice cried out, "Your name,
young priest, your name. You are a fine fellow!" By
and by he was called to a higher court for denouncing
government somewhat severely in its nomination of three
bishops. In 1831 he, with M. de la Mennais, was indicted
by government before the Court of Assize. His coadjutor
employed able and effective counsel, but Lacordaire appeared again as his own; his speech was certainly a remarkable and bold one; he interwove with it somewhat
of the story from the context, scarcely irrelevant, of his
own conversion; and certainly the course of his argument
was one with which Nonconformists in this country may
have profound sympathy, it was a protest upon the danger
of the appointment of officers of religion by the civil power;
the Attorney-General had laid stress upon the term *oppres-*

sors, applied by Lacordaire to the government. Lacordaire exclaimed :

Our oppressors ! The expression has hurt you. You have called me to account for it; you have looked at my hands to see whether they were bruised by manacles. My hands are free, Mr. Attorney-General, but my hands are not myself. Myself, is my thought, my speech, and know it, this self is fettered in my country. You do not, indeed, bind my hands; and even did you, the matter would be but a trifling one. But if you do not tie up my hands, you shackle my thought, you do not allow me to teach—me, to whom it has been said "*Docete.*" The seal of your laws is upon my lips, when will it be broken ? I have consequently called you my oppressors, and I dread bishops from your hand !

It was a trial in the cause of freedom. At midnight both the defendants were acquitted ; the crowds surrounded and cheered the victors. Count de Montalembert, a very young man then, lingers with pathetic affectionateness upon his walk home that night, along the quays and banks of the Seine, with his beloved friend, congratulating him and hailing him as the future orator. In fact, we linger with a great deal of pleasure ourselves, upon the work the young priest was doing. The Government Inspector had ordered that some choristers should be sent away, and not receive gratuitous instruction ; it seemed to Lacordaire, and his friends, Montalembert and De la Mennais, that this was an occasion for putting the rights of the citizens to a test ; they constituted themselves an agency for the defence of religious liberty. Lacordaire announced in the *Avenir*, that "seeing liberty was not given, it must be taken :" so the three of them opened a free school in 1831, having given notice to the Prefect of Police ; each of them having gathered together, taught a class of about twenty children. In a few days came the Commissary, and ordered them all to quit. He first began with the children, saying : "In the name of the law I summon you to leave." The Abbé Lacordaire said : "In the name of your parents, whose authority I hold, I order you to stay." The little rebels cried out, "We will stay." Easier said than done. The police forced both children and masters to leave. Lacordaire, however, who seems to have been the leader of the fight, still objected ; he had rented the room, therefore, he said, it was his dwelling ; he had provided himself with a bed there, it was his lodging ; he sat himself upon it. "You go," said he, "I'll remain the night here with the law and with my rights." But the touch of the Police overmastered this reasoning, and he was compelled to leave. For this misdemeanor all were prosecuted. While the prosecution was pending the father of Count de Montalembert died ; this brought the prosecution of the young Count before the House of Peers, and as it was in its action against the Priest and Count indivisible, the Abbé Lacordaire appeared before the Chamber of Peers to defend himself and friend ; they were found guilty, but only fined one hundred francs. "A small price," says the Count, "to pay for the honor and advantage of having forced upon the attention of the public a question involving the life or death of freedom." This was a remarkable year to the young men, the year of their close friendship and brave united action. As it died, the young Abbé wrote to his biographer, "However cruel Time be, he will never blight the charms of the year which has just closed, that year will be eternally to my heart like a virgin just expired." Meantime, with all this glory, the *Avenir* was not a paying affair. Material resources were few, and they became exhausted by law-suits and publications ; and it would seem Church and State looked alike somewhat scowlingly upon it. The sentiments of De la Mennais were developing in a direction where Lacordaire was not likely to follow. The first had the shapeless and indefinite longings of free impulses, but Lacordaire was a Christian, a priest, and a child of the Church. Their efforts had not been smiled upon by Rome, so together they sought Rome, that they might receive the guiding word of the Holy Father. Holy Father received them respectfully, even affectionately, but as to the matter in hand, quite silently. This silence Lacordaire interpreted as the condemnation, if not of their principles, then, of their tendencies, by the voice of the Church. Like a true priest of Rome, he resigned himself to the thwarting and the disappointment. "Obedience is painful," he wrote to his friend Montalembert, "but experience has taught me that, sooner or later, it is rewarded, and that God alone knows what is good for us ; the light breaks in upon him who submits, as upon one who opens his eyes." The two Abbés parted company then ; the course of De la Mennais certainly was disastrous. I believe his honest endeavor was to *see*. Lacordaire said, "The Church does not say to you *See ;* this power does not belong to her ; she says to you, *Believe,*" and Lacordaire was right. It may seem strange that I find so much that touches my sympathy in the course taken by a Popish priest. In fact, whilst our reasons might differ, it strikes us that all intelligent minds reach a point in their history, when they have to summon themselves to a determination like that which claimed and compelled Lacordaire to plunge on thoughtlessly through what seems to be the light, as though light alone gave the power of seeing, and then to hand over the spirit to what the Abbé well-styled the most fearful bondage of all, "the bondage of the mind"—or to take shelter, as he took shelter, in the conviction, that as there exists in the world a necessity for a power to protect the weak mind against the strong mind, God has appointed it, not in seeking for peace and liberty along the highways of grief and slavery, but in prayer, and in the offices of the Church. Of course, my hearers will not understand me as implying only the offices of the Romish Church ; any church seeking to Christ as the shelter of weak souls. Lacordaire was a Papist—he found his rest therefore in the voice of the Romish ritual—he bowed himself to his religious authorities—he felt there was something to obey, and he obeyed. It might be well for all of us if we had some centre to which we felt we owed the debt of religious obedience. Although, however, he quitted the company of the Abbé De la Mennais, so much his senior, to whom he had yet professed his most earnest and tender advice, he did not so renounce Montalembert, reminding us of the intensity with which, in similar circumstances and for a like end, Ignatius Loyola followed Xavier.

Montalembert, with a reserved and subdued affection, re-fers to the way in which he was followed by his friend, seek-ing him out with logic, with keen and touching eloquence, with a mixture of severity and humble affection, and with irresistible frankness and sweetness. At a much later pe-riod of his life, Lacordaire defined a priest to be "firm as a diamond, softer than a mother." "Such," says Montalem-bert, "he himself seems to me. I was the prisoner of error and pride, and he freed me ; and I was able to cast into the depths of that soul a look, at first troubled and irritated, but, since then and now, bathed in tears of undying gratitude."

Lacordaire was not only acquainted with the phenomena of knowledge, he was still more profoundly acquainted with the phenomena of faith ; thus he established the eternal re-lation between himself and his revering disciple.

Hitherto, as compared with the life he subsequently led, and the vast prominency of his fame, Lacordaire had wrought in obscurity. Returning from Rome to Paris, he still continued in obscurity ; and, when the cholera broke out, with his cool, calm courage, he devoted himself in a tem-porary hospital to the sick and the dying. We know how manifest at that time, was the ill-feeling in Paris towards the clergy: the Administration declined the assistance of the Archbishop of Paris. While priests could not show themselves in their cassocks, Lacordaire was, however, tolerated. He wrote from the hospital, "There are here neither Sisters of Charity, nor Chaplain, nor ordinary Clergy. My presence, and that of two other priests was tolerated. The smallest portion of the work falls to us ; each day I glean but a scanty crop for eternity." So he labored. He wished to bury himself in the depths of the country to live for a small flock. He wrote to Montalembert, he hoped to "bless his children before he died ;" but the Archbishop of Paris kept him in his diocese ; in apartments in the Convent of the Visitation he lived. His mother came to live there with him, and died in his arms ; and then he seems to have derived much sympathy from the celebrated Madame Swetchine. This lady filled to him the place of his mother, out of the treasures of her lofty and upright soul. She died a short time before he did. His days in Paris seem to have been very much of a solitude : the Convent was a retreat to him. "There," says Montalembert, "I saw him growing in calmness and recollection, in prayer, study, and charity." Lacordaire testifies, "Solitude begins to reign around me ; it is my element, my life ; nothing is achieved without solitude."

Hitherto he had never preached ; he preached first in the Church of St. Roch, in the spring of 1833. Montalembert heard him first, and testifies that he failed completely. "We all said on leaving, 'He is a talented man, but will never make a preacher.'" The preacher himself said, "I shall continue to live solitary ; I have enough of nothing that goes to make up a preacher."* A few months after, he

* The reader will remember when Robert Hall delivered his first address, he suddenly paused, covered his face with his hands, exclaiming, "Oh ! I've lost all my ideas," and the second attempt was accompanied by a like failure.

was incomparably the greatest preacher in Europe—the
most magnificent eagle of eloquence since the time of Bossuet ; for it so happened, that as his thoughtful sympathies, and earnestness, and holiness were known to a few
youths of the most unpretending of the Paris colleges, the
College Stanislaus, he was asked to deliver himself in what
is styled Conferences to them ; he promised to do so. At
the second conference the chapel was unable to hold the
crowd. The third, a temporary gallery was erected. His
enemies became busy : he had emerged again from obscurity ; he was denounced at Rome ; denounced to the Government ; and denounced to the Archbishop of Paris. He
was charged with heresy and impiety. Some of the priests,
who in fact never did like him to the close of his career,
charged him with Atheism ; it was said, that in some of
his conferences, he had not pronounced the name of Jesus
Christ one single time ; he replied to this concisely, " I
scorn the annoyance given to me ; I fulfil my duty as a
man and a priest ; I live alone in continual study, calm,
trustful in God and the future." Others did not hesitate
to scoff. To them upon due occasion, he said, " Gentlemen, God has made you witty, very witty, indeed, to show
how little He cares for the wit of man." The Archbishop
of Paris seems to have behaved with remarkable courage.
He was memorialized by a deputation of law-students to
find a larger church for the preacher, and he called upon
him to mount the pulpit of Notre Dame. Montalembert
scarcely rises to exaggeration when he says, that "by his
conferences in Notre Dame, he immortalized that pulpit ;"
and, certainly, I suppose that the most vivid recollections
printed upon any minds by the mention of Notre Dame,
are associated with the thronging crowds who listened in
1835 and 1836 to those conferences, which I will suppose
to be in all my hearers' hands ; to me they have been long
thoroughly familiar ; and making allowance for their ves-

ture of Romanism, they may be mentioned as the most admirable grappling line thrown from the modern pulpit over the consciousness of the intelligent and cultivated mind of the present generation.

He was thirty-three years of age ; in the midst of his fame, he fled from Paris to Rome, and startled all his friends ere long by plunging into one of the severest and most ascetic orders of the church ; he assumed the white robe of St. Dominic ; he became one of the friar-preachers, and devoted himself to an effort for the resurrection of religious orders ; he plunged down, also, into the deep volumes of St. Thomas. "Would that I had long ago drunk of those deep waters," says the monk. Five years passed away before he appeared again in Paris ; he appeared then at Notre Dame, with shaven head and white habit, in the midst of six thousand young men. He, also, always regarded himself as especially the preacher to young men. And from year to year he appeared, gathering immense audiences ; while in the provinces, founding his religious orders, and seeking to obtain freedom from the impositions of the Government, especially for the white habit of the Dominican. I confess, I have little sympathy with the brand of St. Dominic myself, perfectly aware of the wonderful beings that order has produced, nor less aware of its cruelty and saturnalia of abominable crime. With this, however, here we have nothing to do ; the order has produced men among the most affectionately holy of our race ; and of these Pere Lacordaire is one. In 1846, on announcing his attention of speaking on the familiar life of Christ, he exclaimed, in what may, perhaps, be well called a cry of supernatural tenderness—

Lord Jesus ; during the ten years that I have been preaching to this audience, Thou wert ever at the bottom of my discourses ; but, to-day, at last, I come more directly to Thyself, to that Divine face which is daily the object of my contemplation, to those sacred feet which I have so often kissed; to those loving hands which have so often blessed me; to that life, whose fragrance I have inhaled from my cradle, which my boyhood denied, which my youth again learned to love, and which my manhood adores and preaches to every creature. O Father! O Master! O Lover! O Jesus! help me more than ever, since being nearer to Thee, my audience must feel, and I must draw from my heart accents indicative of thy admirable proximity.*

The words, the method of Lacordaire, cannot be unknown to my hearers. The Conferences of Notre Dame are to be met with everywhere. They are especially bold and striking—in their generalizations they are perhaps too dazzling; but they were delivered to vast audiences; they were not the result of great art and preparation, but thought out; they were taken down in short-hand, and corrected the day after for the press; this will save many of the words from the appearance of inflation; we could not have endured had the words received the careful revision and chiselling of the study. Let the following illustrations suffice :

THE HUMAN MYSTERY.

In fine, if I desire to know what will be the end of this terrible struggle, if I think of the destinies of man beaten about by an incomprehensible tempest, it is then that the ignorance and confusion of the ideas of the world are clearly shown. A man is born; will he be happy or miserable, good or bad? The world does not know. An empire is founded; how long will it endure? What will be the various chances of its duration? The world does not know. A war commences; who will be victorious, who will be vanquished? The world does not know. A swallow perches upon a roof: where is it going? The world does not know. A leaf falls; where does it go? The world does not know. The world does not know the destiny of a single hair, how should it know the destiny of mankind?

Oh! ourselves; let us each look into ourselves, recall to our

* First Conference of 1846.

thoughts the amazing mystery of our life. How do we stand with regard to truth and error? How many things have we believed true which we now believe to be false, how many false which we now believe true! And who will tell us what our intelligence will be to-morrow? And whence comes it that we might be on the right hand or on the left? And our existence, what is its history since Adam? What were our fathers? Where and how shall we die? perhaps this evening or to-morrow—we know not. And our heart! Ah! here above all the consideration of ourselves becomes grievous, and the abyss of good and evil appears to us in all its length and breadth and depth. What a wonderful mixture of good and bad actions, of odious and sublime thoughts, of devotedness and of selfishness! Are we angels or demons? And what a marvellous chaos is also the society in which we are born! The sound of tempests surrounded our cradle; we have passed through a thousand contradictory opinions. Some say that everything is perishing, others that all is rising into life; some that we are entering upon a new feature, others that we are only repeating sad and ancient tragedies. And in fine, to crown all, have we chosen our part with reference to our eternal destiny? Young men of this age, do you know where you will be in that of the immutable and the infinite? Look at these walls: what profound faith built them? And you are full of doubt! And yet I am speaking to reasonable beings, to the kings of creation, the masterpiece of nature, and nothing is comparable to their grandeur but their ignorance of themselves, but the impenetrable mystery in which they are plunged. They know everything excepting what they are.

Well! I bring you good tidings; this knowledge which the world does not possess exists. It exists, for how could the Author of things leave His creatures in such unnatural ignorance and uncertainty? It exists in the world, although it comes not from the world.

THE NATIONS AND THE BIBLE.

Who will venture to compare any community constituted by a sacred book with the Christian community? Look first at China; what has she done? By what deeds has she revealed herself to the world? Where are the traces of her arms; where the furrows of her ships? Where her doctrinal propaganda? Have you ever met the Chinese on the great highways of the world? This people, dead in an inactive pride, is shut up within itself, and has not even once during three thousand years felt an electric shock of love and genius. Come nearer, look at India; all the conquerors and all the merchants have been there. She has given gold, pearls, diamonds, ivory to all who have desired them; she still feeds the ambition of the British people with her luxurious riches; but do you know anything else of her, except her sensuality, equal to her humiliating dependence? There remain the nations into whose hands Mahomet placed the scimitar and Islamism, and they have certainly made illustrious use of the one and of the other. Yet, where are they? After having invaded Europe by its two extremities and conquered our Crusades, as the war became learned we perceive their glory waning; and the success of their arms hiding no longer the wretchedness of their civilisation, we look on, not at their decadence, but at their last gasp. Look now to yourselves, Gentlemen, contemplate yourselves; you, the sons of the Bible. You are nothing by your territory; Europe is but a plot of ground by the side of Africa and Asia, and yet they are your colors and your flags which I meet with on all the seas, in the islands, and in the ports of the whole world. You are present from one pole to the other by your navigators, your merchants, your soldiers, your missionaries, your consuls. It is you who give peace or war to nations, who bear the destinies of mankind in the folds of your narrow robe. Descend upon the public place, lift up your voice. I hear the old and the new continents in agitation; they ask, Who, then, is in commotion? It is you, sons of the Bible! That language which travels so far is yours; it has brethren and sisters in all the capitals; it gathers together all passions and all devotedness. If a man from the planks of an adventurous bark, who speaks your language and bears your image, reaches some distant shore, it is at once seen that the great human power has appeared there. By the brightness of his look, by his manner of treading the ground, the earth recognises the Christian, and its savage inhabitant bows his head and exclaims, These are the children of the sun, those whom our traditions promised to us, and for whom we waited.

What activity! What power! What glory! And all that, is yourselves; and the Bible has made you what you are. If, then, nations are constituted by reason of the truth contained in their sacred books, and if the Christian nations surpass all the others, as angels surpass all created natures, it follows that the highest degree of truth is contained in the Christian books.

It is no part of my purpose to follow minutely the life of the preacher. From year to year he emerged from his retreat and appeared in Nôtre Dame. In 1848, hoping much, and still faithful to his first convictions, he took decided part with Lamartine. He was even returned with tumultuous joy as one of the deputies. He only held the post, however, for ten days, confessing that politics were not to his taste, nor administrative ability amongst his powers. Our readers will also remember that he excited the anger and irritability of the Ultramontane party by vindicating the Italian revolution of the same year ; for this his friendly biographer deems it necessary to apologise. When circumstances so marvellously changed in Paris, and the fatal *coup d' état* was struck, Lacordaire bade farewell for ever to Nôtre Dame, and only preached once again in Paris, in the Church of St. Roch, where, nineteen years before, he had stammered out his first sermon and failed. He came to preach before the Archbishop of Paris and Cardinal Donnet. He took for his text the words of David on his deathbed to his son Solomon, " *Esto vir ;*" in our translation— "Show thyself a man." In the course of his sermon he said,

The practice of the greatness of the Gospel is incompatible with meanness of character. . . . . . It is well that we should know what we mean by making Christians; whether we intend to make real men or vulgar men ; whether for us man is the *homo*, whom the ancients derived from *humus*, earth, slime ; or the *vir*, the man who is something more than earth, who has courage, soul, virtue, *virtus*. . . . . A man may have a great mind and a vulgar soul, an intellect capable of enlightening his age, and a soul capable of dishonoring it: he may be a great man in mind, and a wretch at heart. He who employs vile means even to do good, even to save his country, is never anything but a villain.*

It may well be believed that such words would not be palatable to such a government, and more especially coming from a conspicuous church, and from an eminent man. His great faithful soul revolted from the baseness of the Paris priesthood, which had crawled down to every trick of servility and meanness, crying down all the rights of political liberty, declaring that liberty of conscience ought to be restricted in proportion as truth prevailed, and lauding the Inquisition. Lacordaire was faithful to those days, in which, from the pulpit of Nôtre Dame, and in the presence of the Archbishop, he had said, "Whoever in his cry for right excepts a single man—whoever consents to the slavery of a single man, be he white or black, were it only to extend to the unlawful binding of a single hair of his head, that man is not sincere. Catholics, know this well, if you want liberty for yourselves, you must will it for all men under heaven." Now, in the charge of the enslavement of France, he said, "I hope to live and die a penitent Catholic, an impenitent Liberal;" and his letters from Sorèze bear out all the noble words he ever uttered in his life : he says, "I am indeed solitary, but I am with my duty, and that is enough. One of the consolations of my present life is to live only with God and children ; the latter have their faults, but they have as yet betrayed and dishonored nothing."

For one single day he appeared again in the ranks of illustrious men in Paris, when he was received into the

---

* This passage was construed as a demonstration against the Emperor Napoleon III., whose course, it will be remembered, excited such deep and bitter indignation in England at that time.

French Academy ; but he hastened back to his youthful audience at Sorèze ; many hundreds of miles from the French capital he preached from week to week in the college chapel, with as much care and affection as in Paris to the mighty multitude.   He prepared also his *Letters to a Young Man on the Christian Life.*   As he advanced farther into life his modesty, always remarkable, increased.   A self-depreciation went side by side with a profound appreciation of sacred trust.   He knew also more of that detachment of heart, the foundation of all wisdom.   Death met him comparatively in early life ; for a long time he was the victim of pain—even of tortures ; he lay long in great and solemn silence.   After the manner of his Church, he spent hours together with his eyes fixed upon the crucifix, and he said to one who visited him, " I am unable to pray to Him, but I look upon Him."   His last words were, " My God, open to me, open to *me.*"

It is impossible to read as much of his life as I have read and know without being sacredly and painfully affected by it.   He seems to me always to have moved beneath the recollection and impression of deep internal sorrows ; indeed, he says, " There is a dart which we must always carry in the soul ; we must try not to lean on the side where it is, without ever thinking of taking it out."   His oratory was affected by this sense of pain.   Montalembert speaks of his accent and its touching power.   To us, no doubt, as we read his orations there seems something occasionally almost inflated ; the fault of Bossuet reappears, but we have so much more sympathy with the topics of Lacordaire than with any upon which Bossuet ever spoke.   His first conferences are the most earnest and determined effort of the pulpit to put itself *en rapport* with the youthful intelligence of the age with which we are acquainted.   They have, no doubt, many of the vices of French expression, vivid generalization and bold assertion, and they are often unjust to Protestantism, but frequently the words, like a stroke of lightning, reveal to the eye the whole subject.

I have indeed felt and seen something bearing resemblance to it in my experience in the speech of a well-known orator in our midst, famous twenty-five years since for his power over young men. I believe, if I were to give my impression of the power and style of Father Lacordaire, I should astonish some hearers, and perhaps make Count Montalembert somewhat indignant by describing him as a Thomas Binney, with an additional flash of quicksilver in the blood, a higher fence of solitude in the life, and a broader platform from which to throw his voice over the Church; greatly alike in this, that they have both sought to bring themselves into vigorous relation to the intelligence of the age.

Pre-eminently beyond most preachers of this age must Thomas Binney be spoken of as the preacher to the young, to the thoughtful and the earnest of the young—to young men and young women; in a word, to noble, earnest-hearted manhood. He evidently has more sympathy with mental than merely emotional sorrows; for sentimental sorrows he perhaps has no sympathy; for the seeming of suffering which so largely afflicts many Christian souls, and needs—as it is a seeming itself—the ministry and consolation which seems, he has no sympathy; all about him and about his words is thoroughly human and thoroughly real: in all he says he lives, and therefore he understands and speaks to living souls; thus no man has done more to bring to an end that sentimental style of talk which proffers consolations never felt, to souls by whom they are never needed. Nothing more prominently distinguishes his preaching than its humanness—its reality and truth. It is the case, no doubt, there are many states of mind and heart he has not known or felt; but I believe he has never attempted to speak to them.

I have had repeated to me a tradition of our preacher. Called somewhere to address some students, a very demure and well-intentioned brother was fated to precede him. He divided his homily into two parts—"And first," said he, "young men, remember that you are to be men of one book, the Bible ; that is the book you have to read and expound, and you must know no other ; and remember as you pass through great cities, pray 'Turn away mine eyes from beholding vanity ;' let your eyes look straight on ; the shops are nothing to you, their shows, their prices, and their gauds," etc., etc. When Mr. Binney rose, he said, he was so "unfortunate as to have to give to them advice exactly opposite to that they had just heard ; hence," he said, "although the reading of other men may be slight, for amusement, or professional, you must read everything. Look at all books—bad books, that, if necessary, you may brand them, or point the bad page to the readers of them ; good books, that you may commend them ; then, as you walk through the streets, having prayed in the study, keep your eyes open there ; look at all things—prices and people—how they buy and how they sell, the sellers and the purchasers, the hours of labor and the hours of rest ; try to look at all, try to know the whole tariff of trade, and do not be afraid to find in it all matter for your sermon. You are teachers ! Commend 'yourselves to every man's conscience in the sight of God.' Know then the world's thoughts and the world's ways, that you may be the world's masters and ministers." These words must have greatly astonished the first tedious brother, but how much more human and good ?

It is said when St. Francis entered a town to preach, all the clergy went forth to meet him, accompanied by the youth, the women, and the children, waving their branches of greeting triumphantly before him. The preaching of the minister of the Weigh House would never awaken any

such homage ; but then, St. Francis spoke to a larger congregation, as when he began his great sermon in the square
in Spoleto with the words, "Angeli, homines, dæmones."
The preacher who omits all apostrophe to the angels and
devils, and contents himself with talking to men—he cannot expect so mighty a mustering. Much more after the
order of homage accorded to Mr. Binney was that paid to
St. Jerome when he preached in Padua and Milan, and
other cities ; the doctors and masters ceased their lectures,
saying to their scholars,—"Go, hear the preacher of the
best sentences and the worst rhetoric ; gather the fruit and
neglect the leaves ;" and that is a better compliment than·
to say, "Go, and hear what a rustling there is among the
leaves, and as to the fruit, if there be any, try to get it."

For to Mr. Binney's style I may apply a remark by way
of characterization he has himself used in prefacing one
of his discourses—"It is of that rough, rude order—that
artificial and somewhat exaggerated sort of utterance,
which *I designedly adopt* when writing what is to be read to
a mixed multitude." Artificial, in the ordinary sense of
the word, his style can never be said to be, only in the fact
of a conscious usage of forms of expression which it is
well known will strike and tell. It is often the case that
a man describing a style of thought or argument describes
his own ; this, too, he has done when he says,—"An illustration is not a mere prettiness, an ornamental phrase that
might be left out without detriment to the train of thought,
it is something which really *lights up* that train of thought,
and enables the reader or hearer to *see* the aim as well as
feel the force of the logic, when the understanding, having
done its work, passion and genius shall crown the whole
with some vivid illustration, which shall make it stand out
with a distinctness that shall never be forgotten ! *It is one
great faculty of the mind, holding up a lighted torch to the
workmanship of another."* This is a very fair description

12*

of all the greater efforts of our writer, and of his usual style in the pulpit. It is a rare thing indeed to find in union such a force of thought so wholly free from dialectic bands, and winged by so much passion, yet with no action, ever breaking against the calm and dignity of the lofty purpose ; there are no prettinesses in the style—no elegant tropology, or fancy dandyism of dress and adornment. Everything there seems necessary—passion and thought hold each other in check, and so produce a truly admirable unity ; hence thought never seems cold, because it is winged by genius, and the genius is never undisciplined or wild, because it is compelled to keep the pace of the more serious and orderly thought.

This orderly procession of thought leading on and up the attendant train of all the faculties, is the great charm of the preaching of Thomas Binney, and it may be said he is only happy when he sees clearly ; and happy are those moments to the hearers, too, when the understanding and the emotions are in *rapport*. The reason, at any time, any speech is uneffective upon the hearers is because either the statement is not clearly seen or clearly felt—with Mr. Binney, eminently not to see clearly is to be unhappy in ministration. But all speakers who speak not merely words of rote must well know that state in which the mind is pursuing its way in public, attempting to set forth thoughts perhaps rather pondered than either perceived or felt ; the mind arrives at a certain stage of its journey, where it drops the spark which sets fire to the concealed, the hitherto unknown wealth, there are juices and spices for the incense, their is fuel for the flame, there is oil for the lamp. Admirably has Mr. Binney himself described this state when he speaks of ministers "who are never visited by gushes of light irradiating the word—never filled with emotions of solemn rapture from the vivid impressions and enjoyment of its truths," the argument is in a blaze. And this is indeed the value of preparation, clear, long, and earnest, for the pulpit, or for the great occasion ; then, if the mind is free, or capable of freedom, and the self-possession of the soul be equal to its instincts, then the notes and papers all discarded, or only in brief prompting hints before the eye—then when long preparation has toned down all the superfluous and meretricious adornments, or appendages of the subject, then how sublime is the power! Of course the free mind, the heart that lives its teachings and its uttered impulses, to whom it is impossible to preach traditions, must often fail—fail perhaps beneath the very weight of "the burden of the Word of the Lord." But even in the failure of such souls there is the sign of that which is greater than the finest successes of other men ; even as we have seen, when Robert Hall broke down in the pulpit in his first efforts, his failure sent old Dr. Ryland to his knees in prayer, that so promising a spirit might be kept for the Church.

Sacredly and seriously prepared ; the order of the thought established in the mind, and the emotions felt, but held in leash, ready for the spring—surely this gives some conception of the way in which men may preach ; and while there is, perhaps, no necessity that this should be the ordinary process of preparation, yet men who have really been prophets, and have had communion with souls, have usually prepared thus, and thus men must prepare if they would have their preaching to become a power. Hence, although Mr. Binney's books are mostly small, they are thought books. A sermon is sometimes a closely compacted compendium of the process of thought, and the delineation of truth on the subject of which he treats. Far from being mere sermons in the ordinary sense—that is, a slight, sketchy illustration of a text—they often, like the sermons of Barrow, exhaust a subject, thus—"The Law our Schoolmaster," thus, "Salvation by Fire and Fullness," thus, "Life and Immortality brought to Light;" each is an edifice of Christian theology. But Mr. Binney rears for himself; scholastic, scientific theology is unknown here; the preacher's soul, the Bible, and the Spirit build together, and alone.

And here, perhaps, I may stop for a few moments, and indulge my hearers and myself with two or three illustrative readings of those moods of power to which we have referred. We may take the following as a fair illustration of Mr. Binney's *argumentative and philosophical method* in the pulpit:

THE THEORY OF THE MYTHICAL ORIGIN OF CHRISTIANITY.

The hypothesis is something of this sort—The writings of the Old and New Testaments are the utterance and embodiment of the inner subjective life of the Hebrew race. "Thus and thus was it," as these books in their own style relate, that the great mystery of the universe shaped itself to their conceptions. "Thus and thus" they thought about the visible and the invisible, the heavens and the earth, God and man, the infinite and eternal, duty and sin, guilt and forgiveness. Throwing their internal impressions into the form of a splendid ritualism, and associating this with rude myths of flaming mount and supernatural voices that gave to it a divine origin and descent— "thus and thus it was," that this singular people at once made palpable to themselves, by visible objects, their subjective ideas of spiritual truth, and indicated the profound earnestness of their souls by their full persuasion of heavenly guidance. At a subsequent period, stimulated by the recent appearance and extraordinary character of an illustrious individual—to many of his contemporaries a great prophet—to even modern unbelievers a person singularly gifted and singularly virtuous—the best if not the wisest of men—"thus and thus it was," in the second portion of their writings that this same people, or large portions of them, with certain powerful minds as their leaders, threw their strong subjective conceptions of spiritual truth into the supposed facts of the history of Jesus, and the Christian interpretation of the Jewish ritual—an interpretation which attributed to it a previously prophetic design, and superseded it by an asserted supernatural fulfilment. The impression of the greatness, and the memory of the transcendent virtue, of Jesus, so deepened and grew in the minds of His contemporaries, and of those who were immediately affected by them, that there came at last to be no adequate mode in which this deep feeling and these sacred and reverential memories could be bodied forth, but in an imaginary miraculous record of his life—in something superhuman being associated with his person—and in the extraordinary notion of his having in some way given a reality to the spiritual idea of the old law.

Without dwelling on the extreme improbability of this—this making into honest and truthful men, persons, by no means fools, who "professed" to record actual miracles, and "pretended" to direct intercourse with heaven — without dwelling upon this, let us allow for a moment the hypothesis referred to —let us accept it as the solution of the facts—and then notice, briefly, one or two of the things that would seem to result from it. In the first place, it must certainly be confessed that, taking all the facts—the way in which the several pieces constituting what we called the Bible were composed—the sort of book they make when put together—the connection between the two series of writings, and the two supposed religious dispensations —taking these and kindred things, and looking fairly and honestly at them, it must certainly be conceded that anything parallel to such facts is not to be met with in the history of the world. True or false, the Jewish and Christian religions are the most wonderful things of which there is any account in the records of the race. What an extraordinary people that Hebrew people must have been, who in the wilderness commenced, and in subsequent ages perfected, a ritual system embodying in its significance some of the profoundest truths afterwards to be demonstrated by logicians and philosophers—and who did this by no Divine or supernatural assistance, but simply from the impulses of their own inward religious life, which struggled to express itself, and which found utterance in this way! How wonderful that this rude people should go on, perfecting their ideas and multiplying their myths, till they took a new form in the history of Jesus, and in the spiritual or transcendental interpretation of the old ritual system which that introduced! What a marvel it is, too, that the whole thing should have been so constructed, and so carried out, as to seize on the human mind *beyond* Judea—to subdue the most cultivated portions of the human race—to supersede all other myths, theologies, and philosophies with which it came in contact—and to be spreading in the world as a regal power, to the present day!

But, while this general fact is a presumption or something singularly powerful in the genius of the Hebrew people, it should be next noticed, that the extraordinary nature of the Christian interpretation of the Hebrew ritual is itself worthy of specific remark. The idea of taking the tabernacle, or temple, the altar and priesthood, with all the accessories of the ritual service, and giving them a significance—finding for them a design and a reality, that should at once fill the earth and reach up to heaven! —think of *that.* After the prophecies, or supposed prophecies, which for ages had stirred the national heart, filling it with splendid anticipations of a regal and conquering Messiah;—after He was supposed to have come, and then to have departed, and to have so departed as to have disappointed the hopes cherished to the last by His immediate followers;—after this, what an idea it was to turn the very fact which shattered their expectation into a fulcrum on which to fix an engine that should move the world? What an intrepid and sublime *daring* there is in the thought of Messiah the Priest being placed in the foreground of Messiah the King!—the wide earth the place of sacrifice, the cross of ignominy the altar of propitiation, the upper world the holy of holies—the way into it being opened and sanctified by the resuscitated Redeemer, who passes through the veil of the visible heavens, as into the interior of a temple, "there to appear in the presence of God for us"—for *us*, for humanity, and for the accomplishment of those spiritual objects which humanity spiritually needs! However, the truth of all this, objectively considered, may be denied; the whole thing rejected as fanciful— as being nothing more than the imaginative forms in which strongly-excited and fervid minds threw their conceptions of spiritual things, from their inability to find for them fit expression and adequate embodiment in mere language;— however this may be, it must certainly be admitted, that there is a stupendousness about the theory—a magnitude and a magnificence, that should lead to the recognition of it as of something to be classed with the creations of genius!

We shall have a miracle of human genius, instead of one of Divine power;—a prodigy of earth and nature, instead of an actual "sign from heaven!" All things considered, it will be found, I suspect, that to admit the Divine origin of our religion, makes a much smaller demand on our credulity, than to accept the hypothesis for accounting for its existence suggested by philosophic naturalism. Waiving, for the moment, higher motives, we might say, "That, as men, we are believers for the credit of our understanding; as, if we were Jews, we should be disposed to become believers for the credit of our ancient faith.*

I select another citation from Mr. Binney's more *practical* and *devotional method.* In the following extract he is speaking of ministers who do not spiritually succeed because they do not add eminent piety to eminent attainments and endowments. The extract, I may remind my hearers, is from the celebrated sermon entitled, "The Closet and the Church," preached before the Congregational Union of Ministers, from the text "The pastors have become brutish, and have not sought the Lord; therefore, they shall not prosper, and all their flocks shall be scattered."

Whatever their denomination, they are to be supposed to have "entered by their respective doors into the sheep-fold," and not to have "climbed up over the wall," or to have forced admission in any other way. Nor, again, is it to be supposed, that they are destitute either of natural gifts or acquired ability. Their powers may be great, vigorous, and varied. These powers may have been duly trained by academical discipline, enriched by science, purified by taste, brought into contact with all knowledge, and then concentrated on subjects of sacred lore. The men may be distinguished by lofty thoughts, logical acuteness, ready utterance, force of words; with minds as fertile in the lights and illustrations which the imagination supplies, as opulent in the ma-

* "The Law our Schoolmaster," pp. 151–160.

terials of instructive discourse. Farther: it is not to be supposed that their manner in worship is careless or irreverent, or their instructions crude, vapid, repulsive, or destitute of laborious intellectual preparation: it may even be imagined that they strictly adhere to the gravity and decorum of sacred things, and never advance what has not been somewhat carefully reviewed. It is not to be supposed that they deny the truth and inculcate dangerous and deadly error. Their customary topics may be " substantially " evangelical, or, at least, consistent with the verities of Scripture. It need not even be supposed that they are wanting in fervor, variety, or impressiveness. They may have much of the artillery of eloquence at their command ;—may be " sons of thunder," striking to the depths of the conscience and the heart ; or, they may speak in the " still small voice," with the words of love and the accents of tenderness. so that their speech " shall drop like the rain, and distil as the dew." Nor, lastly, are they to be conceived as chargeable with any gross immorality of behavior. Their lives are not to be supposed vicious nor their consciences burdened with great guilt ;—their characters are free from the suspicion of any flagrant impropriety, and their conduct on the whole, in all outward and visible things, equal to the demands of society respecting them. In spite, however, of all that we have enumerated, in spite of personal ability, official order, pulpit accomplishments, grave and decorous " public " devotion, force of utterance, animated feeling, Scriptural topics, moral worth ;—in spite of these and of other excellencies, there is one evil in the habits of these men, which, hidden as it is from the human eye, is real and deadly, and eats " as doth a canker " into all they utter and all they do. *They* " do not prosper," and their flocks are " scattered,—for they have become " brutish," and " have not sought the Lord."

This, then, is the defect that poisons everything ;—they are not men of " frequent, earnest, private devotion." They have great abilites,—" but they do not pray." They are ministers of Christ, according to outward order,—" but they do not pray." They are good, and, perhaps, even great preachers,—" but they do not pray." They are fervent, pungent, persuasive, convincing,—" but they do not pray." They may be zealous and enterprising,—leaders in the movements of public activity,—the first

and foremost in popular excitement,—frequent in their appeals,
—abundant in their labors,—working zealously in various modes
and in divers places,—" but they do not pray." They are men
of integrity, purity, benevolence,—" but they do not pray." And
THIS ONE THING—their " restraining prayer,"—their not " calling upon God,"—their " not seeking after," nor " stirring up
themselves to take hold of" Him,—this, like the want of love
in the Christian character, " stains the glory" of everything
else ;—it renders worthless their genius, talents, and acquisitions, obstructs their own spiritual prosperity, impedes their usefulness, and blasts their success. Though a minister were an
apostle, " and did not pray," his " speech and his preaching "
would *not* be " with the demonstration of the Spirit and of power." " Though he had the gift of prophecy, and understood all
mysteries and all knowledge, and, though he had faith that
could remove mountains, ' and did not pray,' he would be nothing." " Though he gave all his goods to feed the poor, and his
body to be burnt, ' and did not pray,' it would profit him nothing." " Though he spake with the tongues of men and of angels," " and did not pray," he would be but " as sounding brass,
or a tinkling cymbal." He might be " like unto one that hath a
pleasant voice, and a lovely song, and that plays well upon an instrument ; " but the music of the lip and the hand only will
never charm away the evil spirit from Saul; nor can it have in
it that divine and life-giving harmony which " of stones can
raise up children unto Abraham." *

And, at the risk of quoting too freely, I must present my
hearers with the comprehensive and glowing delineation of
the Psalms of David in

THE SERVICE OF SONG.

The songs of Solomon were a thousand and five. But, how
shall we describe those of the PSALMS ? Than Solomon's fewer
in number, but of higher inspiration and richer thought. As
to their " form," they include all varieties of lyric composition ;
they are of every character as to the nature of their subjects,

* Four Discourses.— *The Closet and the Church*, pp. 29-35.

and of all shades and colors of poetic feeling; but, as to their
"essence," they are as a Light from heaven or an Oracle from
the sanctuary :—they discover secrets. Divine and human;—
they lay open the Holy of Holies of both God and man, for they
reveal the hidden things belonging to both, as the life of the
One is developed in the other. The Psalms are the depositories
of the mysteries, the record of the struggles, the wailing when
worsted, the pæans when triumphant of that life. They are the
thousand-voiced heart of the Church, uttering from within, from
the secret depths and chambers of her being, her spiritual consciousness—all that she remembers, experiences, believes; suffers from sin and the flesh, fears from earth or hell, achieves by
heavenly succor, and hopes from God and his Christ. They are
for all time. They never can be outgrown. No Dispensation,
while the world stands and continues what it is, can ever raise
us above the reach or the need of them. They describe every
spiritual vicissitude; they speak to all classes of minds; they
command every natural emotion. They are penitential, jubilant
adorative, deprecatory ;—they are tender, mournful, joyous, majestic; soft as the descent of dew ; low as the whisper of love;
loud as the voice of thunder; terrible as the Almightiness of
God! The effect of some of them in the temple service must
have been immense. Sung by numbers carefully "instructed,"
and accompanied by those who could play "skilfully ;" arranged in parts for "courses" and individuals, who answered each
other in alternate verse;—various voices, single or combined,
being "lifted up," sometimes in specific and "personal" expression, as the high service deepened and advanced,—priests,
Levites, the monarch, the multitude,—there would be every variety of "pleasant movement," and all the forms and forces of
sound, personal recitative ; individual song; dual and semichoral
antiphonal response; burst and swell of voice and instruments;
attenuated cadence ; apostrophe and repeat ; united, full, harmonious combinations. With such a service, and such psalms, it
was natural that the Hebrews should love with enthusiasm and
learn with delight, their national anthems, songs, and melodies ;
nor is it surprising that they were known among the Heathen as
a people possessed of these treasures of verse, and devoted to
their recitation by tongue and harp. Hence it was that their

enemies required of them (whether in seriousness or derision it matters not), "*the words* of a song," and said " sing us one of the songs of Zion."

It is, I presume, an incontestable fact, that genius of the highest order seldom finds its way into the pulpit ; it is true now, as ever, that still "the foolishness of men" is the channel for "the wisdom of God." In the world without the Church there are so many sources of fame and emolument—

> Man may range
> The court, the camp, the vessel, and the mart;
> Sword, gown, gain, glory, offer in exchange
> Pride, fame, ambition, to fill up his heart,
> And few there are whom these will not estrange.
> Man has all these resources.

and none of them point especially to the pulpit at all, and certainly not to the Dissenting Pulpit. The Pulpit of the Church of England has ever been, but for its friction against Dissenting power, notoriously feeble, in comparison with its great power in the cloister and the press. With a few fine exceptions, the great men of the Church of England seem to lay aside all the peculiar attributes of their genius as they enter the pulpit. I admit there are exceptions ; but, considering that the Church exists to teach, how very few the exceptions are. And it must be further said, that a certain restrictiveness has done much to keep down the freedom of soul, which is the inborn heritage of genius. I believe that, in very rare instances only, will genius succeed in the pulpit, perhaps never in the smaller country town ; there is more hope for it even in the small country village, where departure from an established and conventional order of expression is regarded with more charity and toleration. Usually, in the small town, the people require a solemn homage to ancient platitudes, and eschew all new experiences, and suspect the very soundness of the

faith, if it is proved by an argument too original or daring
in its colors or texture. Hence it has come to pass, that
many people, cultured people, suppose that genius has no
home in the Pulpit, and some, that it has no business there.
And yet, how rich in all that belongs to the highest moods
of the human soul is the Pulpit literature of our land.
Surely, the man who should closely look through its lore,
would find no lack of the purest gold ; if in its pages could
not be found the undisciplined fancy of the masters of fic-·
tion (though even this questionable faculty is not wanting),
here are the noblest tones of poetry, the most subtle and
profound touches of feeling ; the most intimate acquaintance with the ways and workings of the human mind and
heart ; here stand in the Pulpit library the words of the
masters of sentences ; the words of the wise ; here are the
ornate, and the more stately and cold ; the monarchs of
parable and illustration—and those who follow the lofty and
consecutive chain of thought to its wondrous and unexpected close ; and, if the Pulpit literature of the present
age does not equal that of the past, it is not wanting some
recent additions giving to us great hopes for the future.

To the order of men of genius eminently does Mr.
Binney belong. In his sermons there is nothing florid,
flickering, or fine ; nothing merely said to finish a period,
or to give a glitter to a paragraph. On the contrary, there
is nothing cold ; there is great idiomatic strength, frequently in his preaching there is great terseness ; but in
the written sermon this yields to argument and to the sustained and resolute conception of the topic.

The author of the *Lamps of the Temple* has introduced
into his sketch of the subject of these remarks many illustrations of his combined humanity and humor. He has
offered, also, an apology. for the introduction of humor
into the Pulpit ; and in this particular has placed Mr.
Binney by the side of some eminent and illustrious names,

especially Latimer and South. I have no need, therefore, to enlarge here by way of defence, but it may suffice to say that Mr. Binney *uses* humor and wit, he does not *abuse* them. In his printed discourses it is not to be expected that many of those racy words will be found which at once relieved the discourse and lightened the argument, and perhaps waked up some drowsy auditor; but in his printed discources there are many of those human touches which can only proceed from the humorous pencil, for human and humor are one. Thus he describes the mere popular preacher as "a strolling star tempting benevolence with a promise of pleasure." (It would be well if many churches would bear in mind the characterization.) My hearers will remember his happy delineation of David—a perfect picture to the hearer's eye through the ear :

DAVID.

The shepherd boy was bold and brave, manly and magnanimous, and had in him, from the first, the slumbering elements of a hero and a king. His harp was the companion of his early prime. Its first inspirations were caught from the music of brooks and groves, as he lay on the verdant and breathing earth, was smiled on through the day by the bright sky, or watched at night by the glowing stars. Even, then, probably, he had mysterious minglings of the Divine Spirit with the impulses of his own; was conscious of cogitations with which none could intermeddle, which would make him at times solitary among numbers, and which were the prelude and prophecy of his future greatness. He became a soldier before he was twenty. Ten years afterwards he was king by the suffrages of his own tribe. During most of the interval, his life was of a nature seriously to peril his habits and principles. He was obliged to use rude, lawless and uncongenial agents. He had to live precariously by gifts or spoil. "He was hunted like a partridge on the mountains." By day providing for sustenance or safety, and sleeping by night in cave or rock, field or forest. And yet this man—in the heat of youth, with a brigand's reputation and a soldier's license—watched carefully his inner self; learned from it as a pupil, and yet ruled it as a king—and found for it con genial employment in the composition of some of the most striking of his psalms. When his companions in arms were carousing or asleep, he sat by his lamp in some still retreat, or "considered the heavens" as they spread above him, or meditated on the law, or engaged in prayer, or held intimate communion with God, and composed and wrote (though he thought not so) what shall sound in the church, and echo through the world, to all time!

But especially we love those pictures in which the humanizing power of the preacher is seen shedding over his subject a pathos and a beautiful tenderness as melting as it was unsuspected. Who can forget that vivid picture of the Catholic girl's

SALVATION BY FIRE.

Look at that poor Catholic girl, there;—doing her penance, and counting her beads; repeating her "aves," and saying her "pater-nosters;" lighting a candle to this saint, or carrying her votive offering to another; wending her way in the dark, wet morning to early mass; conscientiously abstaining from flesh on a Friday; or shutting herself up in conventual sanctity, devoting her life to joyless solitude and bodily mortifications? She is imagining, perhaps, that she is piling up by all this a vast fabric of meritorious deeds, or at least of acceptable Christian virtue. She may expect on account of it to hear from the lips of her heavenly Bridegroom, "Well done, good and faithful" one—"enter thou into the joy of thy Lord." "Thou shalt walk with me in white, for thou art worthy." *We*, however, believe that "she labors in vain, and spends her strength for nought;" that she is building with "wood, hay and stubble;" and that the first beam of the light of eternity will set fire to her worthless structure, and reduce to ashes the labors and sacrifices of her whole life! Be it so. Her "*work* may be burnt;" she may "suffer *loss;*" but *she herself* may be mercifully "*saved.*" In the midst of all that mistaken devotedness to the gathering and amassing of mere lumber as materials for building up a divine life, even in connection with the strange fire of an erring devotion flaming up towards saints and Madonnas, there may be in her soul a central trust in the sacrifice and intercession of the "one Mediator," which shall secure the salvation of the superstitious devotee, at the very moment that she witnesses the destruction of her works. The illustration is an extreme one. I purposely select it because it is so. The greater includes the less.

And, more important by far than the defences in which he engaged for the outworks of Nonconformity, we reckon to be the impulse he gave to a higher strain of devotion within the churches of the Denomination. It is a wonderful thing that the relation of the Minister to the *Service of Song in the House of the Lord* should ever have been broken. Yet nothing is more certain than the fact, that for generations the minister handed over this as a part of the worship in which he had but little concern ; and, in many instances, he principally exercised his influence only to repress all efforts which might be made to restore to the service, harmony and beauty. Very industrious even the energies put forward for a long time for the suppression of all taste and art ; and, inasmuch as Romanism had made beautiful things to be an abomination in religious service, it was thought that a barnlike architecture, and a music where all chords were only used for discordance, were most fitted for the production of Divine impressions. This had long been felt by the churches. The value of the great central man of action is, that he has power and genius to interpret a popular sentiment and to supply a want. This Mr. Binney did. *The Service of Song in the House of the Lord* was greatly instrumental in awakening a new feeling throughout the Denomination, and creating in our midst a sublimed Psalmody. The Prayers of Mr. Binney, too, introduced another element ; too frequently prayer had degenerated into mere confessions of faith, the mere answers

to a catechism—statements of a creed. Perhaps the perfection of prayer would be the preservation of the spirit
of the Liturgy, without the form, combining the special
prayer of the hallowed Christian heart, and the wail of
man as a creature. Prayer is of a region above criticism—
almost above remark. Perhaps the only thing we should
permit ourselves to say is : " Did not our hearts burn
within us ?"—and, in a very eminent degree, both by his
personal power of prayer and by his general aid to the
great work of the sanctuary devotion, Mr. Binney has
aided the Divine services of his Denomination.

Would that I could carry you back to an old scene in the
Weigh House, beginning with my experience nearly a quarter of a century back.   Thither I often went on a Sabbath
evening. The singing always hearty and strong, but profoundly devotional and clear ; the minister standing there
tall, still, collected, and announcing the hymn.   Then the
prayer, always so fresh, and hallowing and real ; then the
sermon, in which somehow everybody felt as if the preacher
were talking with him.   Preaching of all kinds and styles,
but always new, always fresh, to a young mind.   What
scenes I have beheld there ! Sometimes the preacher, standing in perfect, cool, supreme command, holding all the
hearts of the audience in his hand, and doing what he would
with their tears.   Such was his sermon for Robert M‘Ken-
zie, the co-pastor of Dr. Wardlaw, lost in the wreck of the
Pegasus.   Always all along the preaching was heard—

> The still, sad music of humanity.

Scarcely ever did the preacher dilate on Nature, or any of
her majesties : his landscapes were always the heights and
depths of human souls, or the solemn mountain passes and
peaks of abstract thought, and the more gloomsome questions of human history.   Sometimes the sermon was "one
perfect chrysolite" of pure abstract thought, very variously

impressing the hearers ; sometimes a spirit floating in an ether of its own world ; and sometimes, like a spent swimmer, toiling, raftless and buoyless, over and through a difficult sea. At a later period, I heard many of the *Lectures on Proverbs;* truth to say, too, I have beheld scenes of strange humor flowing over that great assembly ; but look whichever way we will, we are compelled to see that tall, commanding figure slowly shaking itself into action, as a lion might shake the dewdrops and the sleep from his mane, after a night in the cave ; the hand slowly passing through the hair on one side of the head ; the speech, now a little more rapid, so rapid that the speaker saves himself from stumbling by picking up the last word, pronouncing it again, and making it the starting point of a new sentence ; then the sentence, or the division, completed ; and the heaving of a long sigh, audible over the whole chapel, and a feeling of indeterminateness from the speaker passing to the hearer ; then some broken words, a careless use of the left hand and the forefinger and thumb of the right hand, engaged as if the preacher, instead of standing in the pulpit, were standing in the compositors' room, throwing type into "pye." Then, perhaps, some dark question casts a strange shadow across his thought. For instance—"Could God by power destroy sin ? Could He by a physical act annihilate it ? Could he make a seraph out of a Tiberias or a Borgia, each retaining his memory and consciousness, as He can make an angel or an archangel out of nothing"?*

And now the wheel is in motion, and words come, blow after blow : and the preacher, as he advances to the close, puts his hand through the centric shock of his, in those days, carelessly worn but beautifully glossy hair ; and soon, with a cogent appeal to practical thought—the end. "The words of the wise are as nails ;" they are also as "rivers of

* "Life and Immortality brought to Life through the Gospel," see page 40.

13

water in a dry place ;" and the reader will believe that those scenes stand out in the memory for the life they communicated. The memory of some of those tones is thrilling yet ; the first surprise of some sudden turn of thought comes upon me now ; I am again one of that vast congregation of young men—the first, perhaps, of that kind ever seen in London ; I feel again, as then I felt, the honor of being born for manhood—born to live in a hard, struggling, much-enduring world. Certainly, in the days of youth, many of my first wider conceptions of the reality and nobleness of life were given to me by Thomas Binney.

FINIS.

INDEX.

INDEX OF TEXTS REFERRED TO

INDEX OF NAMES REFERRED TO

INDEX OF BOOKS REFERRED TO.

M. W. DODD'S
New Books and New Editions.

Watchwords for the Warfare of Life. From Dr. Martin Luther. By the Author of the Schönberg-Cotta Family. One elegant vol. 12mo., cloth extra, bevelled boards, ... $1 75

Mimpriss' Gospel Treasury and Treasury Harmony of the Four Evangelists. With Scripture Illustrations, Copious Notes and Addenda, Analytical and Historical Tables, Indexes, and Map, &c. Crown 8vo; over 900 pages; cloth extra, red edges, . . $3 50

A Harmony of the Gospels. Arranged in Parallel Columns, with Scripture References, Map, &c. By Robert Mimpriss. 16mo., cloth, ... $1 25

Studies on the Gospel Harmony. With Suggestive Questions, Practical Lessons, Analysis, &c., &c. To accompany the above. 16mo., cloth, ... $1 00

The Steps of Jesus. A Narrative Harmony of the Four Evangelists, in the Words of the Authorized Version. 18mo., cloth, . . $0 75
Pocket Edition, ... 35

Simmon's Scripture Manual. Alphabetically and Systematically arranged. Designed to facilitate the finding of proof texts. 12mo., cloth, ... $1 75

Cruden's Complete Concordance. A Dictionary and Alphabetical Index to the Bible. Royal 8vo., with Portrait.—A new style at a reduced price.—Brown cloth extra, bevelled boards, . . . $4 00

Taylor's Apostolic Baptism. Facts and Evidences on Christian Baptism. With 13 engravings, illustrating the modes of Primitive Baptism. By C. Taylor, Editor of Calmet's Dictionary. 12mo., cloth, . $1 25

The Book That Will Suit You; or, A Word For Every One. By Rev. James Smith. 32mo., cloth extra, bevelled boards, red edges, ... $1 00

JUST PUBLISHED.

Lamps, Pitchers, and Trumpets. Lectures on the Vocation of the Preacher. Illustrated by Anecdotes, Biographical, Historical, and Elucidatory, of every order of Pulpit Eloquence from the great Preachers of all ages. By E. Paxton Hood. One vol. large 12mo, ... $1 75

History and Repository of Pulpit Eloquence. (Deceased Divines.) By Henry C. Fish, D.D. A new edition. Two volumes in one; 8vo.; over 1200 pages, with portraits. Cloth extra, bevelled boards, $5 50

UNIFORM WITH

Pulpit Eloquence of the XIXth Century. With seven large steel portraits. 8vo., cloth extra, bevelled boards, . . . $4 00

Before the Throne; or, Daily Devotions for a Child. 32mo., cloth extra, red edges, ... $0 60

A beautiful volume of simple prayers for young children.

M. W. DODD,

506 Broadway, New York.

New Sunday-School Books.

Geneva's Shield. A Story of the Swiss Reformation. By Rc
W. M. Blackburn. 16mo., beautifully illustrated, ... $1 ⁰⁰

The Orphans' Triumphs; or, the Story of Lily and Harrⁿ
Grant. By H. K. P., author of the Kemptons. 16mo., beautifully illustrated, ... $1 25

Paul and Margaret, The Inebriate's Children. A Temperance Story. By H. K. P., 16mo., beautifully illustrated, . . . $1 00

On Both Sides of The Sea. The Sunday-School Edition.
18mo., ... $1 00

NEW EDITIONS.

*The following, for some time out of print, are now issued in new and beau-
tiful styles:—*

Sovereigns of The Bible. By E. R. Steel. With illuminated
title and many illustrations. 16mo., ... $1 50

Oriental and Sacred Scenes. By Fisher Howe. With beau-
tifully-colored plates. 16mo., ... $1 50

The Finland Family; or, Fancies Taken for Facts. By
Susan P. Cornwall. Beautifully bound and illustrated. 16mo., . . $1 25

LATELY PUBLISHED.

Holidays at Roselands. A sequel to Elsie Dinsmore. Beautifully illustrated. *Third Edition just ready.* 16mo., . . . $1 50

Elsie Dinsmore. By Martha Farquharson. Beautifully illustrated. 16mo., *Third Edition,* $1 25

The Little Fox. The Story of McClintock's Arctic Expedition,
told for the Young. Beautifully illustrated, ... $1 00

The Clifford Household. By Mrs. J. F. Moore. Four illustrations. 16mo., ... $1 25

READY IN JUNE.

Uncle John's Flower Gatherers. By Jane Gay Fuller.
Beautifully illustrated with nine engravings. 16mo., cloth extra, . . 1 50

It is believed that this most attractive volume will supply an acknowledged want.
In an interesting narrative is given information, such as children—older ones too—
will enjoy and appreciate, about plants and flowers, and how they grow and bloom.

Philip Brantley's Life Work and How He Found It.
By M. E. M. 16mo., illustrated 1 15

Other works in preparation.

NOTICE.

ANY of our publications will be sent by mail, post paid, oa receipt of the Catalogue price.

A DISCOUNT from Catalogue prices will be made to Ministers, Students, and those ordering *in quantity.*

IN addition to our own publications, we are prepared to supply, on favorable terms, all books in the market.

ATTENTION is invited to our list of BIBLE HELPS and JUVF NILE and SUNDAY-SCHOOL BOOKS, found on the last pages of this Catalogue.

Congregational Sabbath-School and Publishing

Society's Publications (late Massachusetts Sabbath-School Society's), for which we have been for many years New York Agents, constantly on hand, and for sale at Boston prices. The Society's list embraces several hundred volumes of a superior character, and more than fifty Question Books. Catalogues on application

THE PUBLICATIONS OF

J. C. Garrigues & Co.,	American Tract Society, Boston,
R. Carter & Bros.,	American Tract Society, New York,
Henry Hoyt,	American Sunday-School Union,
A. D. F. Randolph & Co.,	Presbyterian Publication Committee,
J. P. Skelly & Co.,	Presbyterian Board of Publication,
Henry A. Young & Co.,	Lutheran Board of Publication,
A. F. Graves,	National Temperance Society,
James S. Claxton,	Evangelical Knowledge Society,
Perkinpine & Higgins,	Methodist Book Concern,
Reformed Church Board of Publication,	And others,

Constantly on hand, and for sale at their own rates.

SPECIAL FACILITIES afforded for supplying Sunday-School Libraries with *carefully selected* books. A circular with full particulars and a list of New S. S. Books sent to any address.

Our stock is full and varied, embracing, with our own books, the latest and best issues of all the Societies and Private Publishers.

N. B. Remit by Check payable to order, Postal Money order, or Registered Letter. The latter method has been improved and is now a perfect protection against loss. All post-offices register letters. Money should not be sent in letters where it can be avoided.

BIBLE HELPS

AND

SUNDAY-SCHOOL TEXT-BOOKS

PUBLISHED BY

M. W. DODD,

506 BROADWAY, NEW YORK.

CRUDEN'S COMPLETE CONCORDANCE TO THE HOLY SCRIPTURES; OR, A DICTIONARY AND ALPHABETICAL INDEX TO THE BIBLE. By ALEXANDER CRUDEN, M.A.

By which, I.—Any verse in the Bible may be readily found by looking for any material word in the verse. To which is added—

II.—The significations of the principal words, by which their true meanings in Scriptures are shown.

III.—An account of Jewish customs and ceremonies illustrative of many portions of the Sacred Record.

IV.—A Concordance to the Proper Names of the Bible, and their meaning in the original.

V.—A Concordance to the Books called the Apocrypha.

To which is appended an original life of the Author, illustrated with an accurate Portrait from a Steel Engraving.

One vol. royal 8vo., cloth extra, bevelled boards, . . . $4 00

Sheep, $5 00 ; Half morocco, ... 6 5c

This is the *genuine* and *entire* edition of Cruden's great work—the only one embracing those features which Cruden himself and the Public, for more than a hundred years, have regarded as *essential* to its completeness and inestimable value. In its *complete* form it has ever been regarded as immeasurably superior to any other work of the kind.

"Cruden's Concordance, in its unabridged and *complete state*, is invaluable to the biblical student, and the abridgments which have been made of it furnish no idea of the thoroughness and fulness of the original and complete work."—*Rev. Thomas De Witt, D.D.*

"It is a low view of such a book to consider it merely as an expedient for *finding a certain verse.* It is in reality a Bible Lexicon. As managed by Cruden, it is also an explanatory dictionary, and his definitions are, in every instance remembered by me, sound and evangelical."—*Rev. James W. Alexander, D.D.*

"The very interesting and useful analysis of the senses, in which the more important words of Scripture are used, gives great value to the work."—*Rev. M. W. Jacobus, D.D.*

"Cruden's Concordance, in its original state, I consider above all price to the student of the Scriptures."—*Rev. Francis Wayland, LL.D., President of Brown University.*

"We never recommend anyone to be satisfied until he is possessed of the full and complete work of Cruden. Let it be your very next investment in Bible Helps. It will pay you as you go along. How a teacher can get through his lessons without it, unless he is gifted with the marvellous memory of a Calvin or a Nathaniel West, we cannot see."—*S. S. Times.*

"We have often been surprised to find intelligent Christians who are daily students of the Divine Record, but who had never had this volume. It ought to be in every household, where every Sabbath-school teacher and scholar and every reader could have access to it."—*New York Observer.*

The Mimpriss System of Graduated Simultaneous Instruction.

THE LIFE OF CHRIST.—Harmonized from the Four Evangelists. A Sunday-School Lesson-Book, in THREE GRADES—Grade First, for the Younger Classes; Grade Second, for Children; Grade Third, for Youth.

In boards, each Grade, . . $0.20 ; $18.00 per hundred.
In Paper, " " . . $0.15 ; $13.00 per hundred.

TEACHERS' MANUAL—For the First, Second, and Third Grades.

Containing Map, Questions, Explanations, Geographical and other information, and an Introduction explaining the System, and showing HOW TO TEACH. 18mo.

In cloth, each Grade, ... $0.60 ; $6.50 per dozen.
In Boards," " . . . . $0.40 ; $4.25 per dozen·

The Life of Christ is completed in One Hundred Lessons, making a Two Year's Course. The Lesson Books and Manuals, as above, contain Fifty Lessons, leaving a Second Volume to complete the Course.

A careful examination of this Series of Lesson-Books by superintendents, teachers, and all interested in elevating the standard of Sunday-School instruction, is earnestly desired. They possess new and important features, and are believed to be in advance of anything yet offered. They are the result of long and patient labor, and are founded on well-tested principles, the Author's works being well known to intelligent Sunday-School workers as the basis of much of the late improvement in Sunday-School instruction.

The System divides the school into three grades, with a higher grade (see next page) for the Bible classes. The subject of the lessons is the same in all the grades, from the lowest to the highest, but adapted in each to the capacity of the scholar.

The Lesson-books, as well as the Manuals, are provided with a Chart of the Holy Land, tracing the journeys of Christ and localizing all the events in his life and ministry. Special attention is paid to the Geography ; the principle being to fix the facts, by associating them with localities.

THE TEACHERS' MANUALS are a new feature, and one peculiar to the System. They contain, with the Questions, &c., in the Scholar's book, full Geographical, Explanatory, and other information, Scripture Parallels, Practical Lessons, and a variety of matter calculated to make the lesson *attractive, instructive, and impressive.* The Introduction is very valuable, furnishing to the Teacher a guide in preparing and teaching the lesson, which will prove of great practical service.

For the Bible Classes.

THE GOSPEL HARMONY.—Having the Text of the Four Evangelists in parallel columns, with Notes, References and Chart. 16mo., ... $1 25

STUDIES ON THE GOSPEL HARMONY.—Containing Suggestive Questions, Scripture Illustrations, Practical Lessons, Exercises in Supplemental Narrative, and Christ our Example. With Chart. 16mo., cloth, $1.00

The above are divided into One Hundred Lessons to correspond with the Lesson-Books; making the Bible-class lesson on the same subject as that studied throughout the school. Unlike the Lesson-Books, they each contain the entire One Hundred lessons or two year's course.

A Cheaper Edition.

THE HARMONY AND STUDIES.—The Frst Fifty Lessons. Bound in one volume, cloth, flexible, $1.10 $12.00 per Dozen.

Teachers' Helps accompanying the System.
For fuller descriptions see Catalogue pages 14 and 15.

THE GOSPEL TREASURY AND TREASURY HARMONY OF THE FOUR EVANGELISTS. With Notes, Practical Reflections, Geographical Notices, Copious Index, Map, &c., &c. Crown 8vo., cloth extra, ... $3 50

This invaluable *Teacher's Help* is especially useful to teachers of this system, and should be in the hands of all who can afford to own a copy. It is divided into one hundred sections, corresponding with the one hundred lessons, and supplies, in one compact volume, just the material needed in preparing the lesson.

THE PATH OF JESUS. With cloth back, folded for the Pocket, ... $0 20

—— For the Wall, mounted on rollers, size 4 x 5 feet, . 7 00

This Chart is the same as that in the Lesson-Books, Manuals, &c., but on larger scales. The pocket size is large enough for class use. The wall size should be owned by every school studying the system, and will be found an invaluable aid to the superintendent or pastor in addressing the school upon the lesson.

THE STEPS OF JESUS. With Chart. 18mo., cloth, $0 75
" " Pocket edition, cloth, flexible, 35

This volume is in the precise words of the authorized version, but arranged to read as a continuous narrative. It may be used to great advantage as a reading book for classes studying the life of Christ, and is especially adapted as a reward or presen' for such

M. W. Dodd's Catalogue.

SIMMONS' SCRIPTURE MANUAL. Alphabetically and Systematically arranged. Designed to facilitate the finding of Proof Texts. By CHARLES SIMMONS, 12mo., . . . $1 75

The texts are printed in full, thus saving the inconvenience of constant reference. The subjects are alphabetically arranged with full cross references, and an ample index is provided.

" The work contains not merely the *proof texts* on the subject to which it refers, but, what appears to my own mind one of its excellences, the texts that *illustrate* these subjects. Though the arrangement of the subjects is alphabetical, in the illustration of the subjects themselves, the author has observed that connection between one truth and another which gives to each its proper place."—*Dr. Spring's Introduction.*

" It is incomparably superior to anything of the kind with which I am acquainted, and its extensive circulation and use cannot but have a happy influence. I have no doubt that the work will soon supersede every other of the kind, as I am clearly of the opinion that it should."—*Rev. Albert Barnes.*

"I consider your text-book to be remarkably suited to the object in view, and likely to be *the Book* which will satisfy not only common people, but ministers and all men of logical mind and cultivated taste. It is my opinion that it will take the place of all other works of the kind, and that nothing else will be called for or attempted for a great while to come."—*Rev. Leonard Woods, D.D.*

"As a help in the selection of proof texts on almost any subject in the Bible, I know of nothing of equal value."—*Rev. Enoch Pond, D.D.*

"A standard work which, like Cruden's Concordance, is not likely to be superseded by anything better We cannot attempt to set forth all the valuable features of this manual. We only urge all Sunday-school teachers and private Christians to get and use it."—*S. S. Times.*

" It is far more copious and reliable than any work of the kind. A better help in the study of the Bible is not accessible."—*Congregationalist.*

" The work is the best of the kind within our knowledge."—*New Englander.*

KING'S QUESTIONS ON THE GOSPELS IN HARMONY, chronologically arranged in 189 separate lessons for Sunday Schools and Bible Classes. By WALTER KING, A.M. 18mo., ... $0 40

―――― The Same, in 3 vols., each, ... 20

· This excellent question book was rewritten several times, and each successive revision tested by actual use in several of the best Sunday Schools in the country for the purpose of discovering any defects or incorporating any improvements suggested by its practical use. Though mainly designed for S. S. Bible classes, it has been introduced with great advantage in Day schools and Families. The arrangement is chronological, the harmony being upon the basis of the best expositors. Many valuable notes are given in the margin. The appendix contains a combined view of thirty of the most interesting scenes. Sectarian allusions are avoided, suiting it to all denominations.

M IMPRISS.—GOSPEL TREASURY AND TREAS URY HARMONY OF THE FOUR EVANGE

LISTS : having the Text in parallel columns. With Scripture Illustrations, Practical Reflections, and Addenda
Geographical, Biographical, Topographical, Historical, and
Critical, illustrating manners, customs, opinions, and localities of the Sacred Narrative, with analytical and historical
tables, and a very copious index : also a chart, with every
event numbered and localized. By ROBERT MIMPRISS.
Crown 8vo., over 900 pp. Cloth extra, red edges, . $3 50
Quarto edition, large type, cloth extra, ... 12 00

It will be found to supply an amount and kind of information not
found in any other volume, and to fill an unoccupied place in the
literature of *Bible Helps.* Its value to Sunday-school teachers and
private students of the Bible especially, is inestimable.

The *Harmony* is according to Greswell, and in the words of the authorized
version.

An *important feature* is the arrangement of the Four Evangelists in parallel
columns, and in *juxtaposition.* This is carried out with great minuteness, giving
a comparison of verses and lines, and even words for consultation at sight. The
arrangement also admits of the Harmony being read as a continuous narrative.

The *Notes* have been carefully selected from the best sources.

The *Geographical* notices are from the most reliable authorities.

The *Addenda* supply a great variety of matter for consultation, illustrating the
text.

The *Scripture Illustrations* are very full, and are calculated to lead to an intelligent knowledge of the Old and New Testaments.

" It is not easy to state in a few words the merits of this extraordinary book. To
say that it is useful, excellent, valuable, and the like, is tame, and far below its
merits. It is in all respects a most unusual book, and the labor in its preparation
must have been immense. It is in its own department without a parallel in the
language, and stands many degrees at the head of its class."—*Primitive Church
Magazine, England.*

" For us who have so earnestly approved the work, and urged it upon the attention of Sunday-school teachers, it is quite unnecessary to add another word. It
ranks among the very first companions of the Bible in bible study. It is a condensed commentary of commentaries, a right-hand helper in the preparation of New-
Testament lessons."—*S. S. Times.*

" No circulation can ever repay in money value the time expended on it. Should
I ever be permitted to go over the same ground again, I expect to derive great
assistance from it."—*Rev. James Hamilton, D.D.*

" The Gospel Treasury prepared by Robert Mimpriss I consider one of the most
valuable helps to a Sunday-school teacher that I have ever seen."—*Rev. Stephen
H. Tyng, D.D.*

" Anything like an adequate idea of the immense amount of information upon
the New Testament incorporated within the compass of this handsome volume, it
is difficult to convey. Within its portable compass we find matter compressed
sufficient to fill ten ordinary demy octavos."—*Sunday-School Teacher's Magazine.*

www.ingramcontent.com/pod-product-compliance
Lightning Source LLC
Chambersburg PA
CBHW060549030726
47498CB00005B/1326